Rustic

Rustleaf

Port Sumac

Scout Burke

Wild
Country

Wolfepointe

Darkwater

Lonepine

Grasslake

Burl

fletarbor   Sandmason

tone

Lillygrove

Oakgrove

Flintrust   Birchflow

Mouse Guard: Legends of the Guard

Archaia Entertainment LLC
www.archaia.com

FOR THE FANS OF MOUSE GUARD

SPECIAL THANKS TO:
JEREMY BASTIAN, TED NAIFEH, ALEX SHEIKMAN,
SEAN RUBIN, ALEX KAIN, TERRY MOORE, GENE HA, LOWELL FRANCIS
JASON SHAWN ALEXANDER, NATE PRIDE, KATIE COOK, GUY DAVIS
KARL KERSCHL, CRAIG ROUSSEAU, MARK SMYLIE,
STEPHEN CHRISTY, PAUL MORRISSEY, MEL CAYLO,
AND PJ BICKETT

Mouse Guard:

Legends of the Guard

Published by Archaia

Archaia Entertainment LLC
1680 Vine Street, Suite 912
Los Angeles, California, 90028, USA

www.archaia.com

MOUSE GUARD: LEGENDS OF THE GUARD

September 2010

FIRST PRINTING

10 9 8 7 6 5 4 3 2 1

ISBN: 1-932386-94-7

ISBN 13: 978-1-932386-94-3

Printed in Korea.

ARCHAIA™

FOREWORD

This project was conceived after Jeremy Bastian and Mark Smylie turned in their pinups for Mouse Guard Fall 1152. I felt they really captured the feeling of my world, and knowing they were both good storytellers, I told them that I would love to have them play in the world of Mouse Guard whenever they wished. The trouble with this plan was how to incorporate any tales they told into my continuity of stories without taking things off track.

So the concept for an anthology book, where the guest stories being told are meant to be out of continuity, came to mind. The more I shared the idea with creators I admired, the more real the project became. Archaia liked the idea, and once we started rounding up names like the folks who contributed to this collection, they gave the OK to start production of a Mouse Guard spinoff series.

My goal was to remain involved telling the pieces of the story that bridge the guest stories. I handpicked the creators, and offered advice and approvals to their stories and artwork. However, with duties in that last category, I tried to remain as hands off as possible. I knew these creators were all good at what they did, I picked them for that very reason. So, I gave them as much freedom with their work as I could. These talented storytellers have added to the Mouse Guard mythos in ways I never could. I appreciate their willingness to do so.

David Petersen

DAVID PETERSEN
MICHIGAN 2010

Story and Contributor Index:

The Battle of the Hawk's Mouse
& the Fox's Mouse: Art & Story: Jeremy Bastian

A Bargain in the Dark: Art & Story: Ted Naifeh

Oleg the Wise: Art & Story: Alex Sheikman, Colors: Scott Keating

Potential: Art: Sean Rubin, Story: Alex Kain

The Shrike and the Toad: Art & Story: Terry Moore

Worley & the Mink: Art: Gene Ha Story: Lowell Francis

A Mouse Named Fox: Art & Story: Katie Cook

The Critic: Art & Story: Guy Davis

The Ballad of Nettledown: Nate Pride

The Raven: Art & Adaptation: Jason Shawn Alexander

The Lion and the Mouse: Art & Story: Craig Rousseau

Bowen's Tale: Art & Story: Karl Kerschl

Crown of Silver, Crown of Gold: Art & Story: Mark Smylie

Additional pages by David Petersen

Additional Lettering by Dave Lanphear

Cover Legends & Extras

On the Cover:

A pair of fangs was kept from each of the heads of the five serpents who had once surrounded all that was. The teeth were hollowed to become warning horns. Ten horns were distributed to the largest settlements in the territories and carved to adorn each location's mark. After twenty winters had past, only five remained: those from Dawnrock, Copperwood, Flintrust, Grasslake, and Ferndale.

It was said that when the five sacred horn blowers combined their efforts the resulting bellow was so loud and resonant it could lure away a rutting elk in springtime.

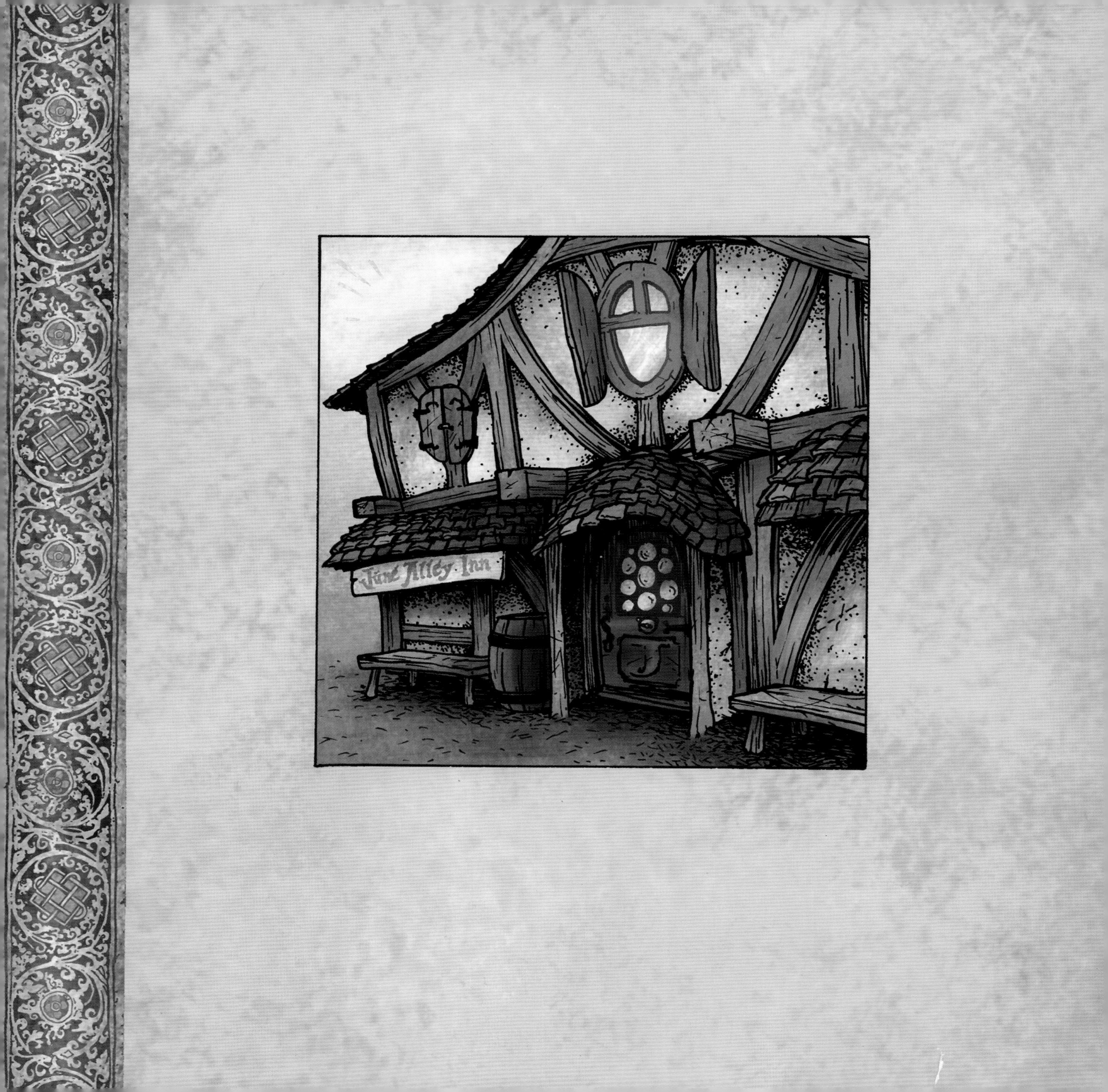
Vine Alley Inn

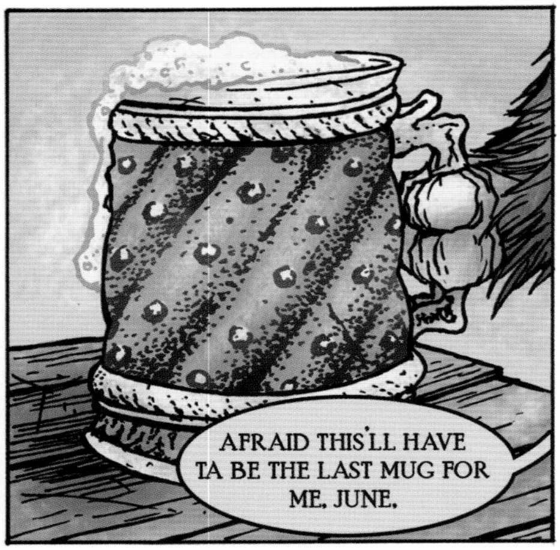
AFRAID THIS'LL HAVE TA BE THE LAST MUG FOR ME, JUNE.

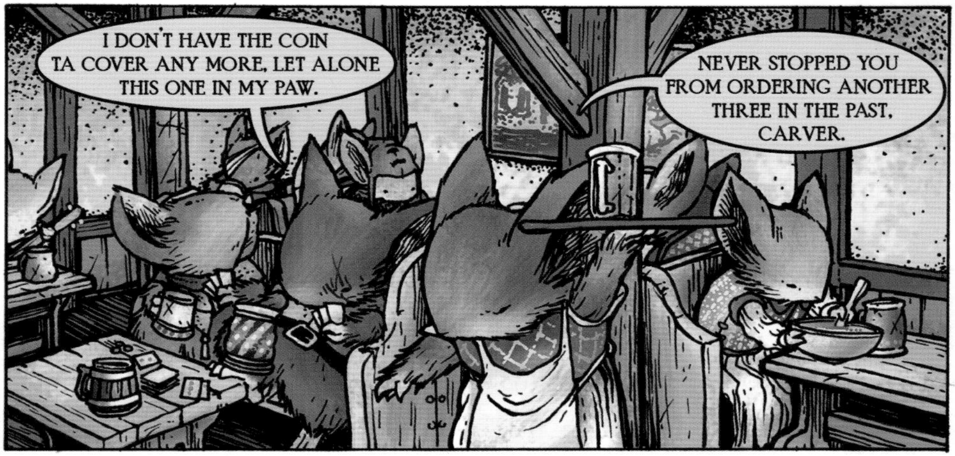
I DON'T HAVE THE COIN TA COVER ANY MORE, LET ALONE THIS ONE IN MY PAW.
NEVER STOPPED YOU FROM ORDERING ANOTHER THREE IN THE PAST, CARVER.

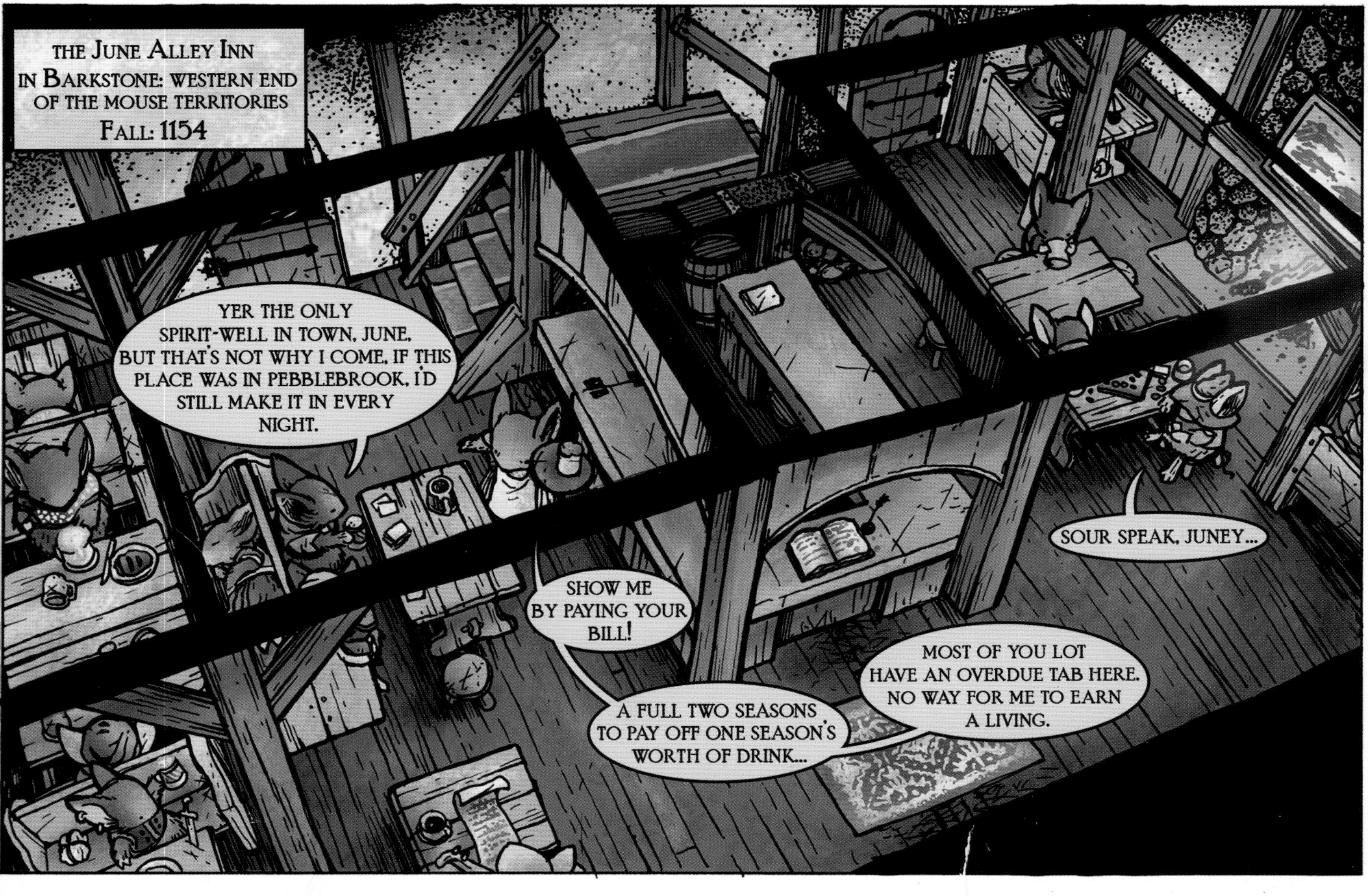
THE JUNE ALLEY INN IN BARKSTONE: WESTERN END OF THE MOUSE TERRITORIES FALL: 1154
YER THE ONLY SPIRIT-WELL IN TOWN, JUNE, BUT THAT'S NOT WHY I COME. IF THIS PLACE WAS IN PEBBLEBROOK, I'D STILL MAKE IT IN EVERY NIGHT.
SHOW ME BY PAYING YOUR BILL!
A FULL TWO SEASONS TO PAY OFF ONE SEASON'S WORTH OF DRINK...
MOST OF YOU LOT HAVE AN OVERDUE TAB HERE. NO WAY FOR ME TO EARN A LIVING.
SOUR SPEAK, JUNEY...

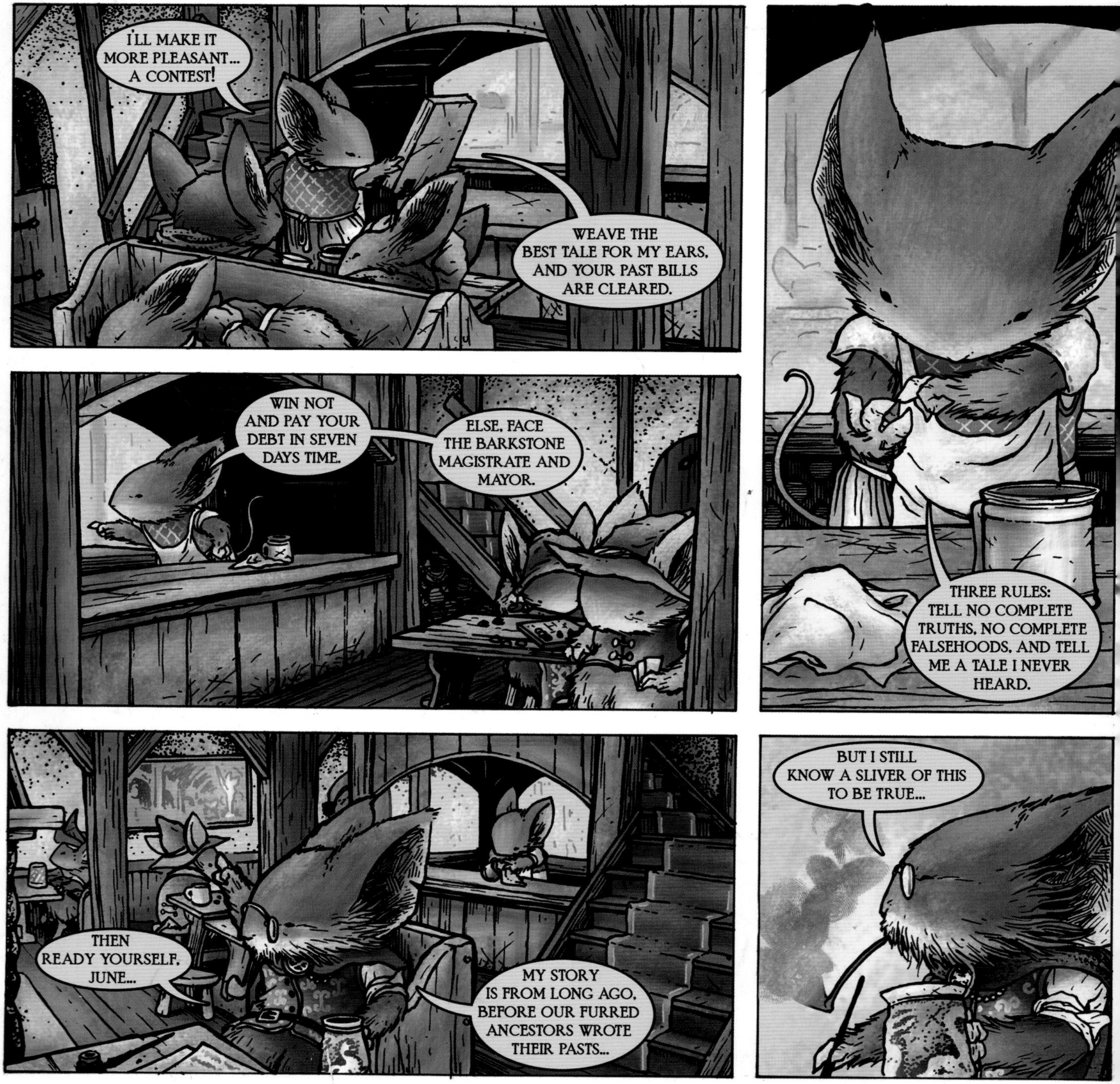
I'LL MAKE IT MORE PLEASANT... A CONTEST!
WEAVE THE BEST TALE FOR MY EARS, AND YOUR PAST BILLS ARE CLEARED.
THREE RULES: TELL NO COMPLETE TRUTHS, NO COMPLETE FALSEHOODS, AND TELL ME A TALE I NEVER HEARD.
WIN NOT AND PAY YOUR DEBT IN SEVEN DAYS TIME.
ELSE, FACE THE BARKSTONE MAGISTRATE AND MAYOR.
THEN READY YOURSELF, JUNE...
MY STORY IS FROM LONG AGO, BEFORE OUR FURRED ANCESTORS WROTE THEIR PASTS...
BUT I STILL KNOW A SLIVER OF THIS TO BE TRUE...

the Battle of

the Hawk's Mouse and the Fox's Mouse

There was a time before the mice of our lands took up cloaks made of cloth and defended their own.

It was common that all creatures employed mouse protectors, for it was well learned that no animal was as cunning, as courageous, as a mouse.

These protectors turned a blind eye to the plight of their own kind and favored, above all, the praise of their masters.

It was during this dark era there lived in a field a hawk and a fox.

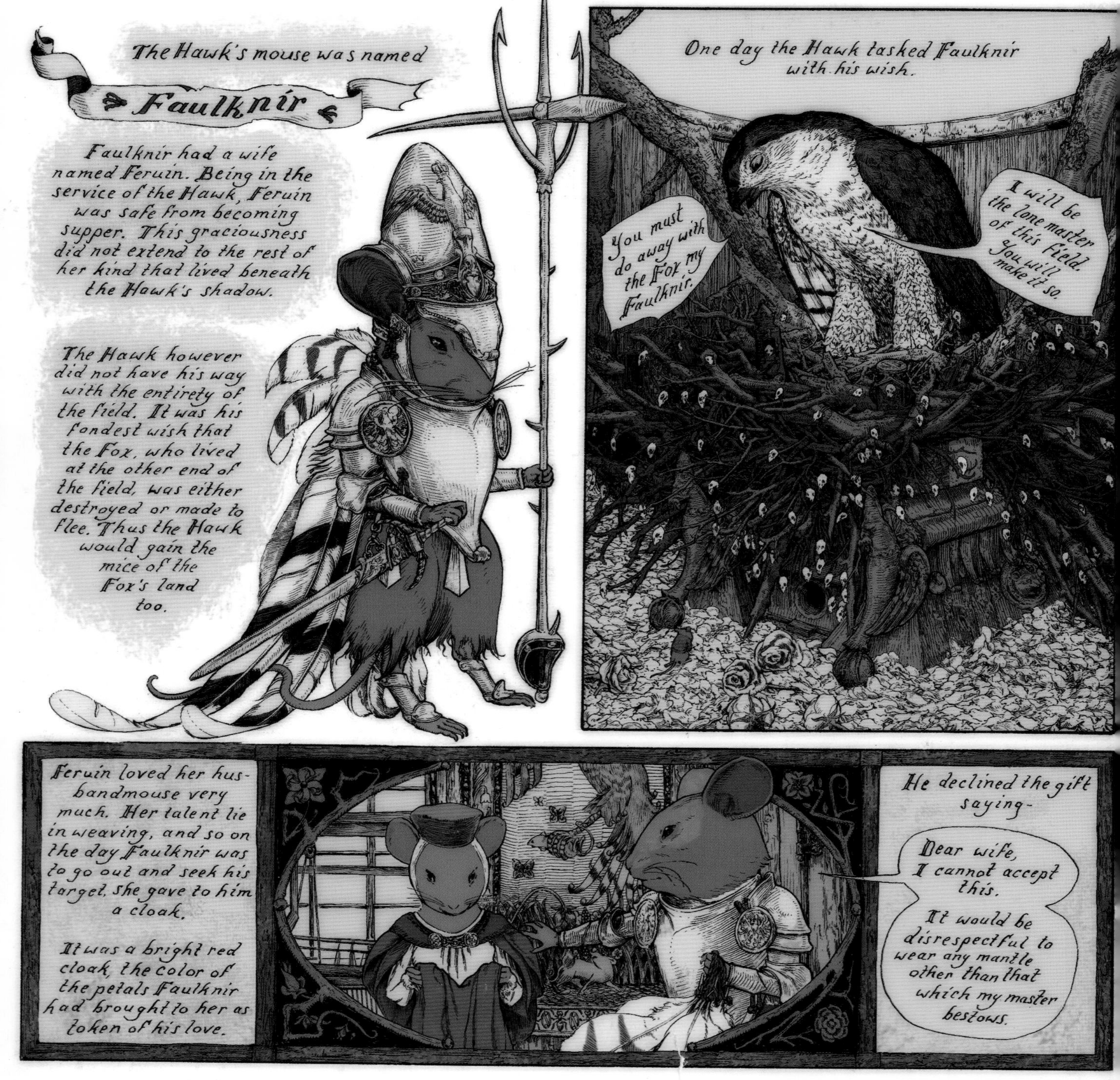
The Hawk's mouse was named
Faulknir
Faulknir had a wife named Feruin. Being in the service of the Hawk, Feruin was safe from becoming supper. This graciousness did not extend to the rest of her kind that lived beneath the Hawk's shadow.
The Hawk however did not have his way with the entirety of the field. It was his fondest wish that the Fox, who lived at the other end of the field, was either destroyed or made to flee. Thus the Hawk would gain the mice of the Fox's land too.
One day the Hawk tasked Faulknir with his wish.
You must do away with the Fox my Faulknir.
I will be the lone master of this field. You will make it so.
Feruin loved her husbandmouse very much. Her talent lie in weaving, and so on the day Faulknir was to go out and seek his target, she gave to him a cloak.
It was a bright red cloak, the color of the petals Faulknir had brought to her as token of his love.
He declined the gift saying-
Dear wife, I cannot accept this.
It would be disrespectful to wear any mantle other than that which my master bestows.

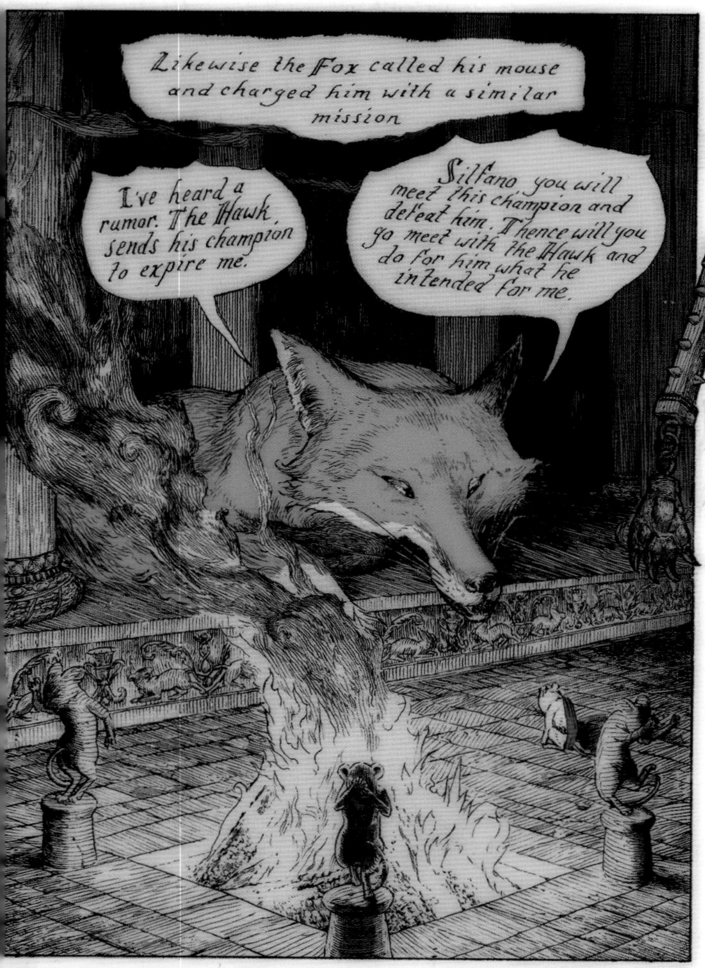
Likewise the Fox called his mouse and charged him with a similar mission
I've heard a rumor. The Hawk sends his champion to expire me.
Silfano, you will meet this champion and defeat him. Thence will you go meet with the Hawk and do for him what he intended for me.

The Fox's mouse was named

Silfano

Silfano's wife was not as fortunate as Feruin, the Fox held his house in a different way. Silfano was allowed an heir. Sefatus, his only son.

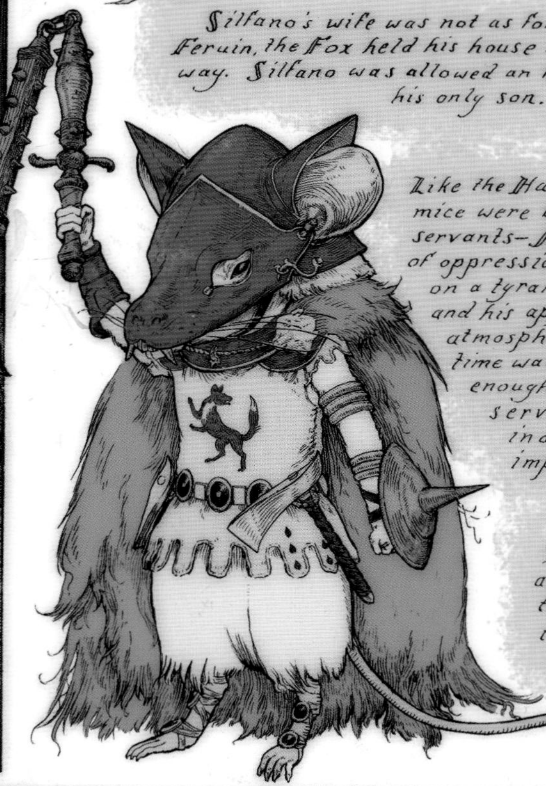

Like the Hawk's domain, mice were brought in as servants–An existance of oppression dependant on a tyrannical lord and his appetite. The atmosphere at the time was perilous enough that such servitude was indeed an improvement.

The Fox was as wanting as the Hawk for the conquest of the field.

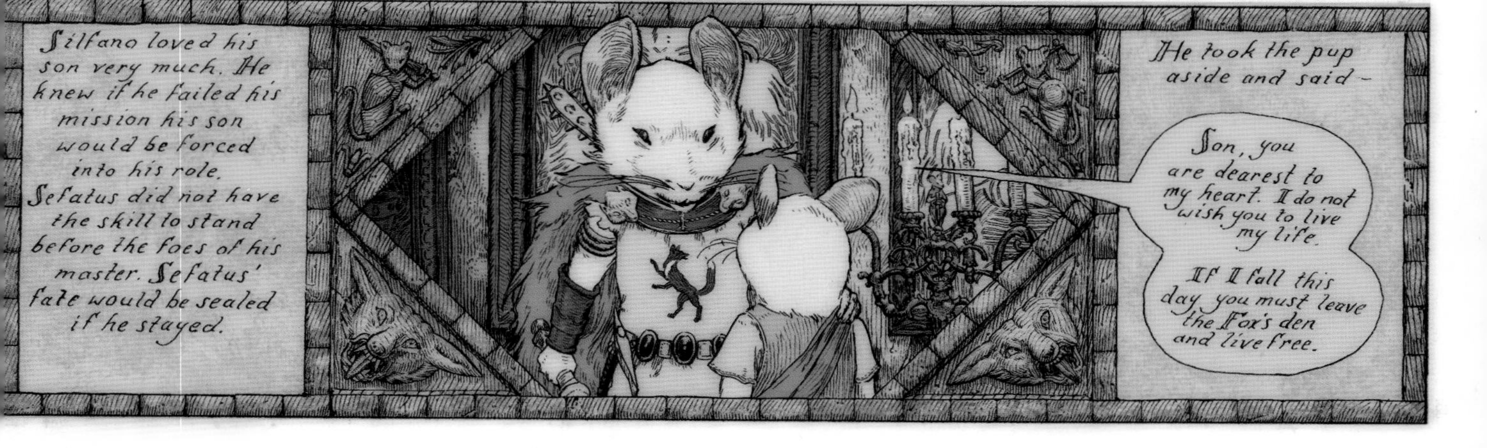
Silfano loved his son very much. He knew if he failed his mission his son would be forced into his role. Sefatus did not have the skill to stand before the foes of his master. Sefatus' fate would be sealed if he stayed.
He took the pup aside and said–
Son, you are dearest to my heart. I do not wish you to live my life.
If I fall this day you must leave the Fox's den and live free.

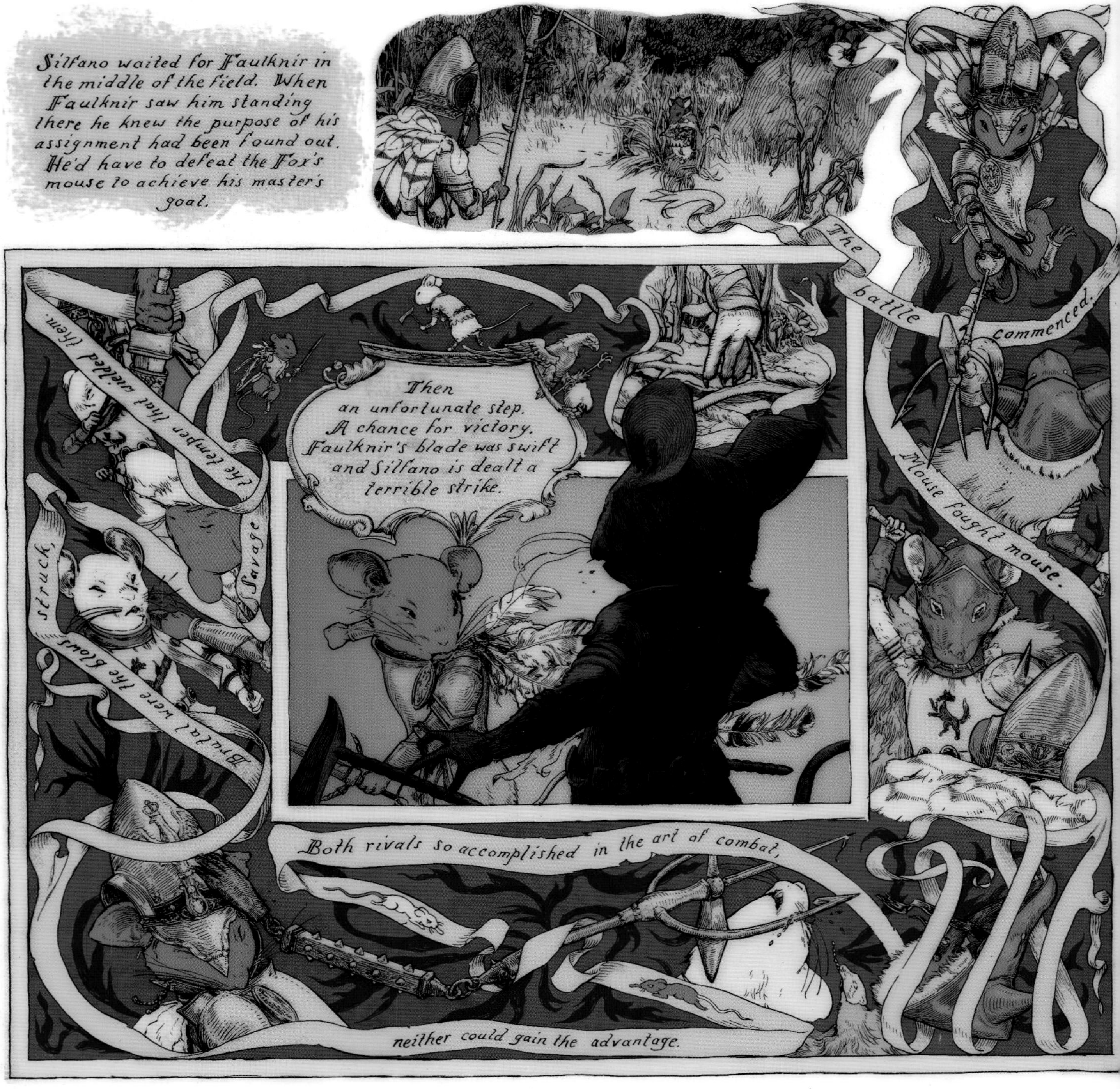
Silfano waited for Faulknir in the middle of the field. When Faulknir saw him standing there he knew the purpose of his assignment had been found out. He'd have to defeat the Fox's mouse to achieve his master's goal.
The battle commenced.
Mouse fought mouse.
Both rivals so accomplished in the art of combat,
neither could gain the advantage.
Brutal were the blows struck,
Savage the temper that wielded them.
Then an unfortunate step. A chance for victory. Faulknir's blade was swift and Silfano is dealt a terrible strike.

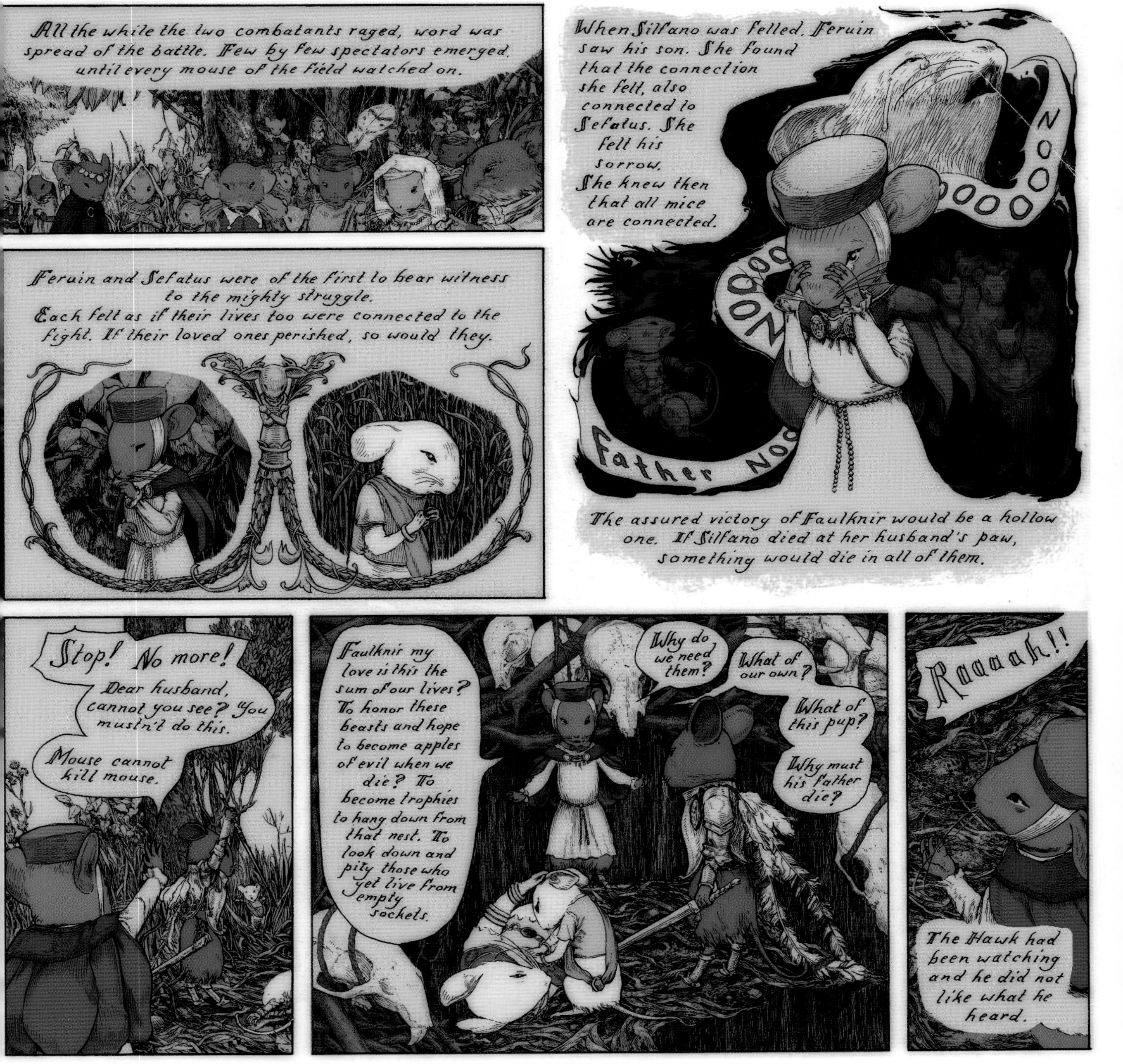

All the while the two combatants raged, word was spread of the battle. Few by few spectators emerged, until every mouse of the field watched on.
Feruin and Sefatus were of the first to bear witness to the mighty struggle. Each felt as if their lives too were connected to the fight. If their loved ones perished, so would they.
When Silfano was felled, Feruin saw his son. She found that the connection she felt, also connected to Sefatus. She felt his sorrow. She knew then that all mice are connected.
NOOOOOOOOOOOOOOO
Father NOOOOOO
The assured victory of Faulknir would be a hollow one. If Silfano died at her husband's paw, something would die in all of them.
Stop! No more!
Dear husband, cannot you see? You mustn't do this.
Mouse cannot kill mouse.
Faulknir my love is this the sum of our lives? To honor these beasts and hope to become apples of evil when we die? To become trophies to hang down from that nest. To look down and pity those who yet live from empty sockets.
Why do we need them?
What of our own?
What of this pup?
Why must his father die?
Raaaah!!
The Hawk had been watching and he did not like what he heard.

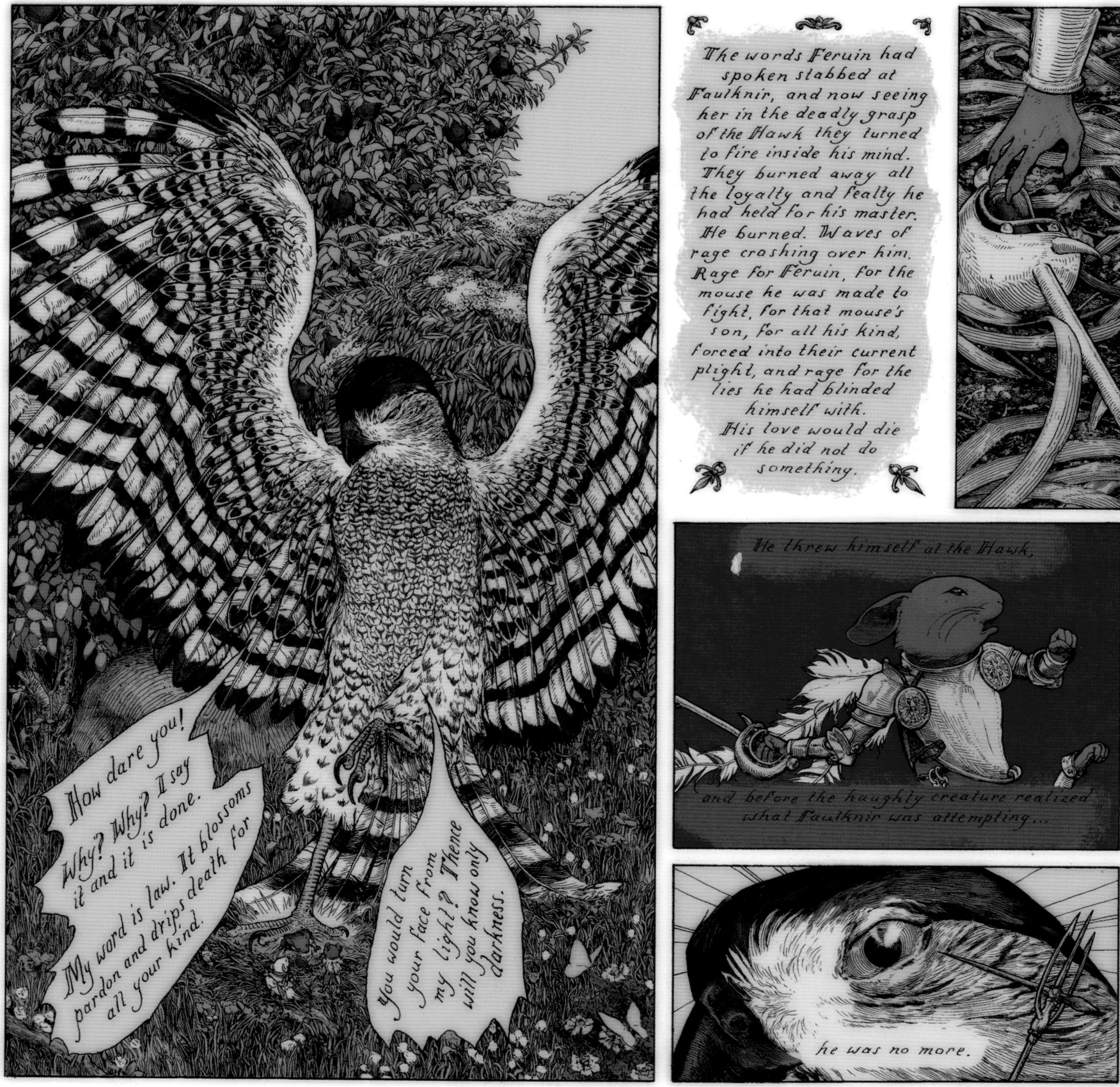

How dare you!
Why? Why? I say it and it is done.
My word is law. It blossoms pardon and drips death for all your kind.
You would turn your face from my light? Thence will you know only darkness.
The words Feruin had spoken stabbed at Faulknir, and now seeing her in the deadly grasp of the Hawk they turned to fire inside his mind. They burned away all the loyalty and fealty he had held for his master. He burned. Waves of rage crashing over him. Rage for Feruin, for the mouse he was made to fight, for that mouse's son, for all his kind, forced into their current plight, and rage for the lies he had blinded himself with. His love would die if he did not do something.
He threw himself at the Hawk,
and before the haughty creature realized what Faulknir was attempting...
he was no more.

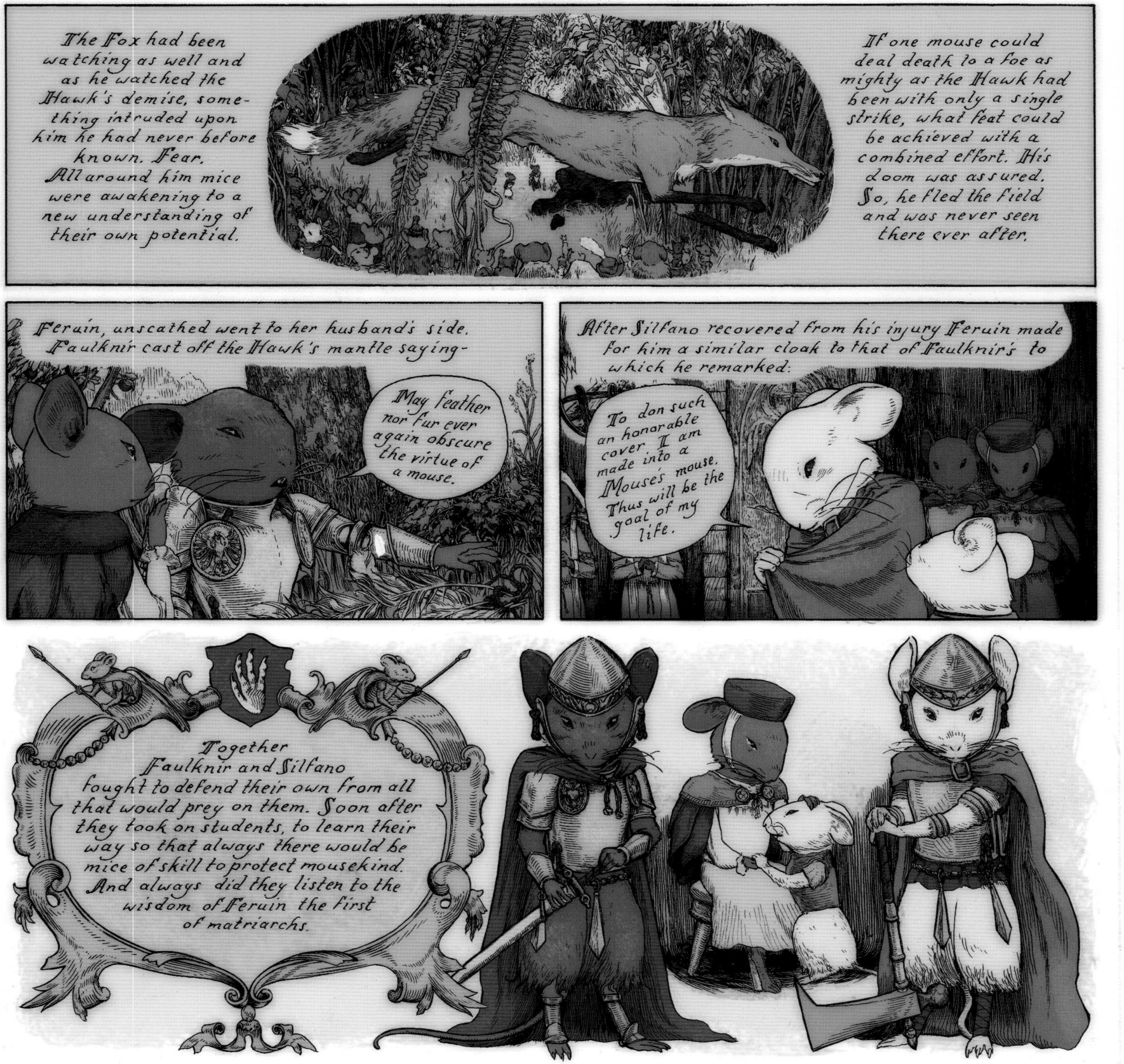
The Fox had been watching as well and as he watched the Hawk's demise, something intruded upon him he had never before known. Fear. All around him mice were awakening to a new understanding of their own potential.
If one mouse could deal death to a foe as mighty as the Hawk had been with only a single strike, what feat could be achieved with a combined effort. His doom was assured. So, he fled the field and was never seen there ever after.
Feruin, unscathed went to her husband's side. Faulknir cast off the Hawk's mantle saying-
May feather nor fur ever again obscure the virtue of a mouse.
After Silfano recovered from his injury Feruin made for him a similar cloak to that of Faulknir's to which he remarked:
To don such an honorable cover I am made into a Mouse's mouse. Thus will be the goal of my life.
Together Faulknir and Silfano fought to defend their own from all that would prey on them. Soon after they took on students, to learn their way so that always there would be mice of skill to protect mousekind. And always did they listen to the wisdom of Feruin the first of matriarchs.

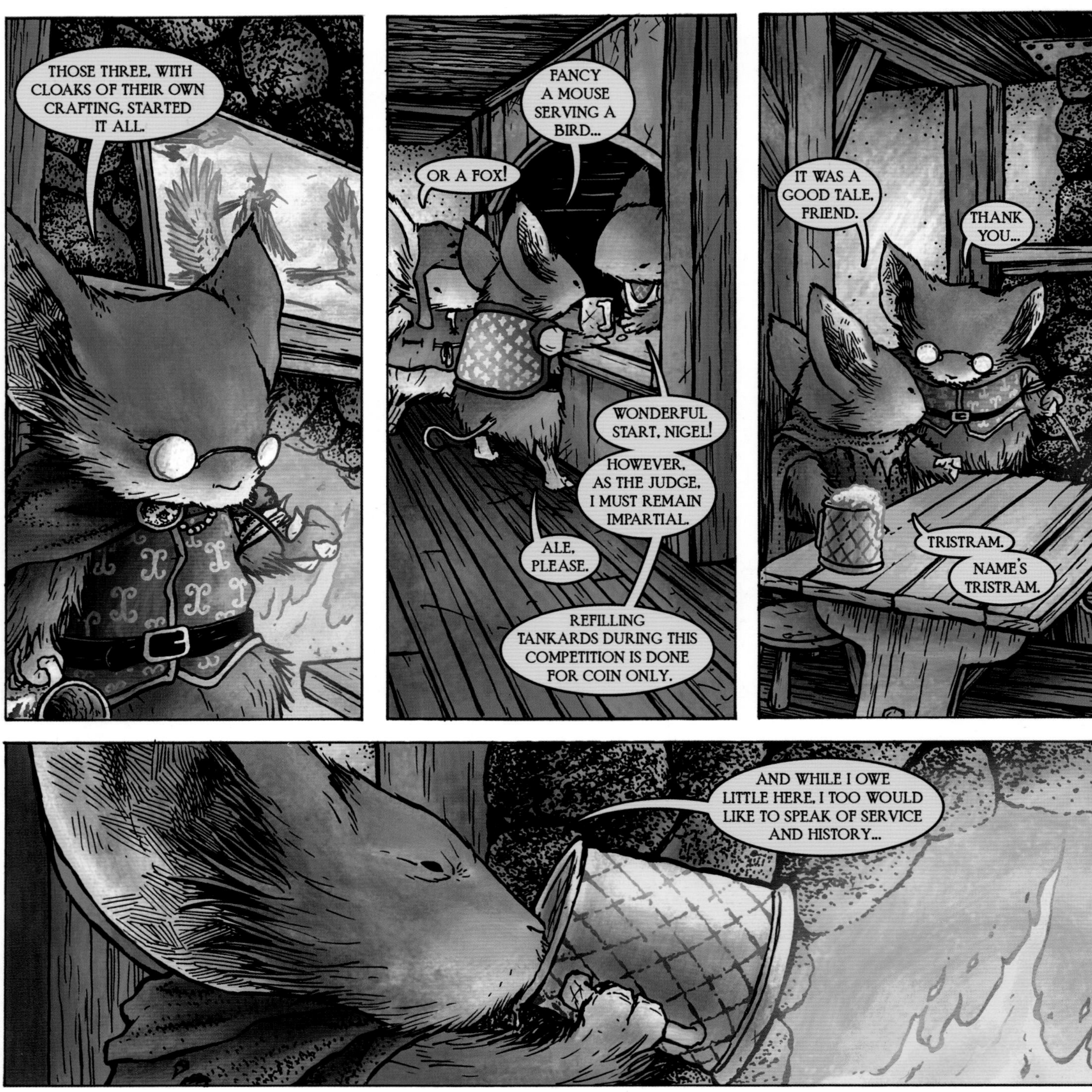
THOSE THREE, WITH CLOAKS OF THEIR OWN CRAFTING, STARTED IT ALL.
FANCY A MOUSE SERVING A BIRD...
OR A FOX!
WONDERFUL START, NIGEL!
HOWEVER, AS THE JUDGE, I MUST REMAIN IMPARTIAL.
ALE, PLEASE.
REFILLING TANKARDS DURING THIS COMPETITION IS DONE FOR COIN ONLY.
IT WAS A GOOD TALE, FRIEND.
THANK YOU...
TRISTRAM.
NAME'S TRISTRAM.
AND WHILE I OWE LITTLE HERE, I TOO WOULD LIKE TO SPEAK OF SERVICE AND HISTORY...

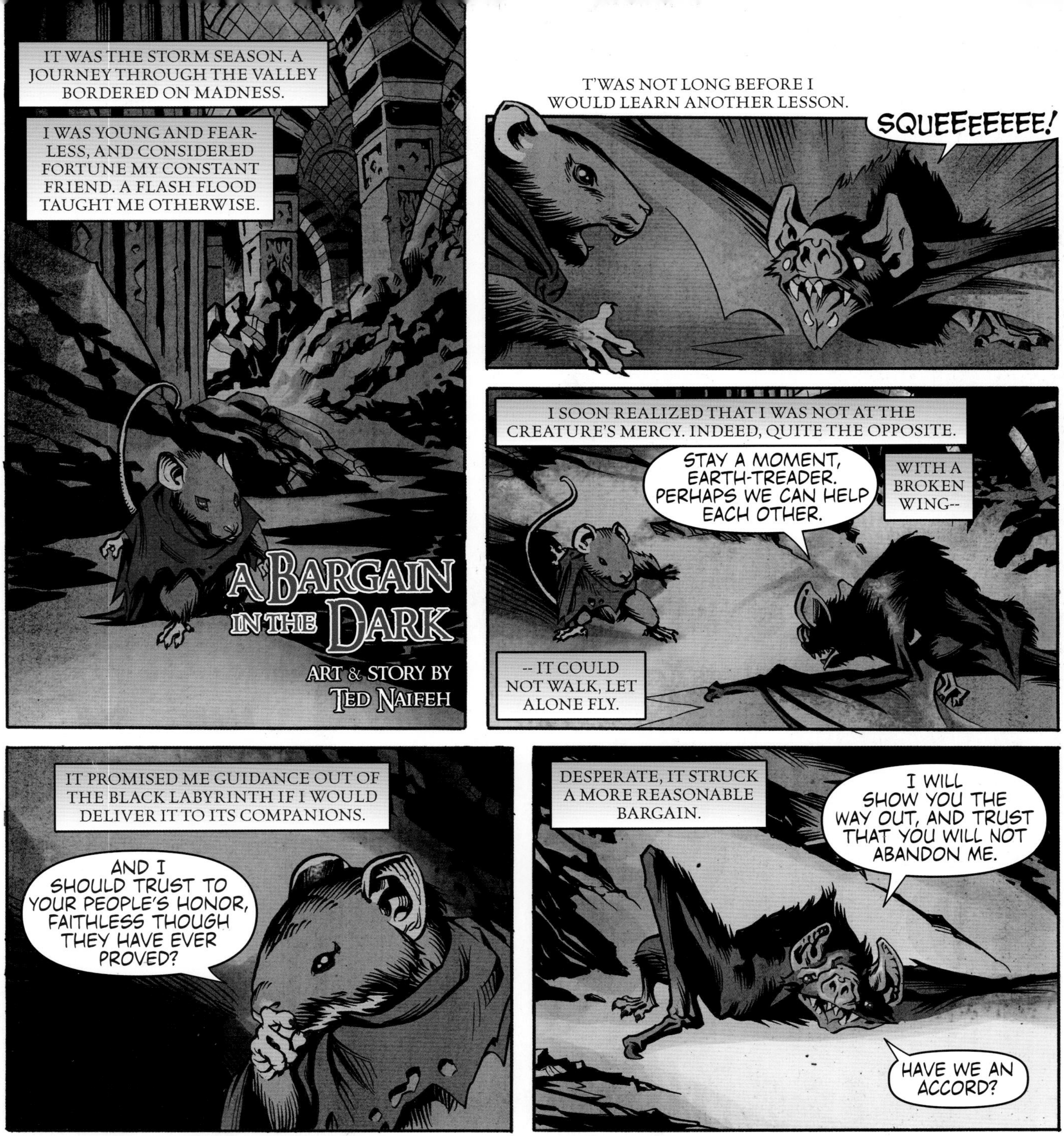
IT WAS THE STORM SEASON. A JOURNEY THROUGH THE VALLEY BORDERED ON MADNESS.
I WAS YOUNG AND FEAR-LESS, AND CONSIDERED FORTUNE MY CONSTANT FRIEND. A FLASH FLOOD TAUGHT ME OTHERWISE.
A BARGAIN IN THE DARK
ART & STORY BY TED NAIFEH
T'WAS NOT LONG BEFORE I WOULD LEARN ANOTHER LESSON.
SQUEEEEEEE!
I SOON REALIZED THAT I WAS NOT AT THE CREATURE'S MERCY. INDEED, QUITE THE OPPOSITE.
STAY A MOMENT, EARTH-TREADER. PERHAPS WE CAN HELP EACH OTHER.
WITH A BROKEN WING--
-- IT COULD NOT WALK, LET ALONE FLY.
IT PROMISED ME GUIDANCE OUT OF THE BLACK LABYRINTH IF I WOULD DELIVER IT TO ITS COMPANIONS.
AND I SHOULD TRUST TO YOUR PEOPLE'S HONOR, FAITHLESS THOUGH THEY HAVE EVER PROVED?
DESPERATE, IT STRUCK A MORE REASONABLE BARGAIN.
I WILL SHOW YOU THE WAY OUT, AND TRUST THAT YOU WILL NOT ABANDON ME.
HAVE WE AN ACCORD?

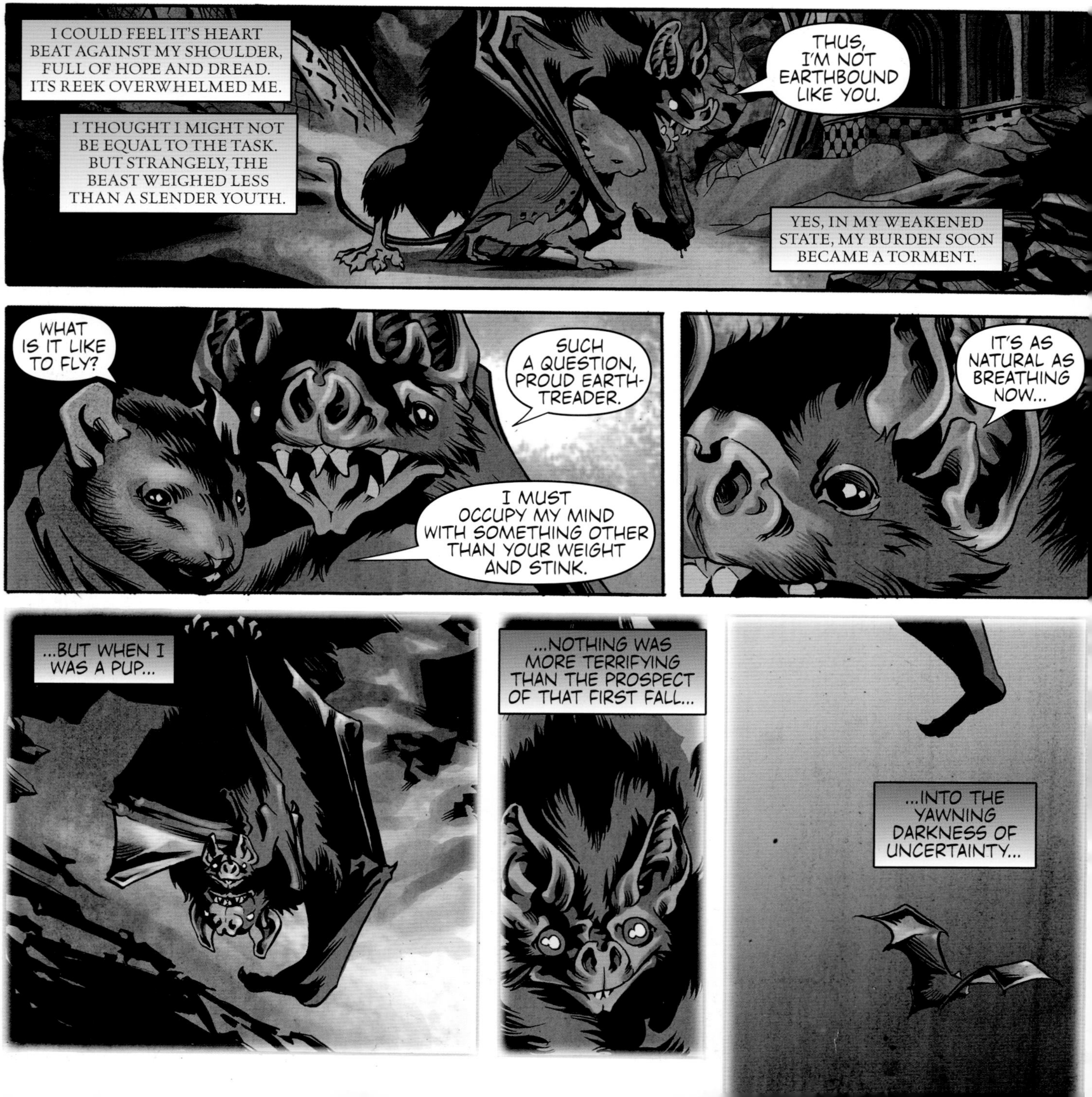
I COULD FEEL IT'S HEART BEAT AGAINST MY SHOULDER, FULL OF HOPE AND DREAD. ITS REEK OVERWHELMED ME.
I THOUGHT I MIGHT NOT BE EQUAL TO THE TASK. BUT STRANGELY, THE BEAST WEIGHED LESS THAN A SLENDER YOUTH.
THUS, I'M NOT EARTHBOUND LIKE YOU.
YES, IN MY WEAKENED STATE, MY BURDEN SOON BECAME A TORMENT.
WHAT IS IT LIKE TO FLY?
SUCH A QUESTION, PROUD EARTH-TREADER.
I MUST OCCUPY MY MIND WITH SOMETHING OTHER THAN YOUR WEIGHT AND STINK.
IT'S AS NATURAL AS BREATHING NOW...
...BUT WHEN I WAS A PUP...
...NOTHING WAS MORE TERRIFYING THAN THE PROSPECT OF THAT FIRST FALL...
...INTO THE YAWNING DARKNESS OF UNCERTAINTY...

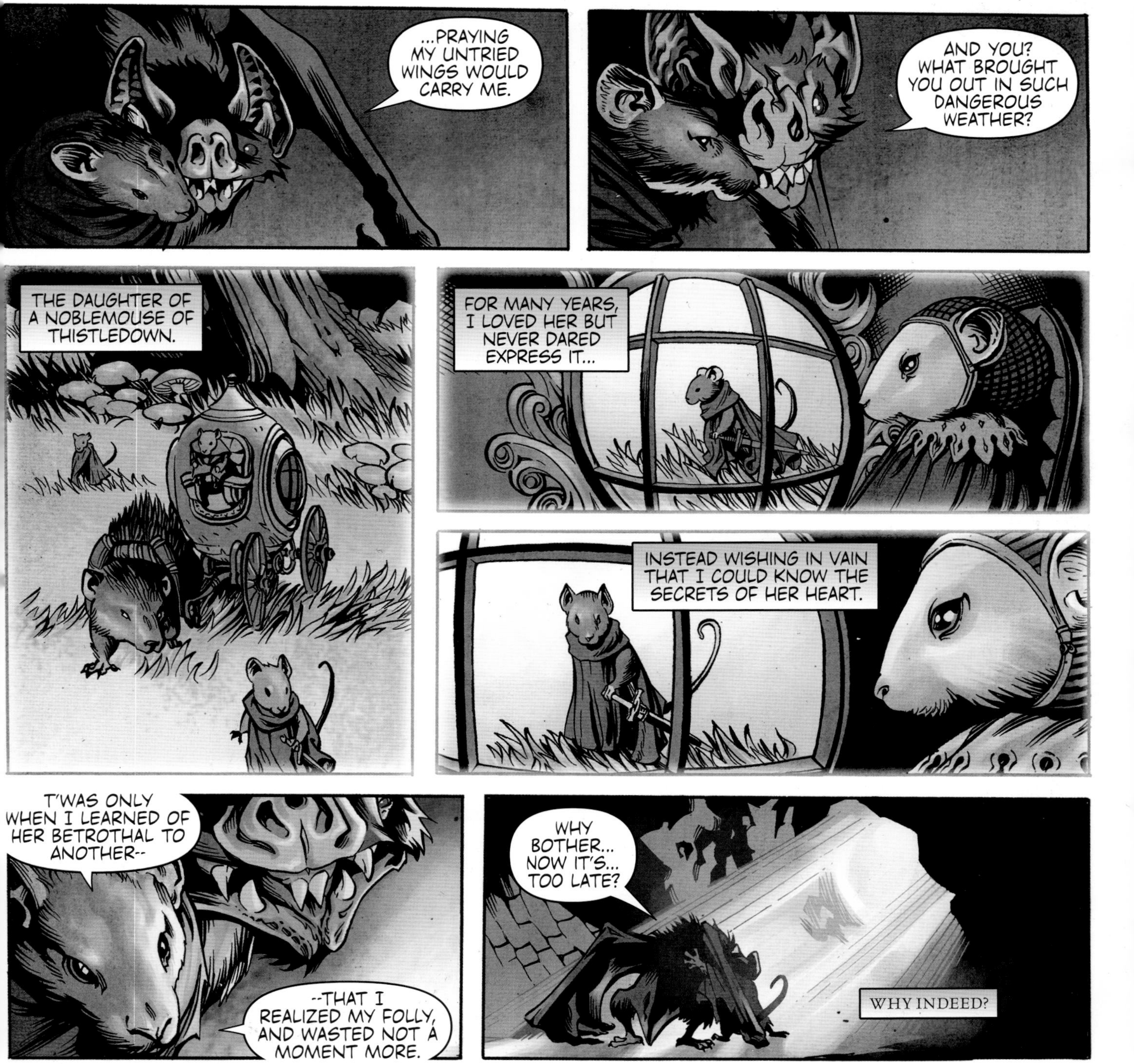
...PRAYING MY UNTRIED WINGS WOULD CARRY ME.
AND YOU? WHAT BROUGHT YOU OUT IN SUCH DANGEROUS WEATHER?
THE DAUGHTER OF A NOBLEMOUSE OF THISTLEDOWN.
FOR MANY YEARS, I LOVED HER BUT NEVER DARED EXPRESS IT...
INSTEAD WISHING IN VAIN THAT I COULD KNOW THE SECRETS OF HER HEART.
T'WAS ONLY WHEN I LEARNED OF HER BETROTHAL TO ANOTHER--
--THAT I REALIZED MY FOLLY, AND WASTED NOT A MOMENT MORE.
WHY BOTHER... NOW IT'S... TOO LATE?
WHY INDEED?

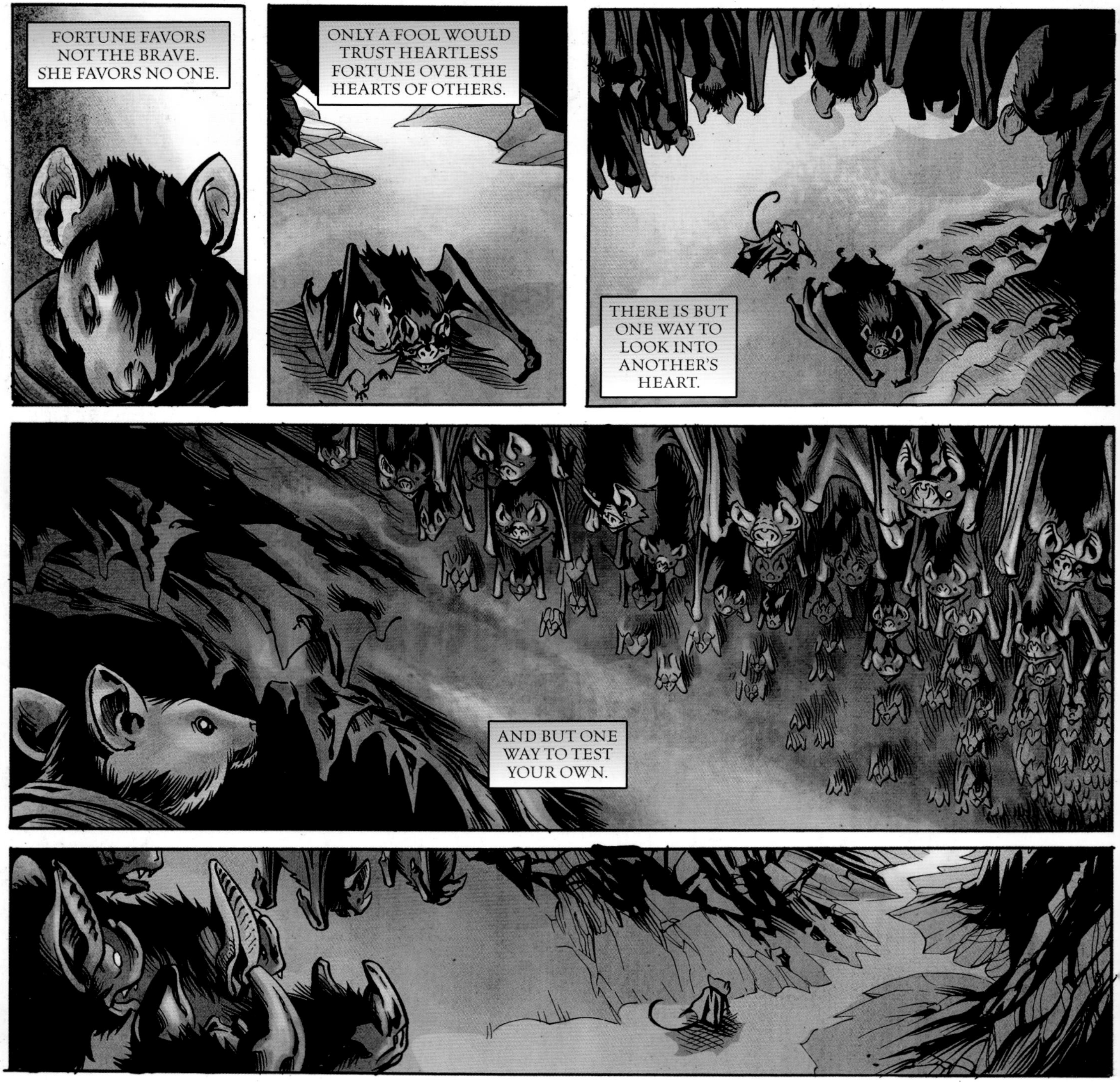
FORTUNE FAVORS NOT THE BRAVE. SHE FAVORS NO ONE.
ONLY A FOOL WOULD TRUST HEARTLESS FORTUNE OVER THE HEARTS OF OTHERS.
THERE IS BUT ONE WAY TO LOOK INTO ANOTHER'S HEART.
AND BUT ONE WAY TO TEST YOUR OWN.

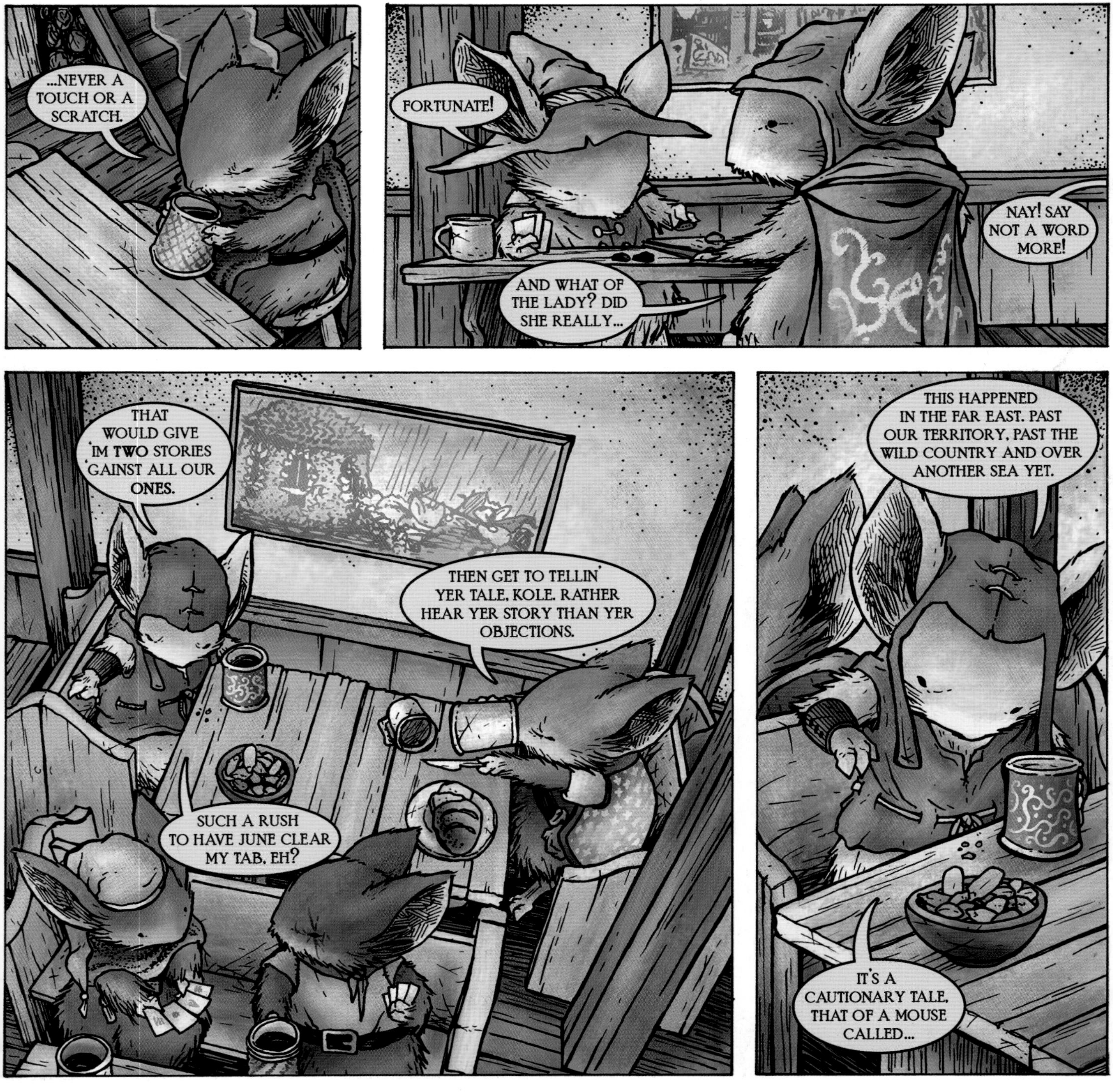
...NEVER A TOUCH OR A SCRATCH.
FORTUNATE!
AND WHAT OF THE LADY? DID SHE REALLY...
NAY! SAY NOT A WORD MORE!
THAT WOULD GIVE 'IM **TWO** STORIES 'GAINST ALL OUR **ONES**.
THEN GET TO TELLIN' YER TALE, KOLE. RATHER HEAR YER STORY THAN YER OBJECTIONS.
SUCH A RUSH TO HAVE JUNE CLEAR MY TAB, EH?
THIS HAPPENED IN THE FAR EAST. PAST OUR TERRITORY, PAST THE WILD COUNTRY AND OVER ANOTHER SEA YET.
IT'S A CAUTIONARY TALE, THAT OF A MOUSE CALLED...

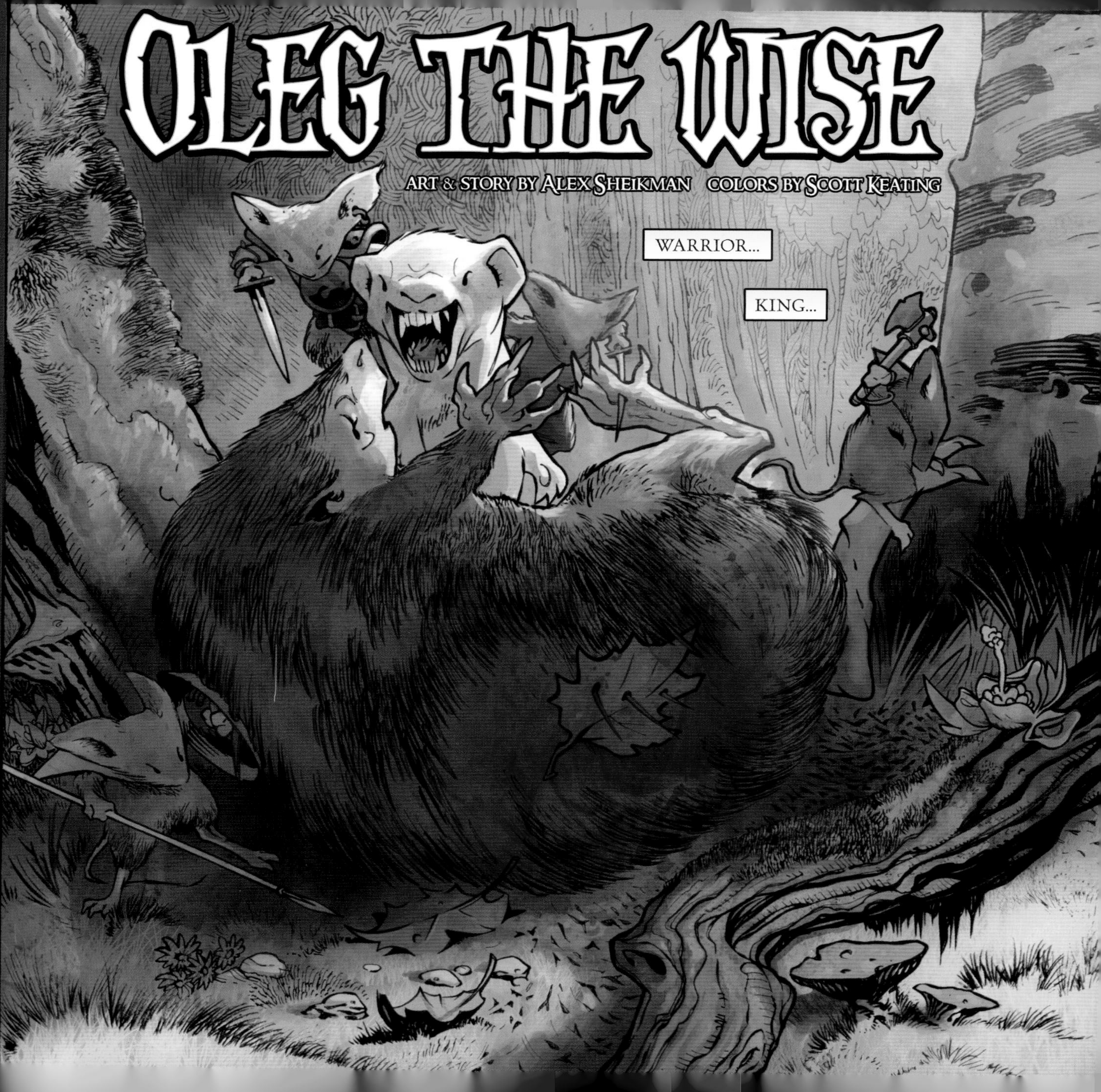
OLEG THE WISE
ART & STORY BY ALEX SHEIKMAN COLORS BY SCOTT KEATING
WARRIOR...
KING...

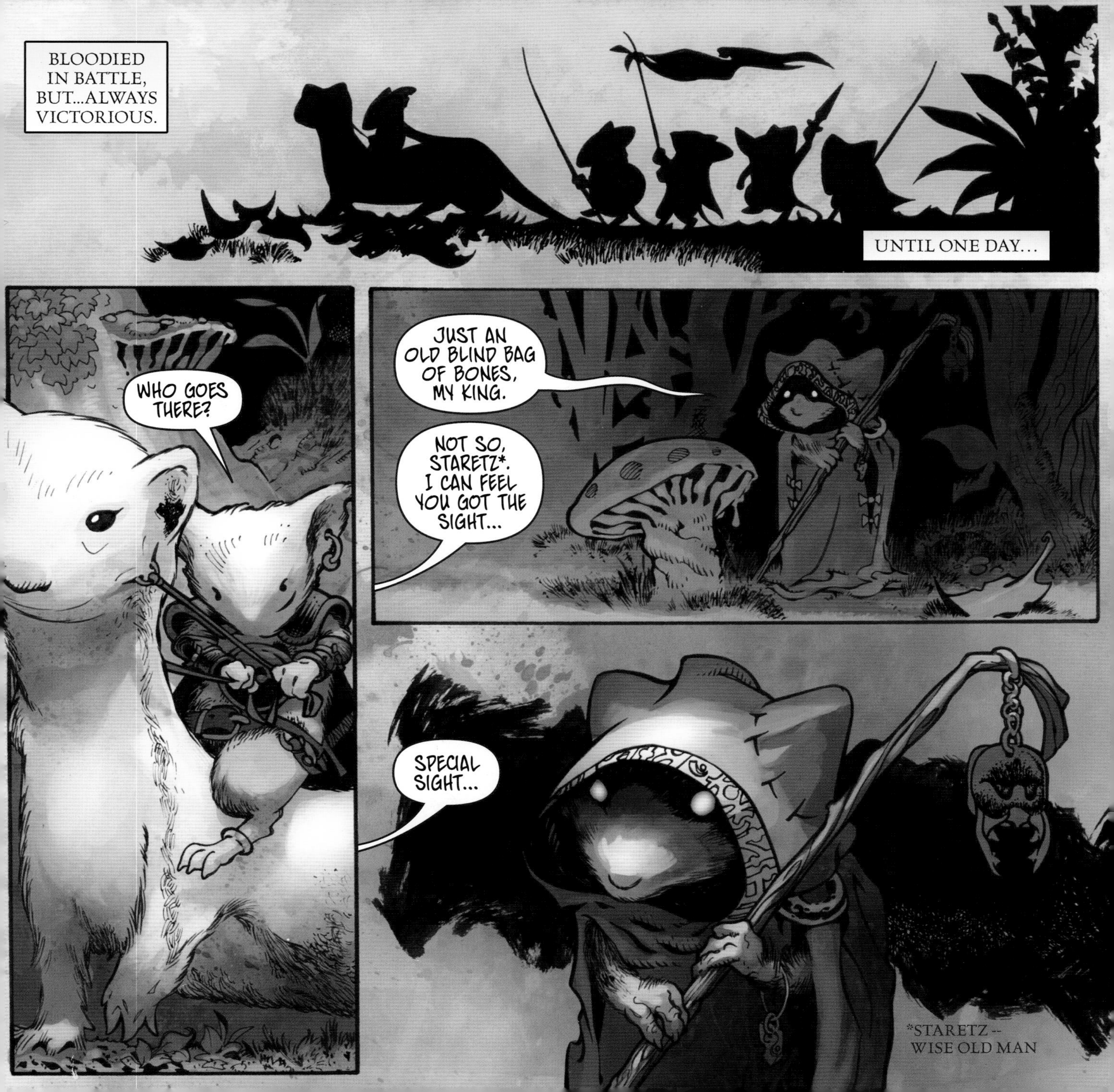
BLOODIED IN BATTLE, BUT...ALWAYS VICTORIOUS.
UNTIL ONE DAY...
WHO GOES THERE?
JUST AN OLD BLIND BAG OF BONES, MY KING.
NOT SO, STARETZ*. I CAN FEEL YOU GOT THE SIGHT...
SPECIAL SIGHT...
*STARETZ -- WISE OLD MAN

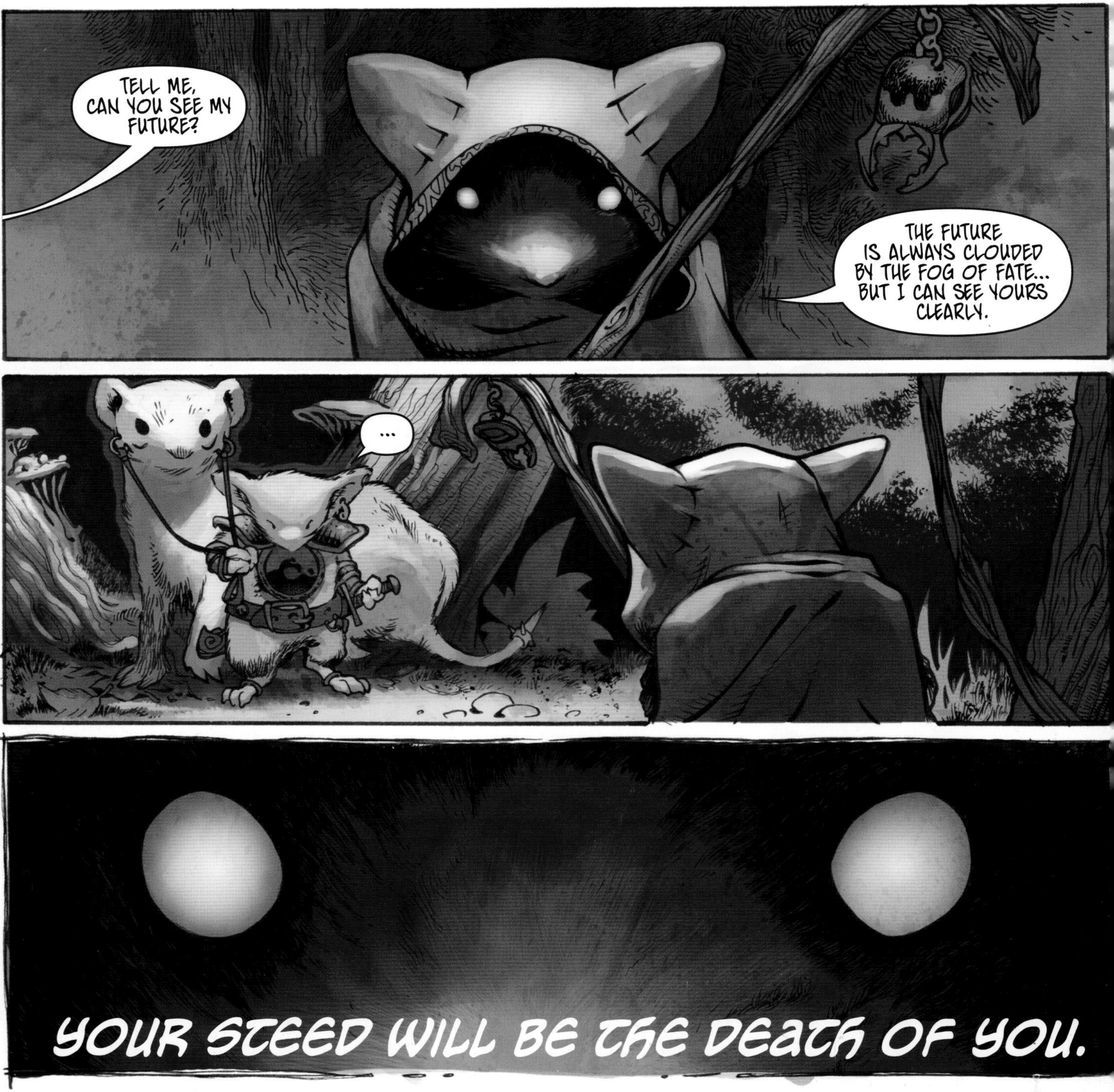
TELL ME, CAN YOU SEE MY FUTURE?
THE FUTURE IS ALWAYS CLOUDED BY THE FOG OF FATE... BUT I CAN SEE YOURS CLEARLY.
...
YOUR STEED WILL BE THE DEATH OF YOU.

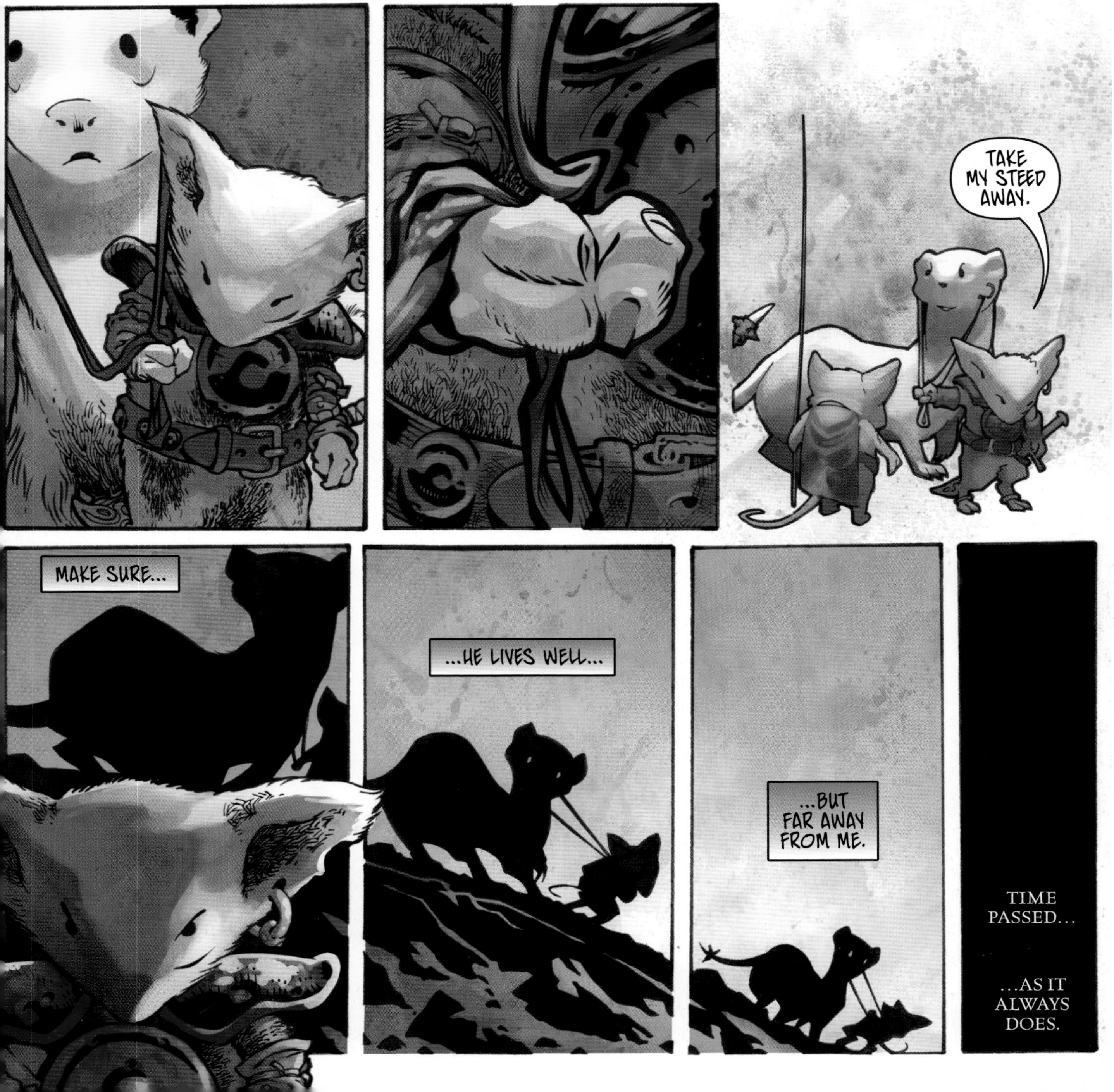
TAKE MY STEED AWAY.
MAKE SURE...
...HE LIVES WELL...
...BUT FAR AWAY FROM ME.
TIME PASSED...
...AS IT ALWAYS DOES.

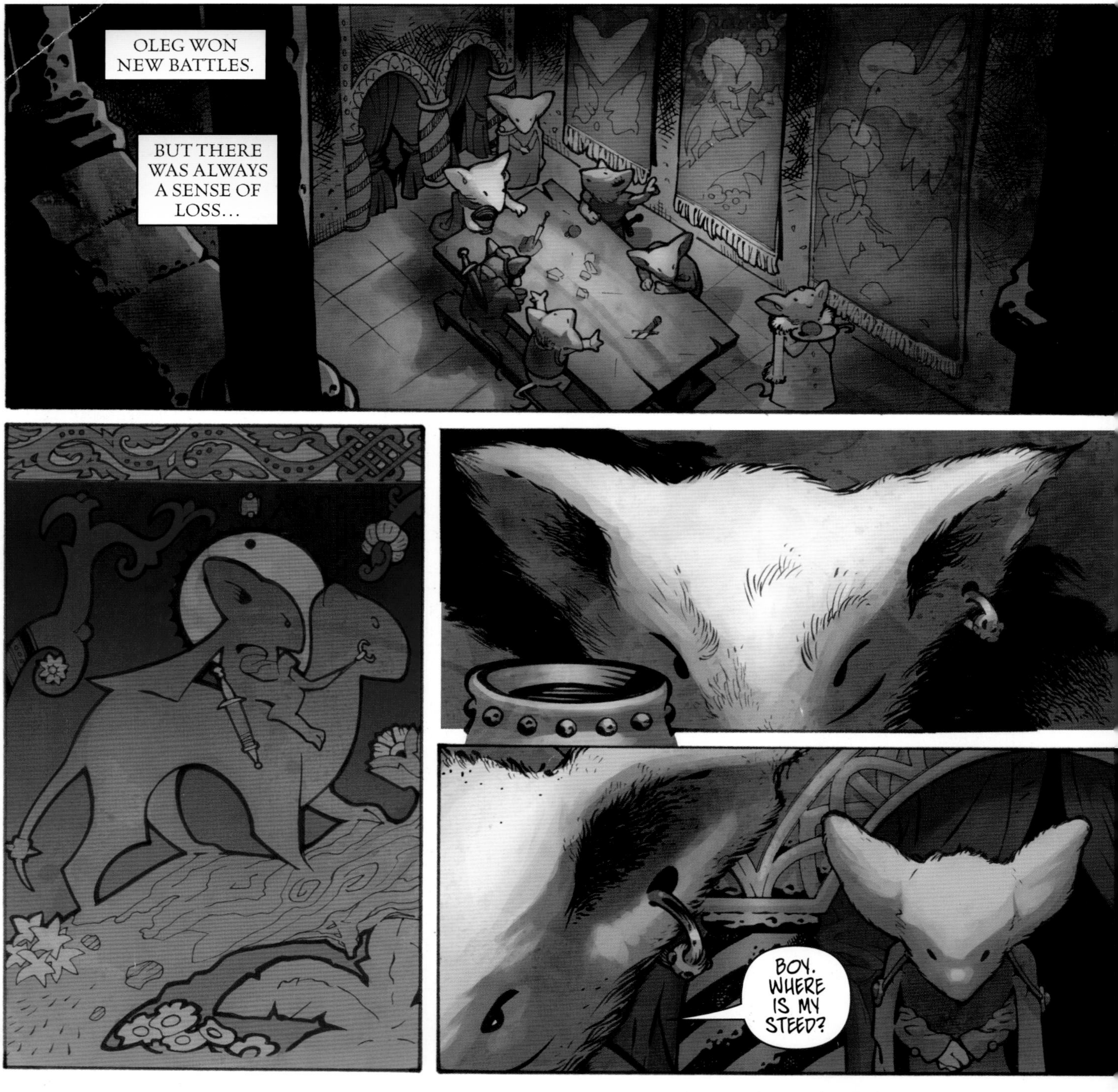
OLEG WON NEW BATTLES.
BUT THERE WAS ALWAYS A SENSE OF LOSS…
BOY. WHERE IS MY STEED?

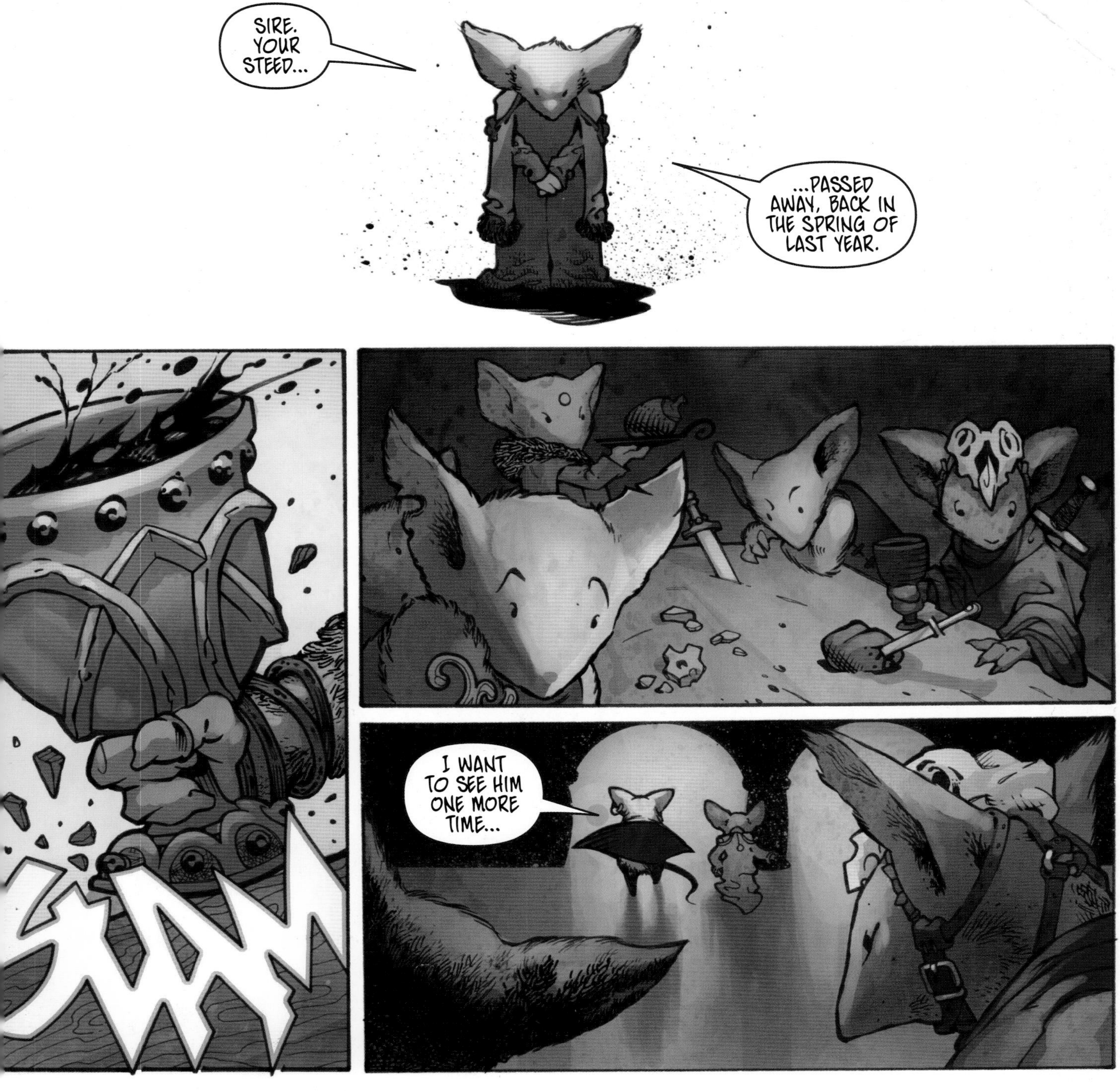
SIRE. YOUR STEED...
...PASSED AWAY, BACK IN THE SPRING OF LAST YEAR.
WAM
I WANT TO SEE HIM ONE MORE TIME...

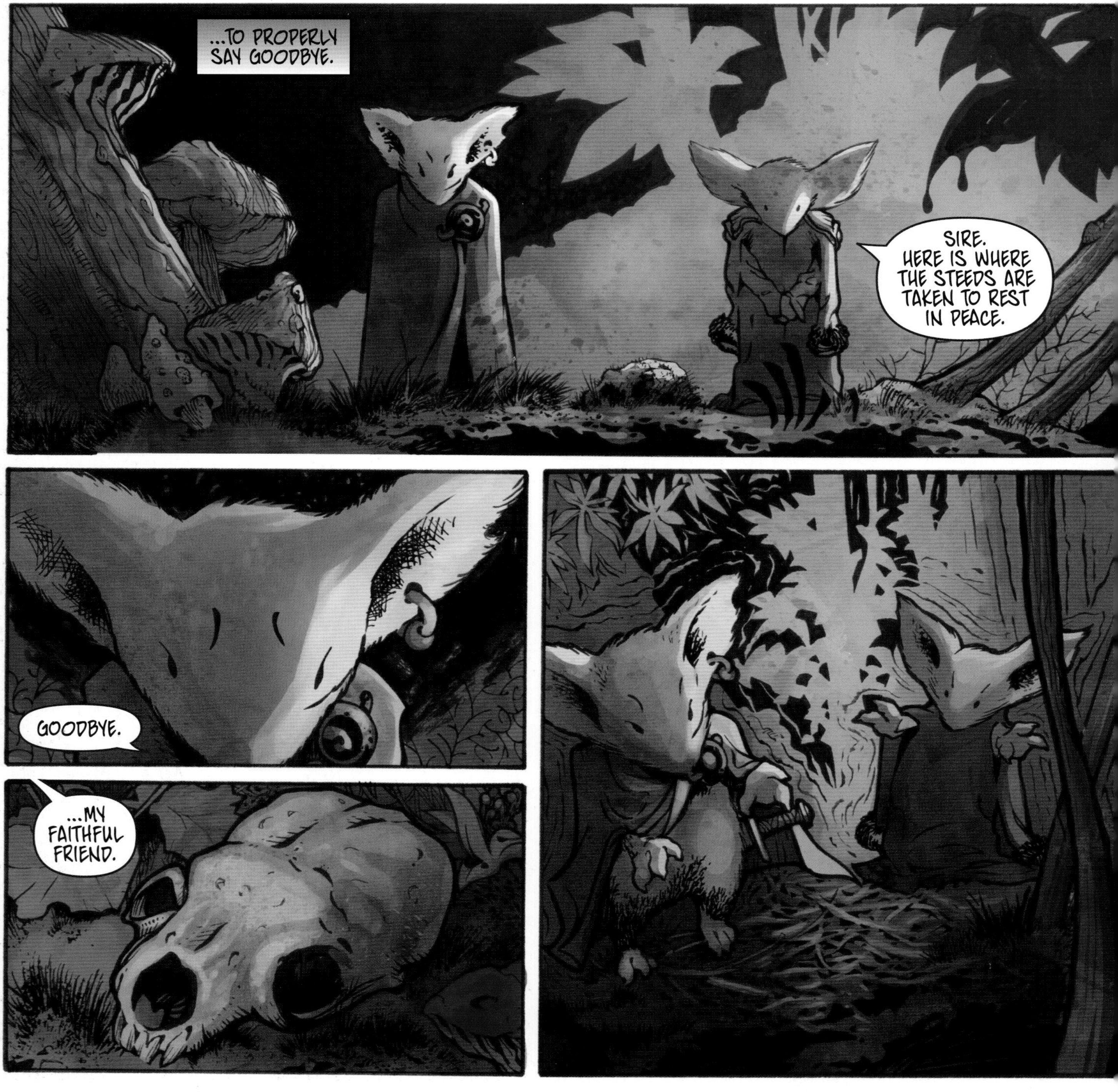
...TO PROPERLY SAY GOODBYE.
SIRE. HERE IS WHERE THE STEEDS ARE TAKEN TO REST IN PEACE.
GOODBYE.
...MY FAITHFUL FRIEND.

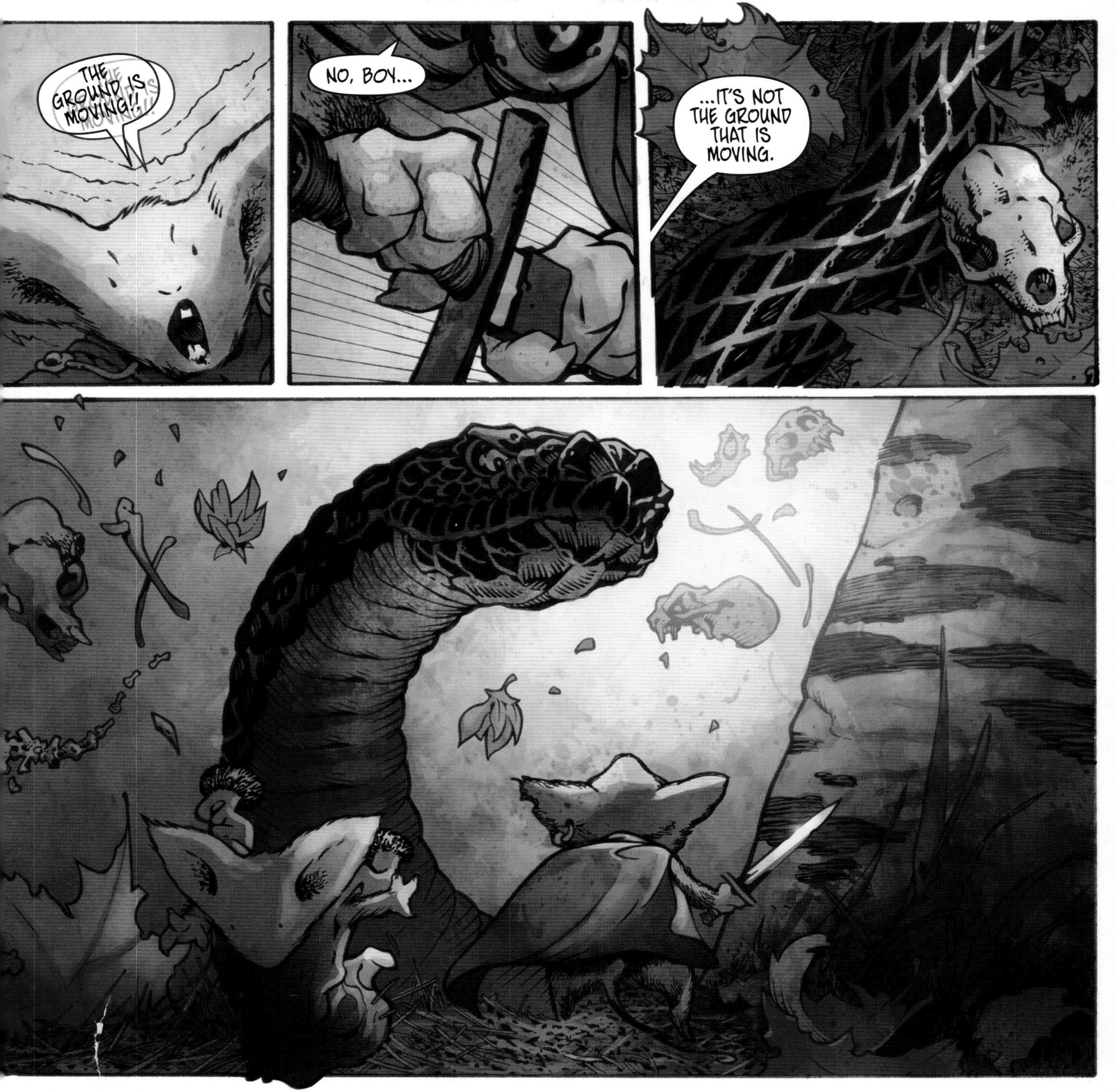
THE GROUND IS MOVING!!
NO, BOY...
...IT'S NOT THE GROUND THAT IS MOVING.

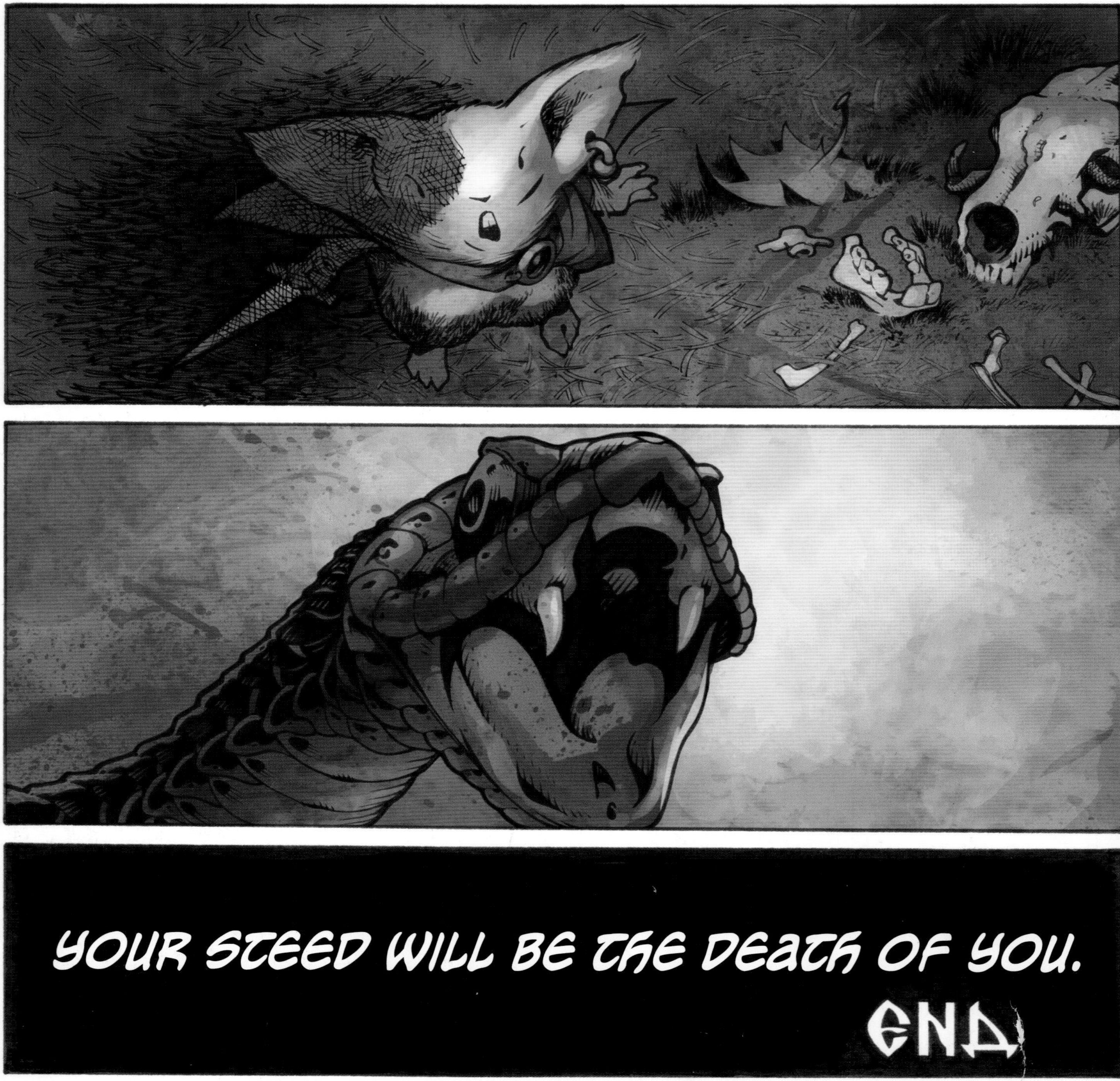
YOUR STEED WILL BE THE DEATH OF YOU.
END

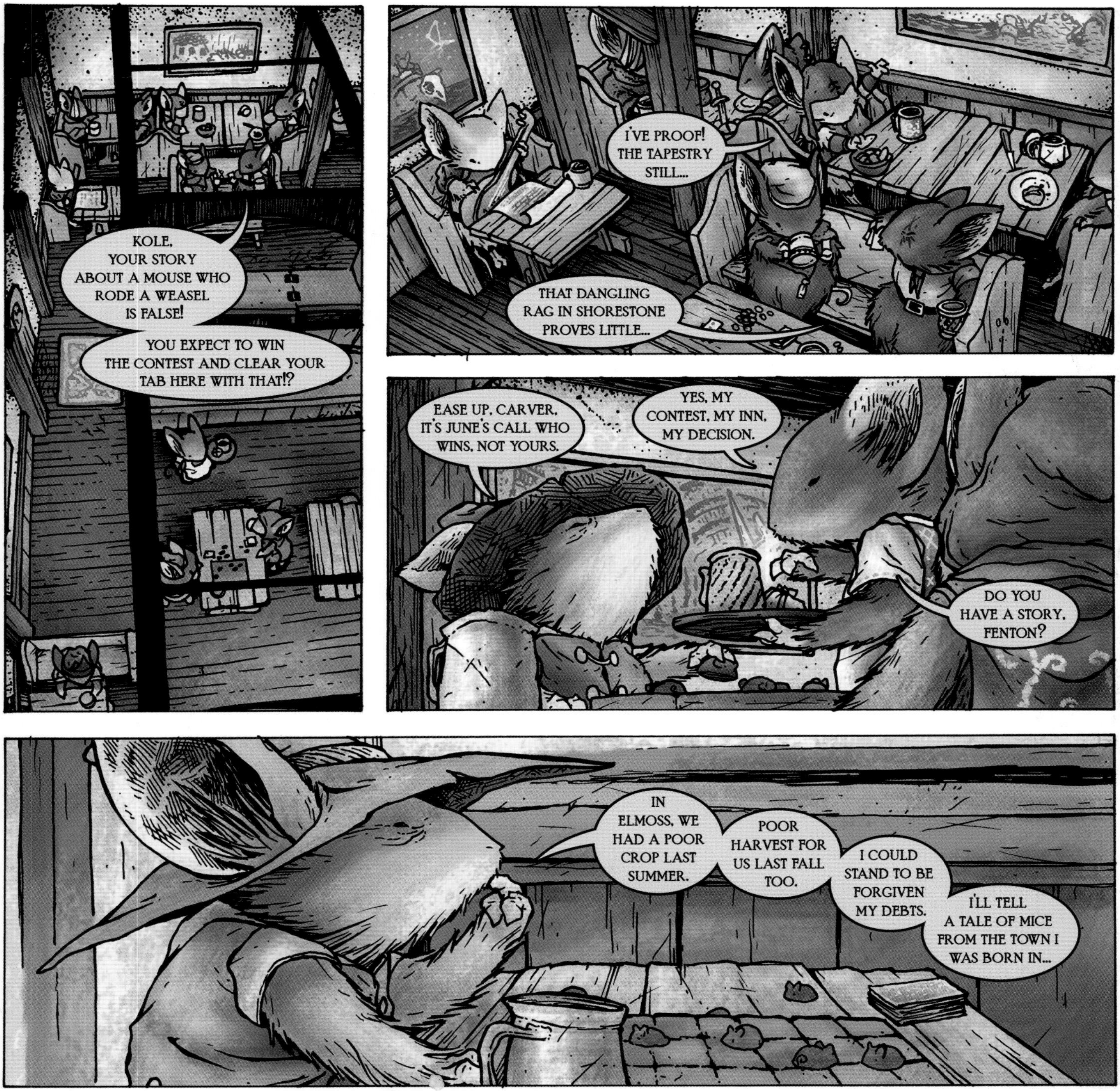
KOLE, YOUR STORY ABOUT A MOUSE WHO RODE A WEASEL IS FALSE!
YOU EXPECT TO WIN THE CONTEST AND CLEAR YOUR TAB HERE WITH THAT!?
I'VE PROOF! THE TAPESTRY STILL...
THAT DANGLING RAG IN SHORESTONE PROVES LITTLE...
EASE UP, CARVER. IT'S JUNE'S CALL WHO WINS, NOT YOURS.
YES, MY CONTEST, MY INN, MY DECISION.
DO YOU HAVE A STORY, FENTON?
IN ELMOSS, WE HAD A POOR CROP LAST SUMMER.
POOR HARVEST FOR US LAST FALL TOO.
I COULD STAND TO BE FORGIVEN MY DEBTS.
I'LL TELL A TALE OF MICE FROM THE TOWN I WAS BORN IN...

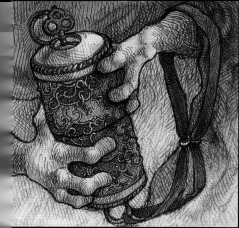

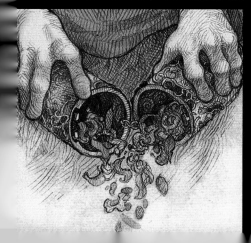

IS IT ALRIGHT FOR THE HERBS TO SCATTER LIKE THAT?

YES. TOO SMALL OF AN AREA, AND THE BEAST WON'T SMELL THEM.

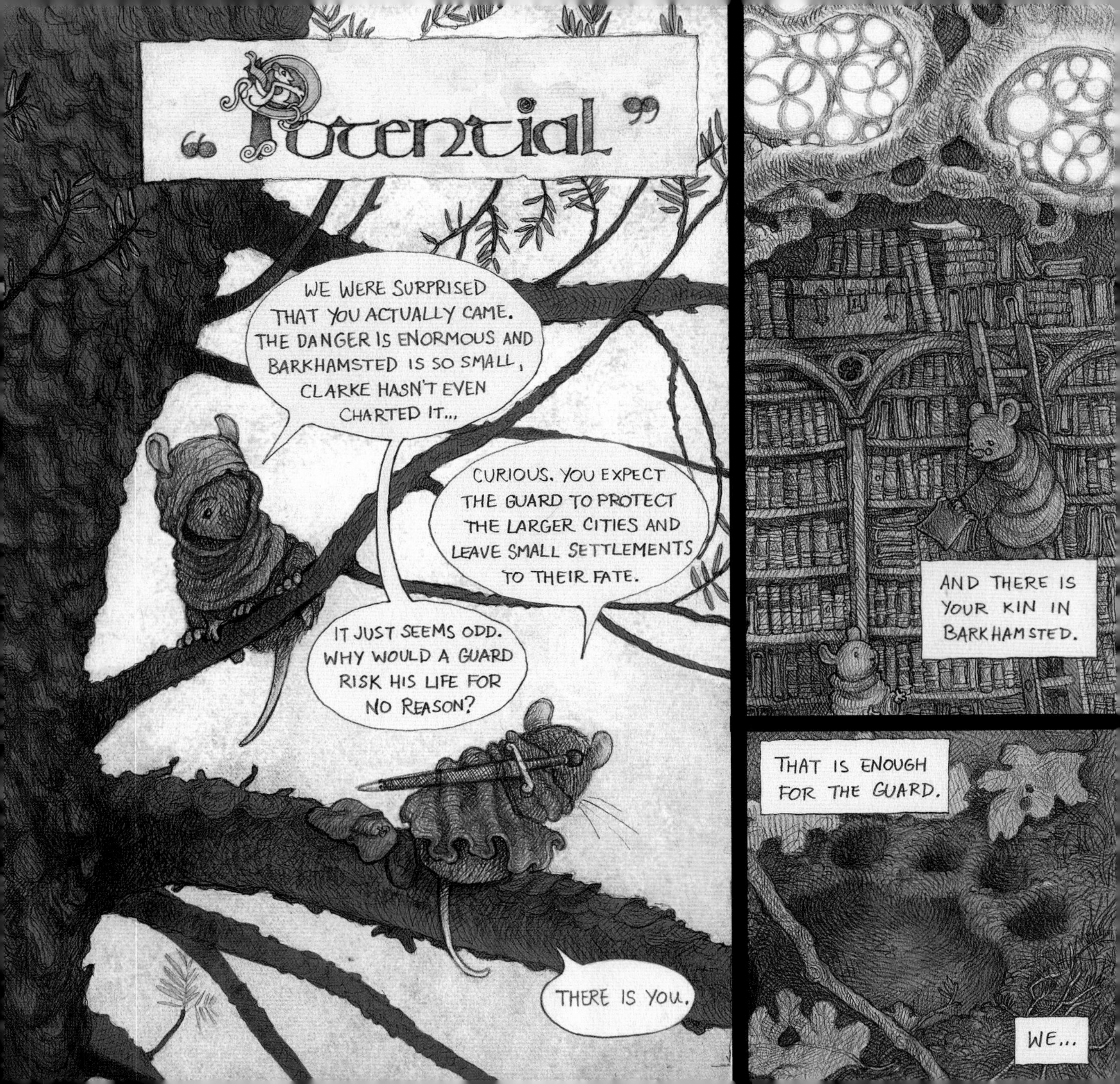
"Potential"
WE WERE SURPRISED THAT YOU ACTUALLY CAME. THE DANGER IS ENORMOUS AND BARKHAMSTED IS SO SMALL, CLARKE HASN'T EVEN CHARTED IT...
IT JUST SEEMS ODD. WHY WOULD A GUARD RISK HIS LIFE FOR NO REASON?
CURIOUS. YOU EXPECT THE GUARD TO PROTECT THE LARGER CITIES AND LEAVE SMALL SETTLEMENTS TO THEIR FATE.
THERE IS YOU.
AND THERE IS YOUR KIN IN BARKHAMSTED.
THAT IS ENOUGH FOR THE GUARD.
WE...

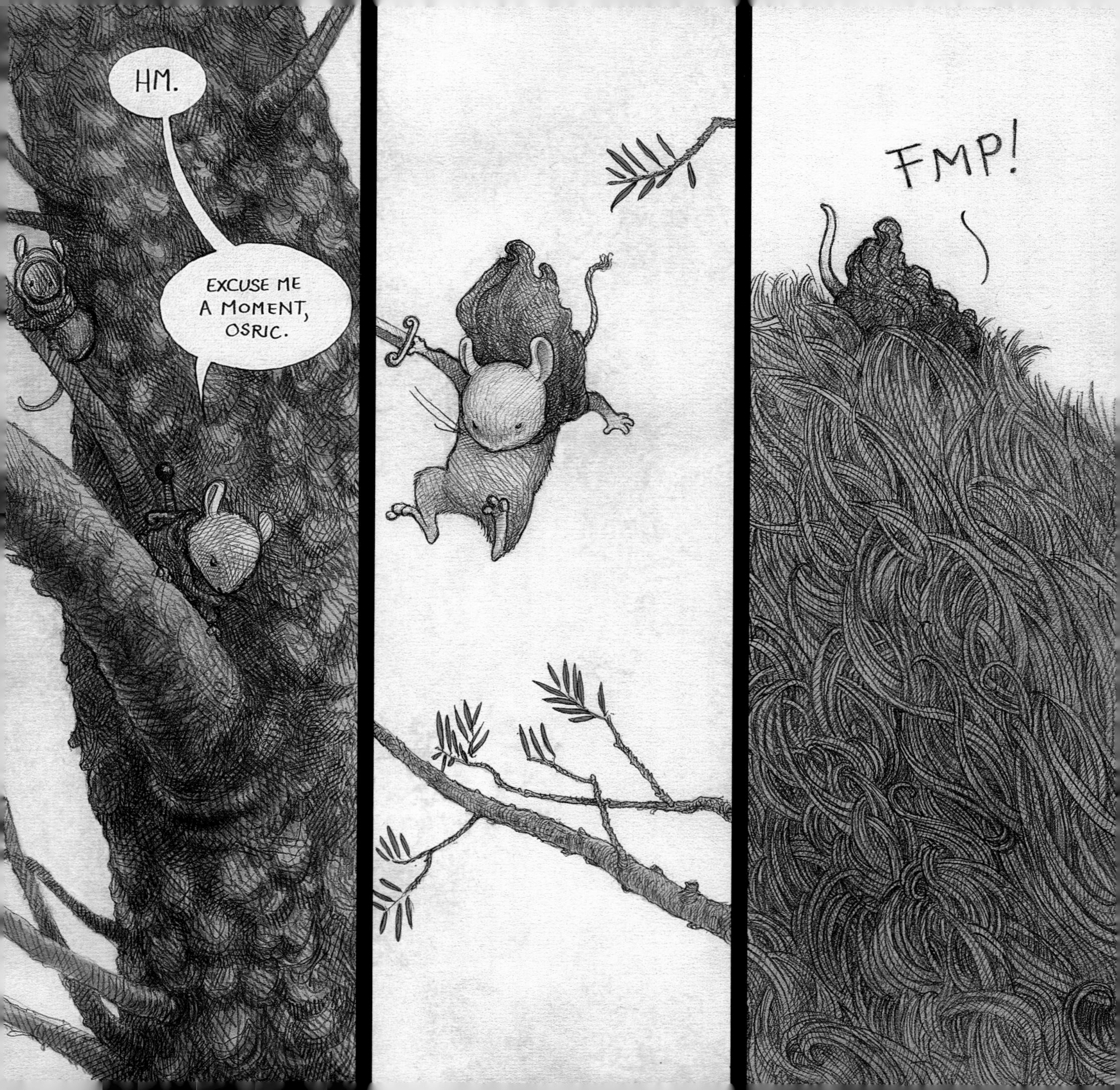
HM.
EXCUSE ME A MOMENT, OSRIC.
FMP!

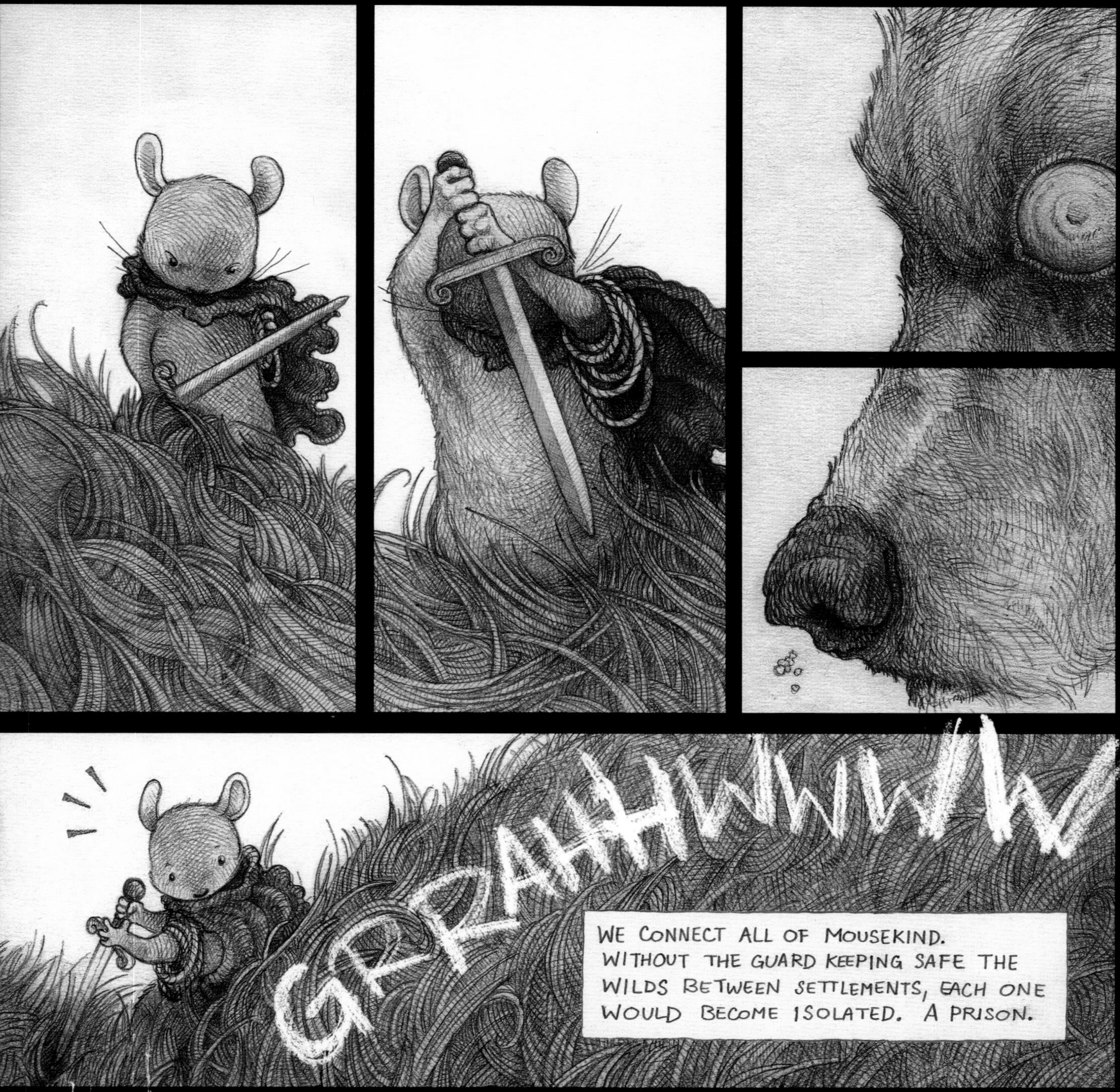
GRRAHHWWWW
WE CONNECT ALL OF MOUSEKIND. WITHOUT THE GUARD KEEPING SAFE THE WILDS BETWEEN SETTLEMENTS, EACH ONE WOULD BECOME ISOLATED. A PRISON.

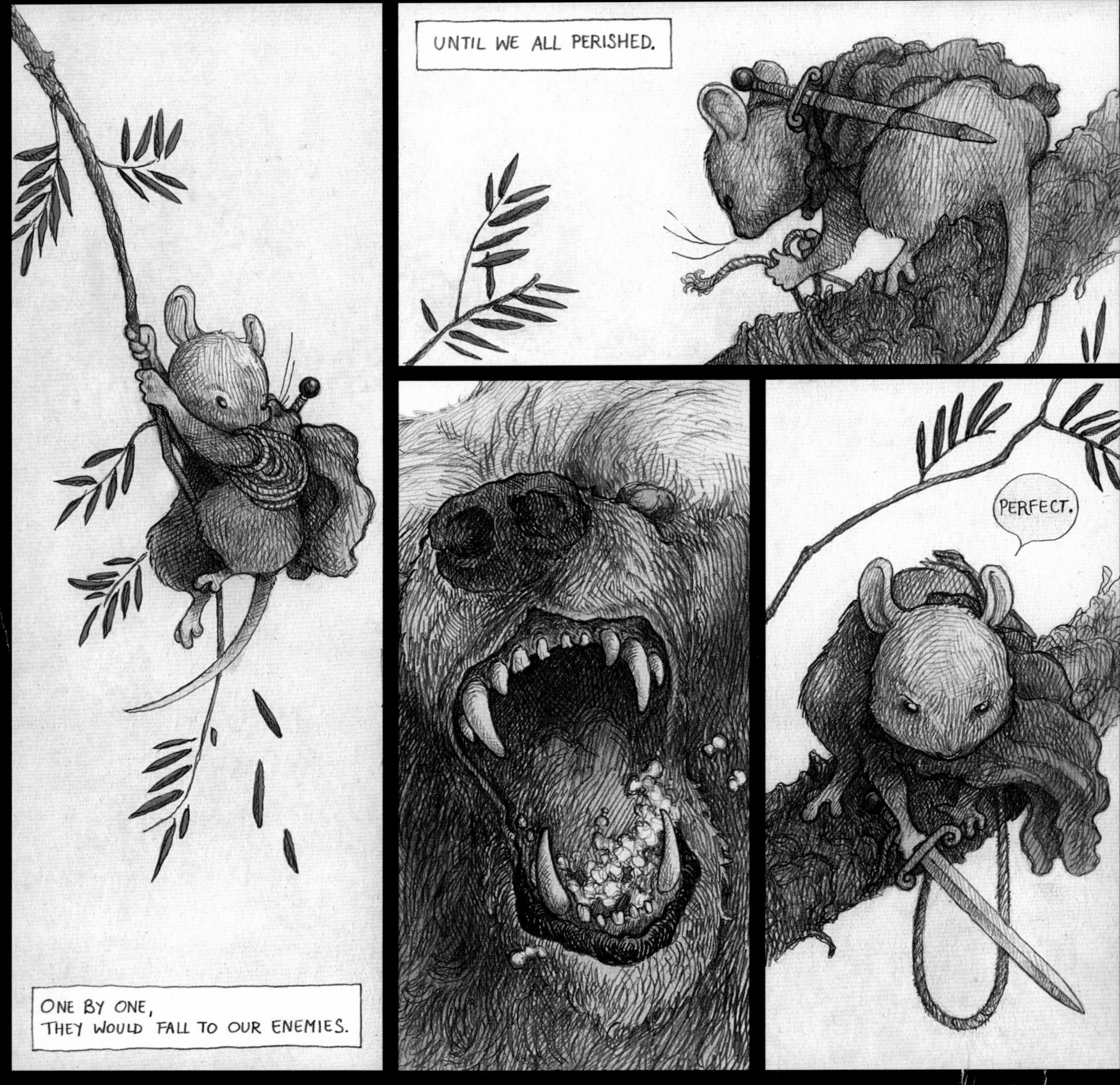
ONE BY ONE,
THEY WOULD FALL TO OUR ENEMIES.
UNTIL WE ALL PERISHED.
PERFECT.

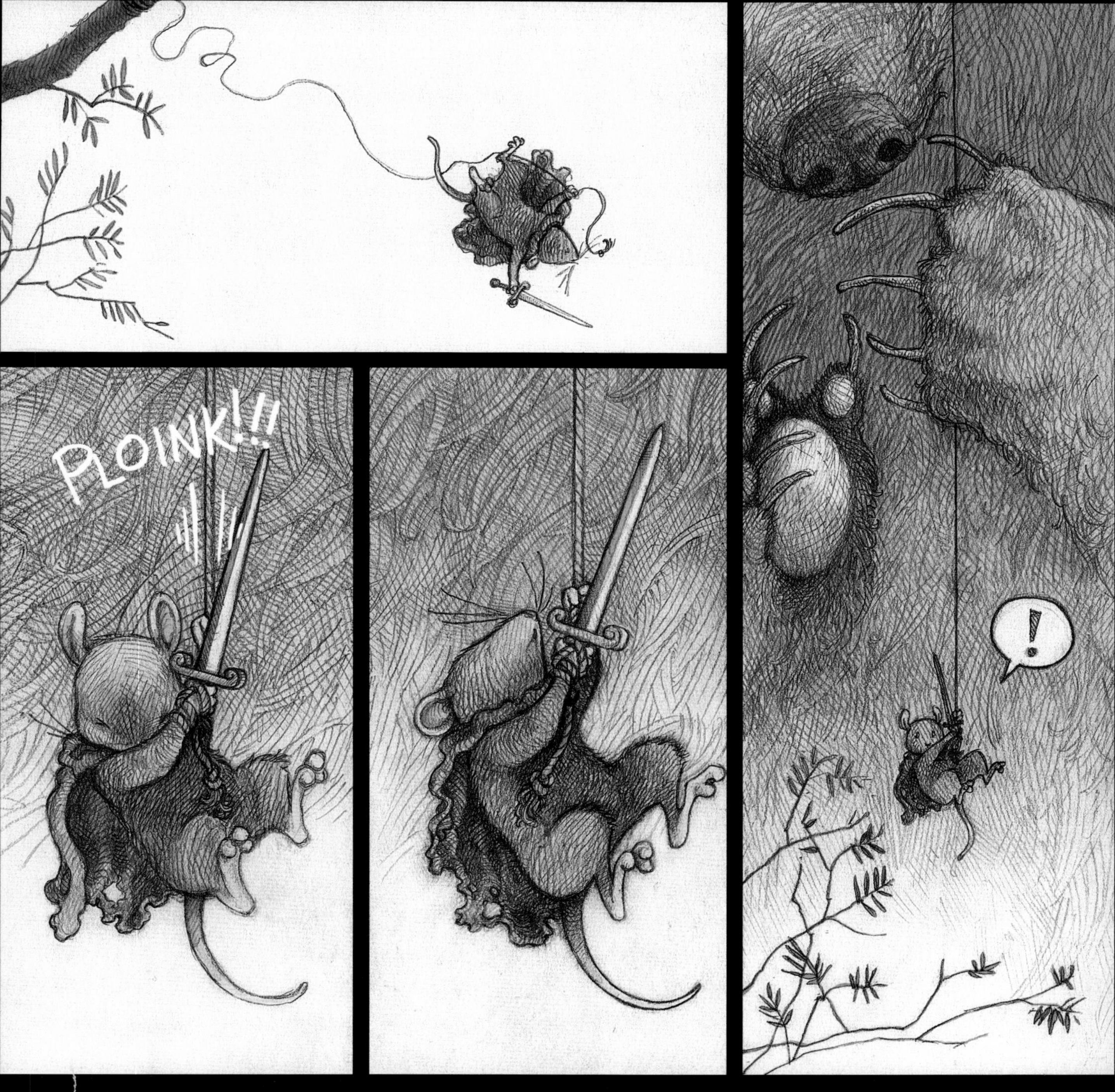
PLOINK!!!
!

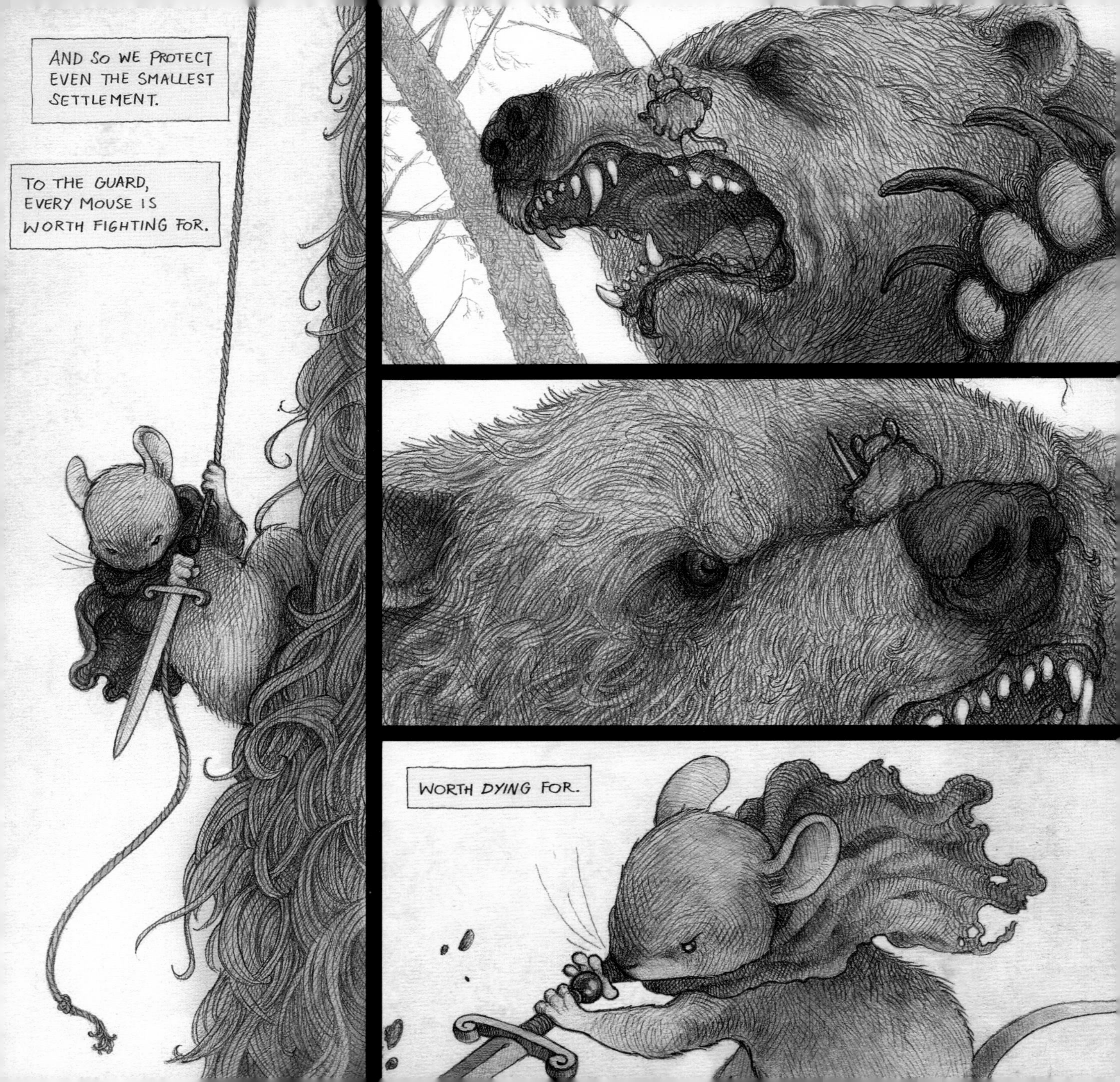
AND SO WE PROTECT EVEN THE SMALLEST SETTLEMENT.
TO THE GUARD, EVERY MOUSE IS WORTH FIGHTING FOR.
WORTH *DYING* FOR.

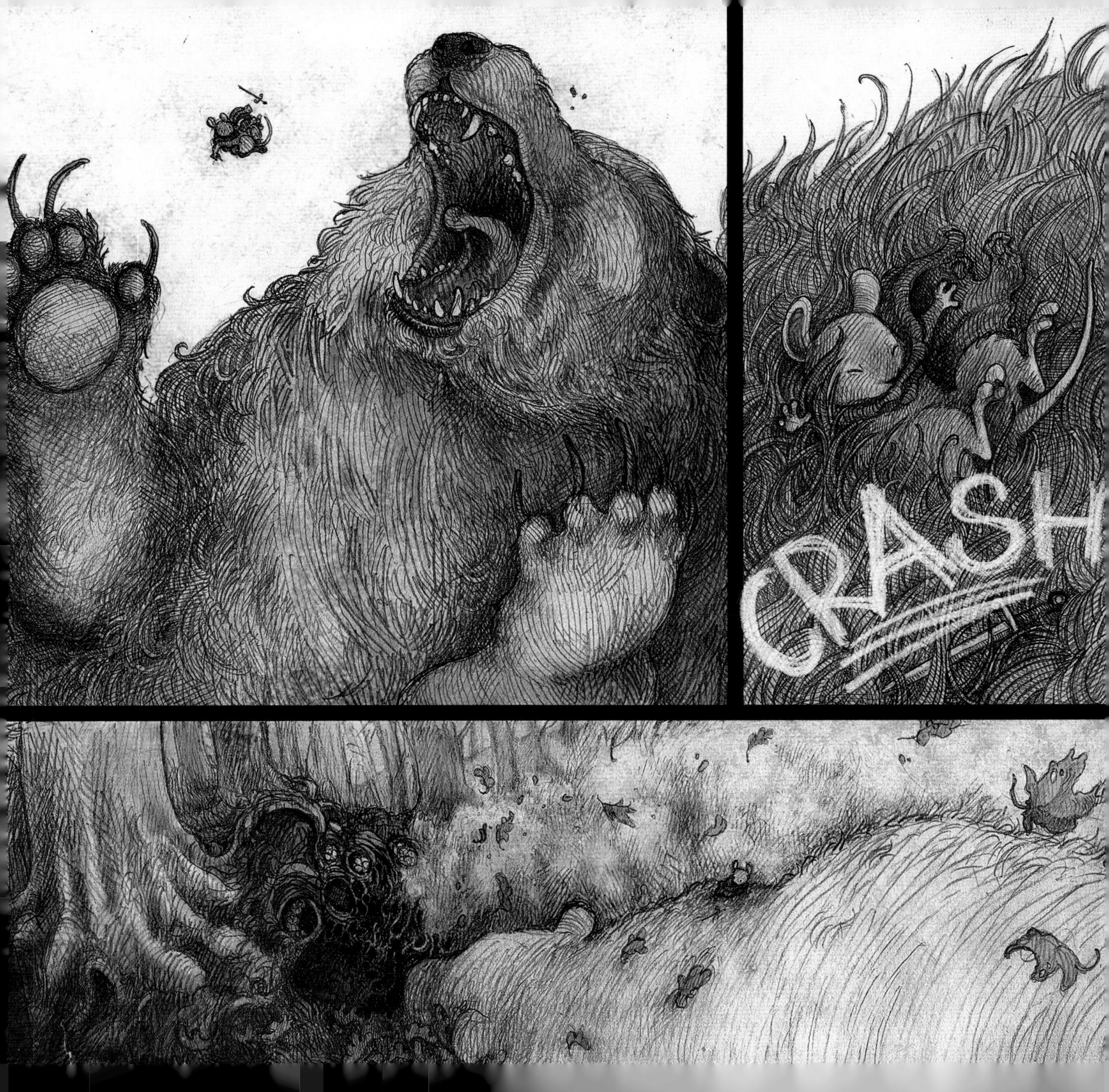
CRASH

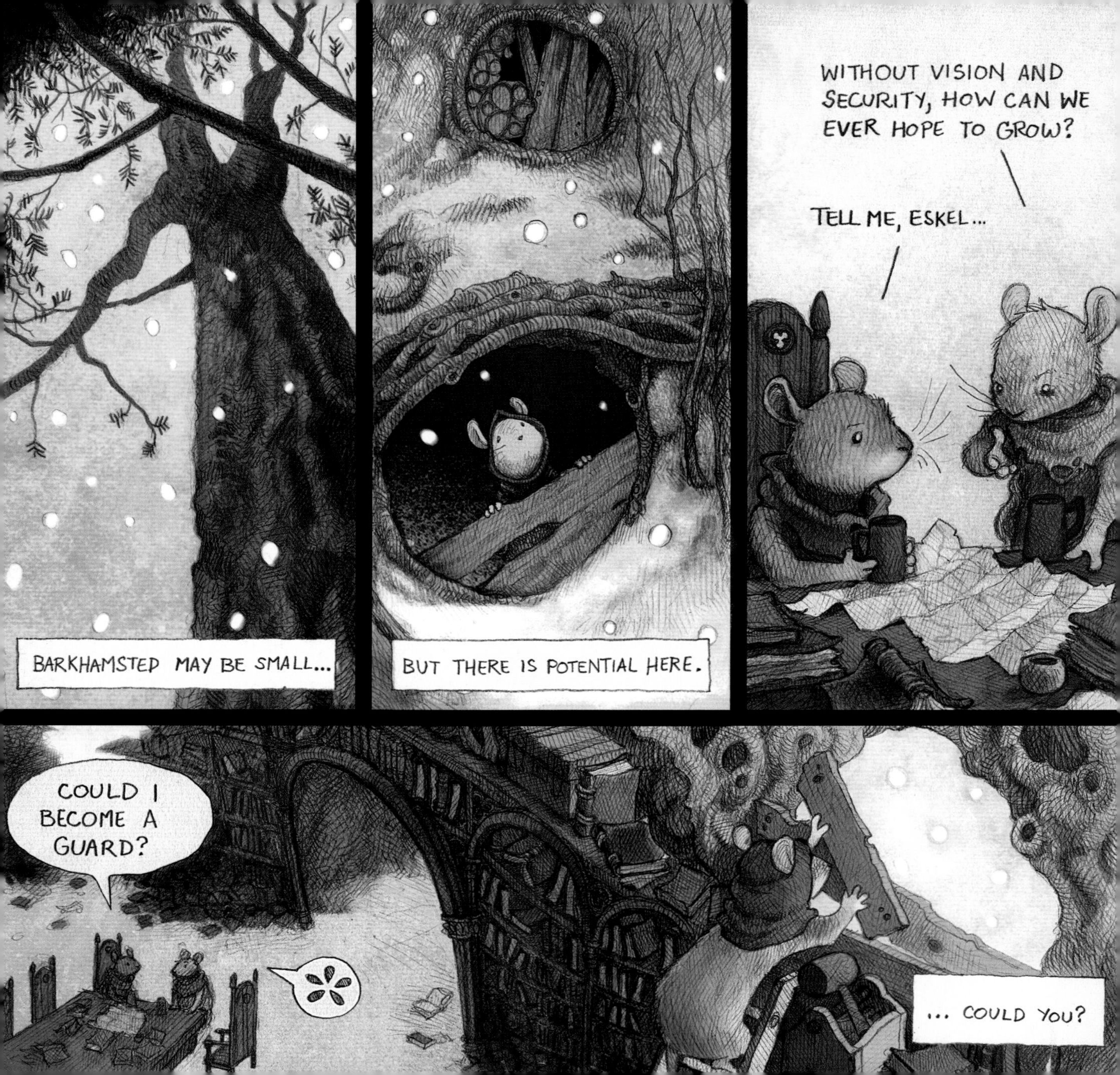
BARKHAMSTED MAY BE SMALL...
BUT THERE IS POTENTIAL HERE.
WITHOUT VISION AND SECURITY, HOW CAN WE EVER HOPE TO GROW?
TELL ME, ESKEL...
COULD I BECOME A GUARD?
... COULD YOU?

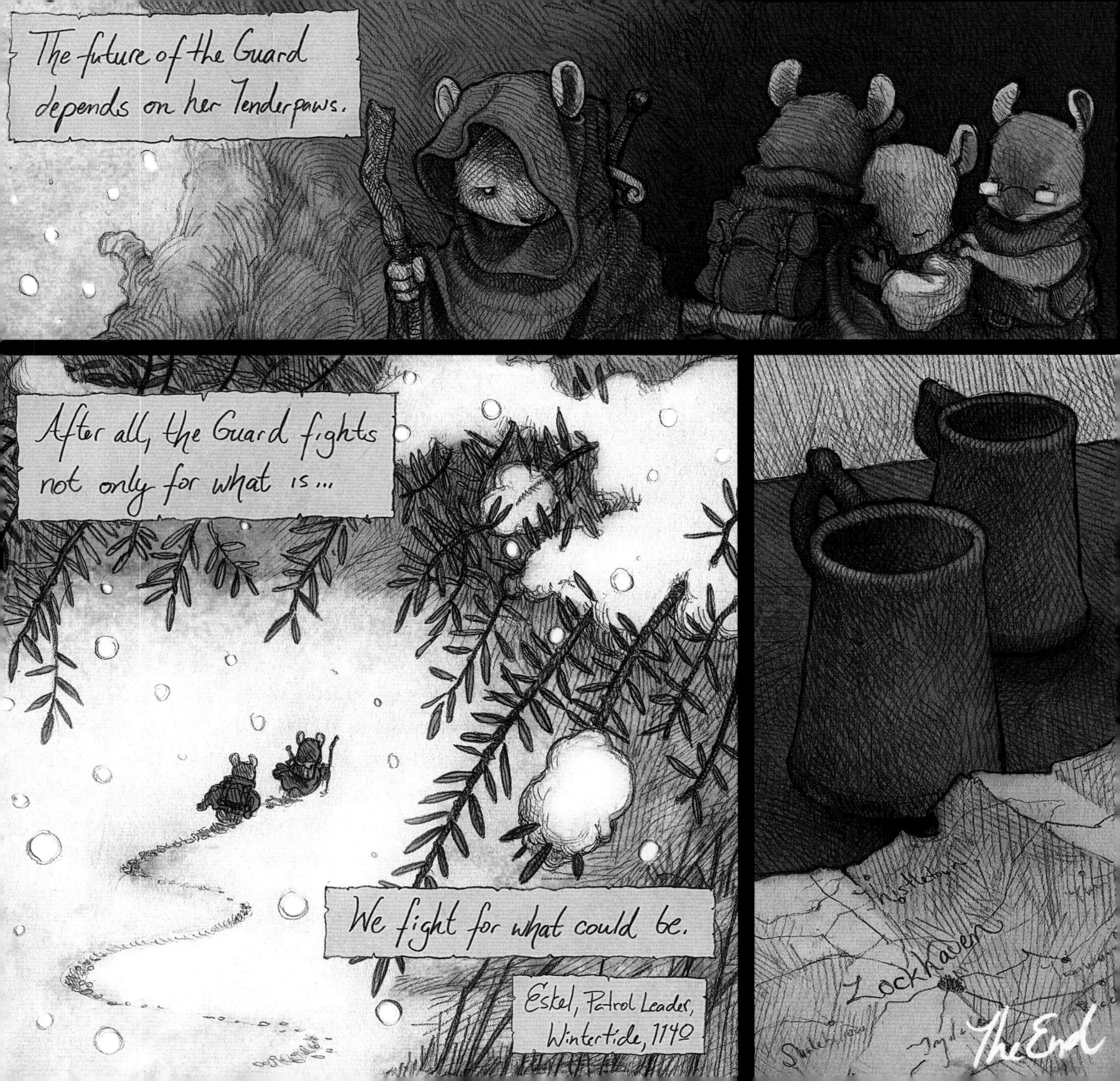
The future of the Guard depends on her Tenderpaws.
After all, the Guard fights not only for what is...
We fight for what could be.
Eskel, Patrol Leader, Wintertide, 1140
Thistletown
Lockhaven
The End

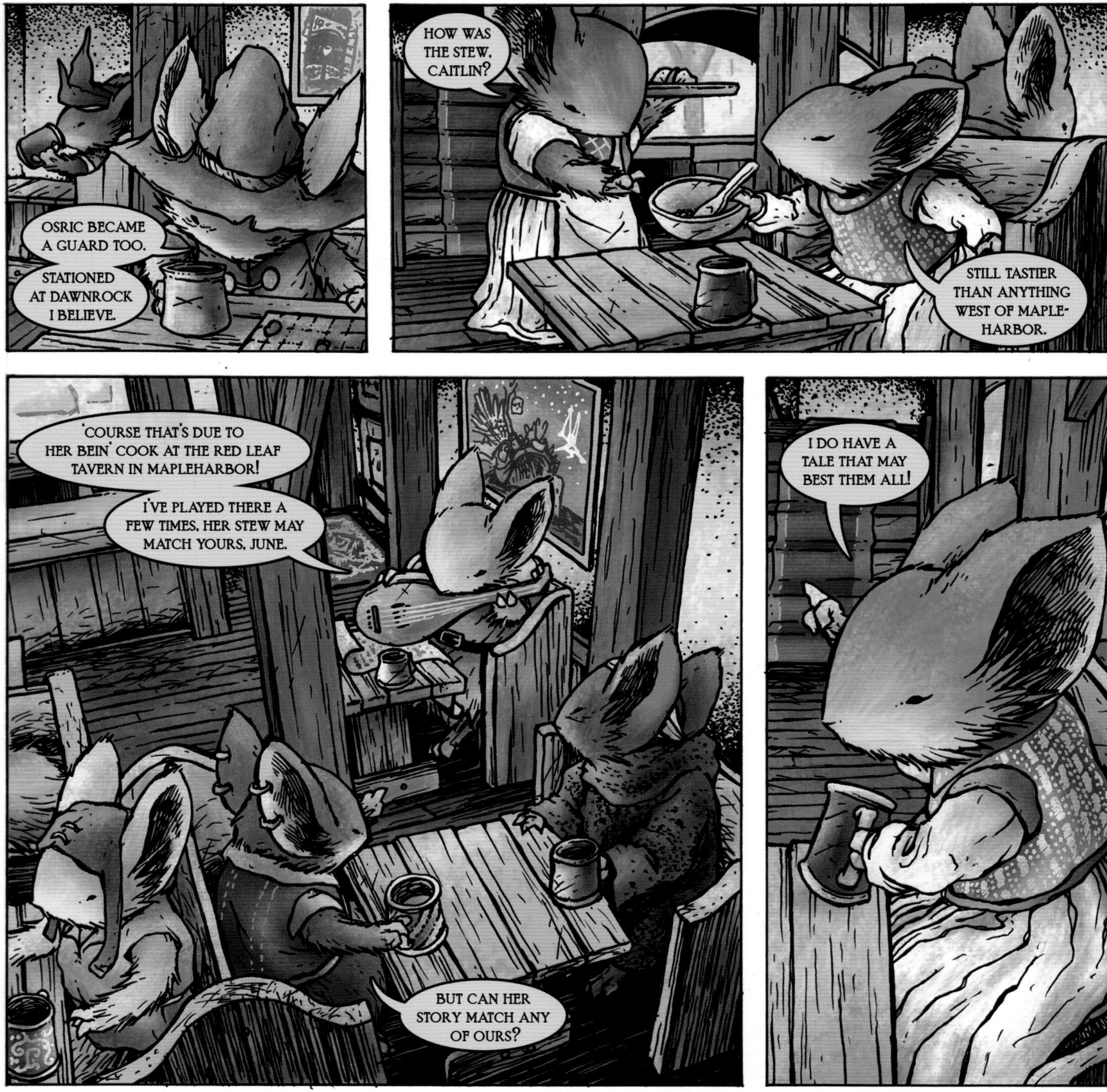
OSRIC BECAME A GUARD TOO.
STATIONED AT DAWNROCK I BELIEVE.
HOW WAS THE STEW, CAITLIN?
STILL TASTIER THAN ANYTHING WEST OF MAPLE-HARBOR.
'COURSE THAT'S DUE TO HER BEIN' COOK AT THE RED LEAF TAVERN IN MAPLEHARBOR!
I'VE PLAYED THERE A FEW TIMES. HER STEW MAY MATCH YOURS, JUNE.
BUT CAN HER STORY MATCH ANY OF OURS?
I DO HAVE A TALE THAT MAY BEST THEM ALL!

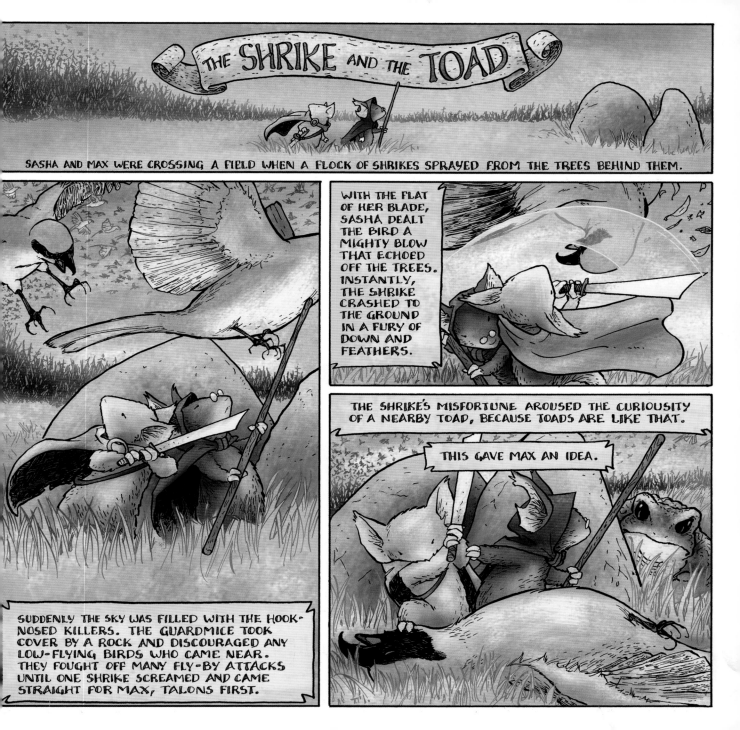

THE SHRIKE AND THE TOAD

SASHA AND MAX WERE CROSSING A FIELD WHEN A FLOCK OF SHRIKES SPRAYED FROM THE TREES BEHIND THEM.

WITH THE FLAT OF HER BLADE, SASHA DEALT THE BIRD A MIGHTY BLOW THAT ECHOED OFF THE TREES. INSTANTLY, THE SHRIKE CRASHED TO THE GROUND IN A FURY OF DOWN AND FEATHERS.

THE SHRIKE'S MISFORTUNE AROUSED THE CURIOUSITY OF A NEARBY TOAD, BECAUSE TOADS ARE LIKE THAT.

THIS GAVE MAX AN IDEA.

SUDDENLY THE SKY WAS FILLED WITH THE HOOK-NOSED KILLERS. THE GUARDMICE TOOK COVER BY A ROCK AND DISCOURAGED ANY LOW-FLYING BIRDS WHO CAME NEAR. THEY FOUGHT OFF MANY FLY-BY ATTACKS UNTIL ONE SHRIKE SCREAMED AND CAME STRAIGHT FOR MAX, TALONS FIRST.

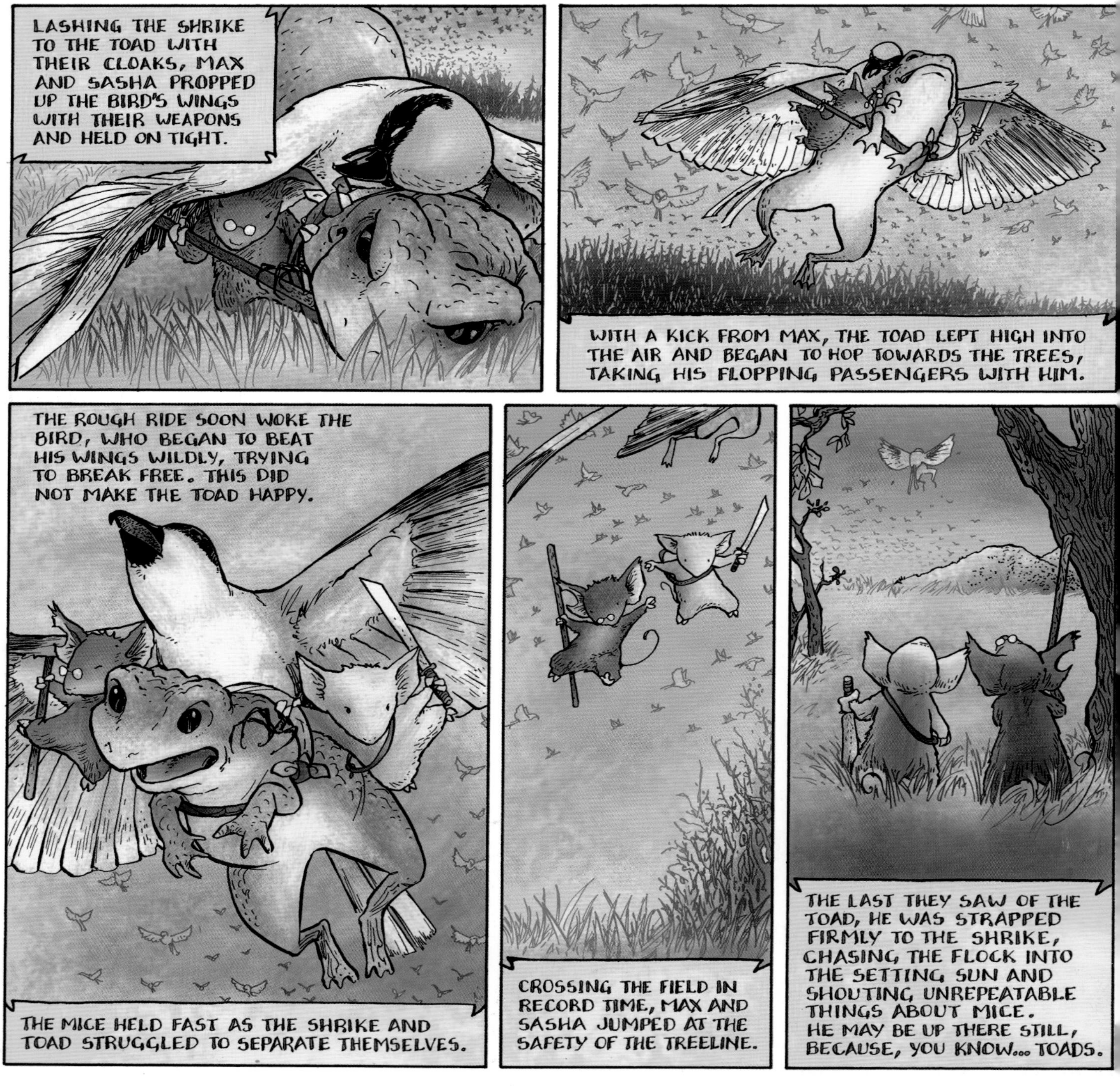
LASHING THE SHRIKE TO THE TOAD WITH THEIR CLOAKS, MAX AND SASHA PROPPED UP THE BIRD'S WINGS WITH THEIR WEAPONS AND HELD ON TIGHT.
WITH A KICK FROM MAX, THE TOAD LEPT HIGH INTO THE AIR AND BEGAN TO HOP TOWARDS THE TREES, TAKING HIS FLOPPING PASSENGERS WITH HIM.
THE ROUGH RIDE SOON WOKE THE BIRD, WHO BEGAN TO BEAT HIS WINGS WILDLY, TRYING TO BREAK FREE. THIS DID NOT MAKE THE TOAD HAPPY.
THE MICE HELD FAST AS THE SHRIKE AND TOAD STRUGGLED TO SEPARATE THEMSELVES.
CROSSING THE FIELD IN RECORD TIME, MAX AND SASHA JUMPED AT THE SAFETY OF THE TREELINE.
THE LAST THEY SAW OF THE TOAD, HE WAS STRAPPED FIRMLY TO THE SHRIKE, CHASING THE FLOCK INTO THE SETTING SUN AND SHOUTING UNREPEATABLE THINGS ABOUT MICE.
HE MAY BE UP THERE STILL, BECAUSE, YOU KNOW... TOADS.

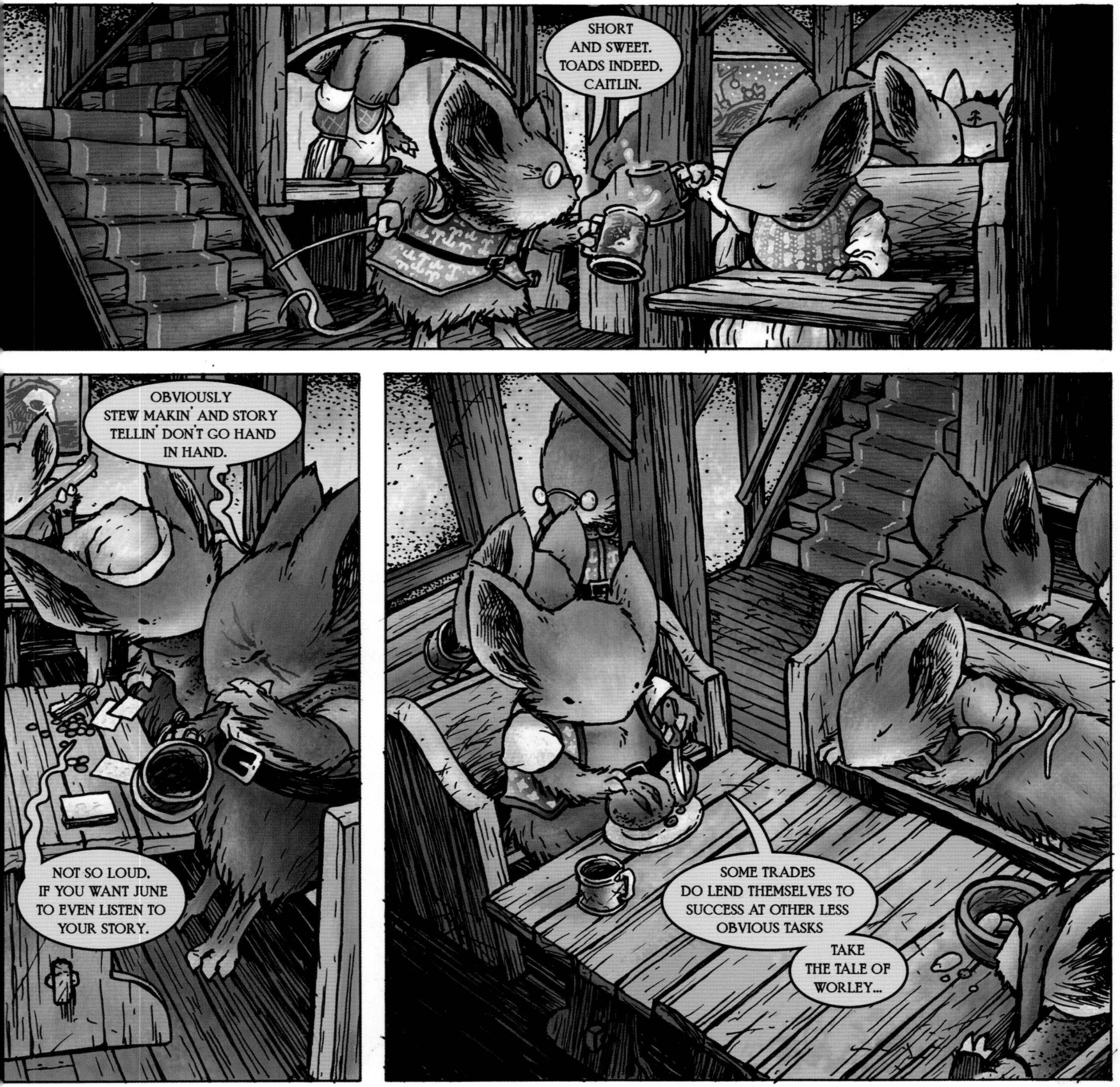
SHORT AND SWEET. TOADS INDEED, CAITLIN.
OBVIOUSLY STEW MAKIN' AND STORY TELLIN' DON'T GO HAND IN HAND.
NOT SO LOUD, IF YOU WANT JUNE TO EVEN LISTEN TO YOUR STORY.
SOME TRADES DO LEND THEMSELVES TO SUCCESS AT OTHER LESS OBVIOUS TASKS
TAKE THE TALE OF WORLEY...

WORLEY CAME FROM LOST WALNUTPECK,
WHERE COWARDICE IS VIRTUE.
BUT THAT WAS NOT FOR HIM.
HE LEFT AS A YOUTH TO SEEK ADVENTURE,
BUT FOUND SOMETHING ELSE.

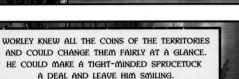

FOR WORLEY BECAME
THE GREATEST AND MOST
STUBBORN BANKER
IN ALL THE TERRITORIES.

WORLEY KNEW ALL THE COINS OF THE TERRITORIES
AND COULD CHANGE THEM FAIRLY AT A GLANCE.
HE COULD MAKE A TIGHT-MINDED SPRUCETUCK
A DEAL AND LEAVE HIM SMILING.

WITH A SHARP MIND HE KEPT
HIS COLLEAGUES' MONEY SAFE.
HE INVESTED CAREFULLY AND
MADE SURE ALL GOT THEIR SHARE
WHEN AN EXPEDITION
CAME HOME SAFE.

AND HE NEVER, EVER LET ANYONE CHEAT HIM...

WORLEY &
THE MINK

ART BY
GENE HA

STORY BY
LOWELL FRANCIS

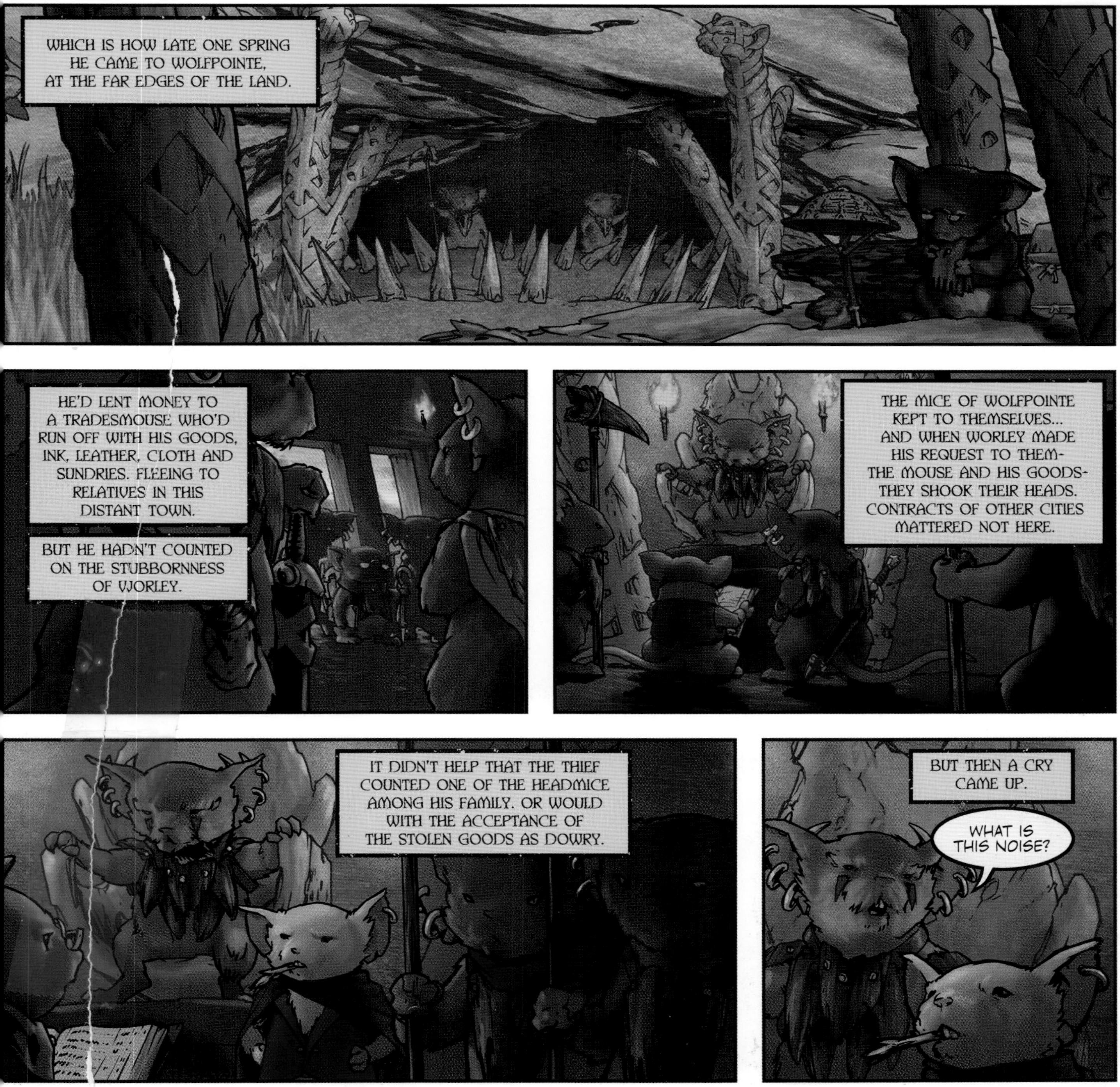
WHICH IS HOW LATE ONE SPRING HE CAME TO WOLFPOINTE, AT THE FAR EDGES OF THE LAND.
HE'D LENT MONEY TO A TRADESMOUSE WHO'D RUN OFF WITH HIS GOODS, INK, LEATHER, CLOTH AND SUNDRIES. FLEEING TO RELATIVES IN THIS DISTANT TOWN.
BUT HE HADN'T COUNTED ON THE STUBBORNNESS OF WORLEY.
THE MICE OF WOLFPOINTE KEPT TO THEMSELVES... AND WHEN WORLEY MADE HIS REQUEST TO THEM- THE MOUSE AND HIS GOODS- THEY SHOOK THEIR HEADS. CONTRACTS OF OTHER CITIES MATTERED NOT HERE.
IT DIDN'T HELP THAT THE THIEF COUNTED ONE OF THE HEADMICE AMONG HIS FAMILY. OR WOULD WITH THE ACCEPTANCE OF THE STOLEN GOODS AS DOWRY.
BUT THEN A CRY CAME UP.
WHAT IS THIS NOISE?

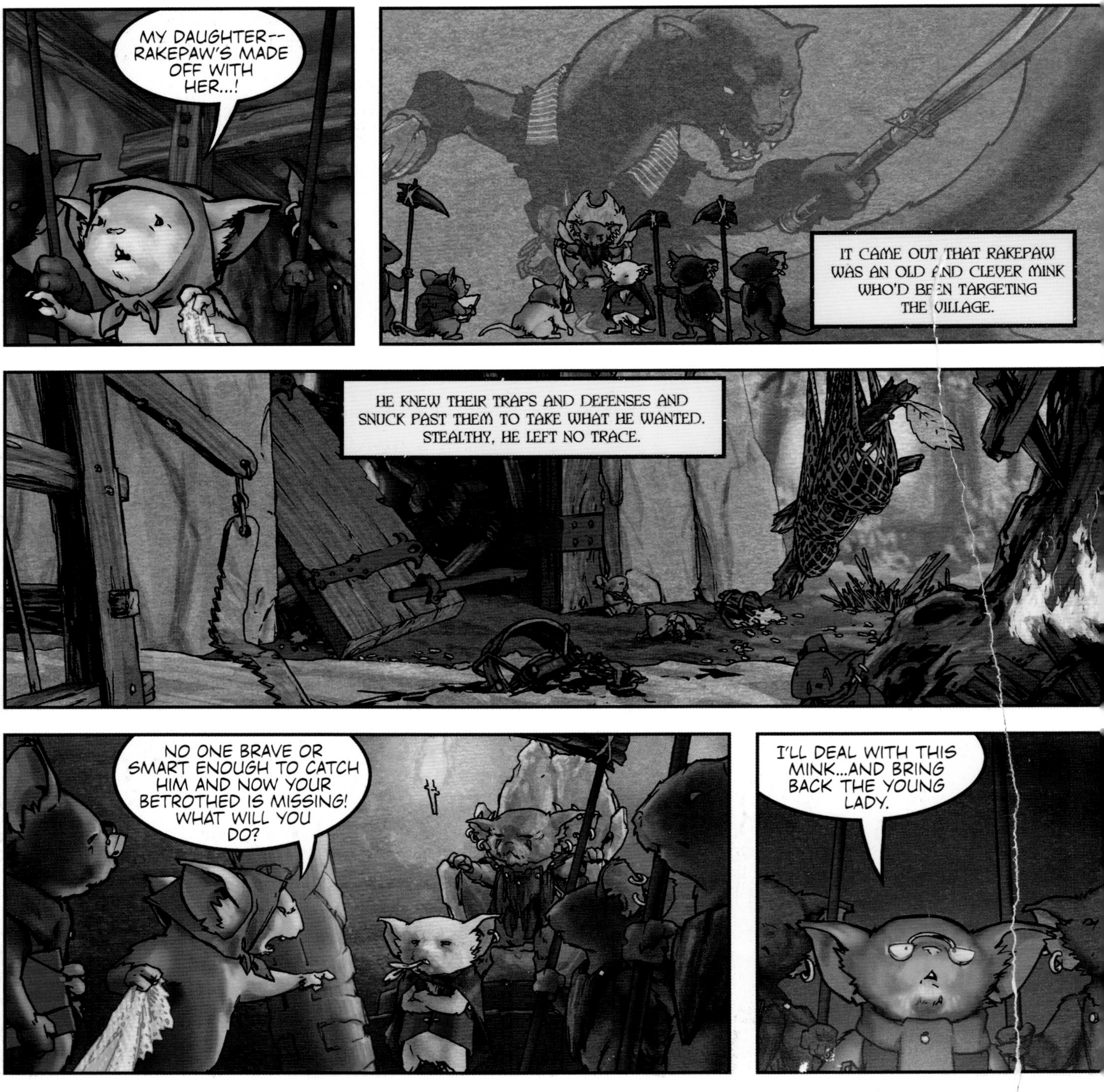
MY DAUGHTER-- RAKEPAW'S MADE OFF WITH HER...!
IT CAME OUT THAT RAKEPAW WAS AN OLD AND CLEVER MINK WHO'D BEEN TARGETING THE VILLAGE.
HE KNEW THEIR TRAPS AND DEFENSES AND SNUCK PAST THEM TO TAKE WHAT HE WANTED. STEALTHY, HE LEFT NO TRACE.
NO ONE BRAVE OR SMART ENOUGH TO CATCH HIM AND NOW YOUR BETROTHED IS MISSING! WHAT WILL YOU DO?
I'LL DEAL WITH THIS MINK...AND BRING BACK THE YOUNG LADY.

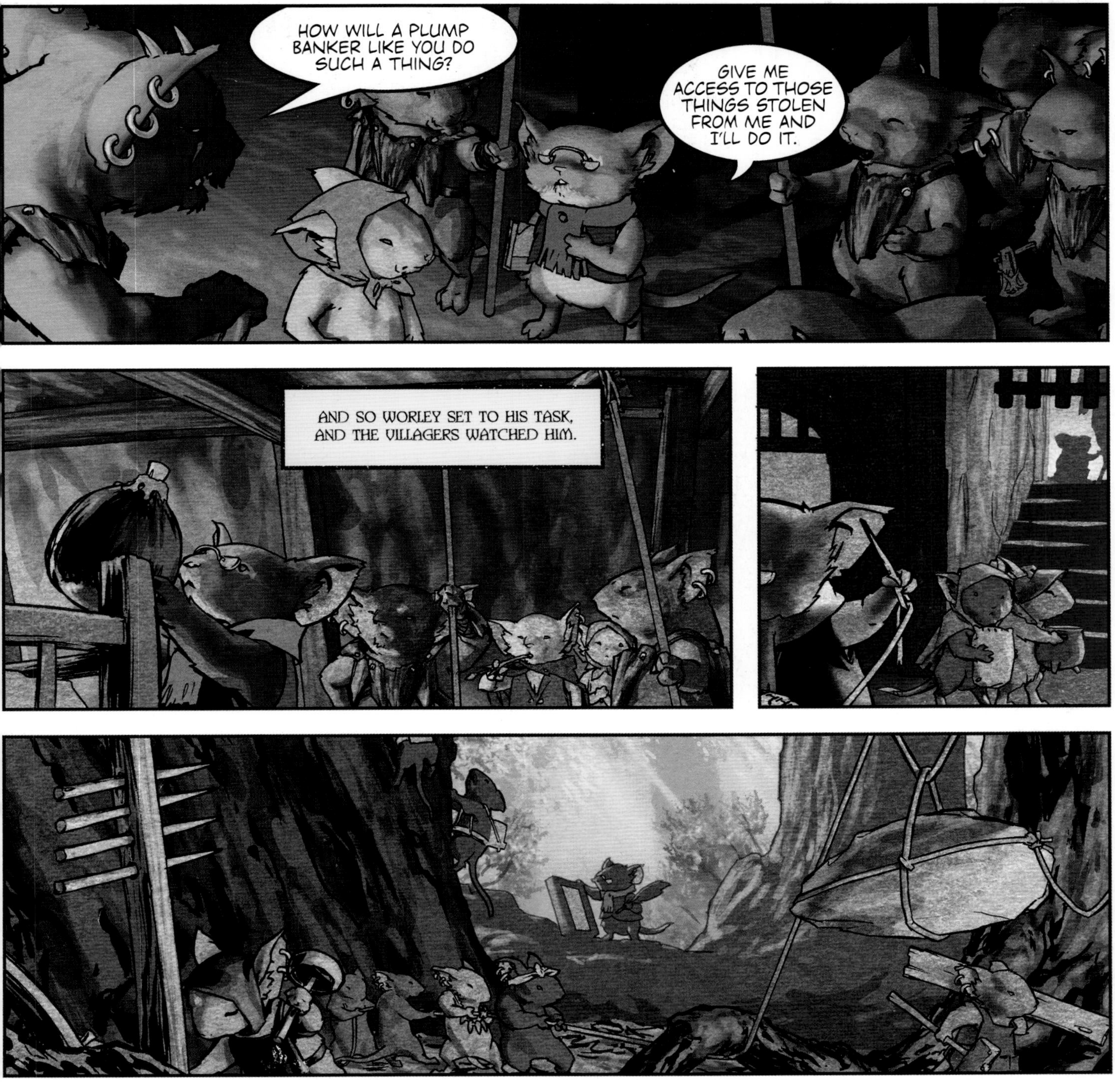
HOW WILL A PLUMP BANKER LIKE YOU DO SUCH A THING?
GIVE ME ACCESS TO THOSE THINGS STOLEN FROM ME AND I'LL DO IT.
AND SO WORLEY SET TO HIS TASK, AND THE VILLAGERS WATCHED HIM.

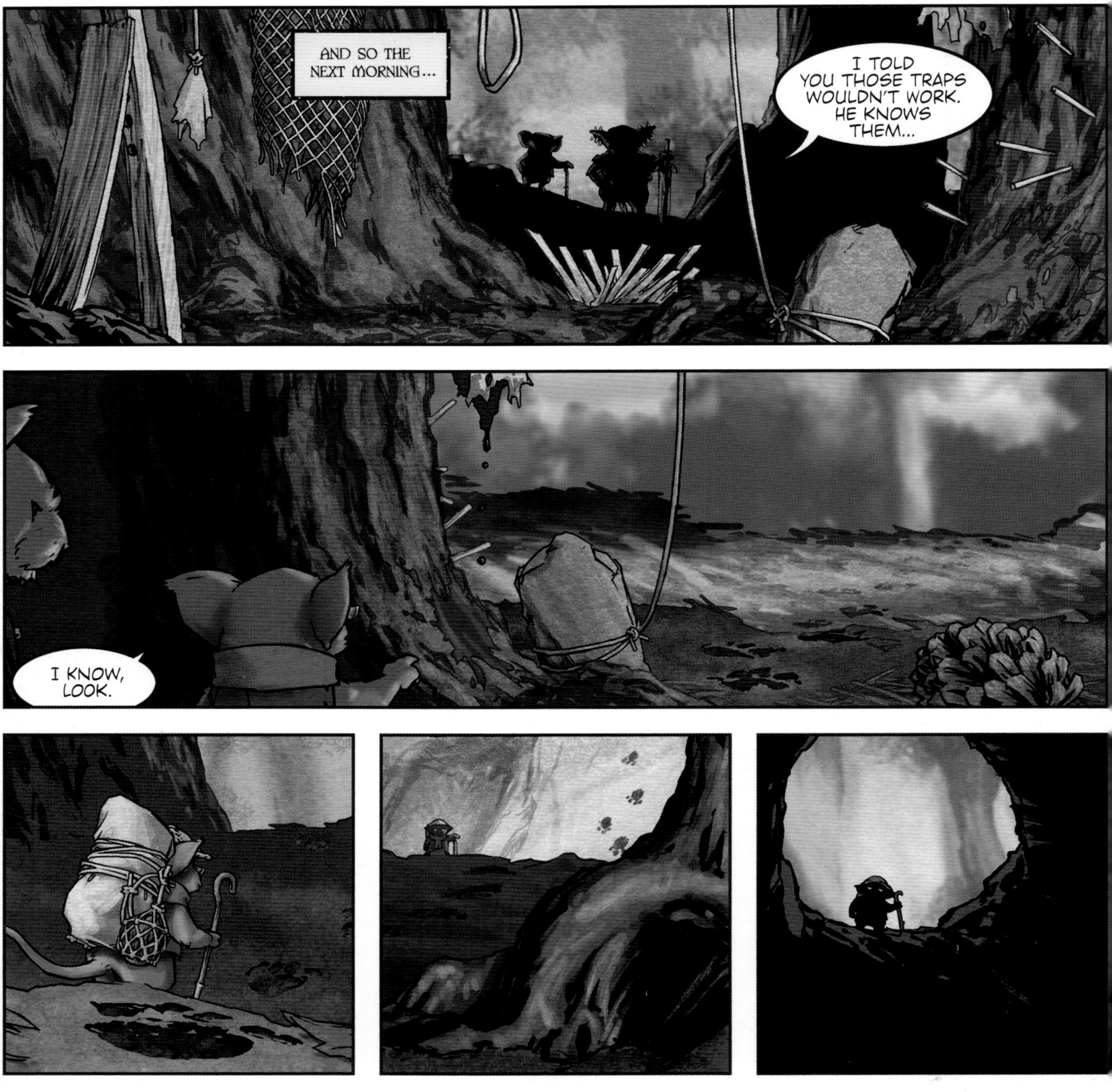
AND SO THE NEXT MORNING...
I TOLD YOU THOSE TRAPS WOULDN'T WORK. HE KNOWS THEM...
I KNOW, LOOK.

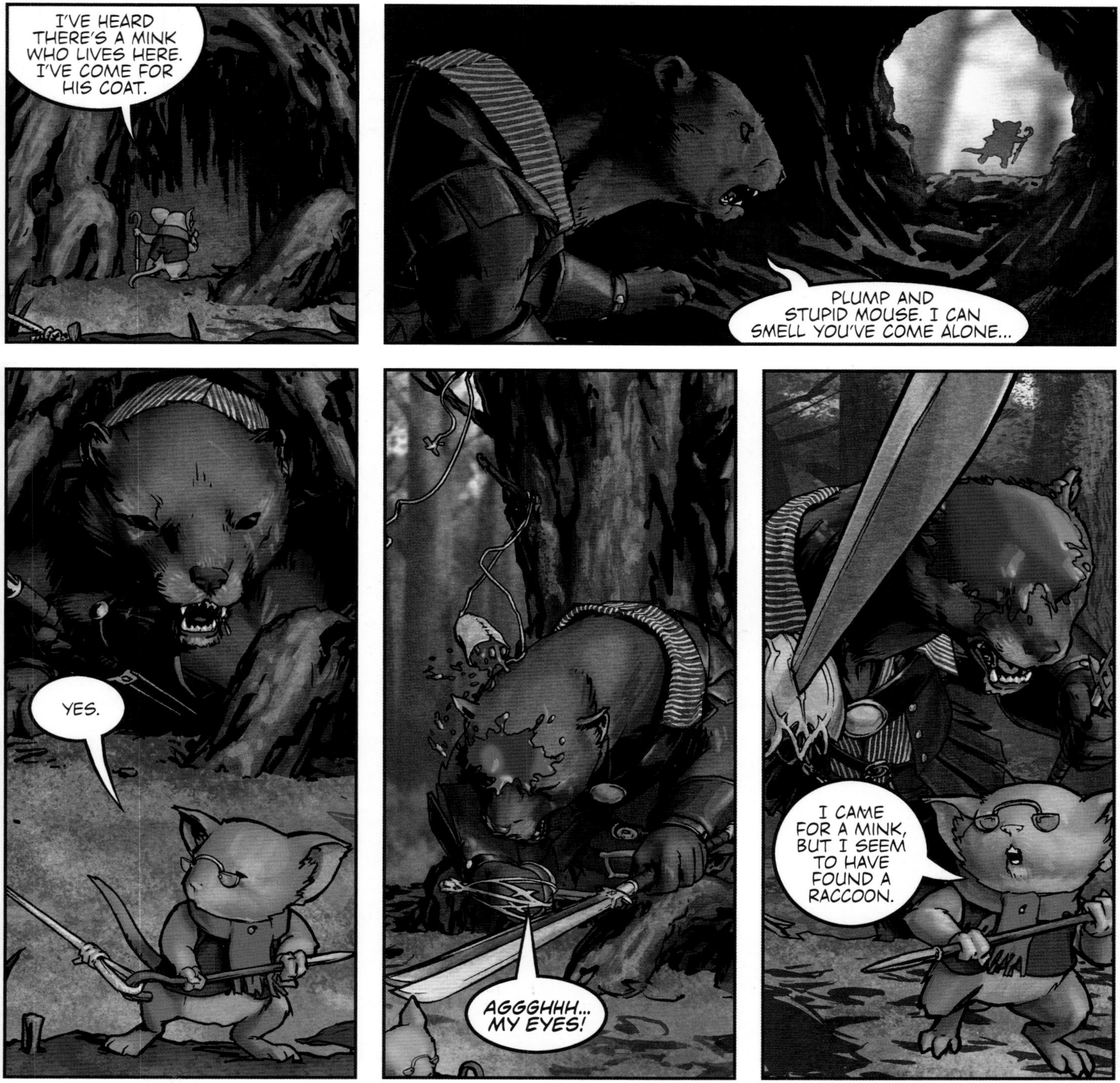
I'VE HEARD THERE'S A MINK WHO LIVES HERE. I'VE COME FOR HIS COAT.
PLUMP AND STUPID MOUSE. I CAN SMELL YOU'VE COME ALONE...
YES.
AGGGHHH... MY EYES!
I CAME FOR A MINK, BUT I SEEM TO HAVE FOUND A RACCOON.

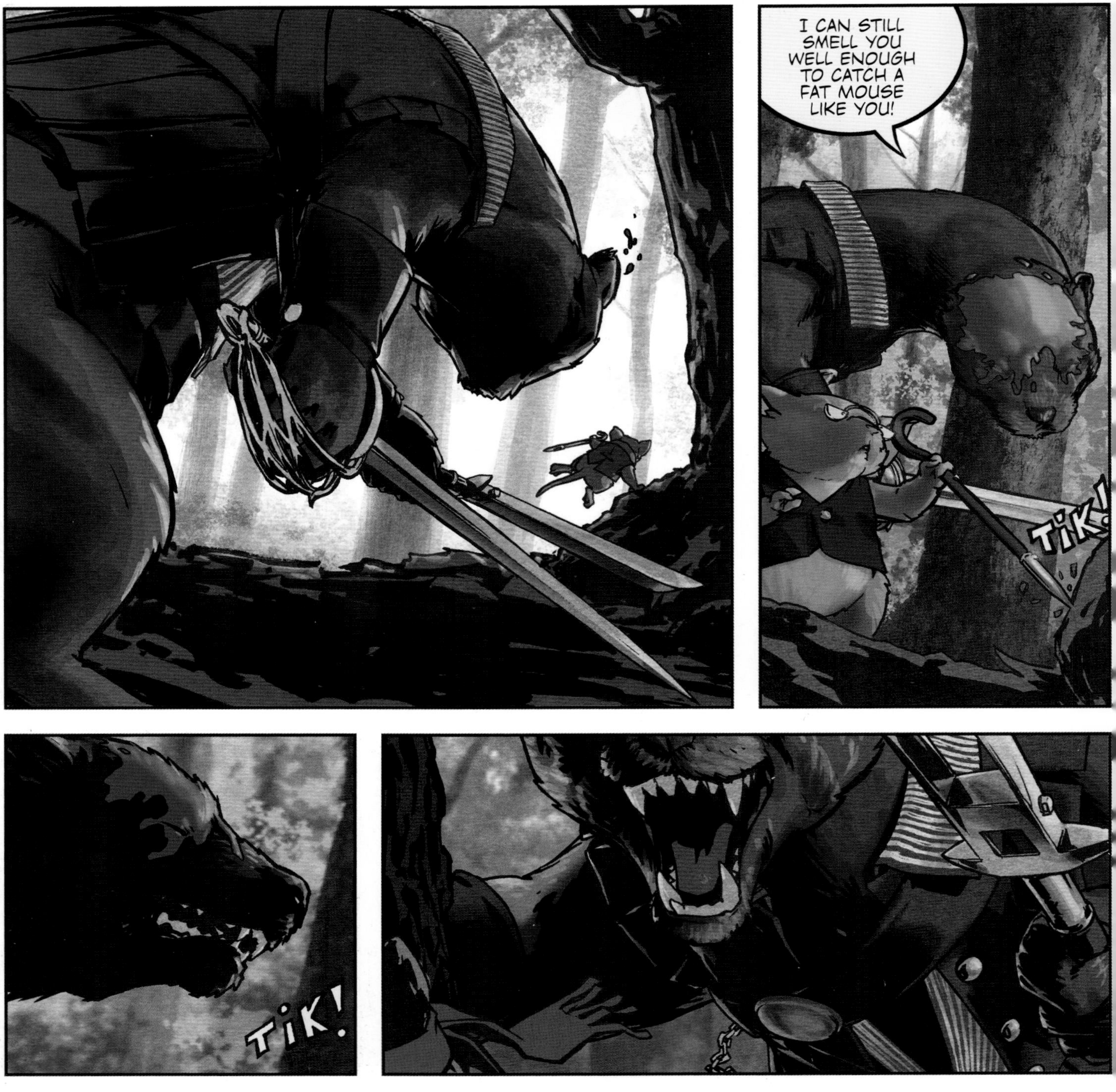
I CAN STILL SMELL YOU WELL ENOUGH TO CATCH A FAT MOUSE LIKE YOU!
TIK!
TIK!

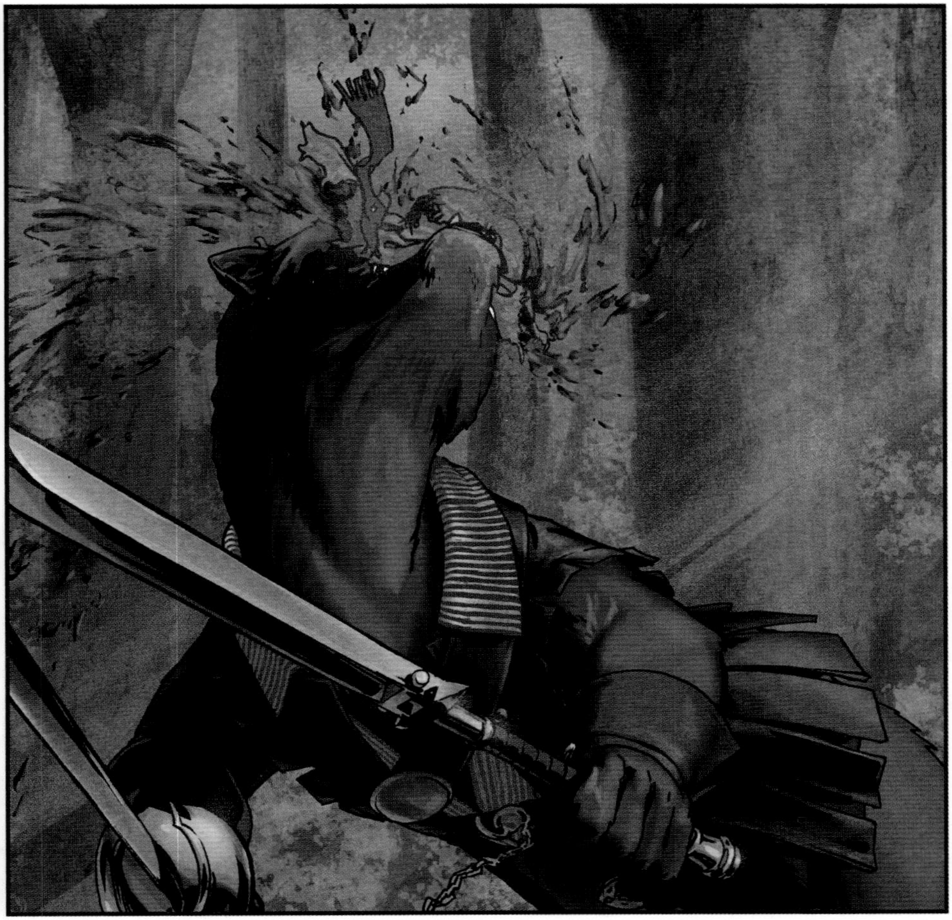

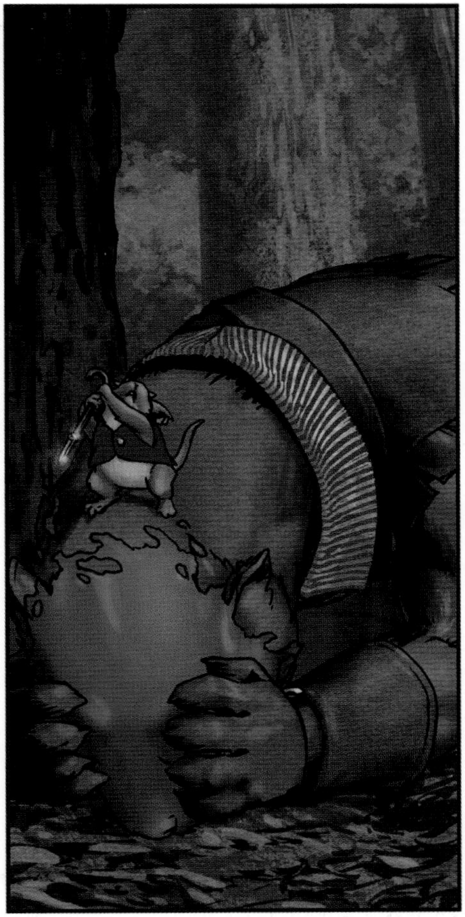

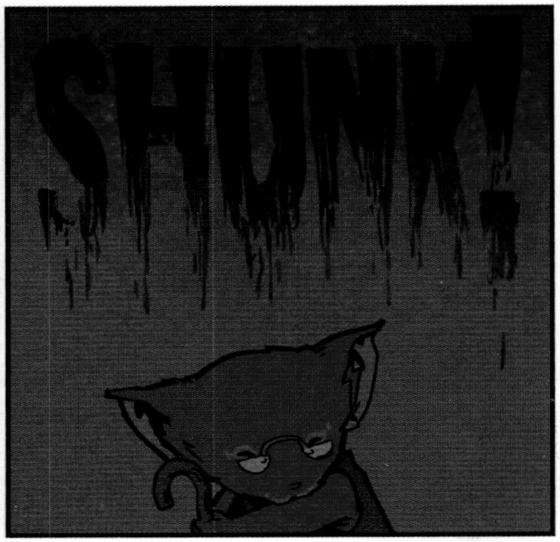
SHUNK!

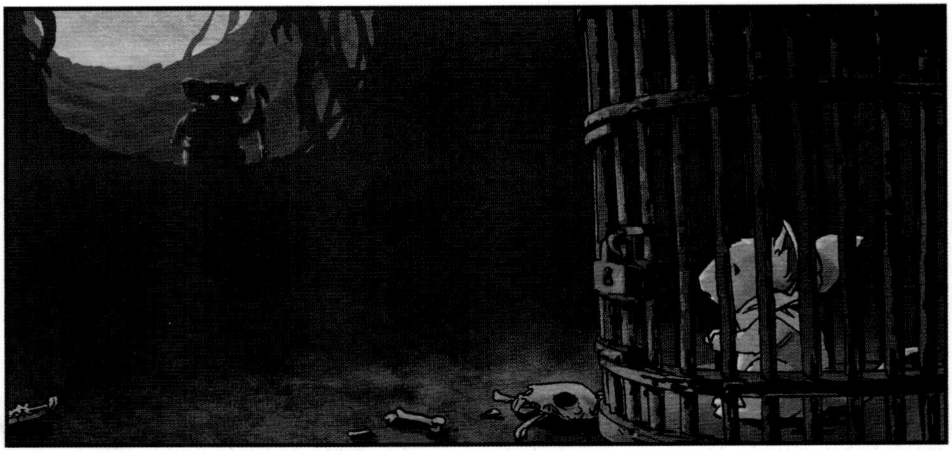

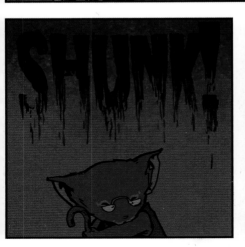

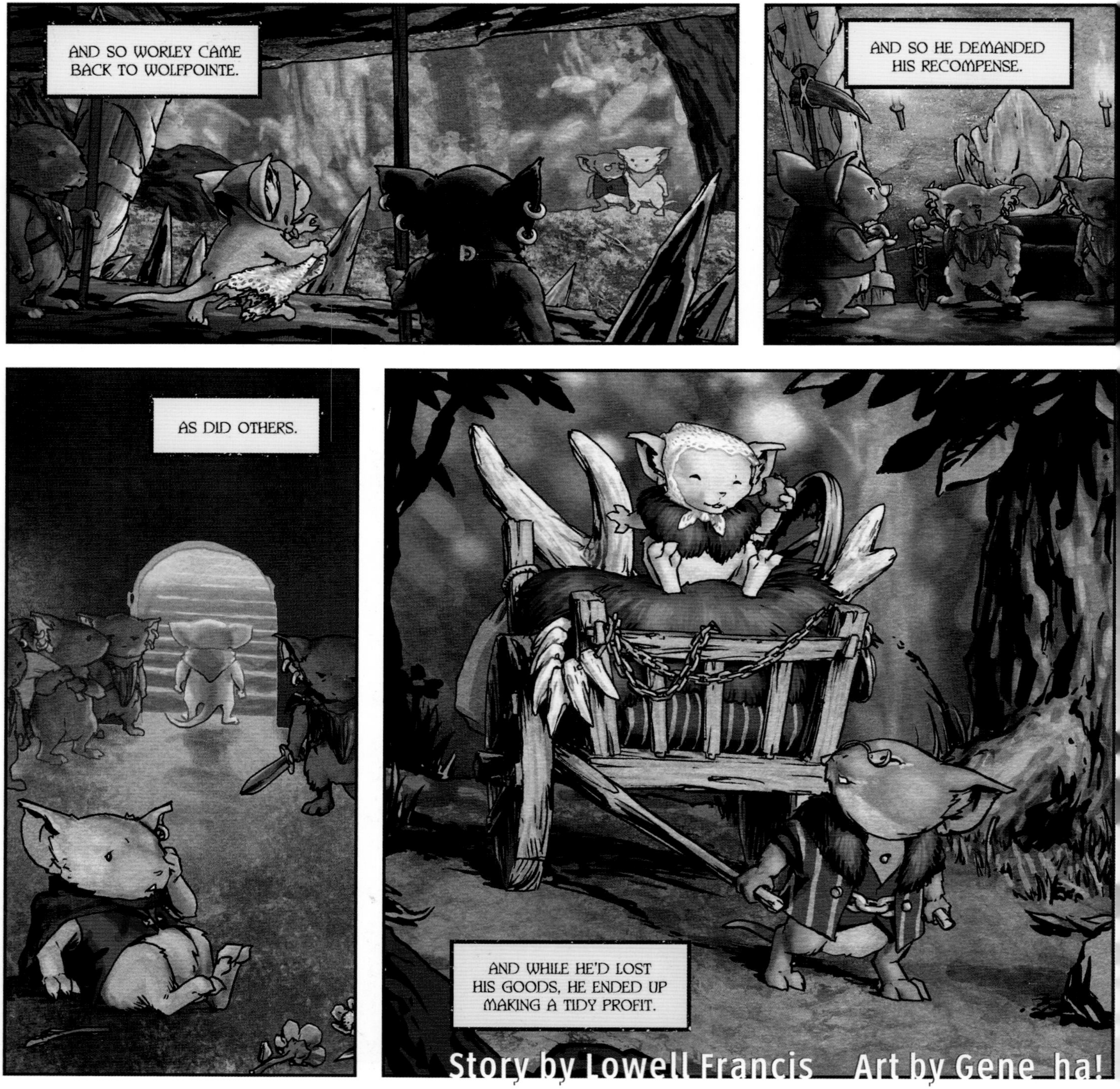
AND SO WORLEY CAME BACK TO WOLFPOINTE.
AND SO HE DEMANDED HIS RECOMPENSE.
AS DID OTHERS.
AND WHILE HE'D LOST HIS GOODS, HE ENDED UP MAKING A TIDY PROFIT.
Story by Lowell Francis Art by Gene ha!

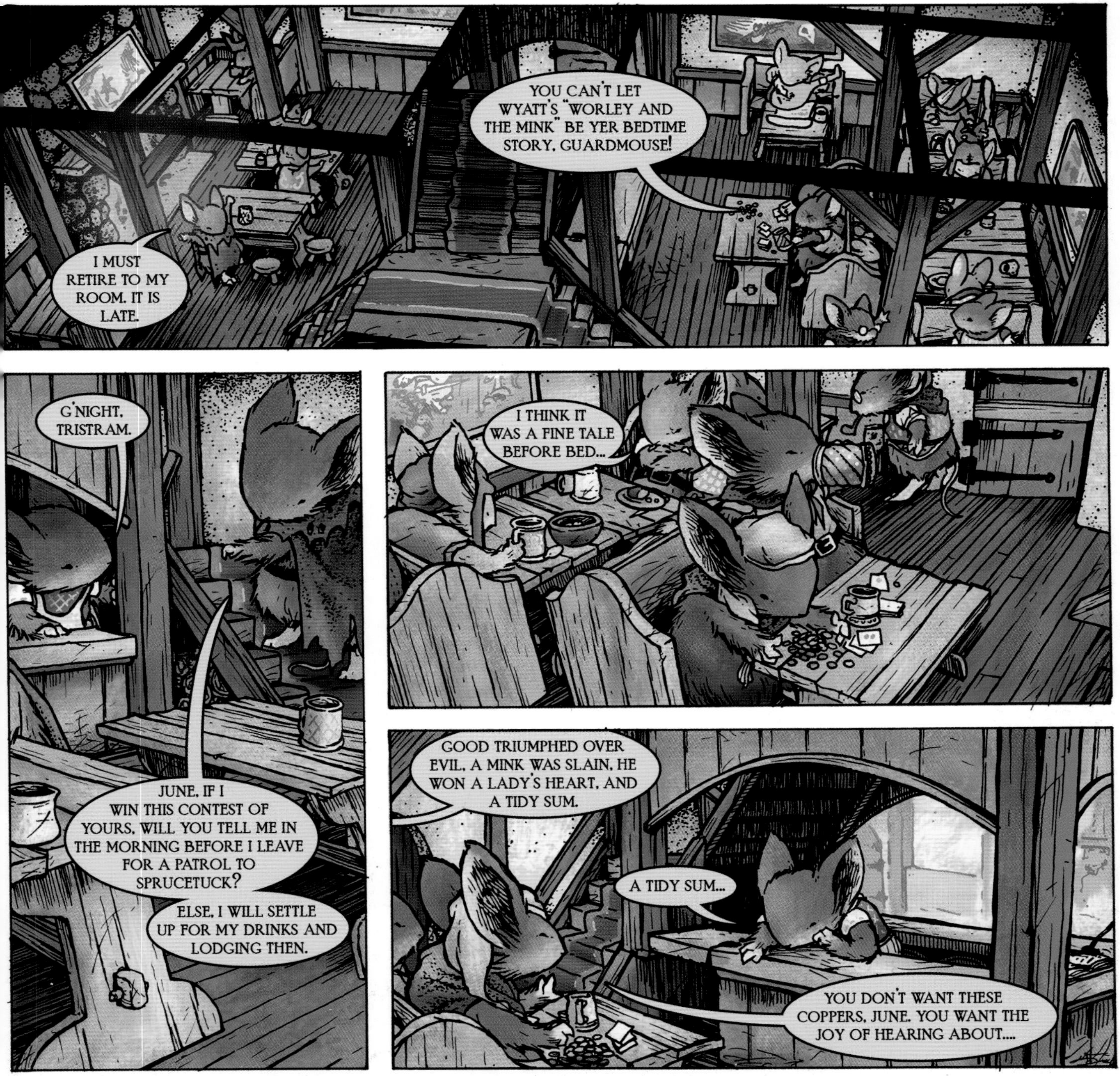

YOU CAN'T LET WYATT'S "WORLEY AND THE MINK" BE YER BEDTIME STORY, GUARDMOUSE!
I MUST RETIRE TO MY ROOM. IT IS LATE.
G'NIGHT, TRISTRAM.
JUNE, IF I WIN THIS CONTEST OF YOURS, WILL YOU TELL ME IN THE MORNING BEFORE I LEAVE FOR A PATROL TO SPRUCETUCK?
ELSE, I WILL SETTLE UP FOR MY DRINKS AND LODGING THEN.
I THINK IT WAS A FINE TALE BEFORE BED...
GOOD TRIUMPHED OVER EVIL, A MINK WAS SLAIN, HE WON A LADY'S HEART, AND A TIDY SUM.
A TIDY SUM...
YOU DON'T WANT THESE COPPERS, JUNE. YOU WANT THE JOY OF HEARING ABOUT....

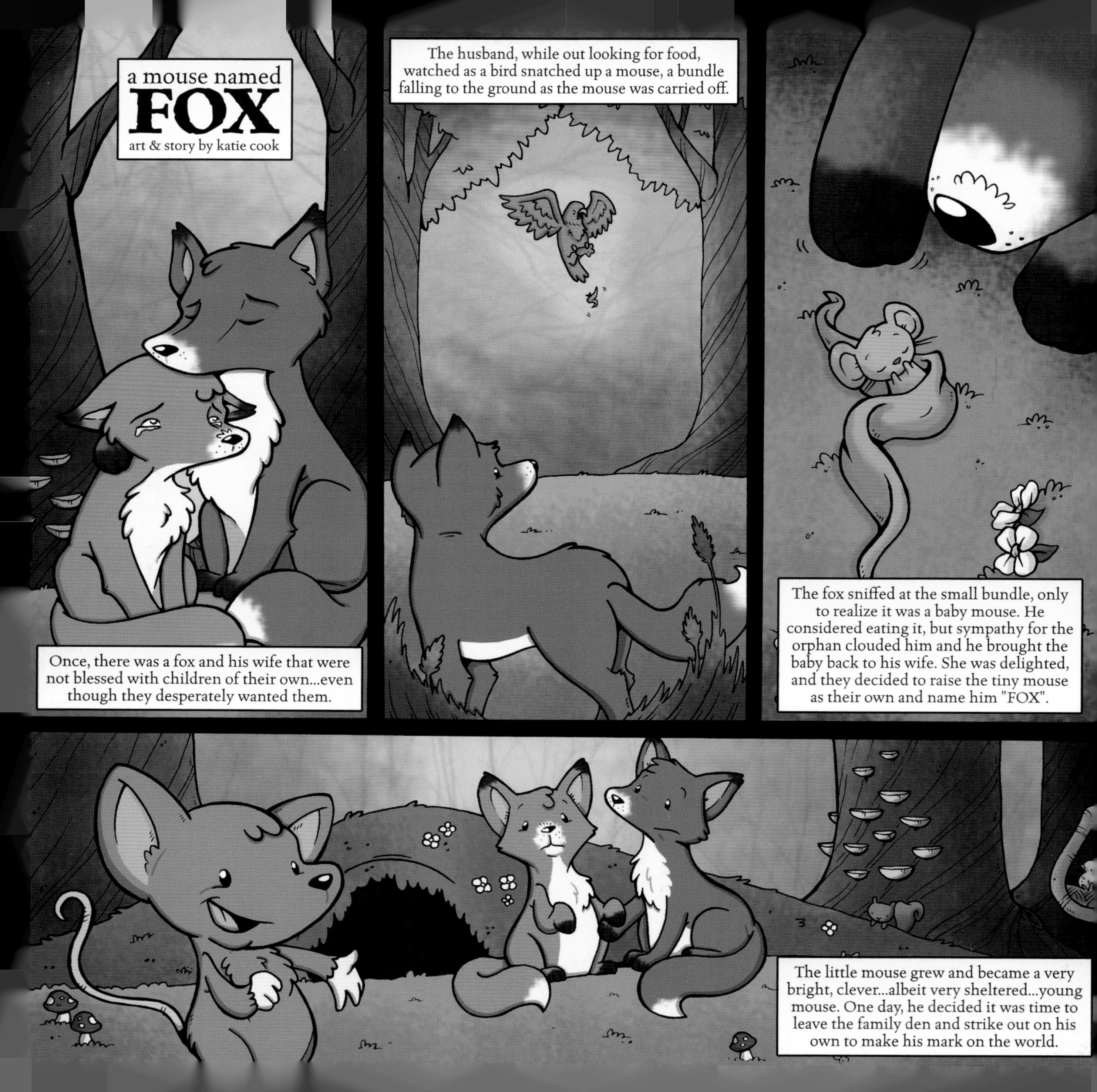
a mouse named
FOX
art & story by katie cook
Once, there was a fox and his wife that were not blessed with children of their own...even though they desperately wanted them.
The husband, while out looking for food, watched as a bird snatched up a mouse, a bundle falling to the ground as the mouse was carried off.
The fox sniffed at the small bundle, only to realize it was a baby mouse. He considered eating it, but sympathy for the orphan clouded him and he brought the baby back to his wife. She was delighted, and they decided to raise the tiny mouse as their own and name him "FOX".
The little mouse grew and became a very bright, clever...albeit very sheltered...young mouse. One day, he decided it was time to leave the family den and strike out on his own to make his mark on the world.

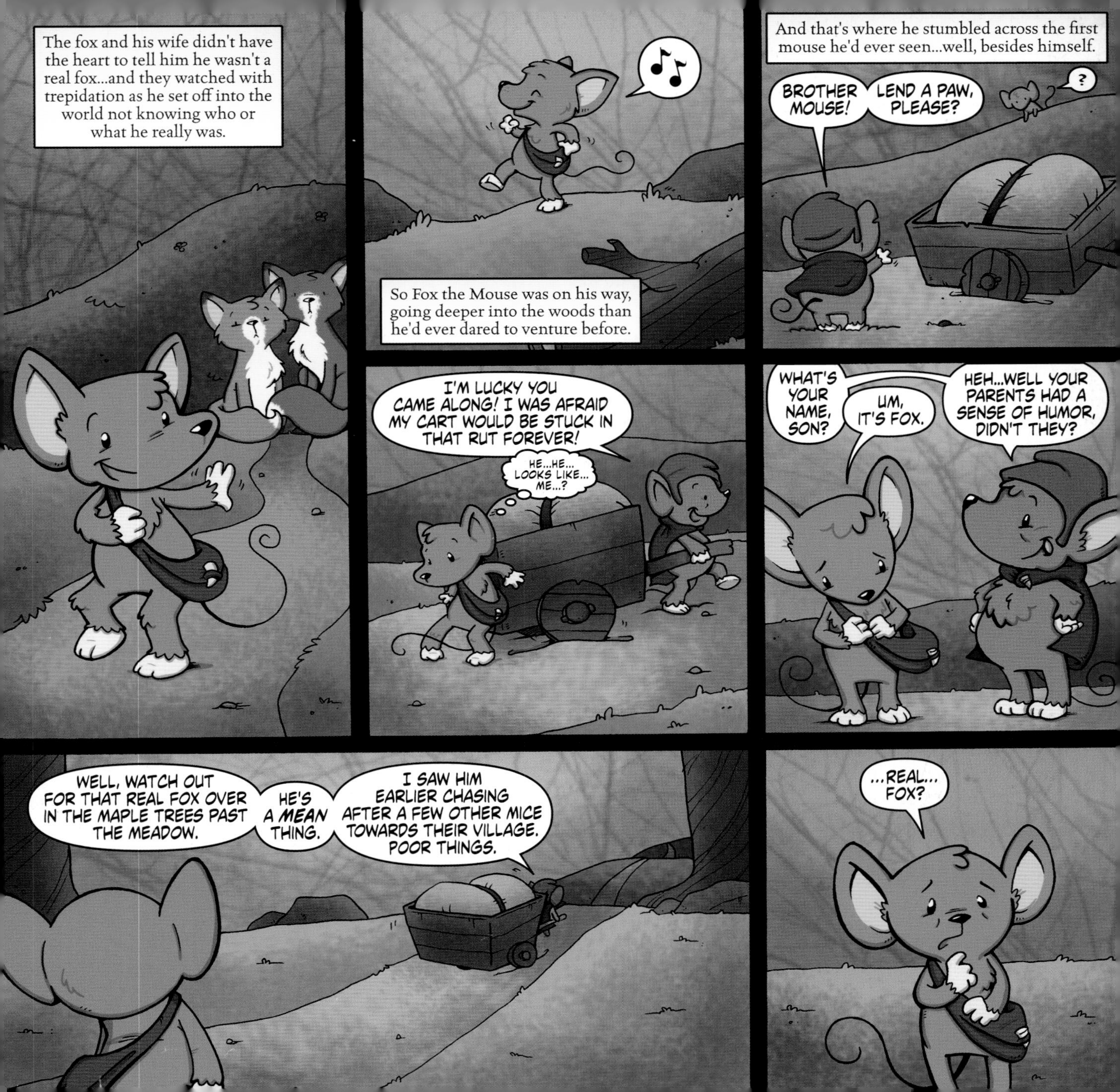

The fox and his wife didn't have the heart to tell him he wasn't a real fox...and they watched with trepidation as he set off into the world not knowing who or what he really was.
So Fox the Mouse was on his way, going deeper into the woods than he'd ever dared to venture before.
And that's where he stumbled across the first mouse he'd ever seen...well, besides himself.
BROTHER MOUSE!
LEND A PAW, PLEASE?
?
I'M LUCKY YOU CAME ALONG! I WAS AFRAID MY CART WOULD BE STUCK IN THAT RUT FOREVER!
HE...HE... LOOKS LIKE... ME...?
WHAT'S YOUR NAME, SON?
UM, IT'S FOX.
HEH...WELL YOUR PARENTS HAD A SENSE OF HUMOR, DIDN'T THEY?
WELL, WATCH OUT FOR THAT REAL FOX OVER IN THE MAPLE TREES PAST THE MEADOW.
HE'S A MEAN THING.
I SAW HIM EARLIER CHASING AFTER A FEW OTHER MICE TOWARDS THEIR VILLAGE. POOR THINGS.
...REAL... FOX?

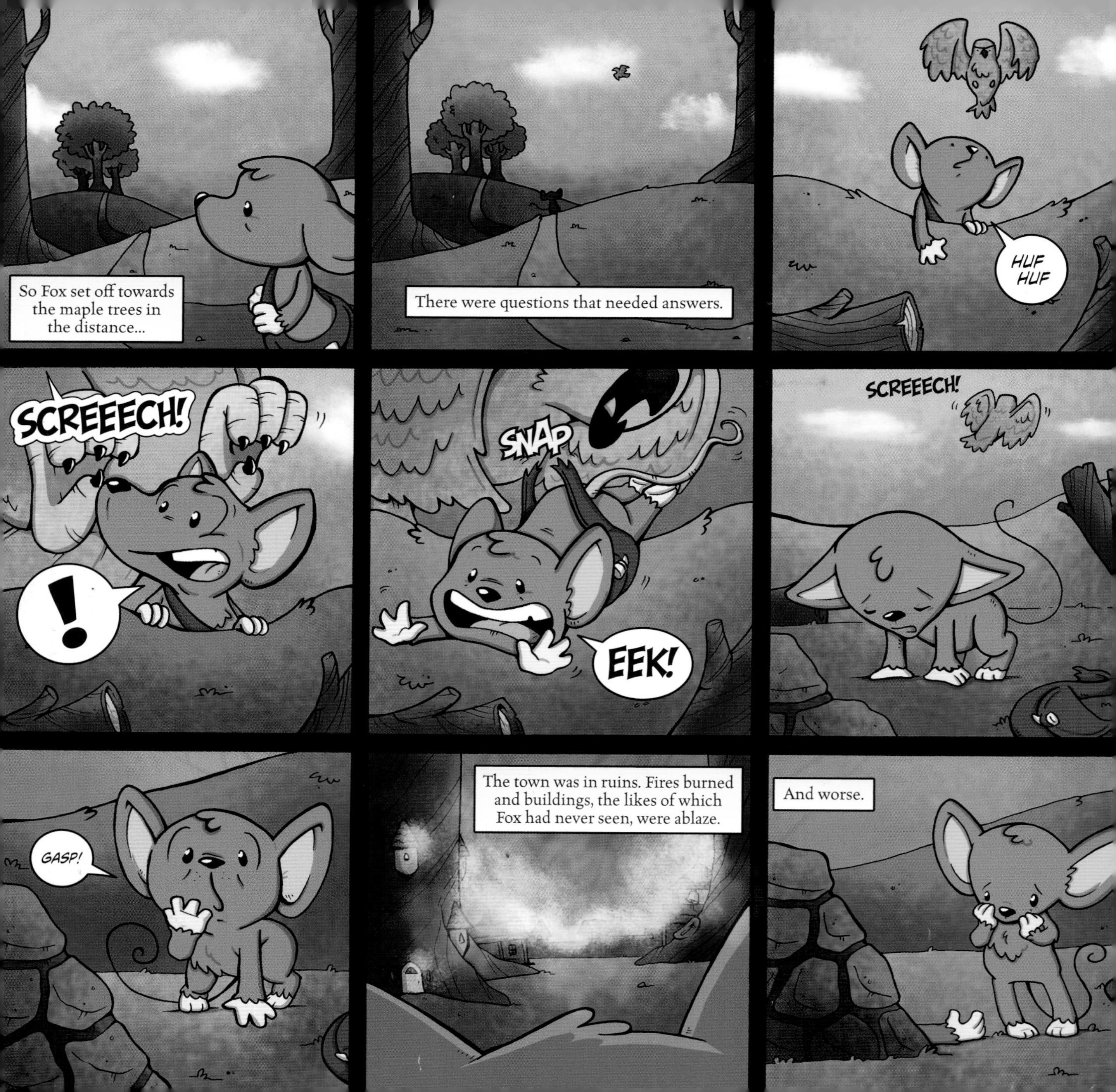
So Fox set off towards the maple trees in the distance...
There were questions that needed answers.
HUF HUF
SCREEECH!
!
SNAP
EEK!
SCREEECH!
GASP!
The town was in ruins. Fires burned and buildings, the likes of which Fox had never seen, were ablaze.
And worse.

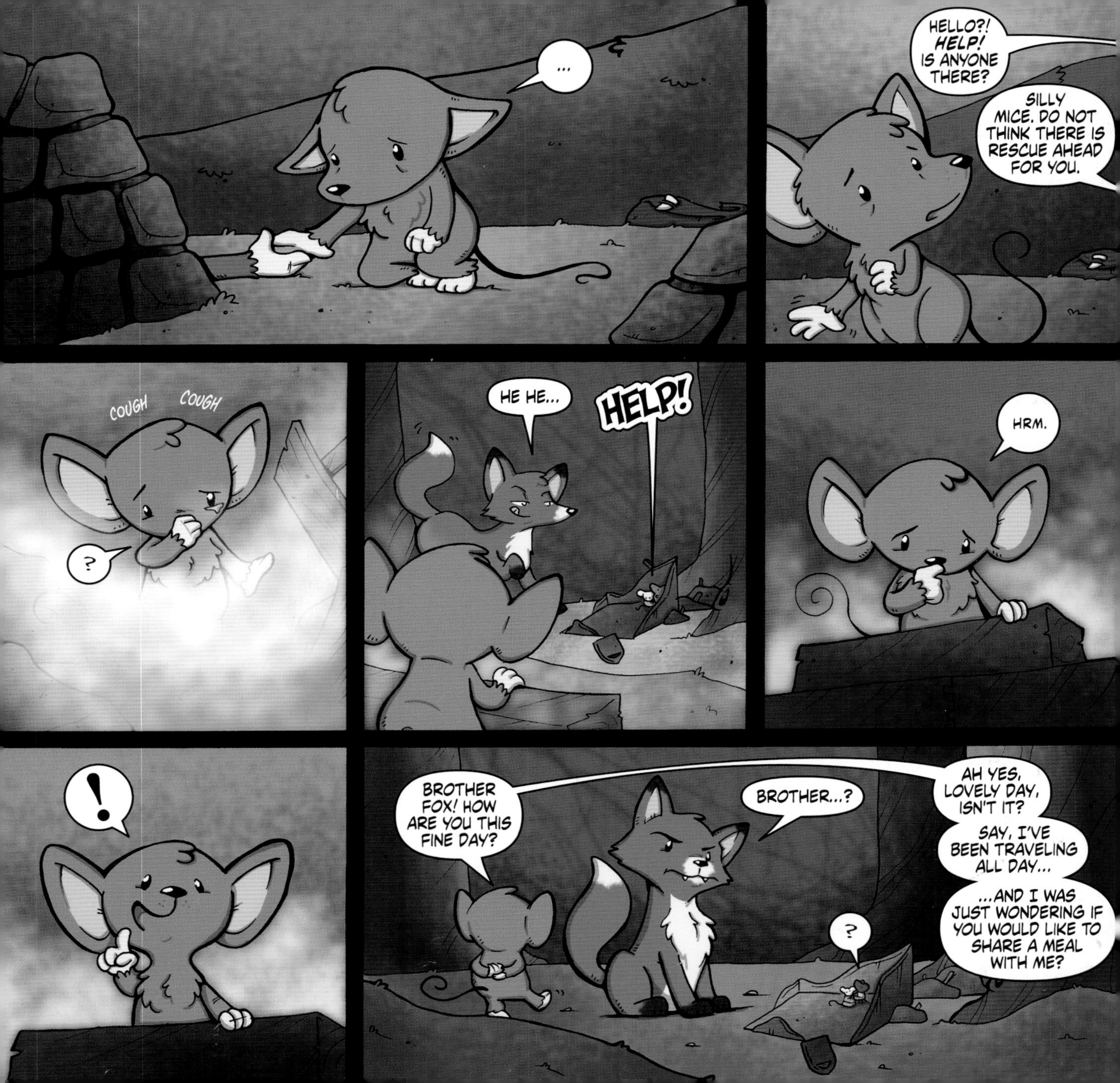
...
HELLO?! HELP! IS ANYONE THERE?
SILLY MICE. DO NOT THINK THERE IS RESCUE AHEAD FOR YOU.
COUGH
COUGH
?
HE HE...
HELP!
HRM.
!
BROTHER FOX! HOW ARE YOU THIS FINE DAY?
BROTHER...?
AH YES, LOVELY DAY, ISN'T IT?
SAY, I'VE BEEN TRAVELING ALL DAY...
...AND I WAS JUST WONDERING IF YOU WOULD LIKE TO SHARE A MEAL WITH ME?
?

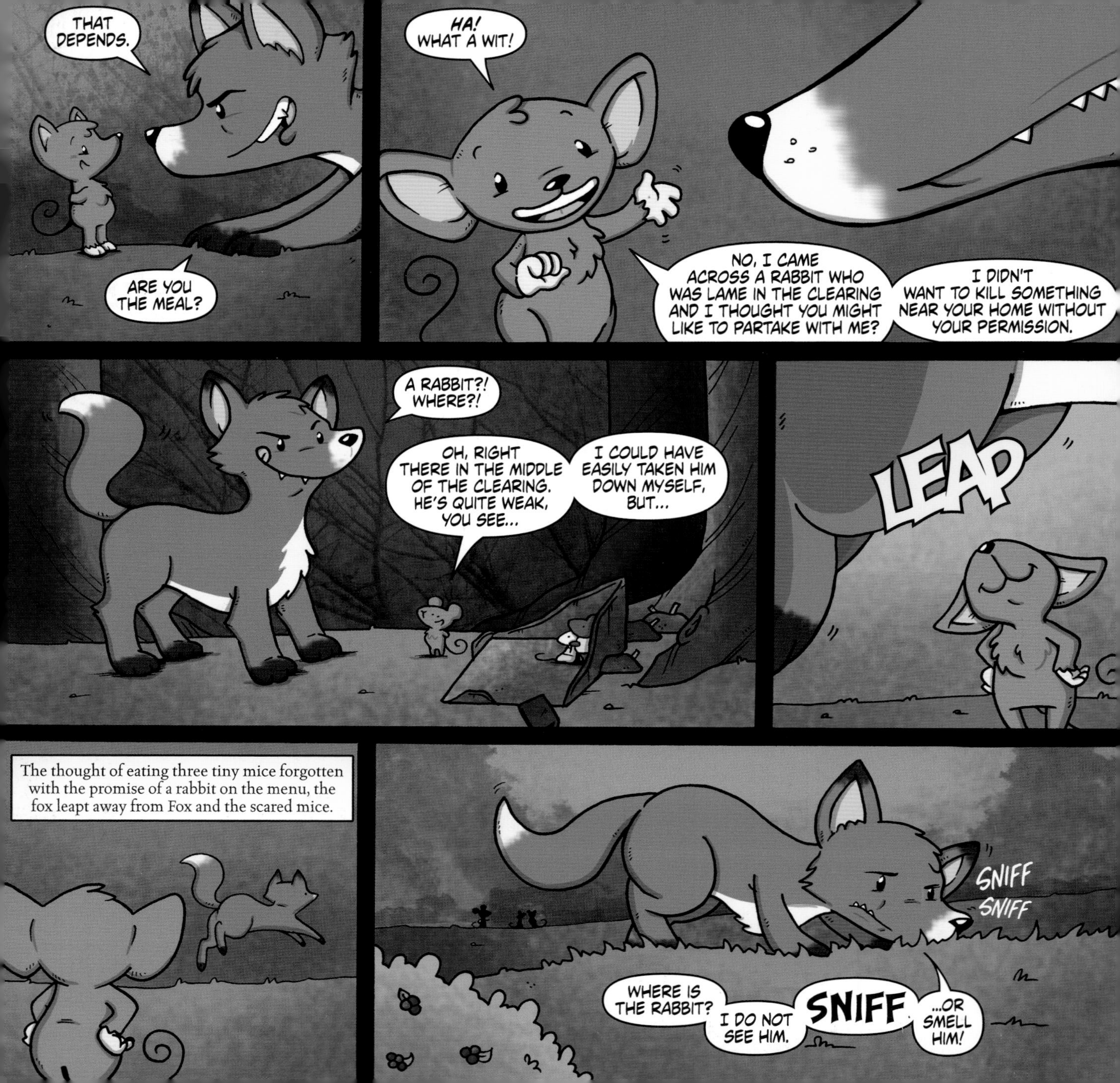
THAT DEPENDS.
ARE YOU THE MEAL?
HA! WHAT A WIT!
NO, I CAME ACROSS A RABBIT WHO WAS LAME IN THE CLEARING AND I THOUGHT YOU MIGHT LIKE TO PARTAKE WITH ME?
I DIDN'T WANT TO KILL SOMETHING NEAR YOUR HOME WITHOUT YOUR PERMISSION.
A RABBIT?! WHERE?!
OH, RIGHT THERE IN THE MIDDLE OF THE CLEARING. HE'S QUITE WEAK, YOU SEE...
I COULD HAVE EASILY TAKEN HIM DOWN MYSELF, BUT...
LEAP
The thought of eating three tiny mice forgotten with the promise of a rabbit on the menu, the fox leapt away from Fox and the scared mice.
SNIFF SNIFF
WHERE IS THE RABBIT?
I DO NOT SEE HIM.
SNIFF
...OR SMELL HIM!

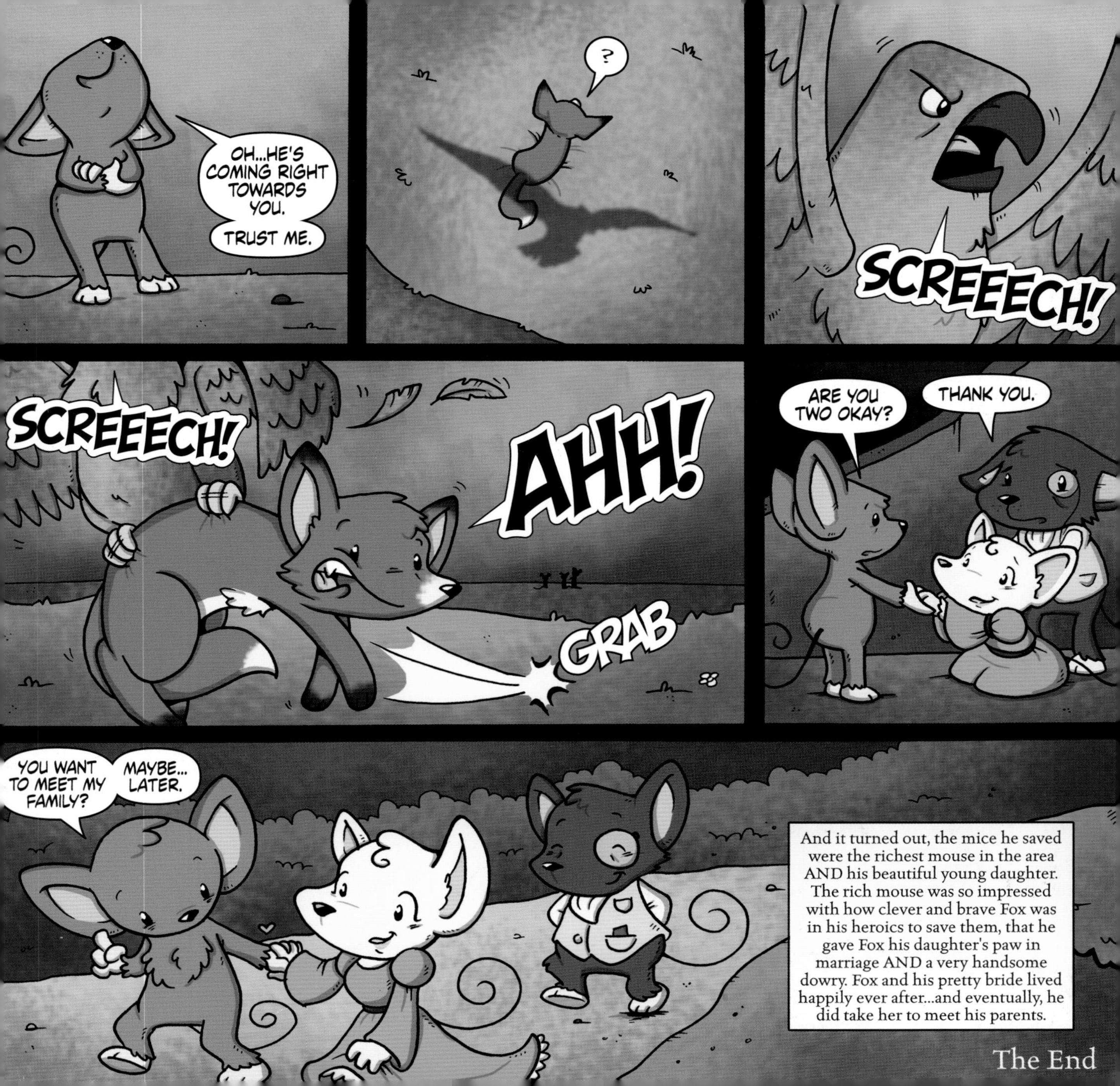

OH...HE'S COMING RIGHT TOWARDS YOU.
TRUST ME.
?
SCREEEECH!
SCREEEECH!
AHH!
GRAB
ARE YOU TWO OKAY?
THANK YOU.
YOU WANT TO MEET MY FAMILY?
MAYBE... LATER.
And it turned out, the mice he saved were the richest mouse in the area AND his beautiful young daughter. The rich mouse was so impressed with how clever and brave Fox was in his heroics to save them, that he gave Fox his daughter's paw in marriage AND a very handsome dowry. Fox and his pretty bride lived happily ever after...and eventually, he did take her to meet his parents.
The End

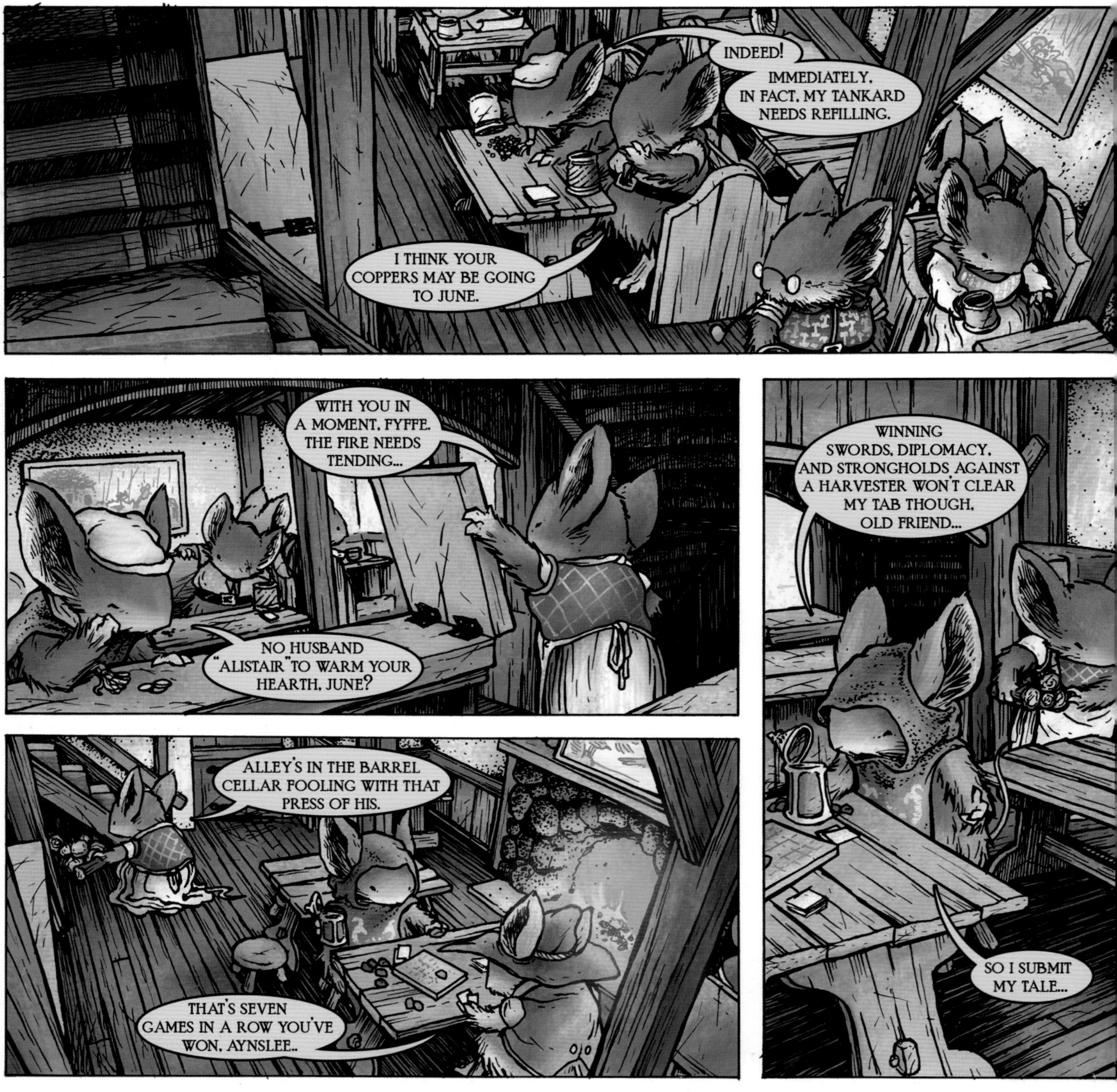
INDEED!
IMMEDIATELY, IN FACT, MY TANKARD NEEDS REFILLING.
I THINK YOUR COPPERS MAY BE GOING TO JUNE.
WITH YOU IN A MOMENT, FYFFE. THE FIRE NEEDS TENDING...
NO HUSBAND "ALISTAIR" TO WARM YOUR HEARTH, JUNE?
ALLEY'S IN THE BARREL CELLAR FOOLING WITH THAT PRESS OF HIS.
THAT'S SEVEN GAMES IN A ROW YOU'VE WON, AYNSLEE..
WINNING SWORDS, DIPLOMACY, AND STRONGHOLDS AGAINST A HARVESTER WON'T CLEAR MY TAB THOUGH, OLD FRIEND...
SO I SUBMIT MY TALE...

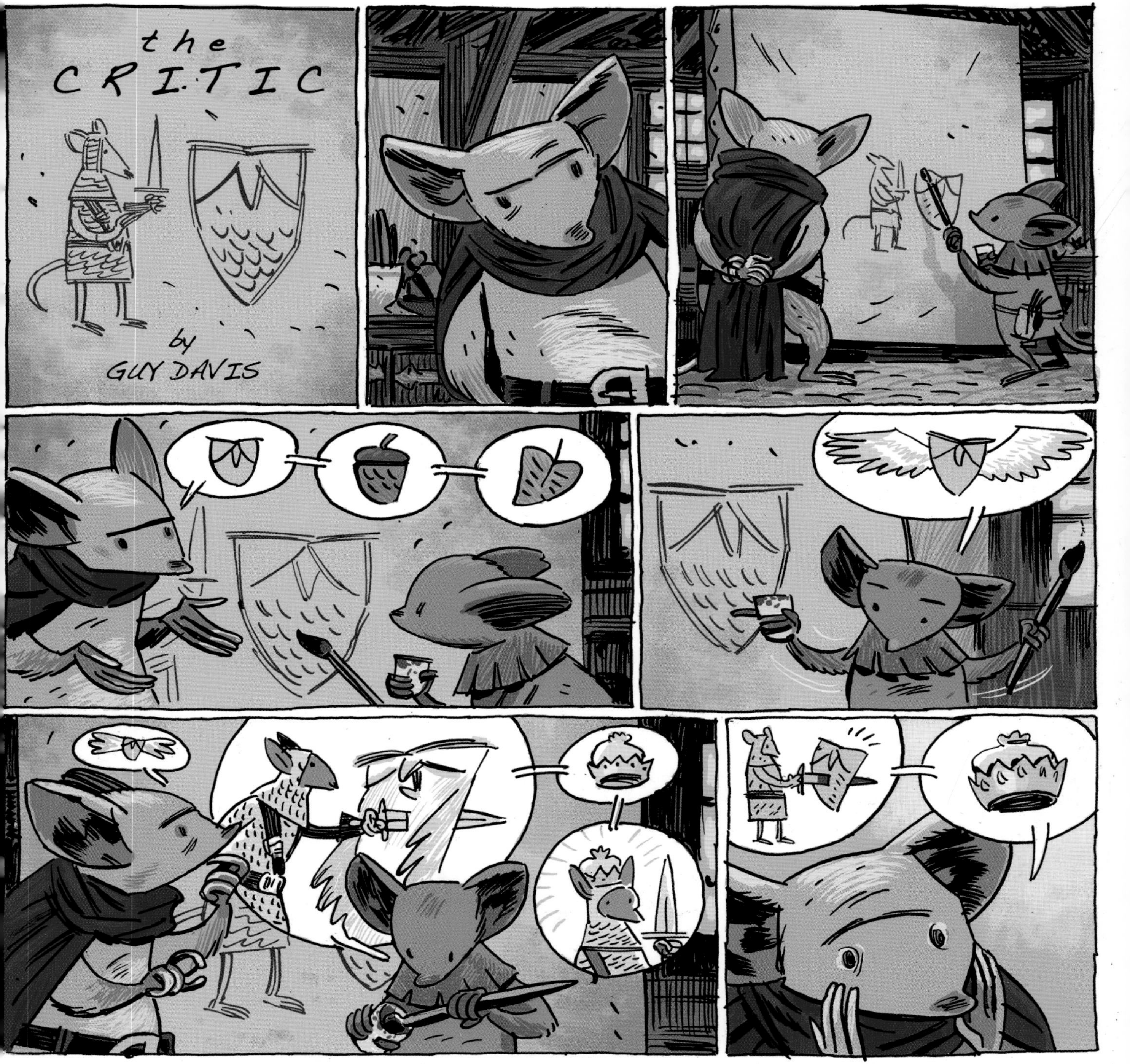
the CRITIC
by GUY DAVIS

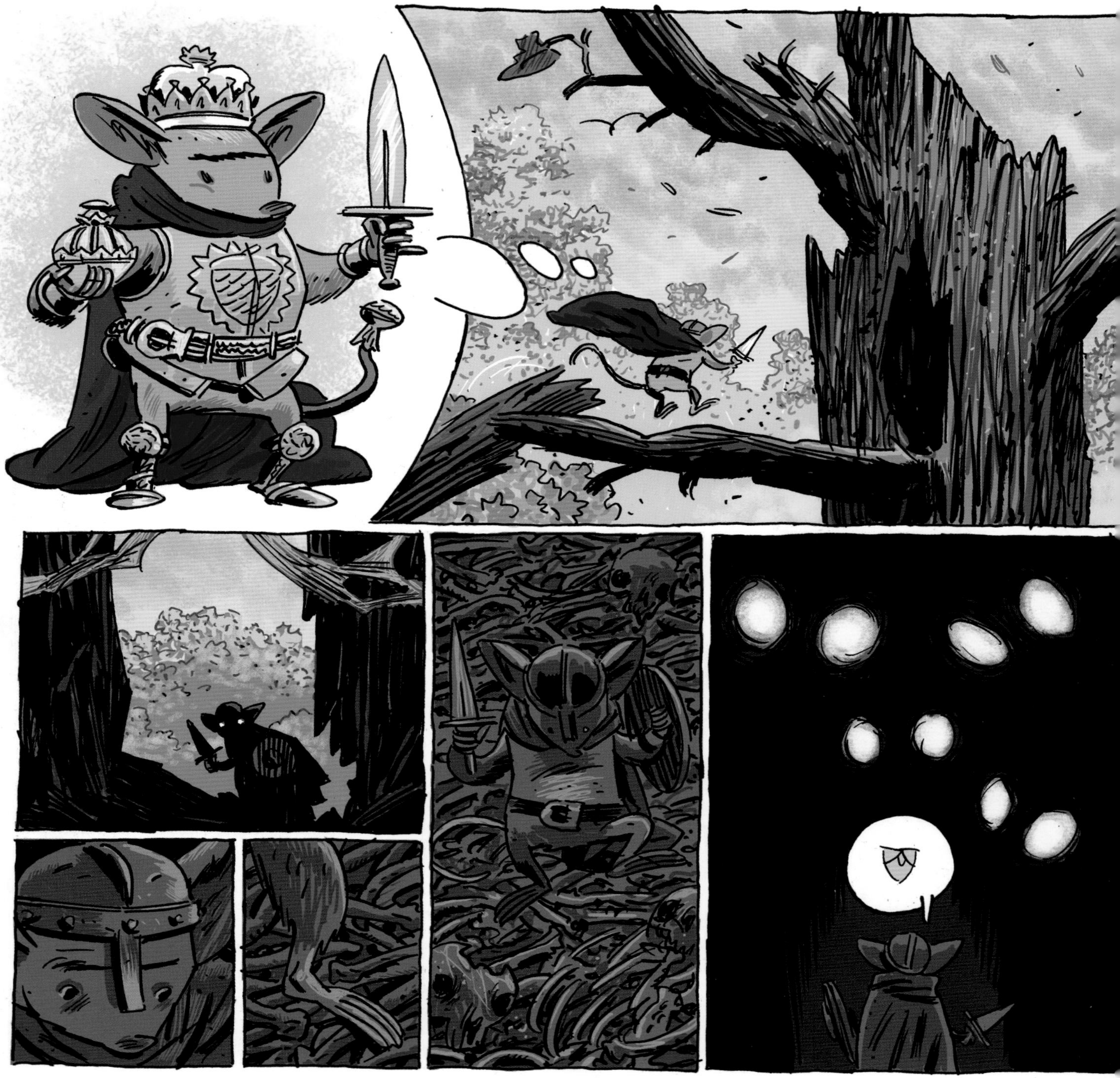

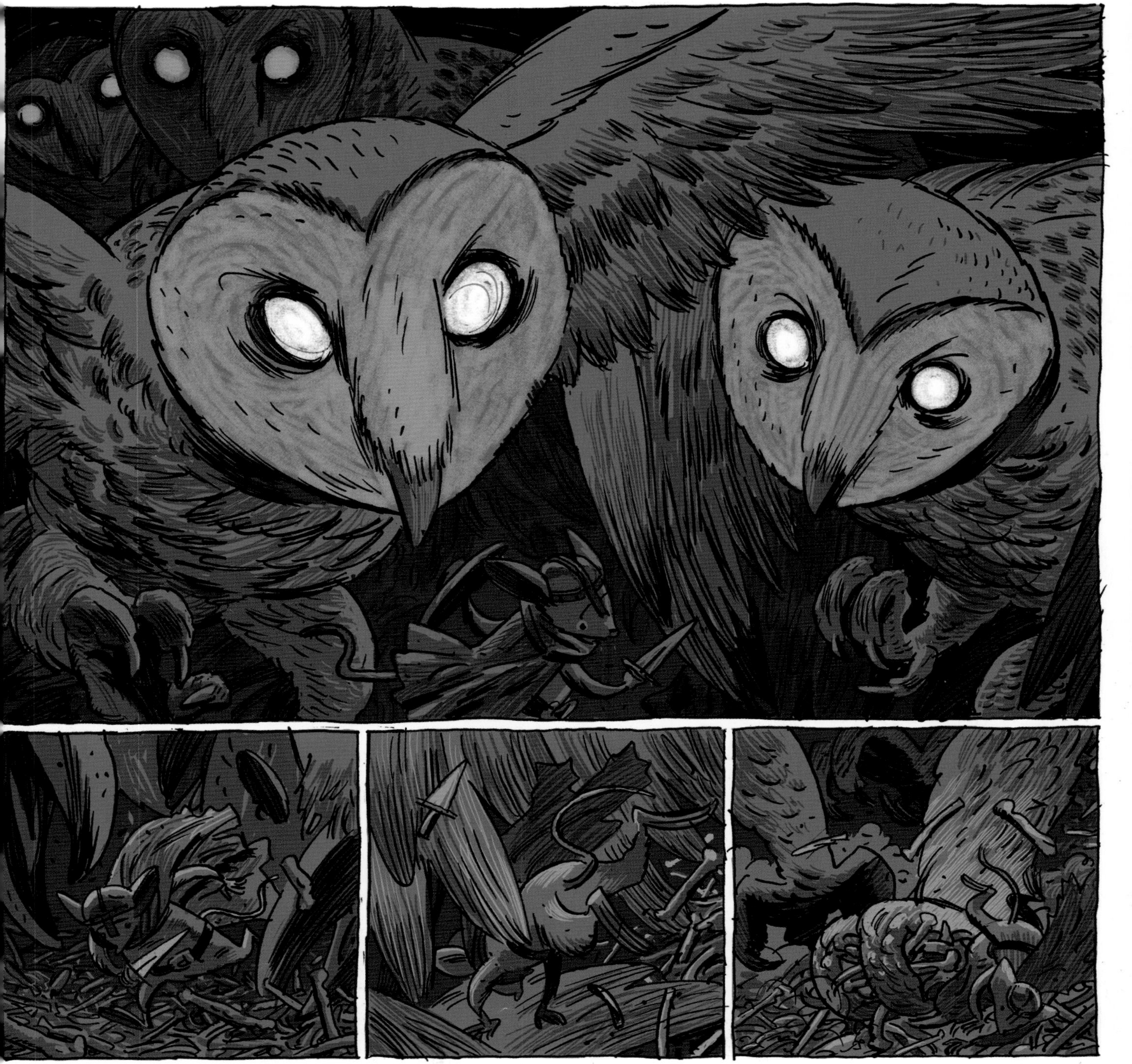

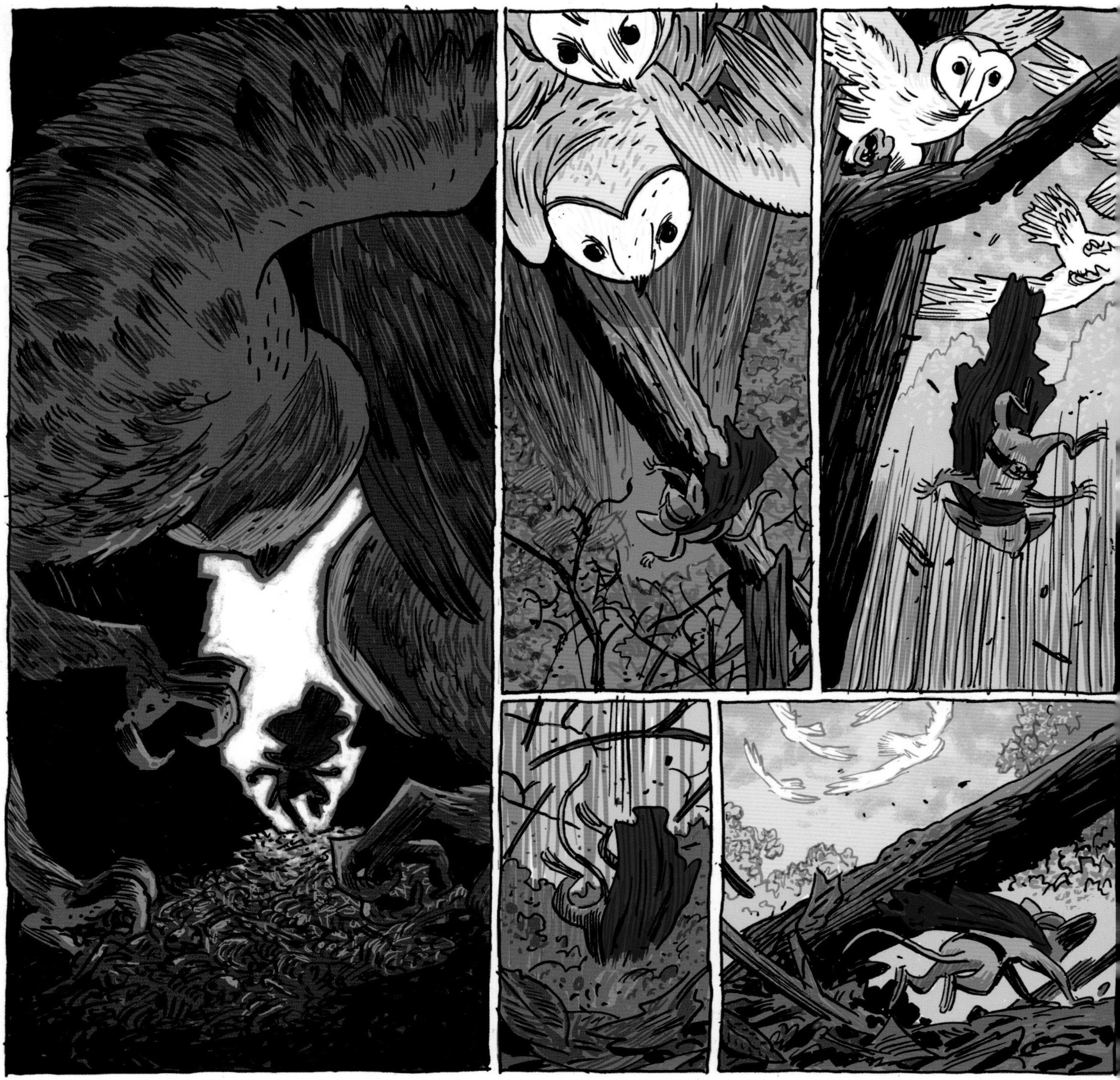

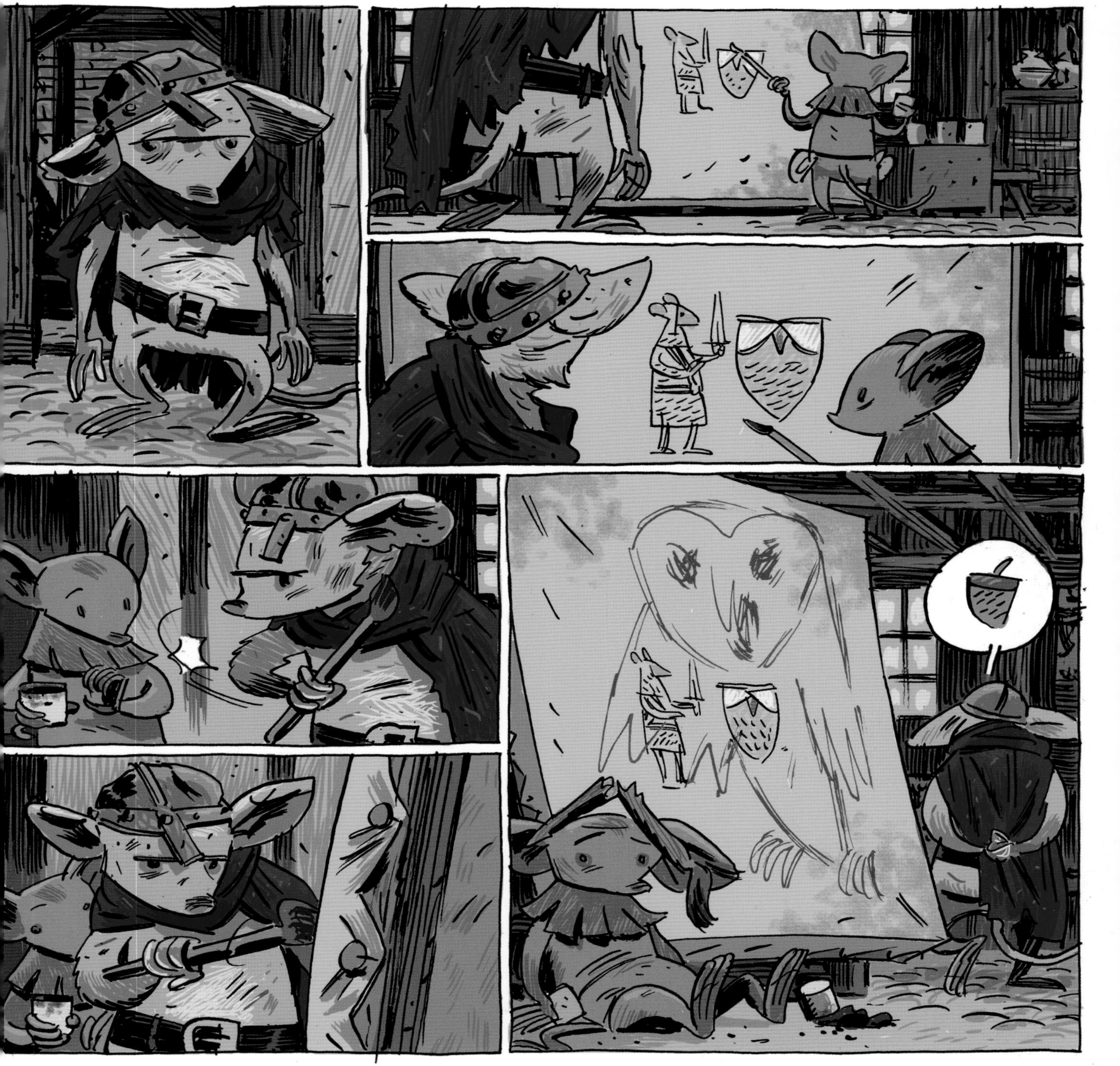

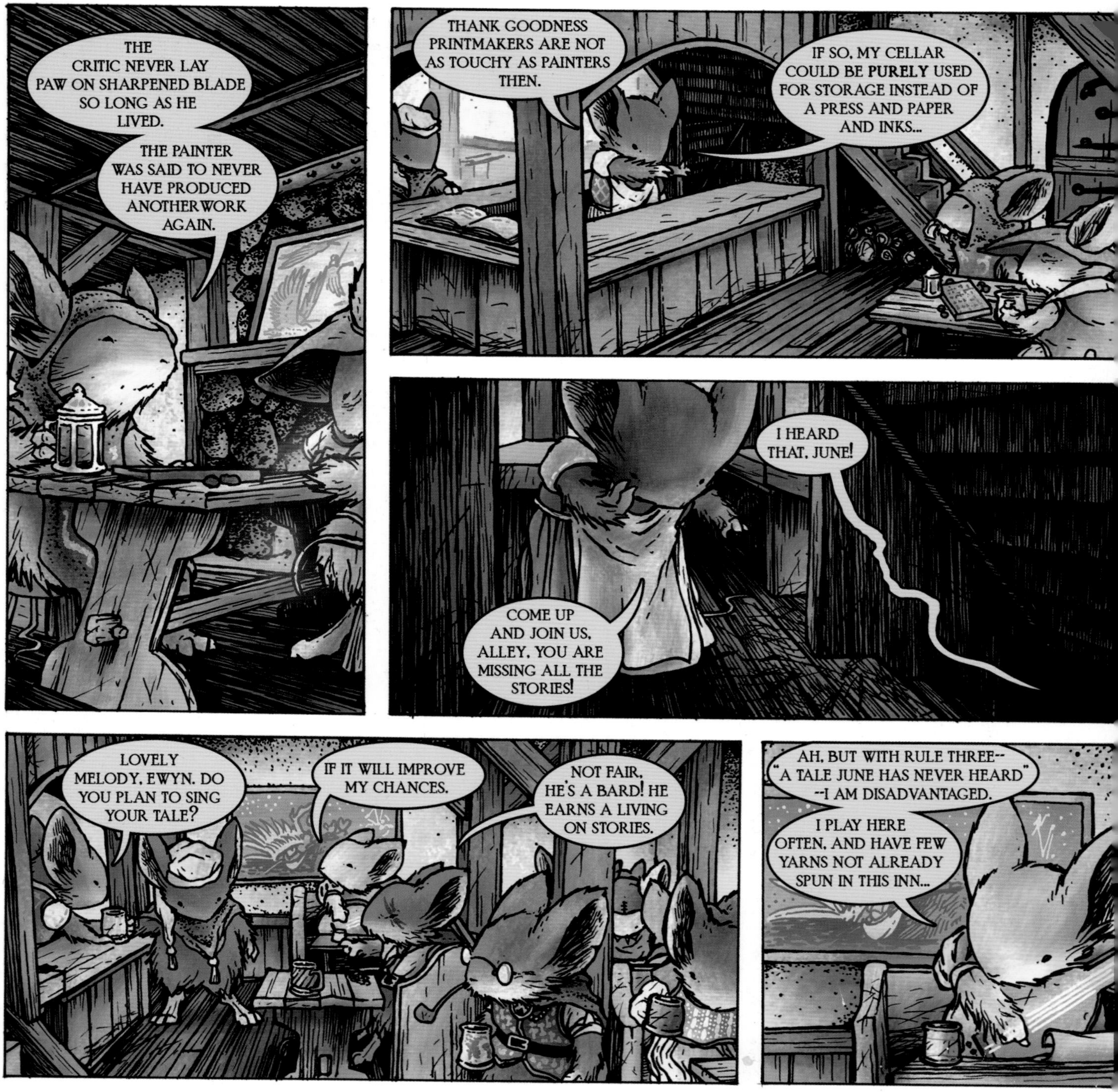
THE CRITIC NEVER LAY PAW ON SHARPENED BLADE SO LONG AS HE LIVED.
THE PAINTER WAS SAID TO NEVER HAVE PRODUCED ANOTHERWORK AGAIN.
THANK GOODNESS PRINTMAKERS ARE NOT AS TOUCHY AS PAINTERS THEN.
IF SO, MY CELLAR COULD BE PURELY USED FOR STORAGE INSTEAD OF A PRESS AND PAPER AND INKS...
COME UP AND JOIN US, ALLEY, YOU ARE MISSING ALL THE STORIES!
I HEARD THAT, JUNE!
LOVELY MELODY, EWYN. DO YOU PLAN TO SING YOUR TALE?
IF IT WILL IMPROVE MY CHANCES.
NOT FAIR, HE'S A BARD! HE EARNS A LIVING ON STORIES.
AH, BUT WITH RULE THREE-- "A TALE JUNE HAS NEVER HEARD" --I AM DISADVANTAGED.
I PLAY HERE OFTEN, AND HAVE FEW YARNS NOT ALREADY SPUN IN THIS INN...

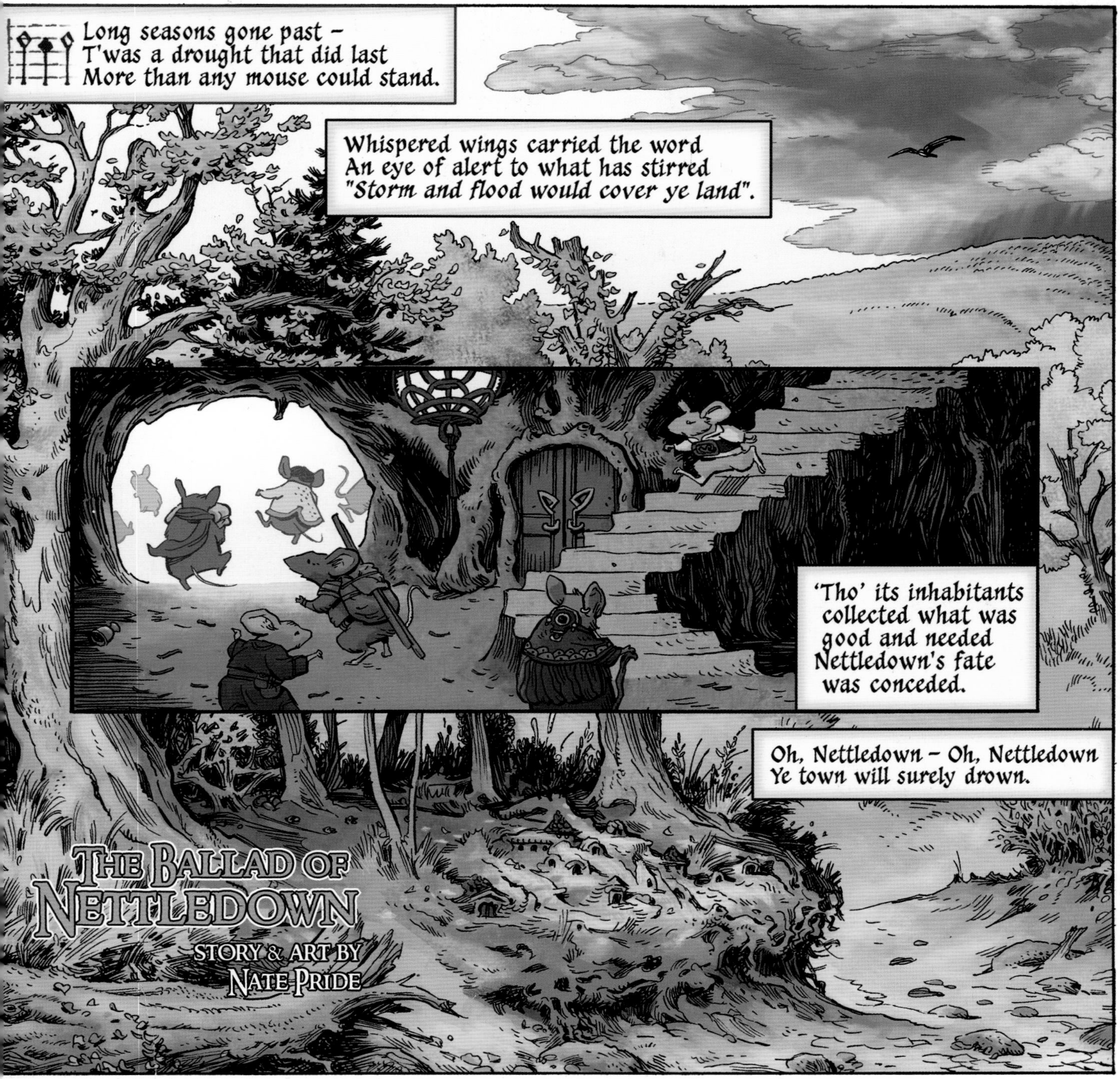
Long seasons gone past -
T'was a drought that did last
More than any mouse could stand.
Whispered wings carried the word
An eye of alert to what has stirred
"Storm and flood would cover ye land".
'Tho' its inhabitants collected what was good and needed Nettledown's fate was conceded.
Oh, Nettledown - Oh, Nettledown
Ye town will surely drown.
THE BALLAD OF NETTLEDOWN
STORY & ART BY NATE PRIDE

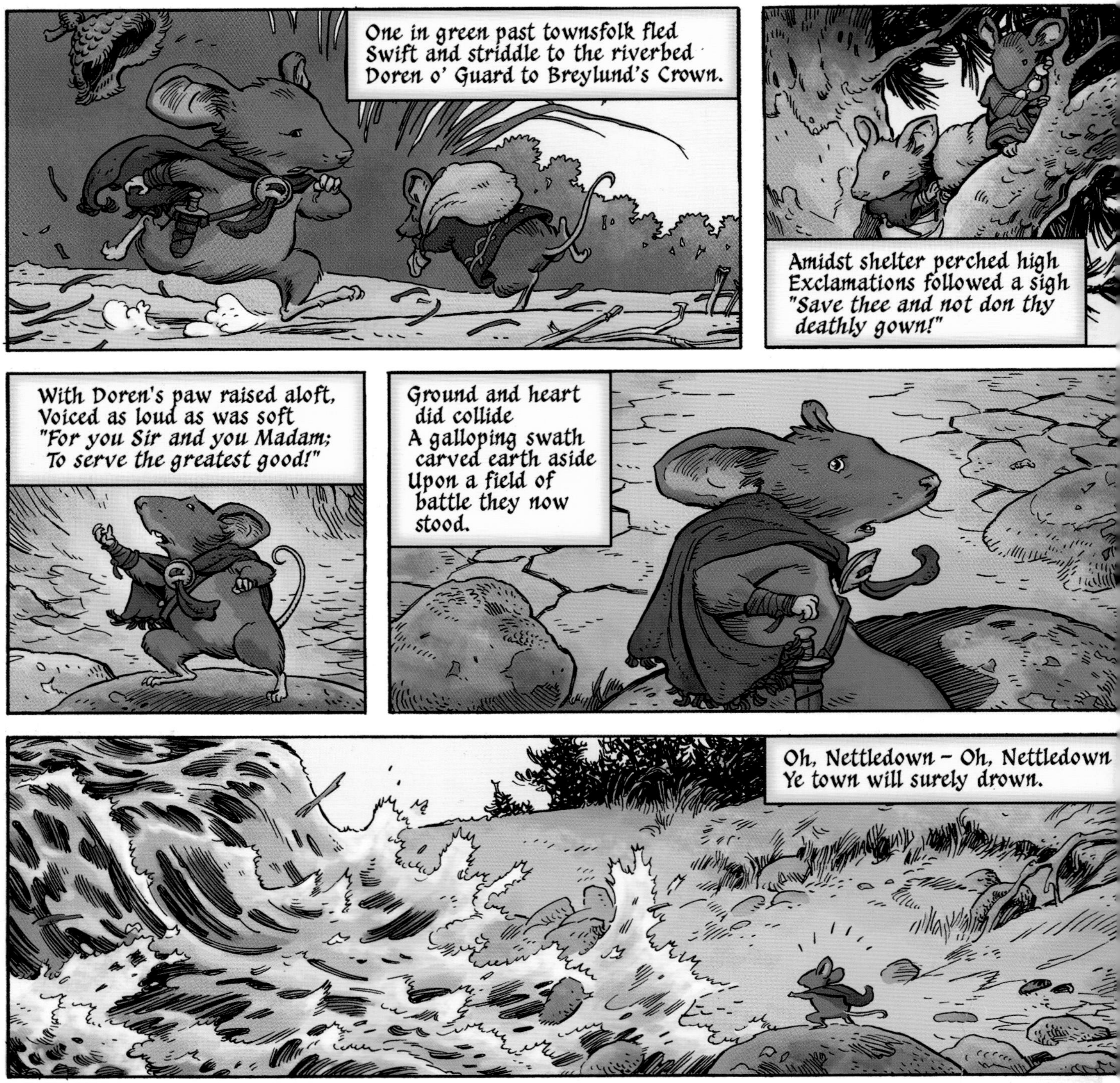
One in green past townsfolk fled
Swift and striddle to the riverbed
Doren o' Guard to Breylund's Crown.
Amidst shelter perched high
Exclamations followed a sigh
"Save thee and not don thy deathly gown!"
With Doren's paw raised aloft,
Voiced as loud as was soft
"For you Sir and you Madam;
To serve the greatest good!"
Ground and heart did collide
A galloping swath carved earth aside
Upon a field of battle they now stood.
Oh, Nettledown – Oh, Nettledown
Ye town will surely drown.

As the crest of water bore down
Doren opened his maw with renown
Swallowing that torrent whole.

Aye, like a thunderous clap
Off his paws and sent Eau-Galle-Glap
As the townsfolk cheered a grateful extol.

Climbing slowly up to awaiting throngs
As the tempest grumbled o'er their songs
Annointed with petals from a river Plum.

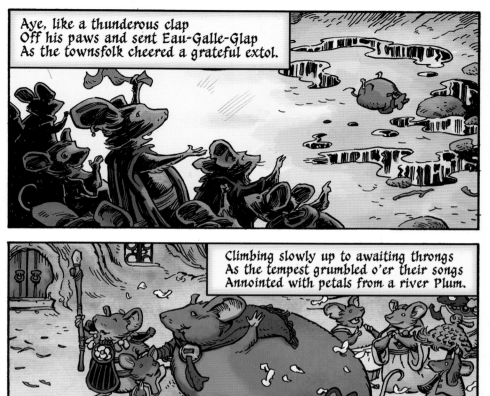

A quarry his chosen destination
Filled with the fruits of his salvation
Would nourish for seasons to come.

Oh, Nettledown – Oh, Nettledown
Ye town t'was nearly drown'd.

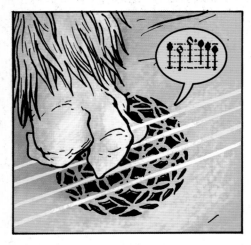

AND THAT, MY GENEROUS BAR MAIDEN, IS HOW THE LAKESIDE TOWN OF NETTLEDOWN AVOIDED TRAGEDY.

OR AS CLOSELY AS I CAN MAKE IT RHYME.

"TRAGEDY"?

THAT FLOOD WOULD HAVE WIPED THEM ALL OUT.

NO SURVIVORS.

NO MEMORY.

YOU SEE, WHEN SOMEONE IS LEFT BEHIND, IT'S THE MEMORY AND LOSS THAT IS THE TRAGEDY.

IT IS A FAR EASIER THING TO MOURN THE FACELESS MASSES...

THAN TO MOURN THE SINGLE LOVE...

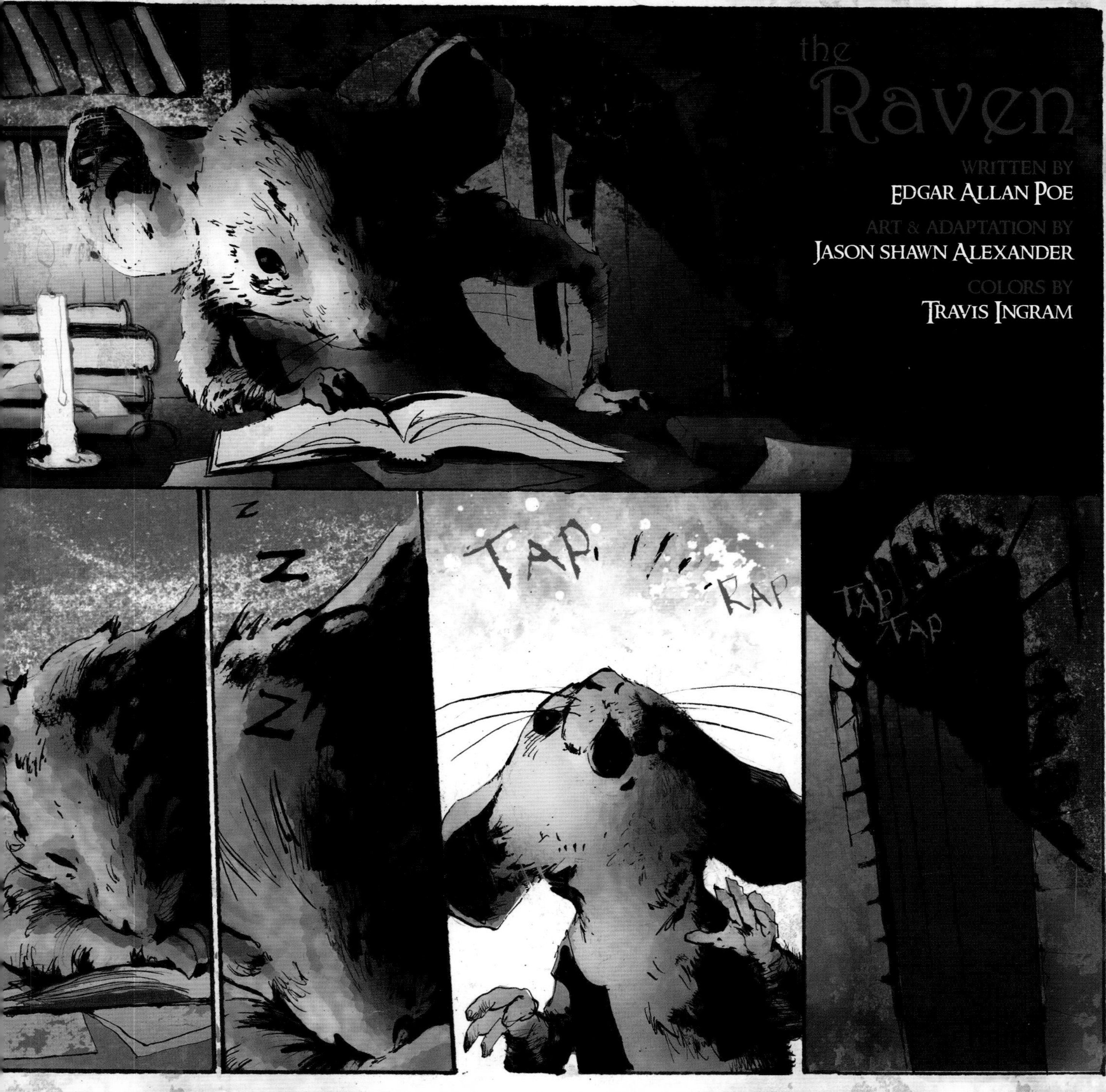

the Raven
WRITTEN BY
EDGAR ALLAN POE
ART & ADAPTATION BY
JASON SHAWN ALEXANDER
COLORS BY
TRAVIS INGRAM
Z
Z
Z
TAP
RAP
TAP
TAP

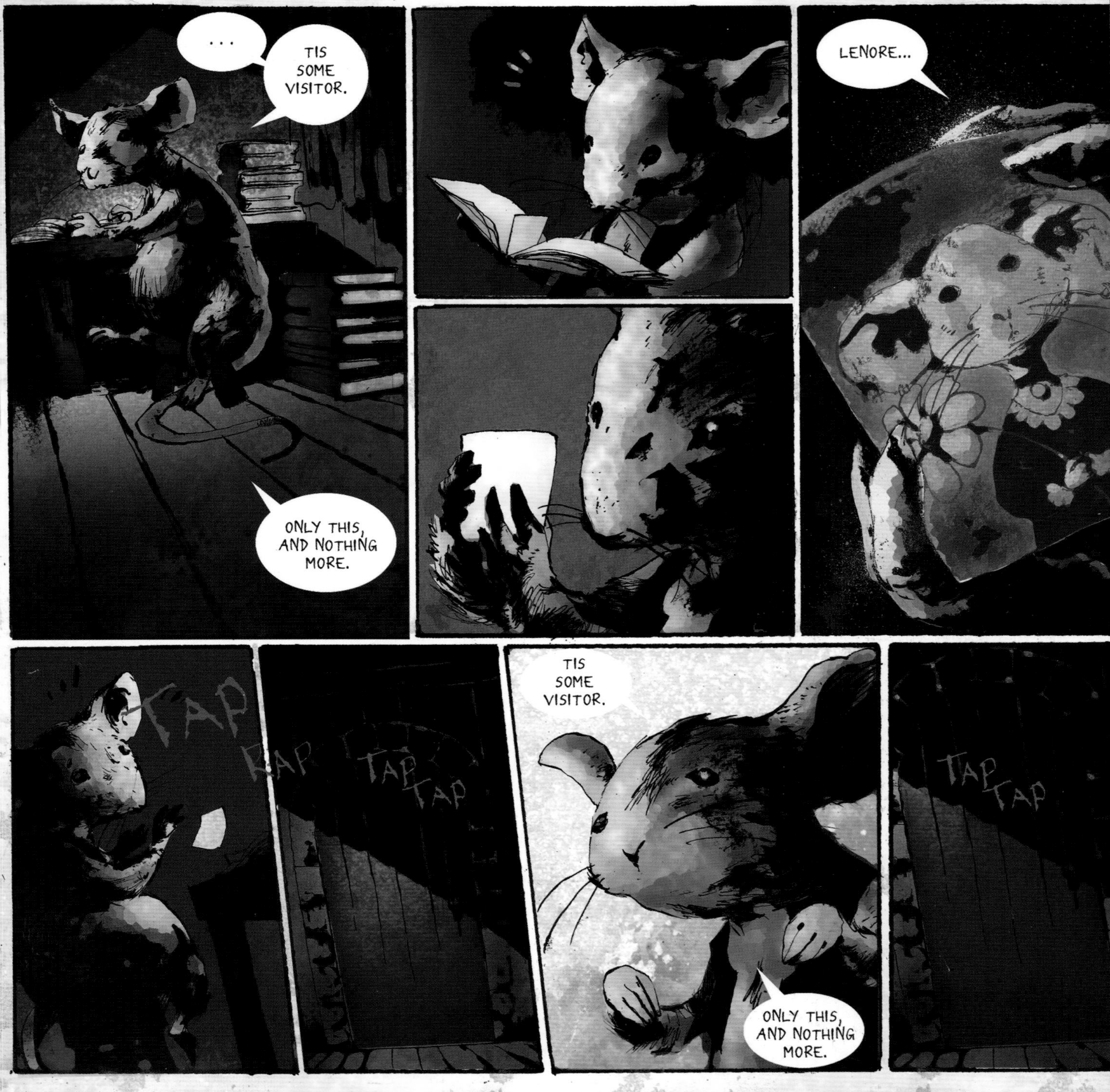
. . .
TIS SOME VISITOR.
ONLY THIS, AND NOTHING MORE.
LENORE...
TAP
RAP
TAP TAP
TIS SOME VISITOR.
ONLY THIS, AND NOTHING MORE.
TAP TAP

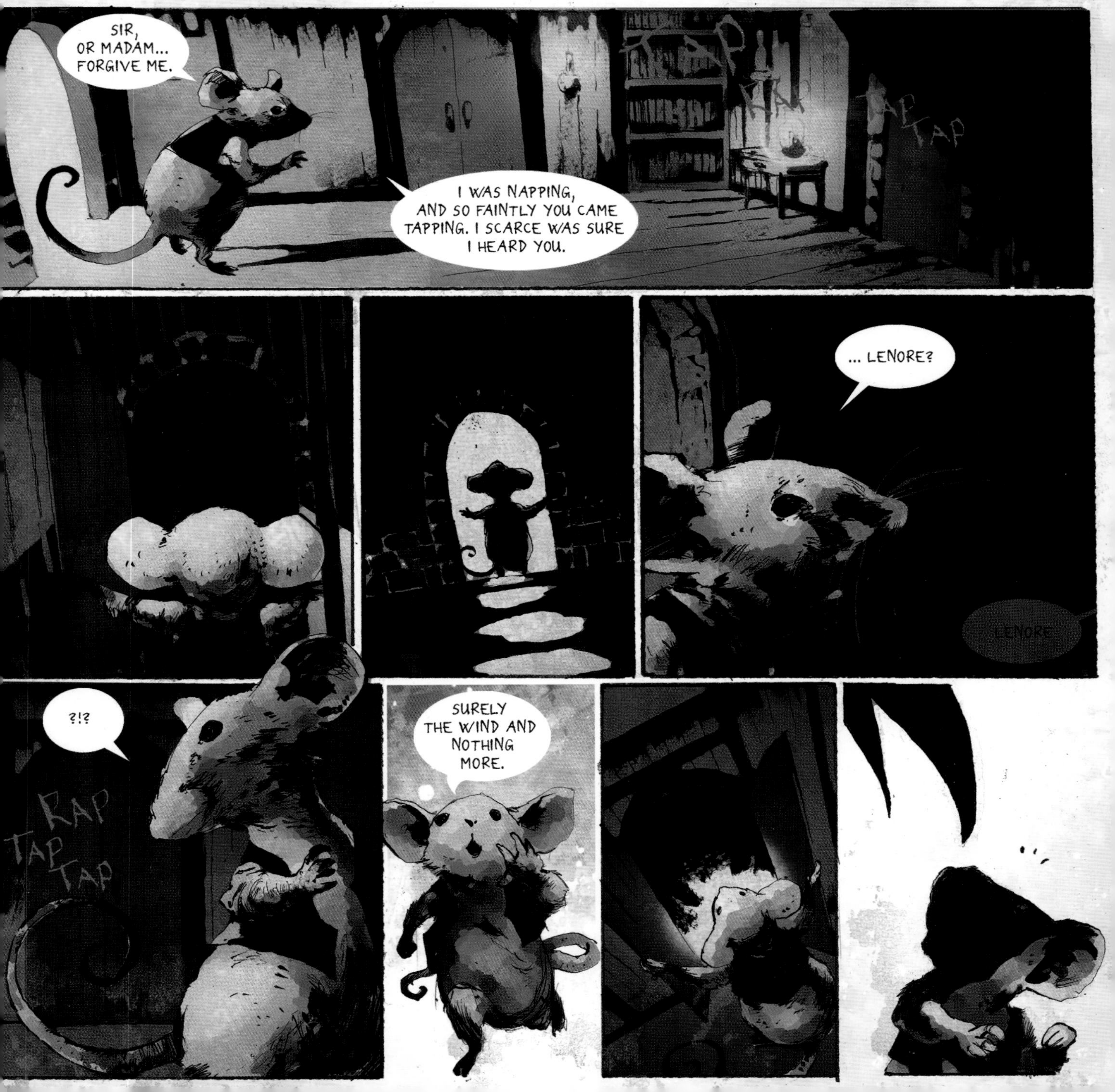
SIR, OR MADAM... FORGIVE ME.
RAP
RAP
TAP TAP
I WAS NAPPING, AND SO FAINTLY YOU CAME TAPPING. I SCARCE WAS SURE I HEARD YOU.
... LENORE?
LENORE
?!?
RAP
TAP
TAP
SURELY THE WIND AND NOTHING MORE.

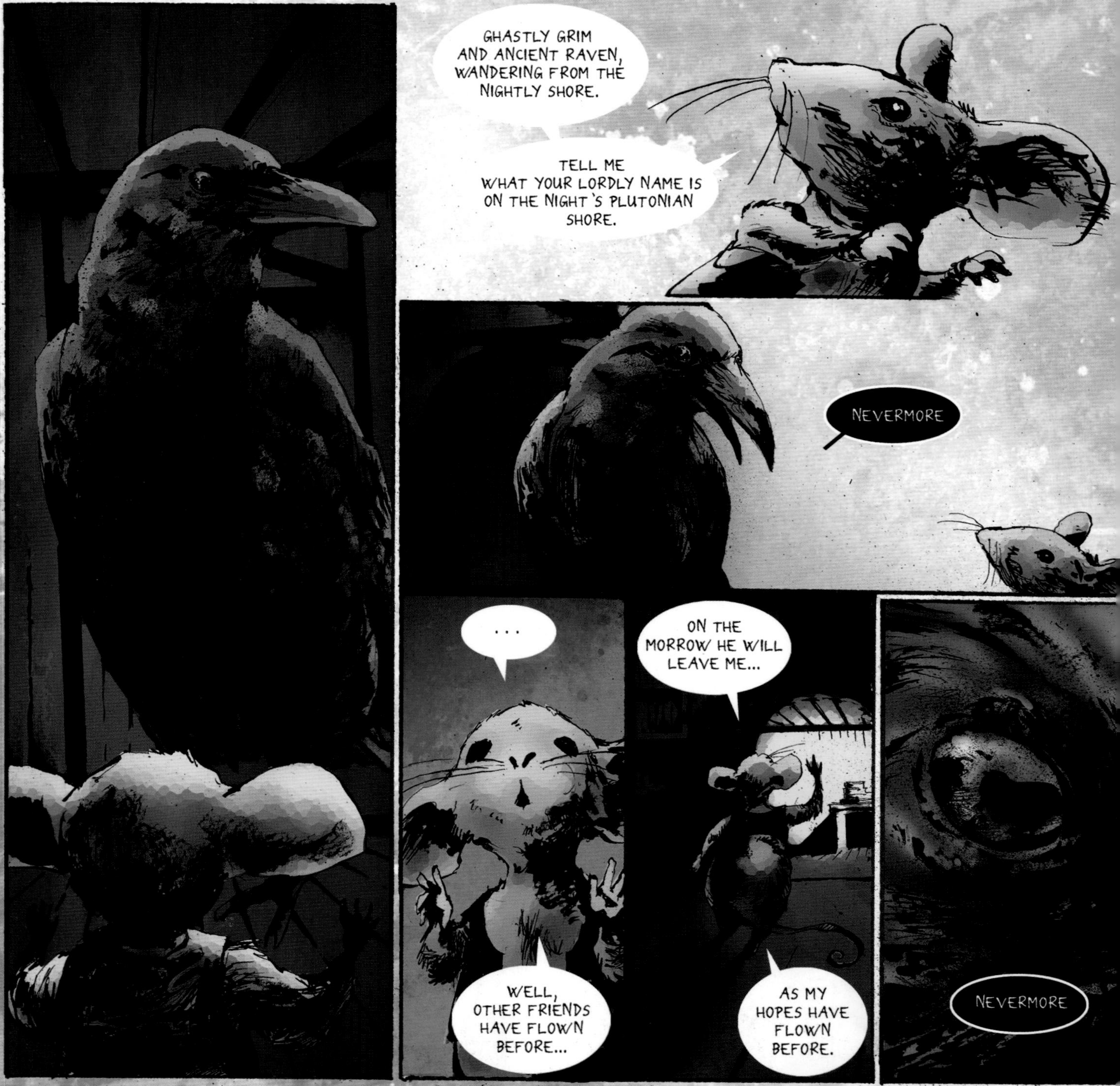
GHASTLY GRIM AND ANCIENT RAVEN, WANDERING FROM THE NIGHTLY SHORE.
TELL ME WHAT YOUR LORDLY NAME IS ON THE NIGHT'S PLUTONIAN SHORE.
NEVERMORE
...
WELL, OTHER FRIENDS HAVE FLOWN BEFORE...
ON THE MORROW HE WILL LEAVE ME...
AS MY HOPES HAVE FLOWN BEFORE.
NEVERMORE

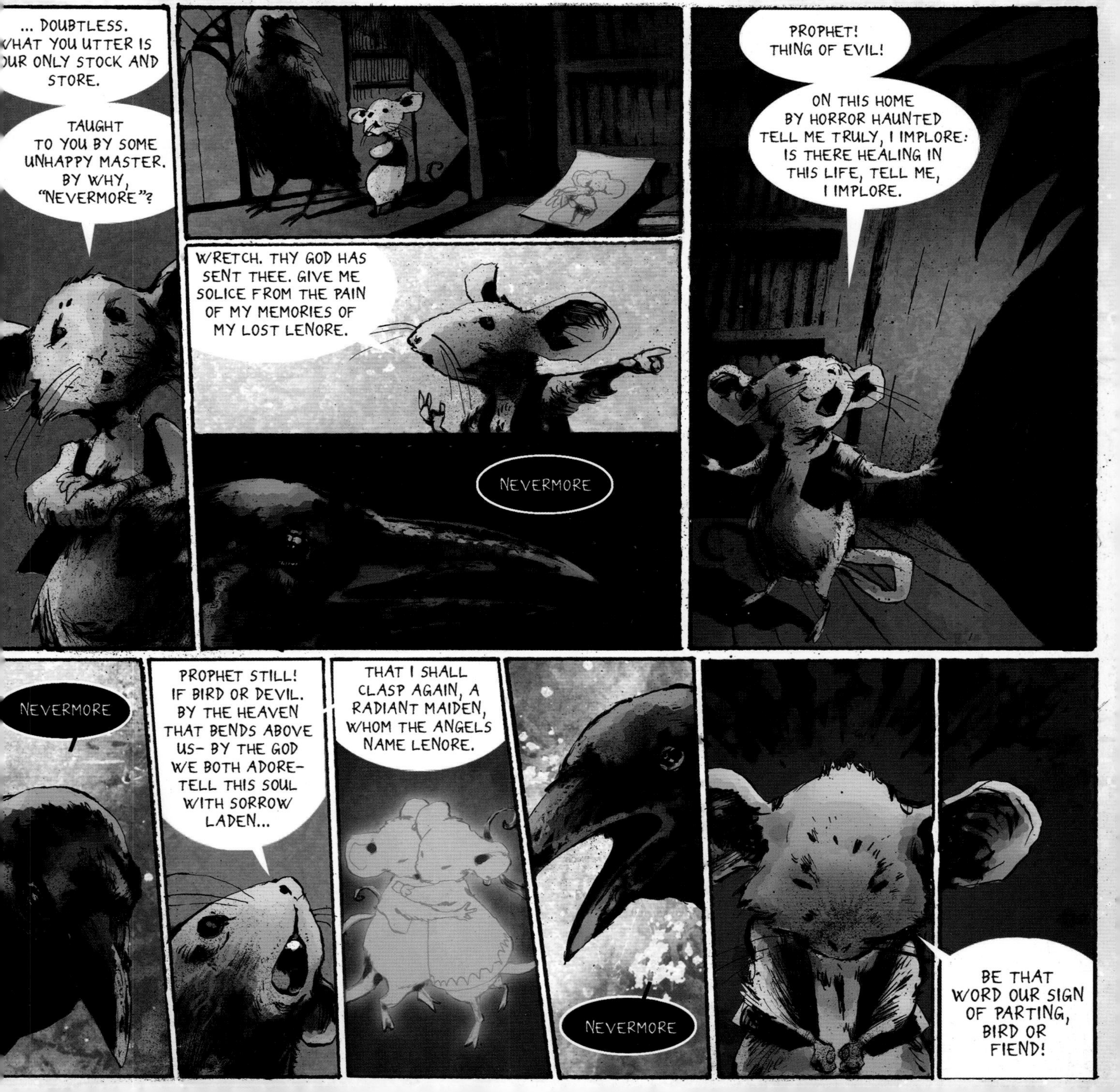
... DOUBTLESS. WHAT YOU UTTER IS OUR ONLY STOCK AND STORE.
TAUGHT TO YOU BY SOME UNHAPPY MASTER. BY WHY, "NEVERMORE"?
WRETCH. THY GOD HAS SENT THEE. GIVE ME SOLICE FROM THE PAIN OF MY MEMORIES OF MY LOST LENORE.
NEVERMORE
PROPHET! THING OF EVIL!
ON THIS HOME BY HORROR HAUNTED TELL ME TRULY, I IMPLORE: IS THERE HEALING IN THIS LIFE, TELL ME, I IMPLORE.
NEVERMORE
PROPHET STILL! IF BIRD OR DEVIL. BY THE HEAVEN THAT BENDS ABOVE US- BY THE GOD WE BOTH ADORE- TELL THIS SOUL WITH SORROW LADEN...
THAT I SHALL CLASP AGAIN, A RADIANT MAIDEN, WHOM THE ANGELS NAME LENORE.
NEVERMORE
BE THAT WORD OUR SIGN OF PARTING, BIRD OR FIEND!

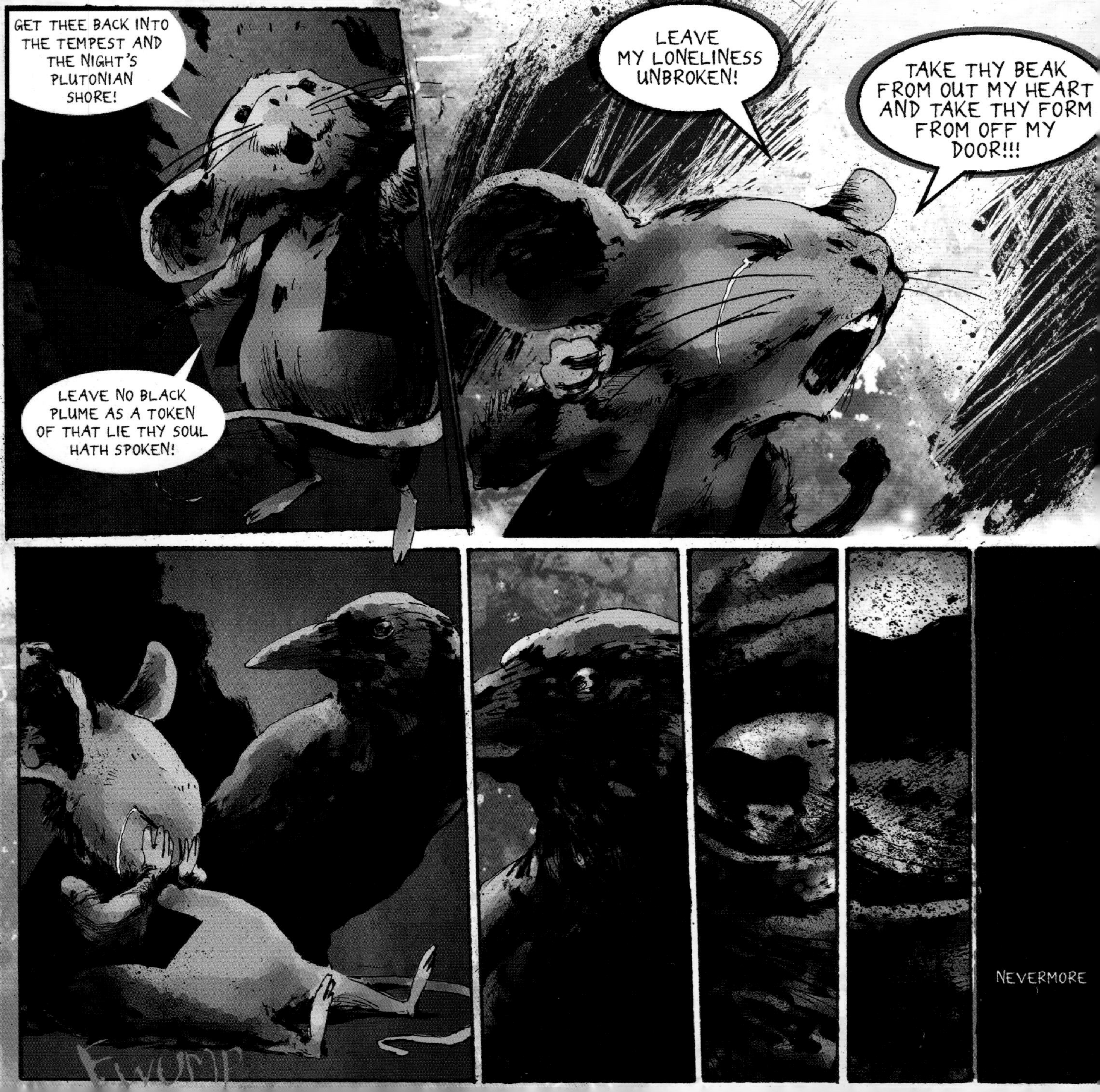
GET THEE BACK INTO THE TEMPEST AND THE NIGHT'S PLUTONIAN SHORE!
LEAVE NO BLACK PLUME AS A TOKEN OF THAT LIE THY SOUL HATH SPOKEN!
LEAVE MY LONELINESS UNBROKEN!
TAKE THY BEAK FROM OUT MY HEART AND TAKE THY FORM FROM OFF MY DOOR!!!
FWUMP
NEVERMORE

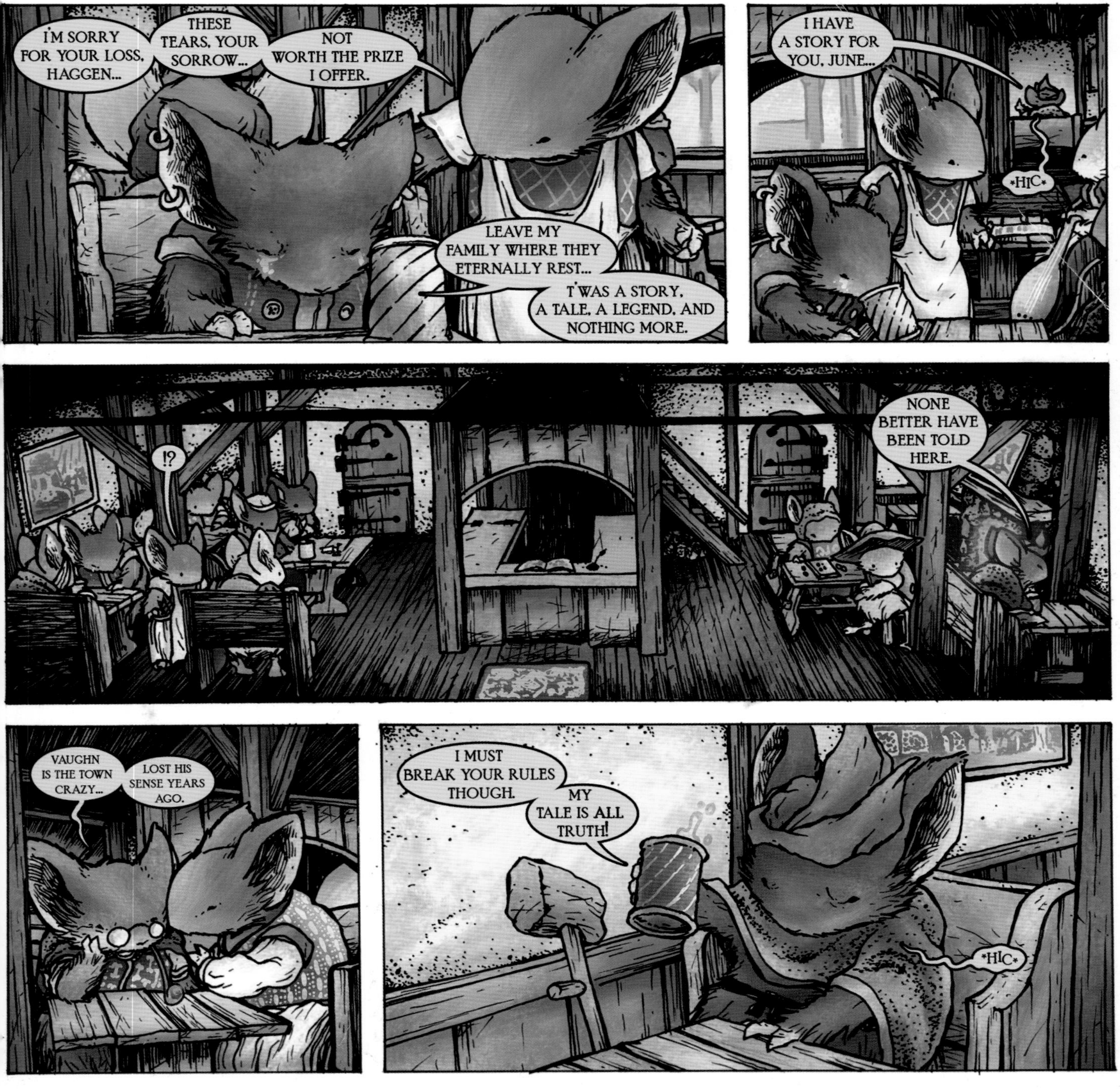
I'M SORRY FOR YOUR LOSS, HAGGEN...
THESE TEARS, YOUR SORROW...
NOT WORTH THE PRIZE I OFFER.
LEAVE MY FAMILY WHERE THEY ETERNALLY REST...
T'WAS A STORY, A TALE, A LEGEND, AND NOTHING MORE.
I HAVE A STORY FOR YOU, JUNE...
HIC
!?
NONE BETTER HAVE BEEN TOLD HERE.
VAUGHN IS THE TOWN CRAZY...
LOST HIS SENSE YEARS AGO.
I MUST BREAK YOUR RULES THOUGH.
MY TALE IS ALL TRUTH!
HIC

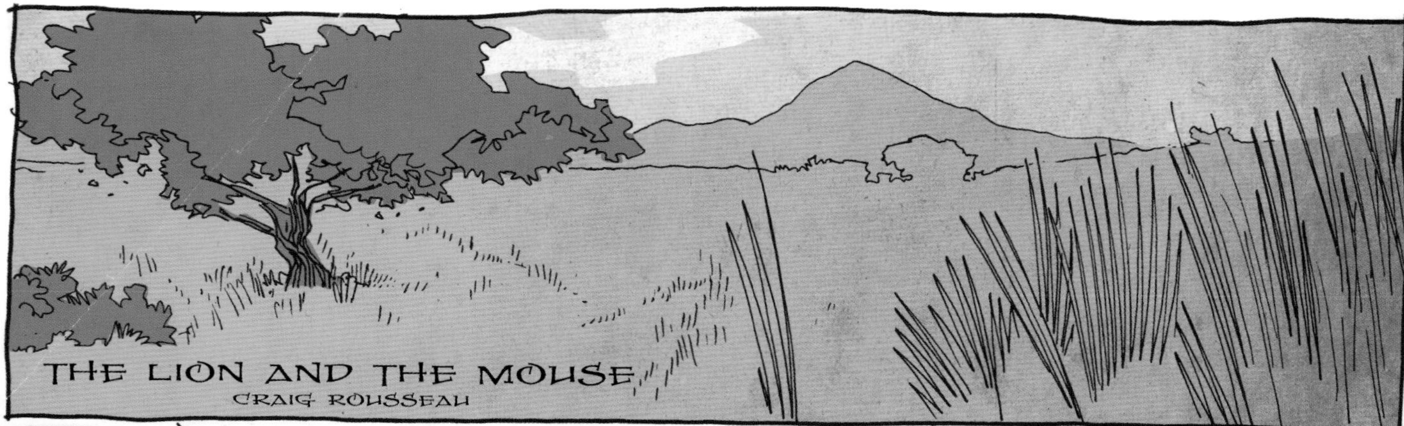
THE LION AND THE MOUSE
CRAIG ROUSSEAU

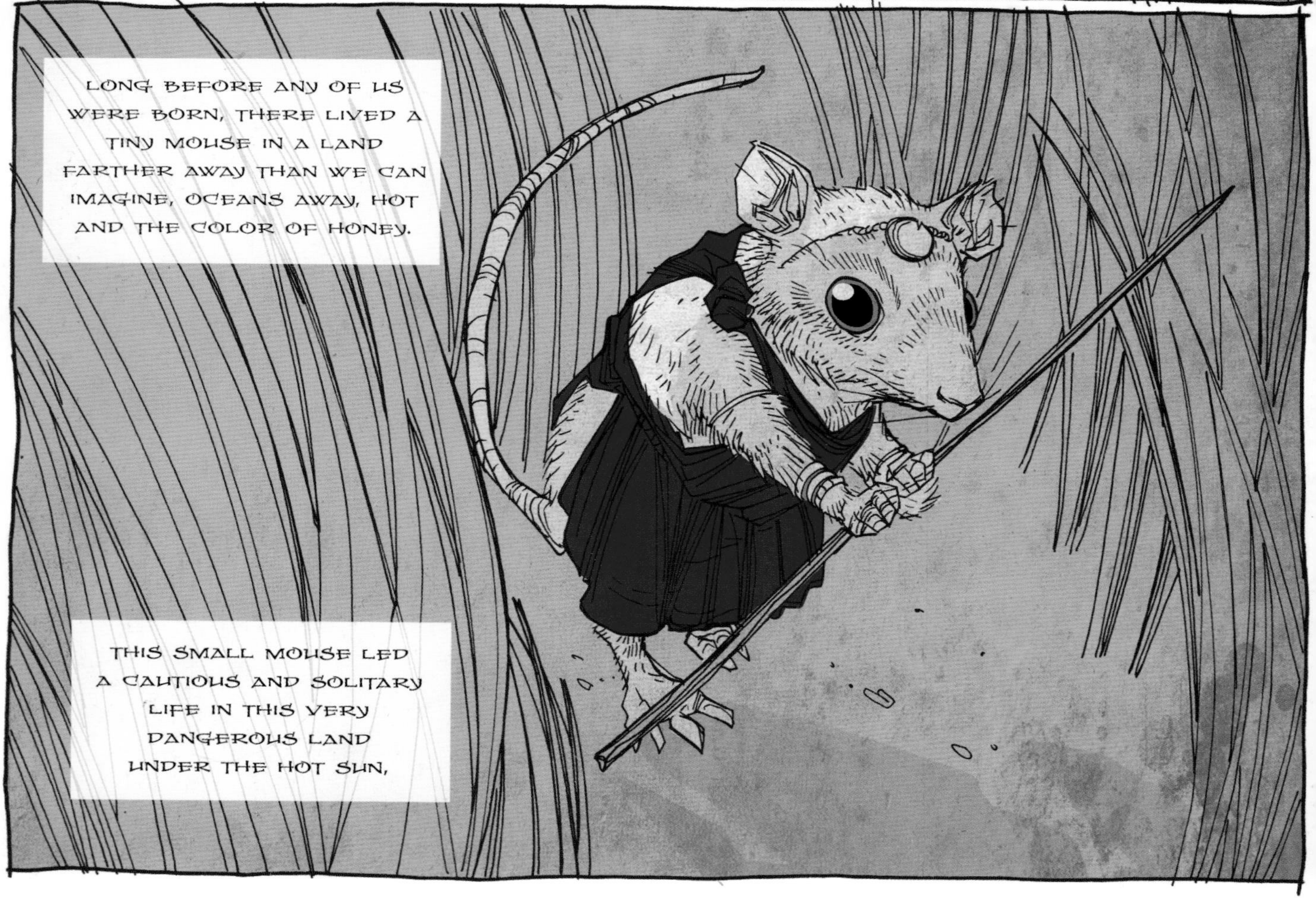
LONG BEFORE ANY OF US WERE BORN, THERE LIVED A TINY MOUSE IN A LAND FARTHER AWAY THAN WE CAN IMAGINE, OCEANS AWAY, HOT AND THE COLOR OF HONEY.
THIS SMALL MOUSE LED A CAUTIOUS AND SOLITARY LIFE IN THIS VERY DANGEROUS LAND UNDER THE HOT SUN,

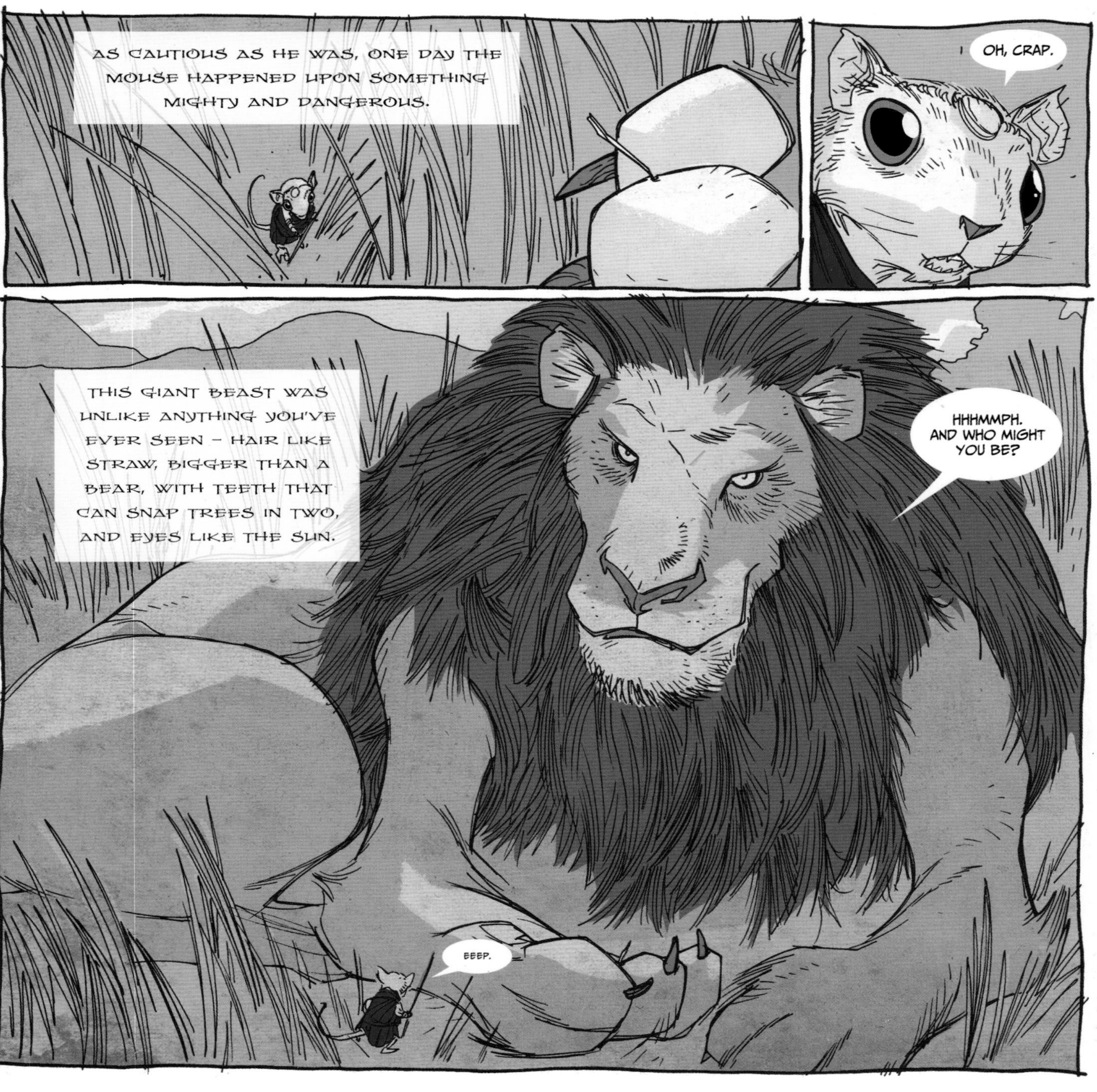
AS CAUTIOUS AS HE WAS, ONE DAY THE MOUSE HAPPENED UPON SOMETHING MIGHTY AND DANGEROUS.
OH, CRAP.
THIS GIANT BEAST WAS UNLIKE ANYTHING YOU'VE EVER SEEN – HAIR LIKE STRAW, BIGGER THAN A BEAR, WITH TEETH THAT CAN SNAP TREES IN TWO, AND EYES LIKE THE SUN.
HHHMMPH. AND WHO MIGHT YOU BE?
EEEP.

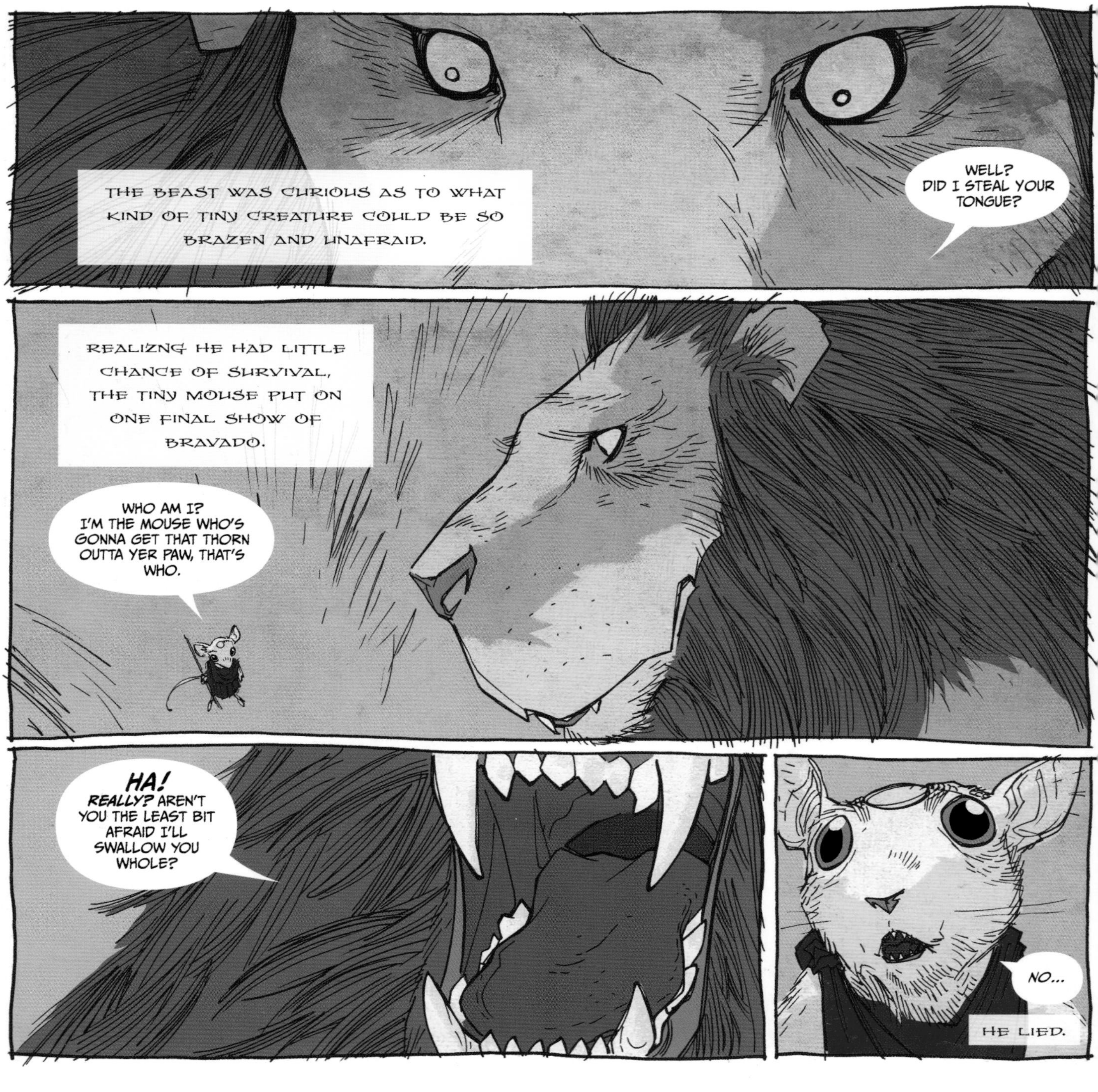
THE BEAST WAS CURIOUS AS TO WHAT KIND OF TINY CREATURE COULD BE SO BRAZEN AND UNAFRAID.
WELL? DID I STEAL YOUR TONGUE?
REALIZNG HE HAD LITTLE CHANCE OF SURVIVAL, THE TINY MOUSE PUT ON ONE FINAL SHOW OF BRAVADO.
WHO AM I? I'M THE MOUSE WHO'S GONNA GET THAT THORN OUTTA YER PAW, THAT'S WHO.
HA! REALLY? AREN'T YOU THE LEAST BIT AFRAID I'LL SWALLOW YOU WHOLE?
NO...
HE LIED.

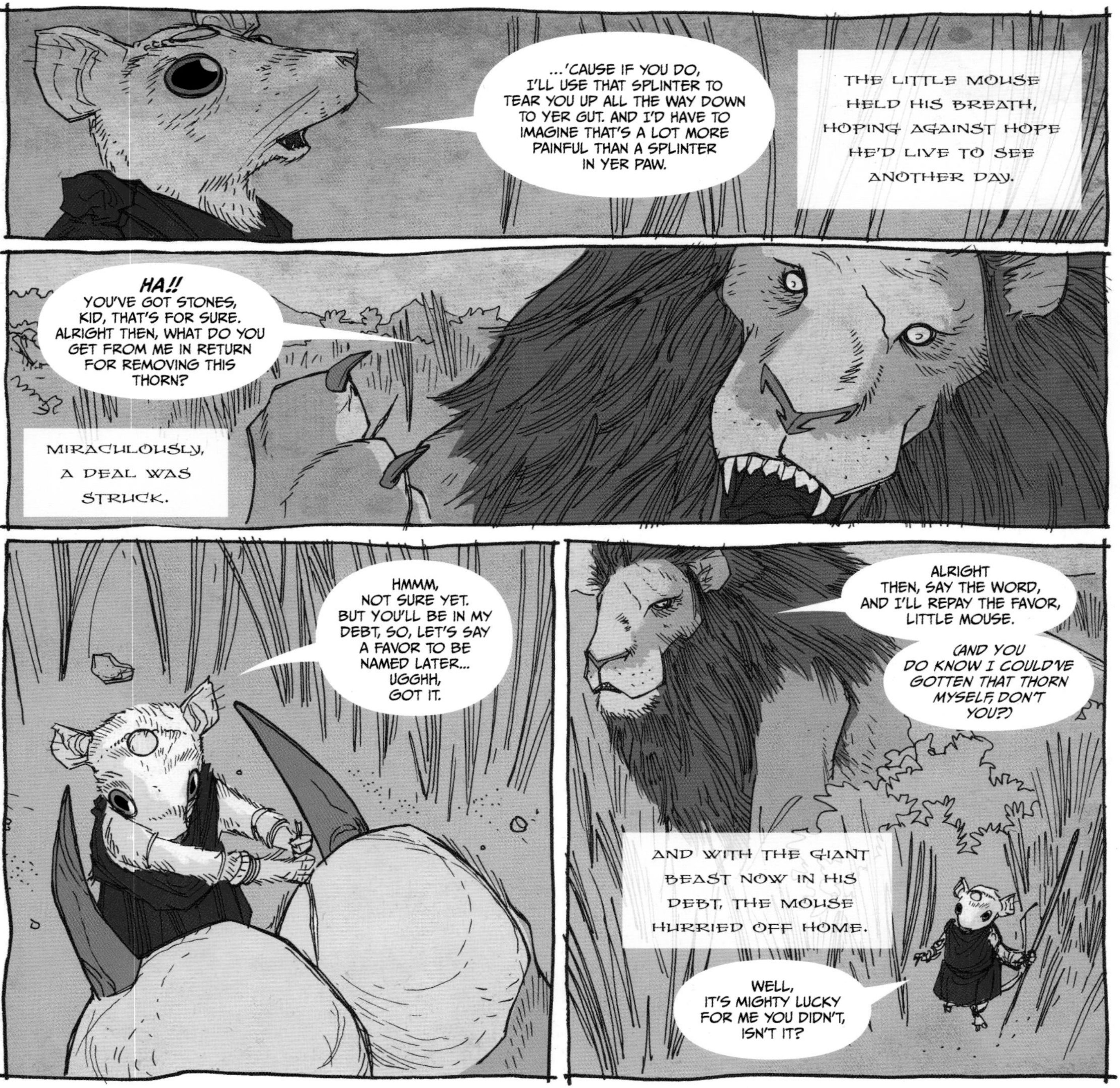
...'CAUSE IF YOU DO, I'LL USE THAT SPLINTER TO TEAR YOU UP ALL THE WAY DOWN TO YER GUT. AND I'D HAVE TO IMAGINE THAT'S A LOT MORE PAINFUL THAN A SPLINTER IN YER PAW.
THE LITTLE MOUSE HELD HIS BREATH, HOPING AGAINST HOPE HE'D LIVE TO SEE ANOTHER DAY.
HA!! YOU'VE GOT STONES, KID, THAT'S FOR SURE. ALRIGHT THEN, WHAT DO YOU GET FROM ME IN RETURN FOR REMOVING THIS THORN?
MIRACULOUSLY, A DEAL WAS STRUCK.
HMMM, NOT SURE YET. BUT YOU'LL BE IN MY DEBT, SO, LET'S SAY A FAVOR TO BE NAMED LATER... UGGHH, GOT IT.
ALRIGHT THEN, SAY THE WORD, AND I'LL REPAY THE FAVOR, LITTLE MOUSE.
(AND YOU DO KNOW I COULD'VE GOTTEN THAT THORN MYSELF, DON'T YOU?)
AND WITH THE GIANT BEAST NOW IN HIS DEBT, THE MOUSE HURRIED OFF HOME.
WELL, IT'S MIGHTY LUCKY FOR ME YOU DIDN'T, ISN'T IT?

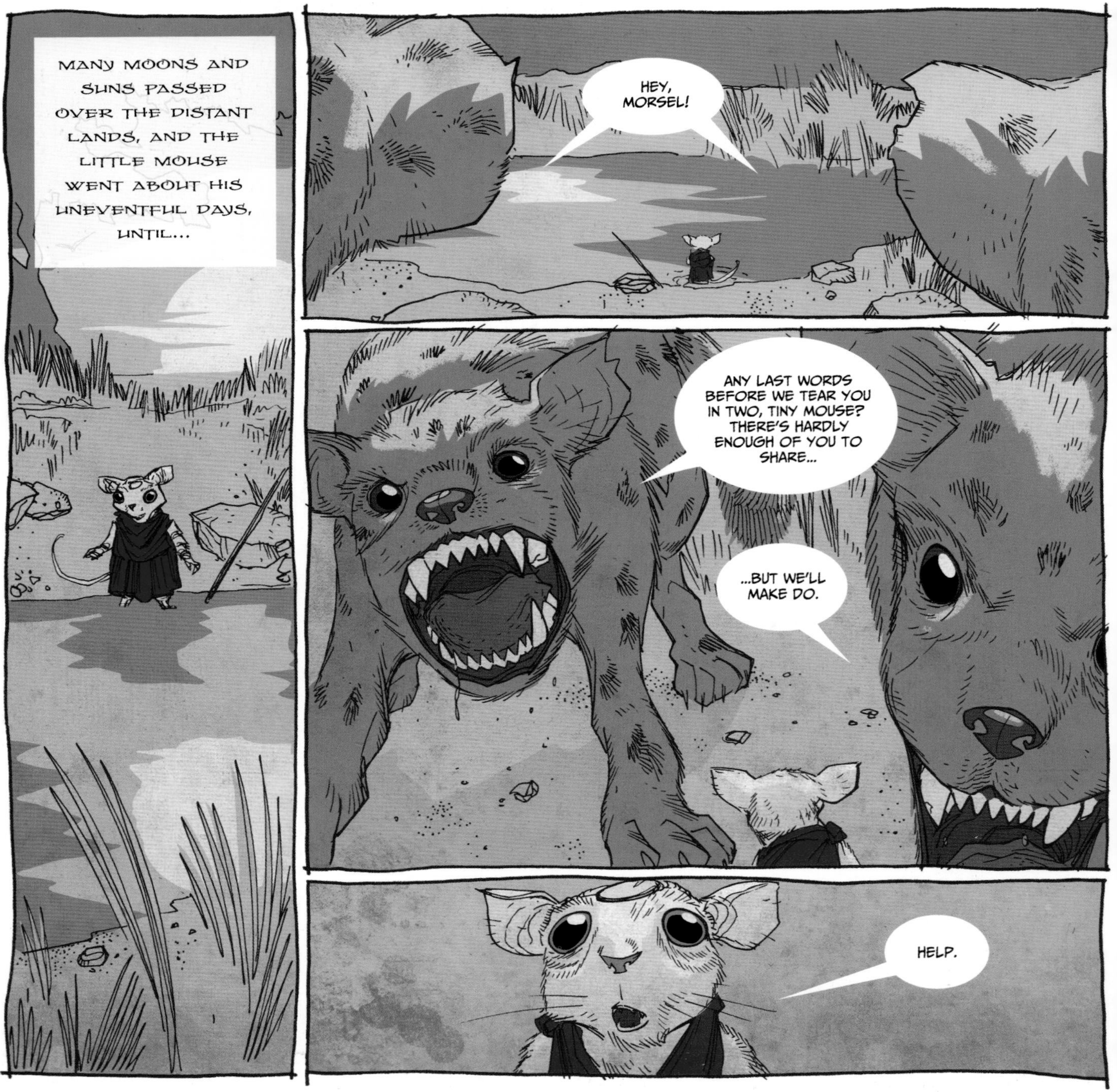
MANY MOONS AND SUNS PASSED OVER THE DISTANT LANDS, AND THE LITTLE MOUSE WENT ABOUT HIS UNEVENTFUL DAYS, UNTIL...
HEY, MORSEL!
ANY LAST WORDS BEFORE WE TEAR YOU IN TWO, TINY MOUSE? THERE'S HARDLY ENOUGH OF YOU TO SHARE...
...BUT WE'LL MAKE DO.
HELP.

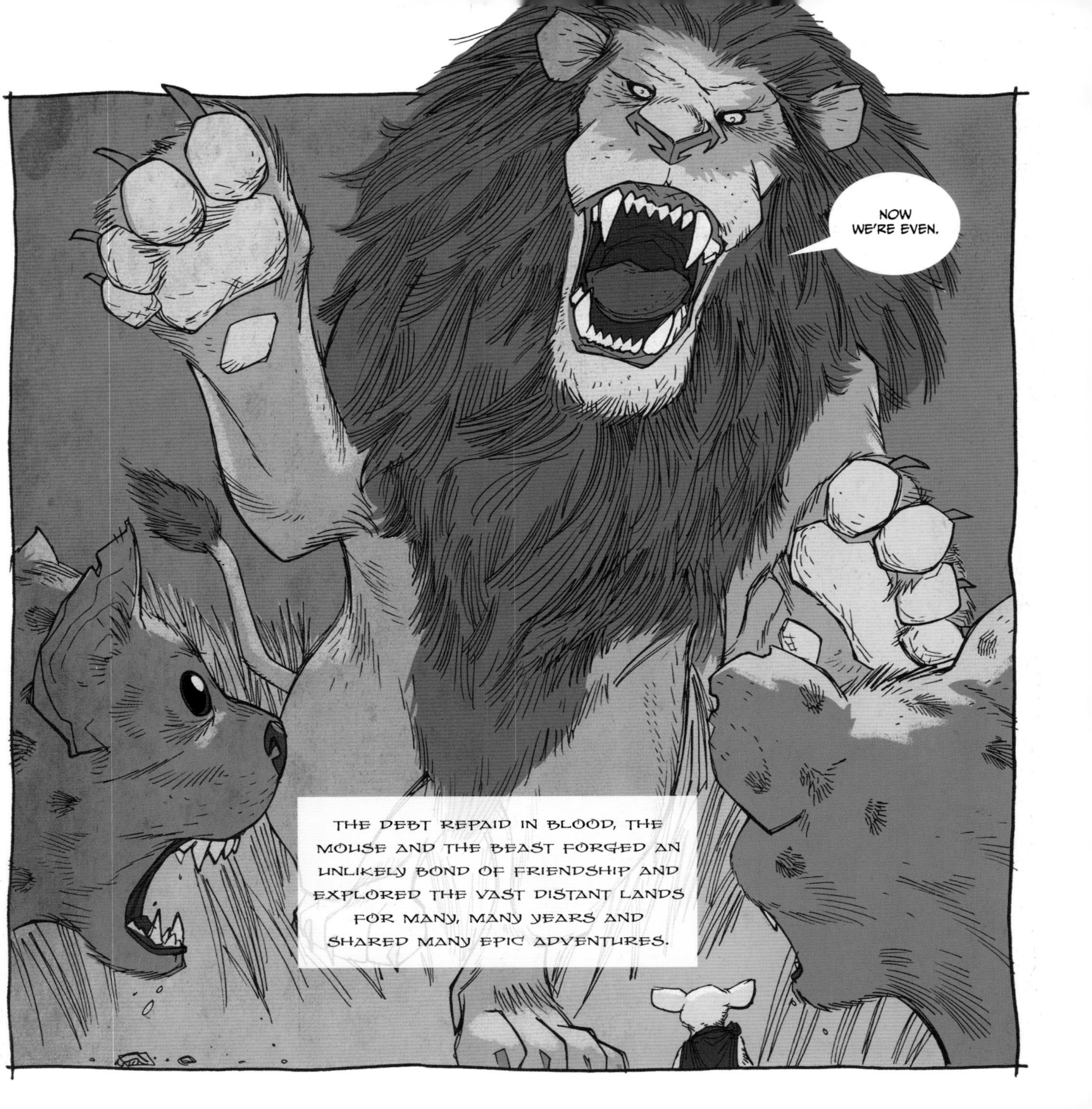
NOW WE'RE EVEN.
THE DEBT REPAID IN BLOOD, THE MOUSE AND THE BEAST FORGED AN UNLIKELY BOND OF FRIENDSHIP AND EXPLORED THE VAST DISTANT LANDS FOR MANY, MANY YEARS AND SHARED MANY EPIC ADVENTURES.

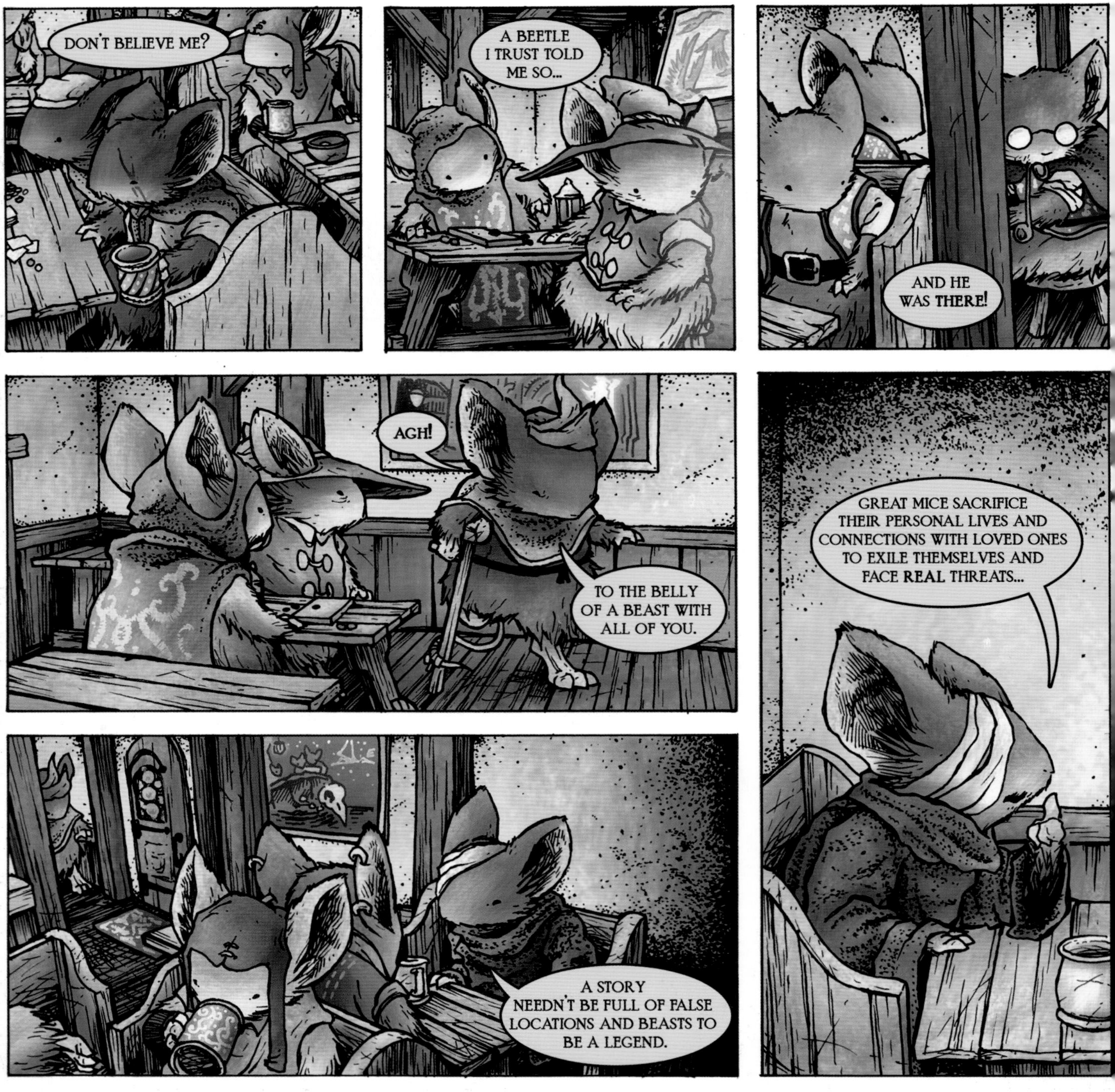
DON'T BELIEVE ME?
A BEETLE I TRUST TOLD ME SO...
AND HE WAS THERE!
AGH!
TO THE BELLY OF A BEAST WITH ALL OF YOU.
A STORY NEEDN'T BE FULL OF FALSE LOCATIONS AND BEASTS TO BE A LEGEND.
GREAT MICE SACRIFICE THEIR PERSONAL LIVES AND CONNECTIONS WITH LOVED ONES TO EXILE THEMSELVES AND FACE REAL THREATS...

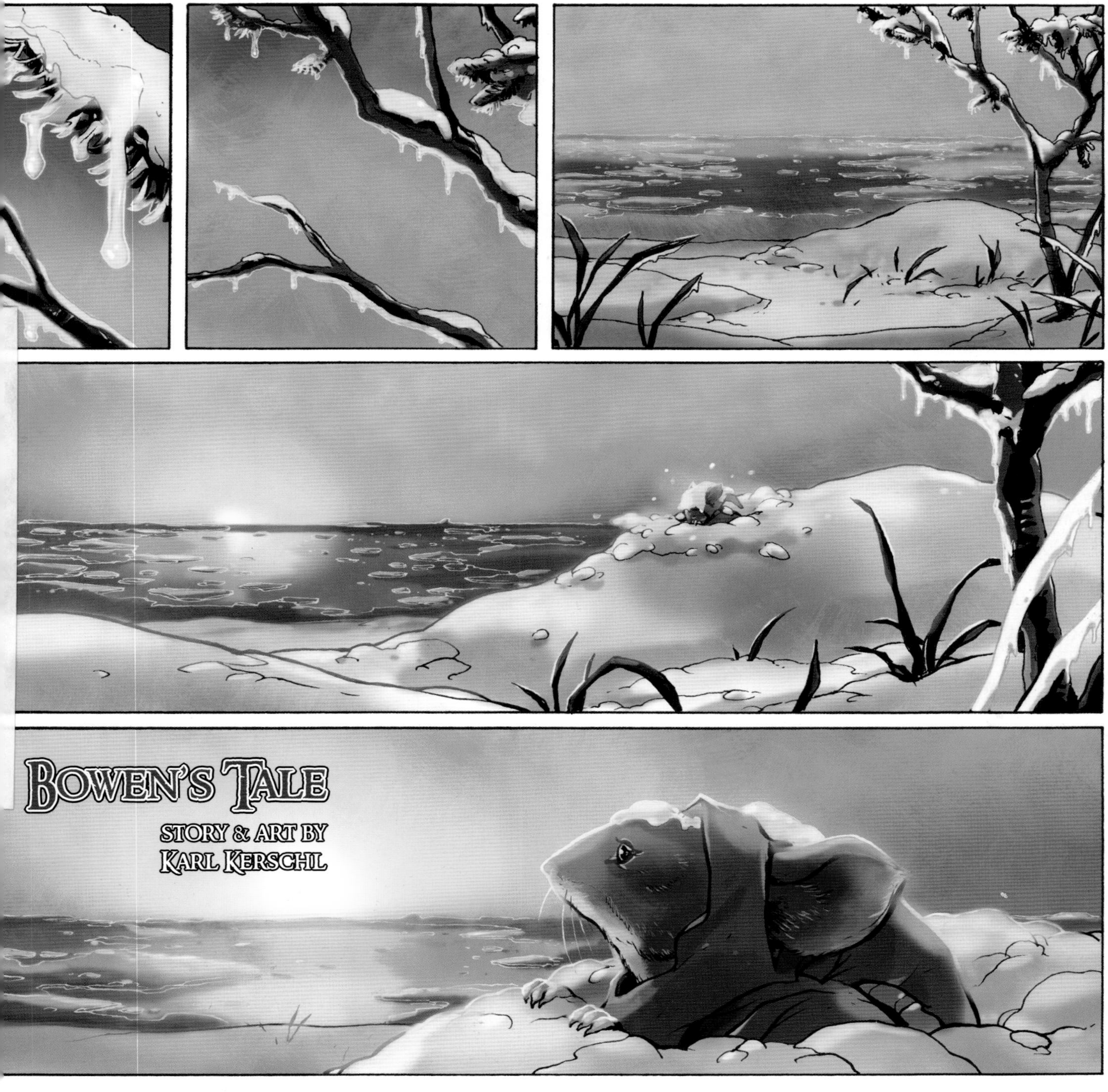
BOWEN'S TALE
STORY & ART BY
KARL KERSCHL

TINK
KSHHHHH

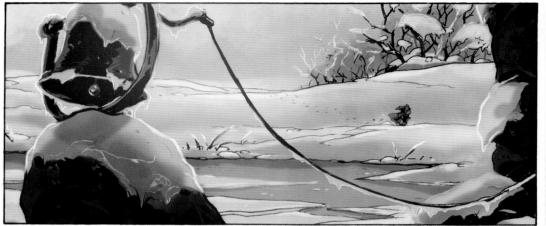

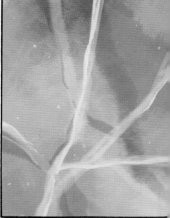

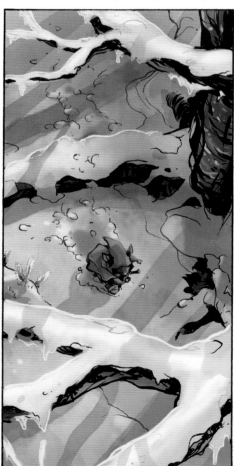

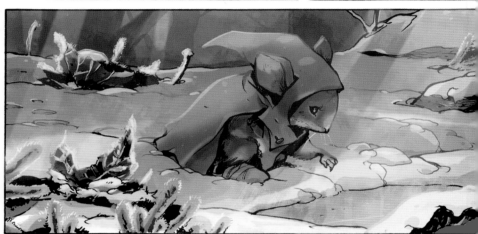

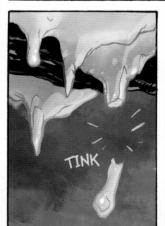

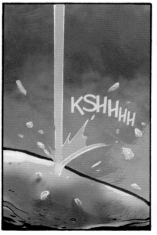

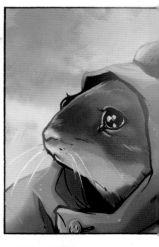

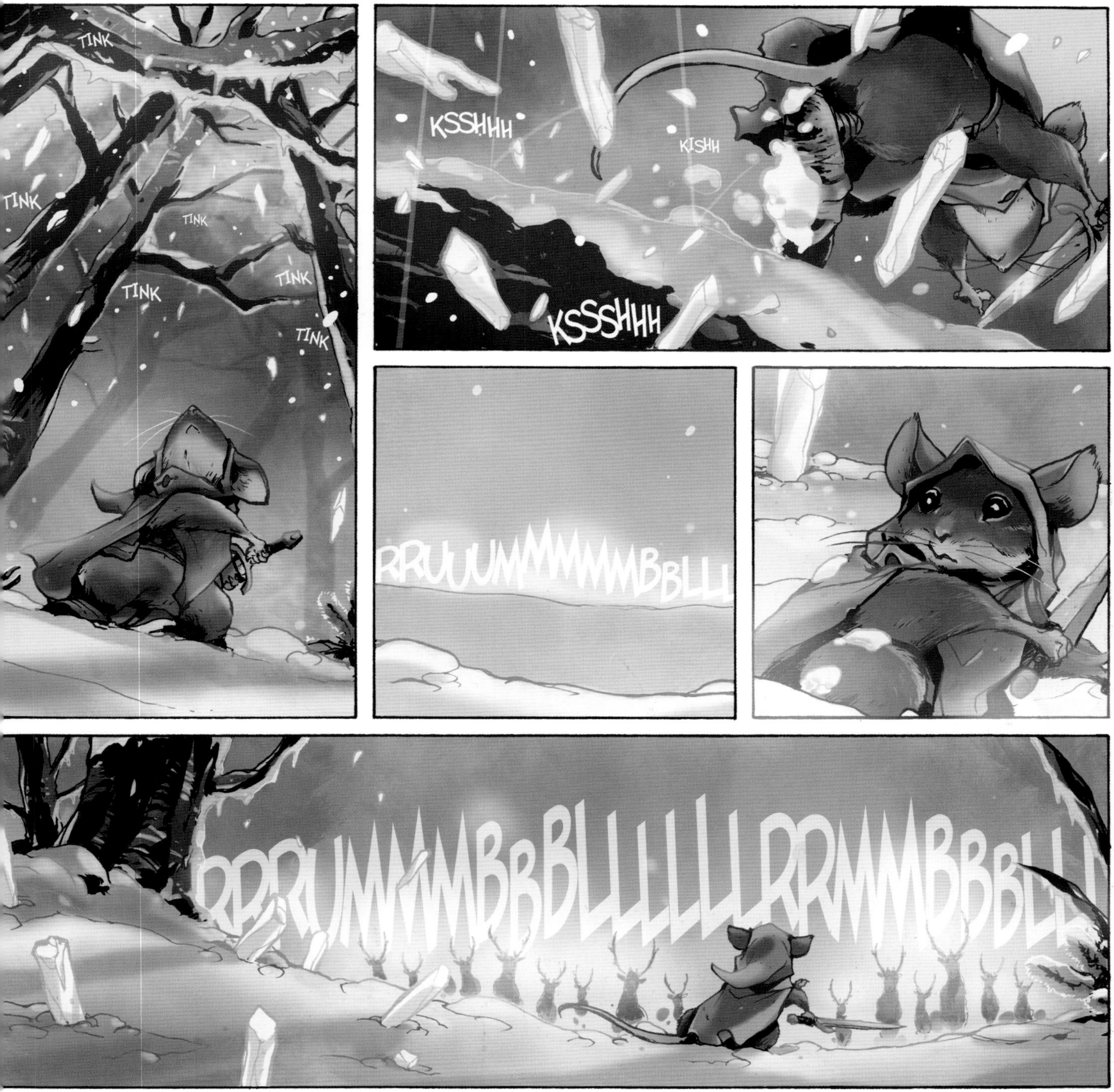
TINK
TINK
TINK
TINK
TINK
TINK
KSSHHH
KISHH
KSSSHHH
RRUUUMMMMMBBLLL
RRRUMMMMBBBLLLLLLRRMMBBBLLL

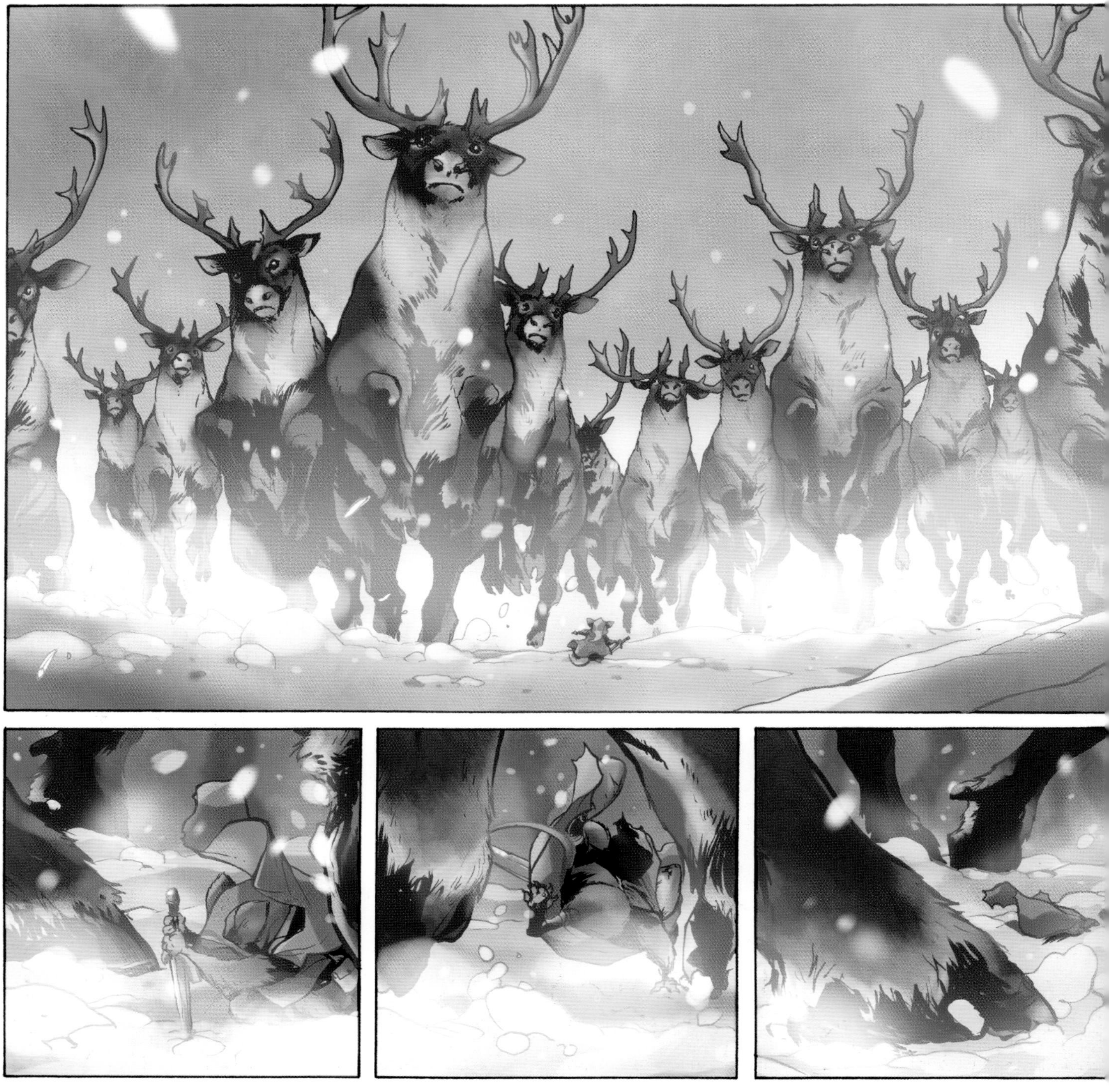

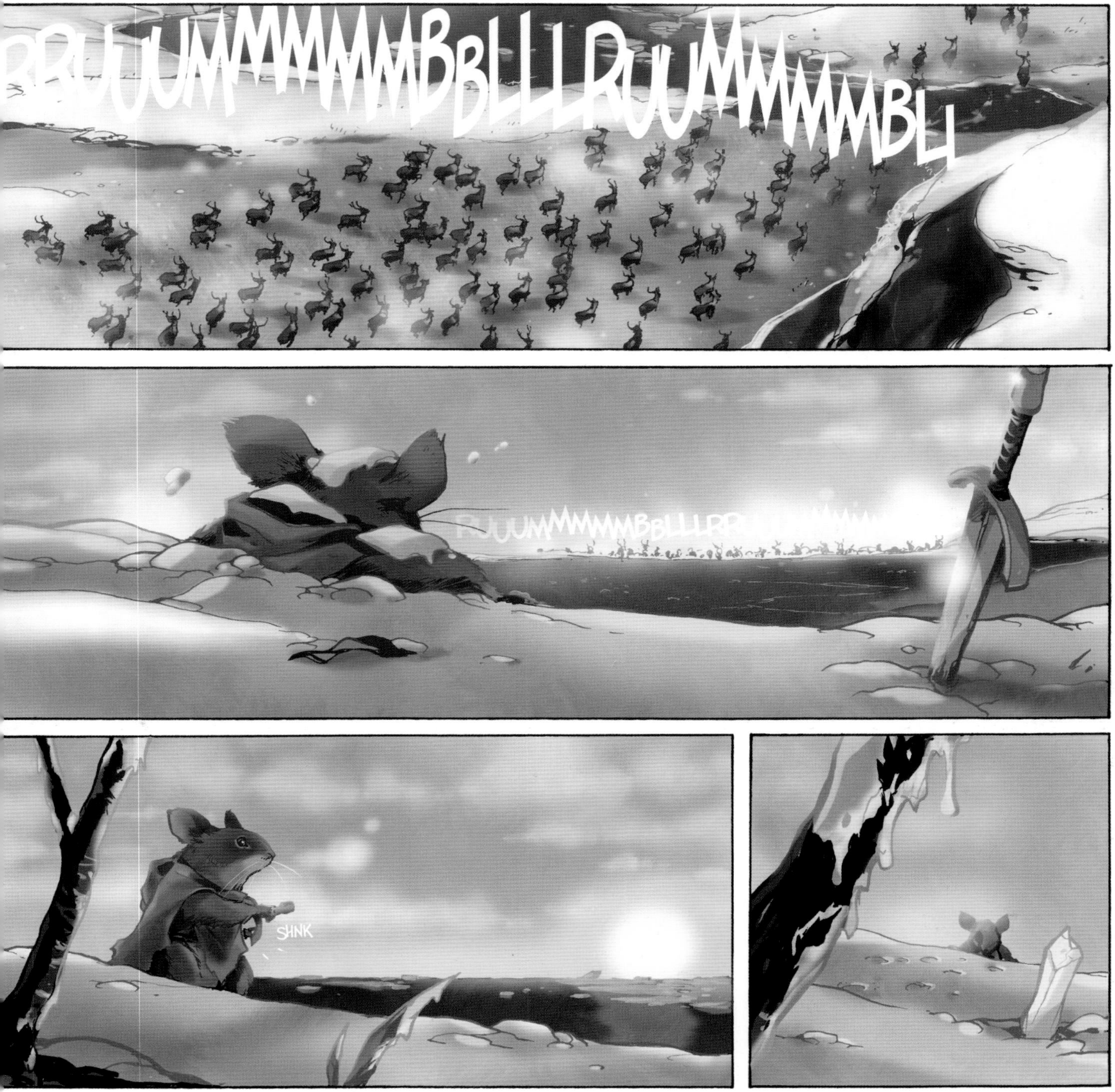
RRUUUMMMMMMBBLLLRUUMMMMMBLL
RUUUMMMMMMBBLLLRR
SHNK

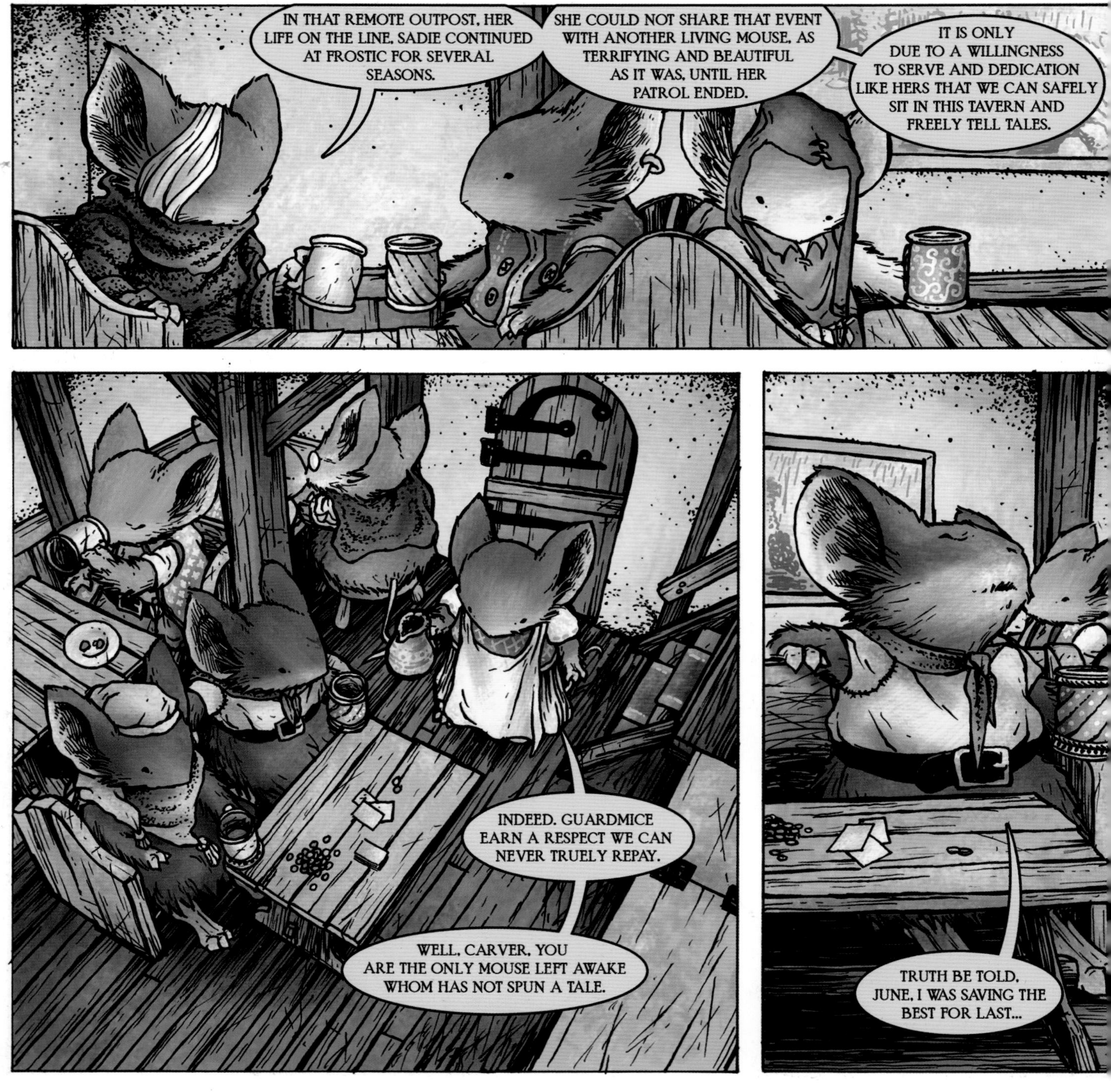
IN THAT REMOTE OUTPOST, HER LIFE ON THE LINE, SADIE CONTINUED AT FROSTIC FOR SEVERAL SEASONS.
SHE COULD NOT SHARE THAT EVENT WITH ANOTHER LIVING MOUSE, AS TERRIFYING AND BEAUTIFUL AS IT WAS, UNTIL HER PATROL ENDED.
IT IS ONLY DUE TO A WILLINGNESS TO SERVE AND DEDICATION LIKE HERS THAT WE CAN SAFELY SIT IN THIS TAVERN AND FREELY TELL TALES.
INDEED. GUARDMICE EARN A RESPECT WE CAN NEVER TRUELY REPAY.
WELL, CARVER, YOU ARE THE ONLY MOUSE LEFT AWAKE WHOM HAS NOT SPUN A TALE.
TRUTH BE TOLD, JUNE, I WAS SAVING THE BEST FOR LAST...

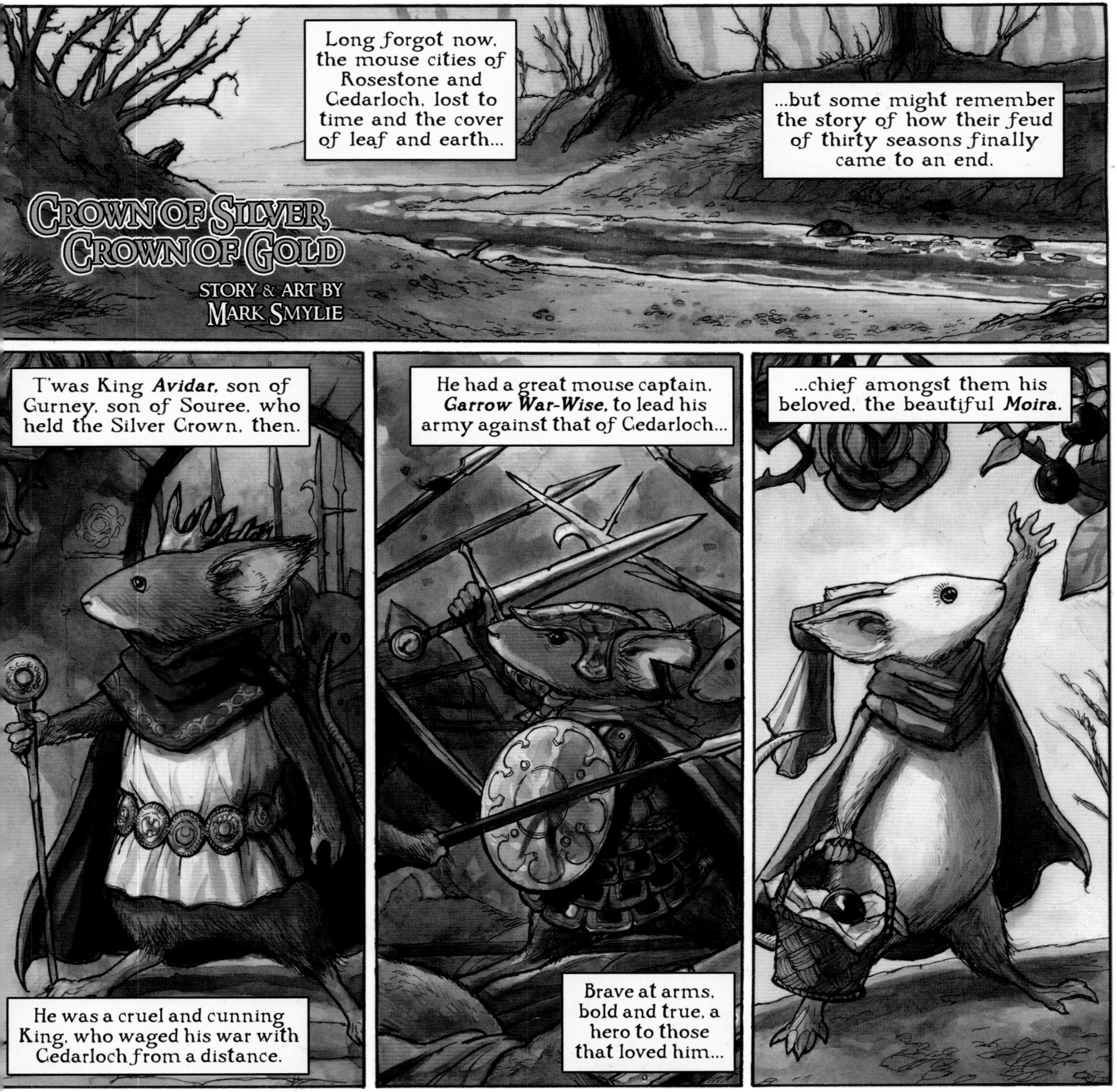
Long forgot now, the mouse cities of Rosestone and Cedarloch, lost to time and the cover of leaf and earth...
...but some might remember the story of how their feud of thirty seasons finally came to an end.
CROWN OF SILVER, CROWN OF GOLD
STORY & ART BY MARK SMYLIE
T'was King Avidar, son of Gurney, son of Souree, who held the Silver Crown, then.
He was a cruel and cunning King, who waged his war with Cedarloch from a distance.
He had a great mouse captain, Garrow War-Wise, to lead his army against that of Cedarloch...
Brave at arms, bold and true, a hero to those that loved him...
...chief amongst them his beloved, the beautiful Moira.

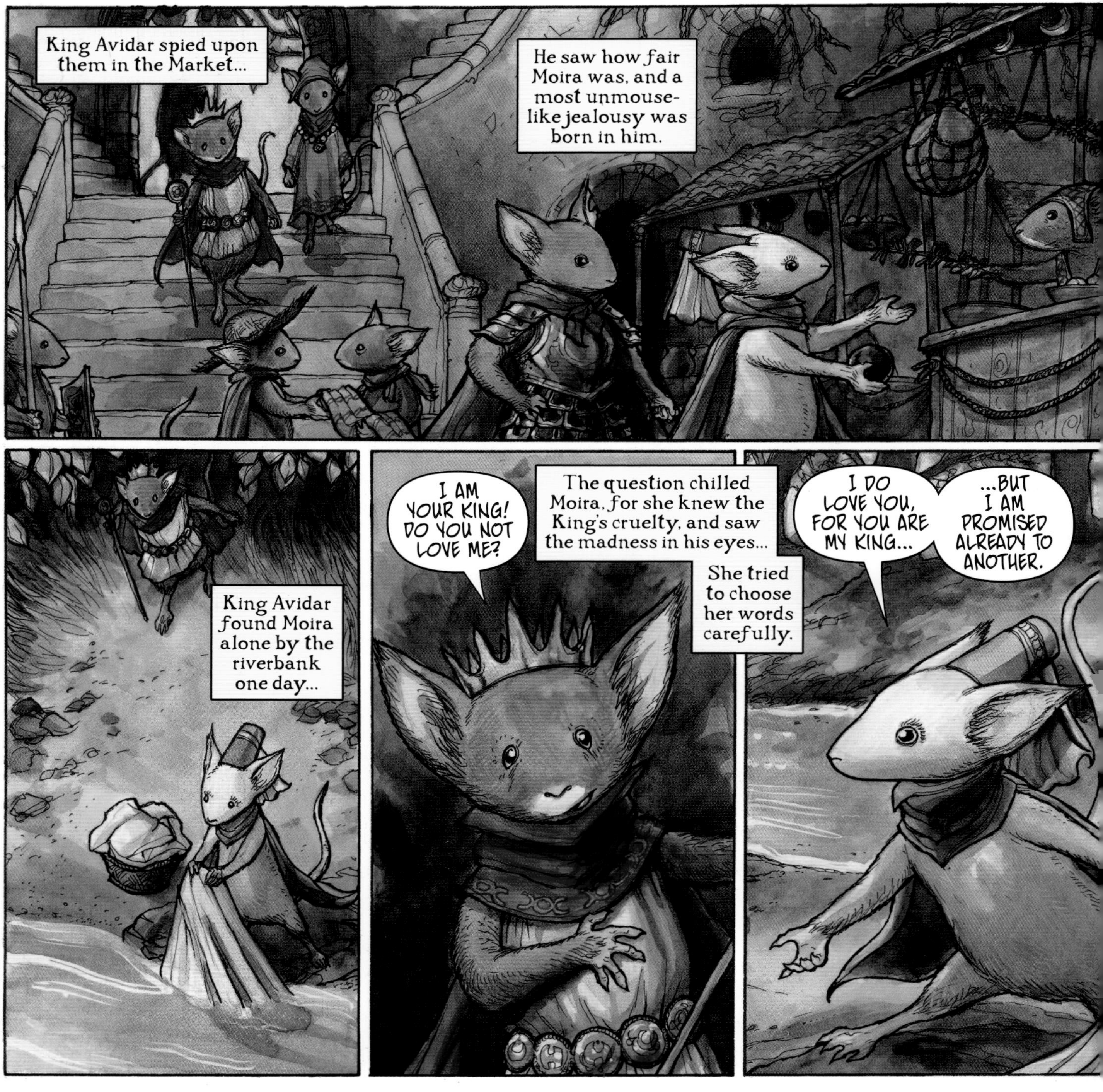
King Avidar spied upon them in the Market...
He saw how fair Moira was, and a most unmouse-like jealousy was born in him.
King Avidar found Moira alone by the riverbank one day...
I AM YOUR KING! DO YOU NOT LOVE ME?
The question chilled Moira, for she knew the King's cruelty, and saw the madness in his eyes...
She tried to choose her words carefully.
I DO LOVE YOU, FOR YOU ARE MY KING...
...BUT I AM PROMISED ALREADY TO ANOTHER.

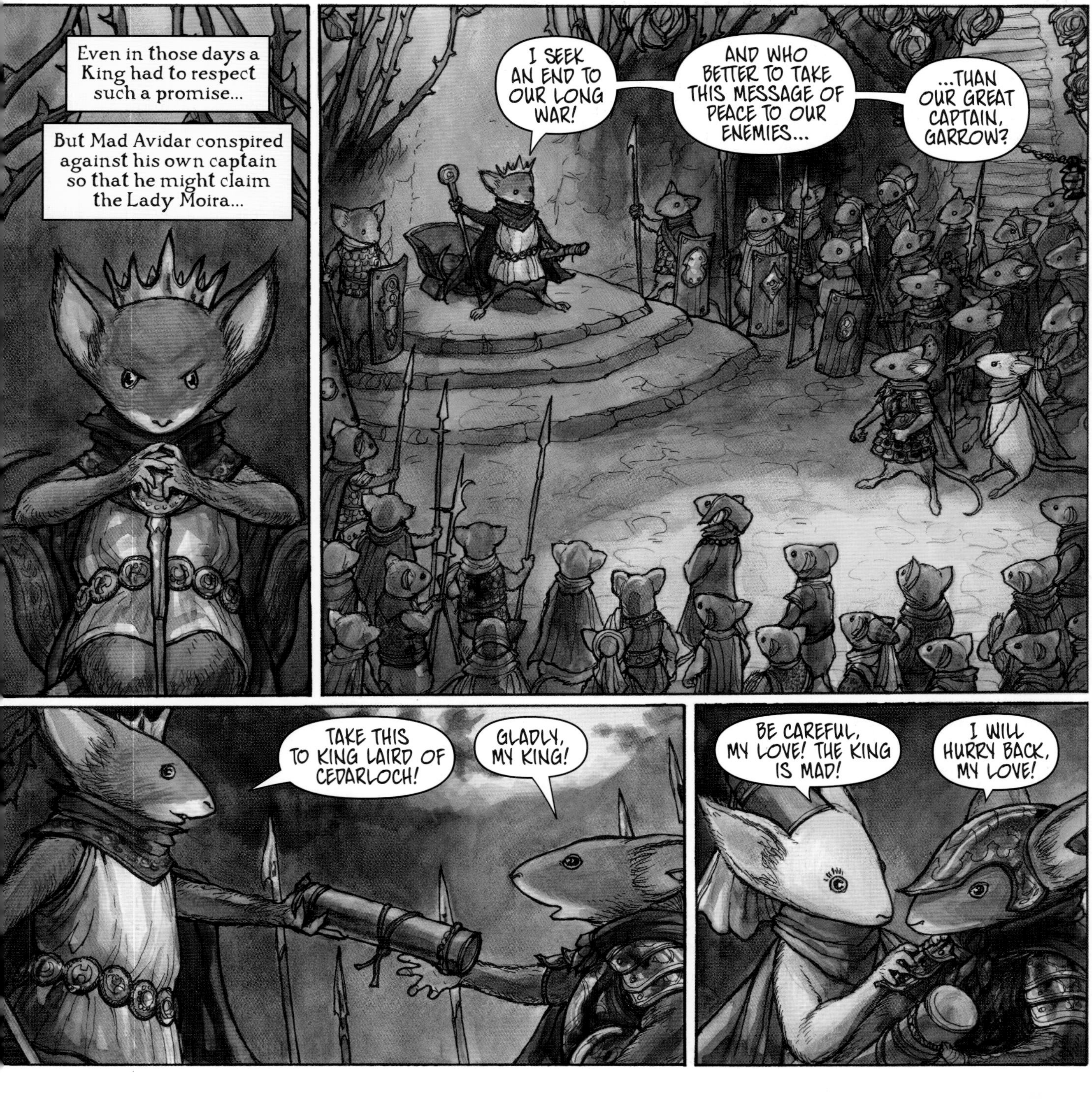
Even in those days a King had to respect such a promise...
But Mad Avidar conspired against his own captain so that he might claim the Lady Moira...
I SEEK AN END TO OUR LONG WAR!
AND WHO BETTER TO TAKE THIS MESSAGE OF PEACE TO OUR ENEMIES...
...THAN OUR GREAT CAPTAIN, GARROW?
TAKE THIS TO KING LAIRD OF CEDARLOCH!
GLADLY, MY KING!
BE CAREFUL, MY LOVE! THE KING IS MAD!
I WILL HURRY BACK, MY LOVE!

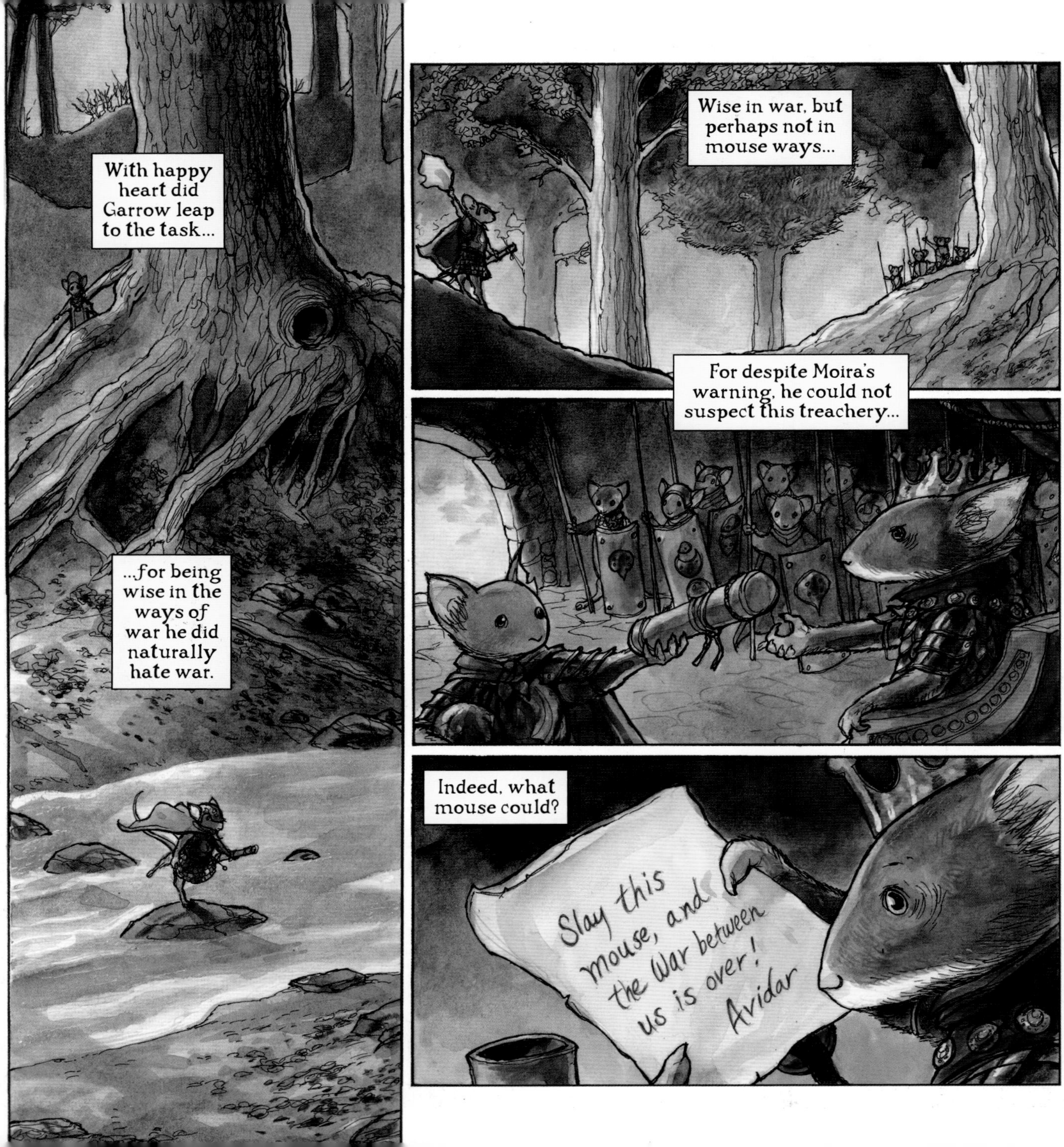

With happy heart did Garrow leap to the task...
...for being wise in the ways of war he did naturally hate war.
Wise in war, but perhaps not in mouse ways...
For despite Moira's warning, he could not suspect this treachery...
Indeed, what mouse could?
Slay this mouse, and the War between us is over! Avidar

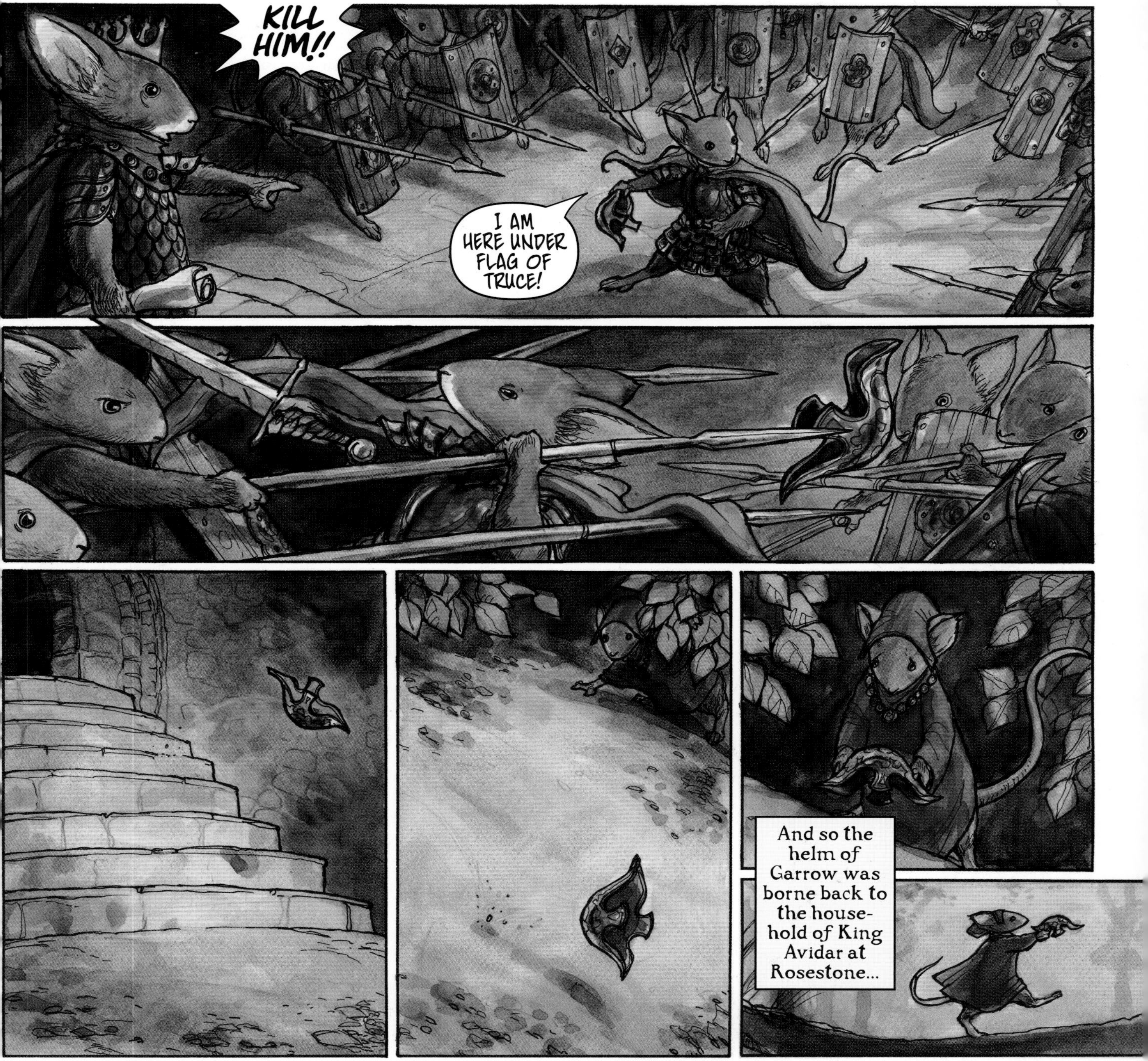
KILL HIM!!
I AM HERE UNDER FLAG OF TRUCE!
And so the helm of Garrow was borne back to the household of King Avidar at Rosestone...

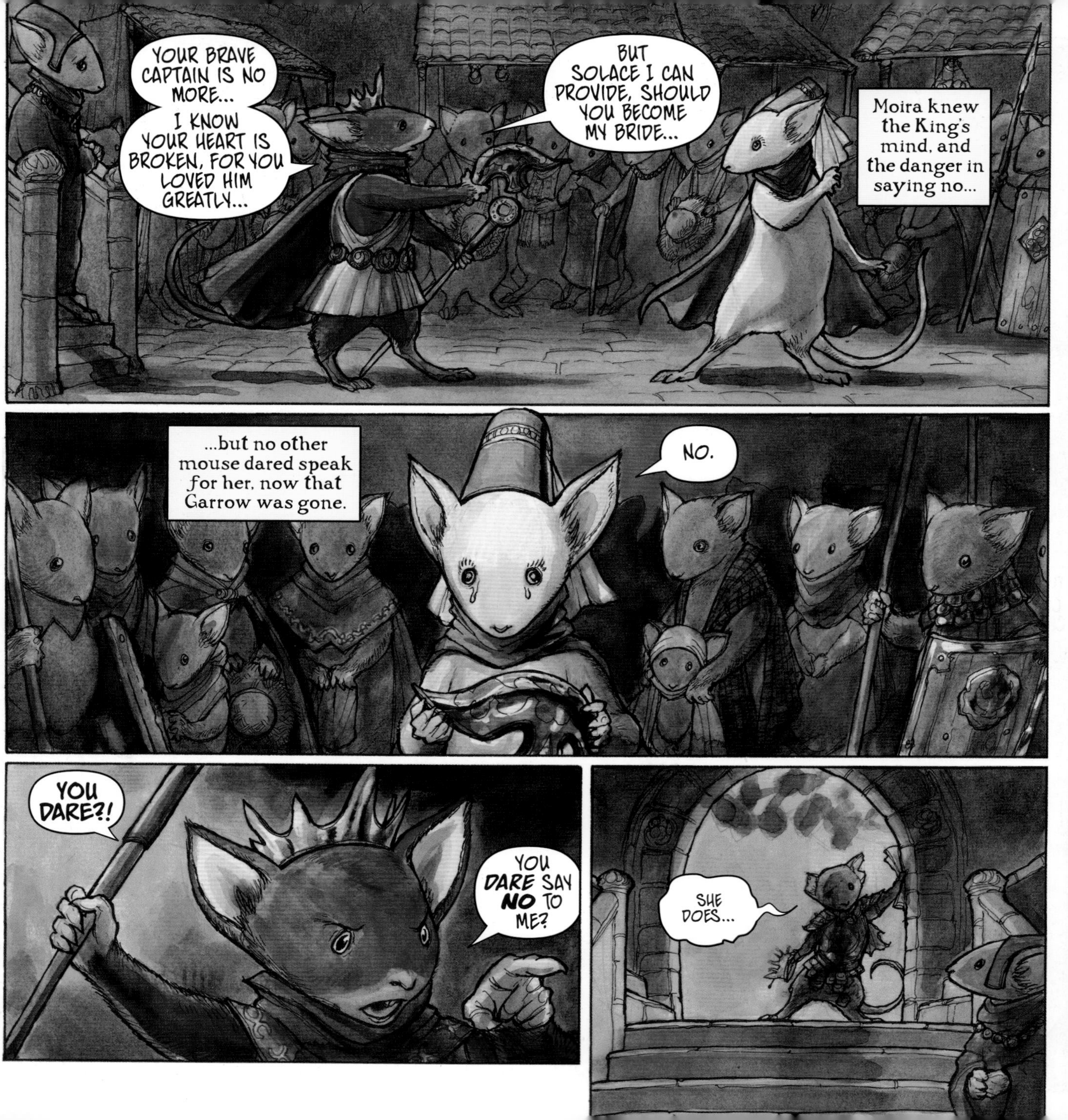
YOUR BRAVE CAPTAIN IS NO MORE...
I KNOW YOUR HEART IS BROKEN, FOR YOU LOVED HIM GREATLY...
BUT SOLACE I CAN PROVIDE, SHOULD YOU BECOME MY BRIDE...
Moira knew the King's mind, and the danger in saying no...
...but no other mouse dared speak for her, now that Garrow was gone.
NO.
YOU DARE?!
YOU DARE SAY NO TO ME?
SHE DOES...

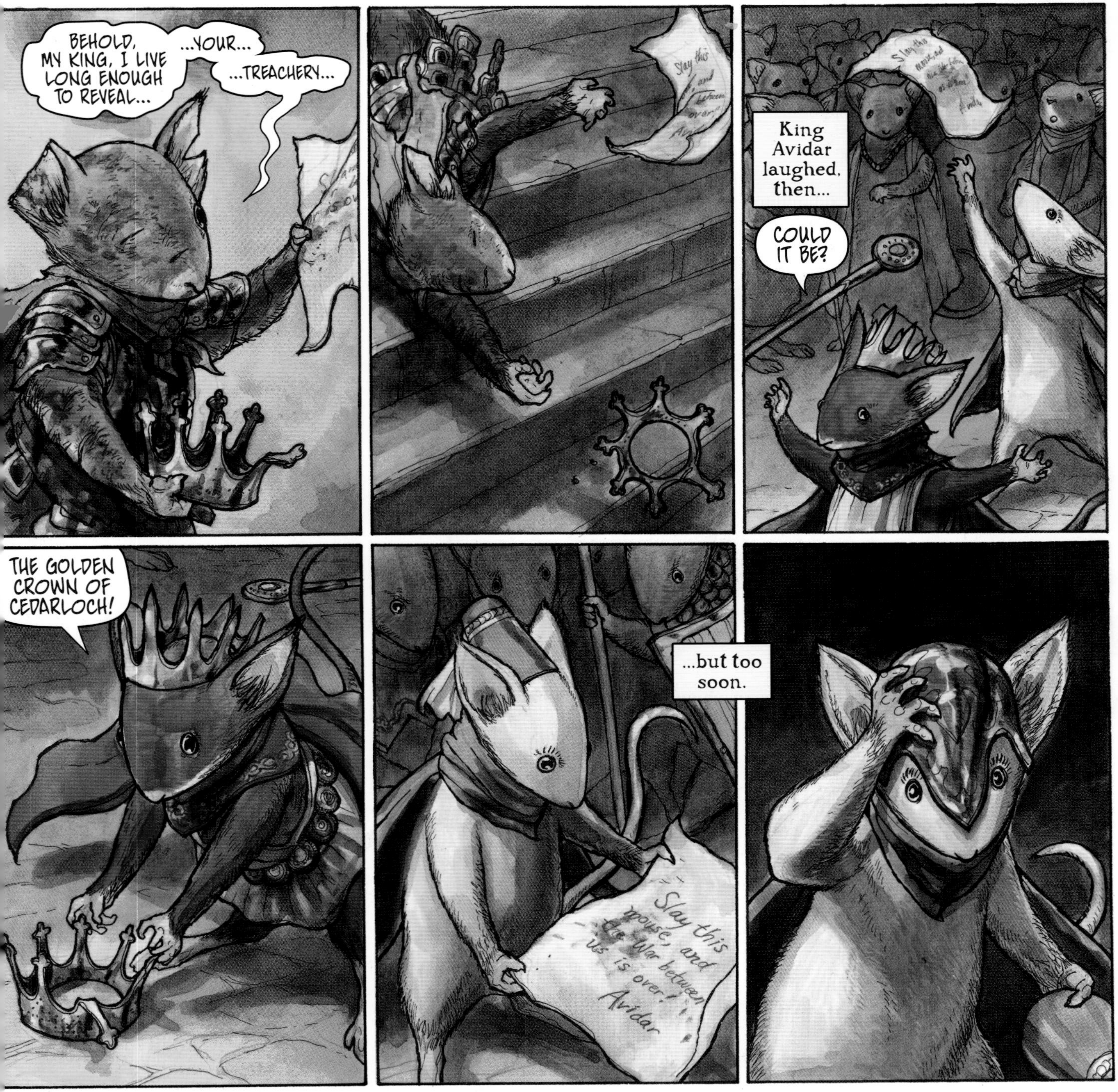
BEHOLD, MY KING, I LIVE LONG ENOUGH TO REVEAL...
...YOUR...
...TREACHERY...
King Avidar laughed, then...
COULD IT BE?
THE GOLDEN CROWN OF CEDARLOCH!
Slay this mouse, and the War between us is over! Avidar
...but too soon.

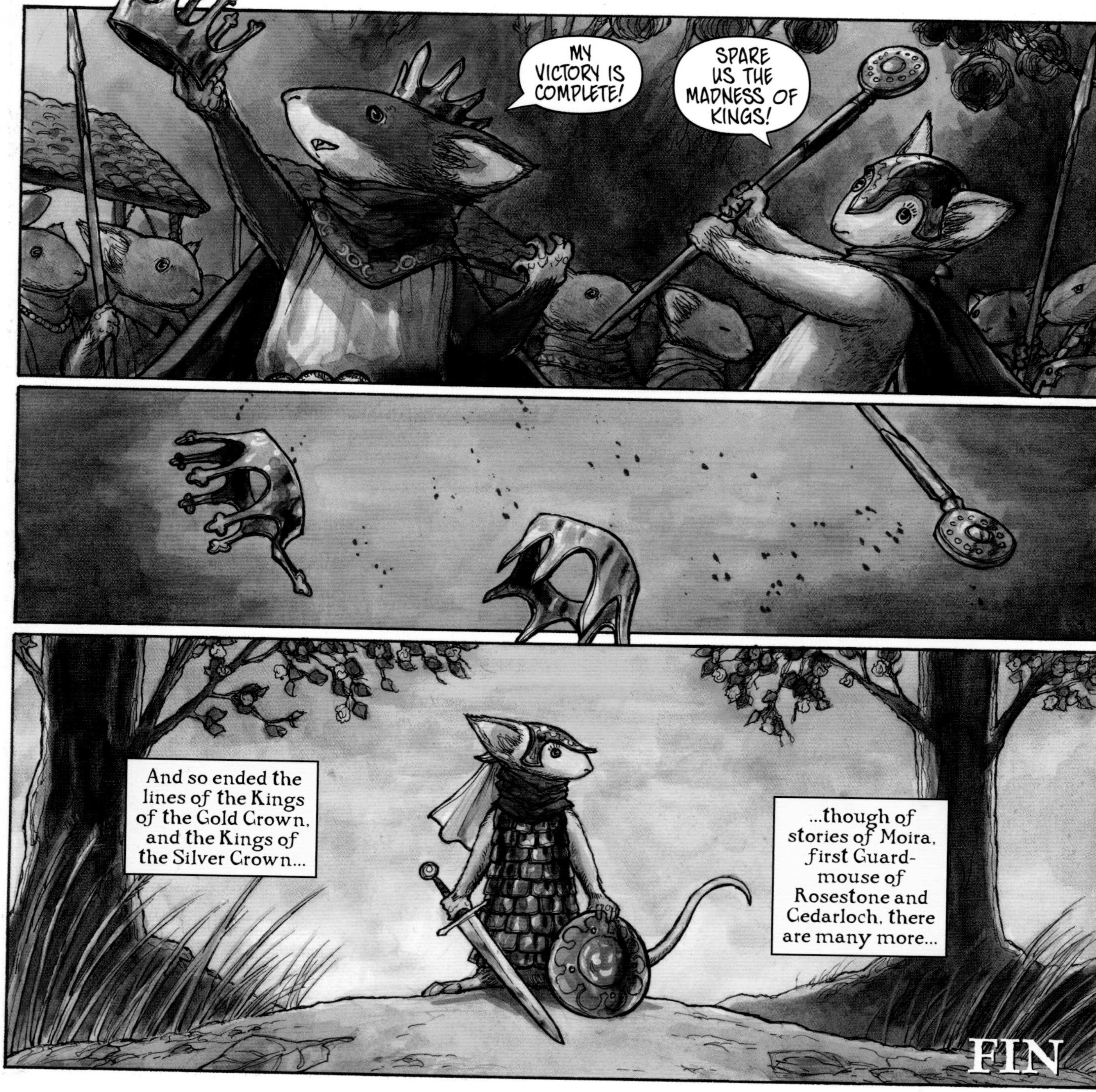
MY VICTORY IS COMPLETE!
SPARE US THE MADNESS OF KINGS!
And so ended the lines of the Kings of the Gold Crown, and the Kings of the Silver Crown...
...though of stories of Moira, first Guard-mouse of Rosestone and Cedarloch, there are many more...
FIN

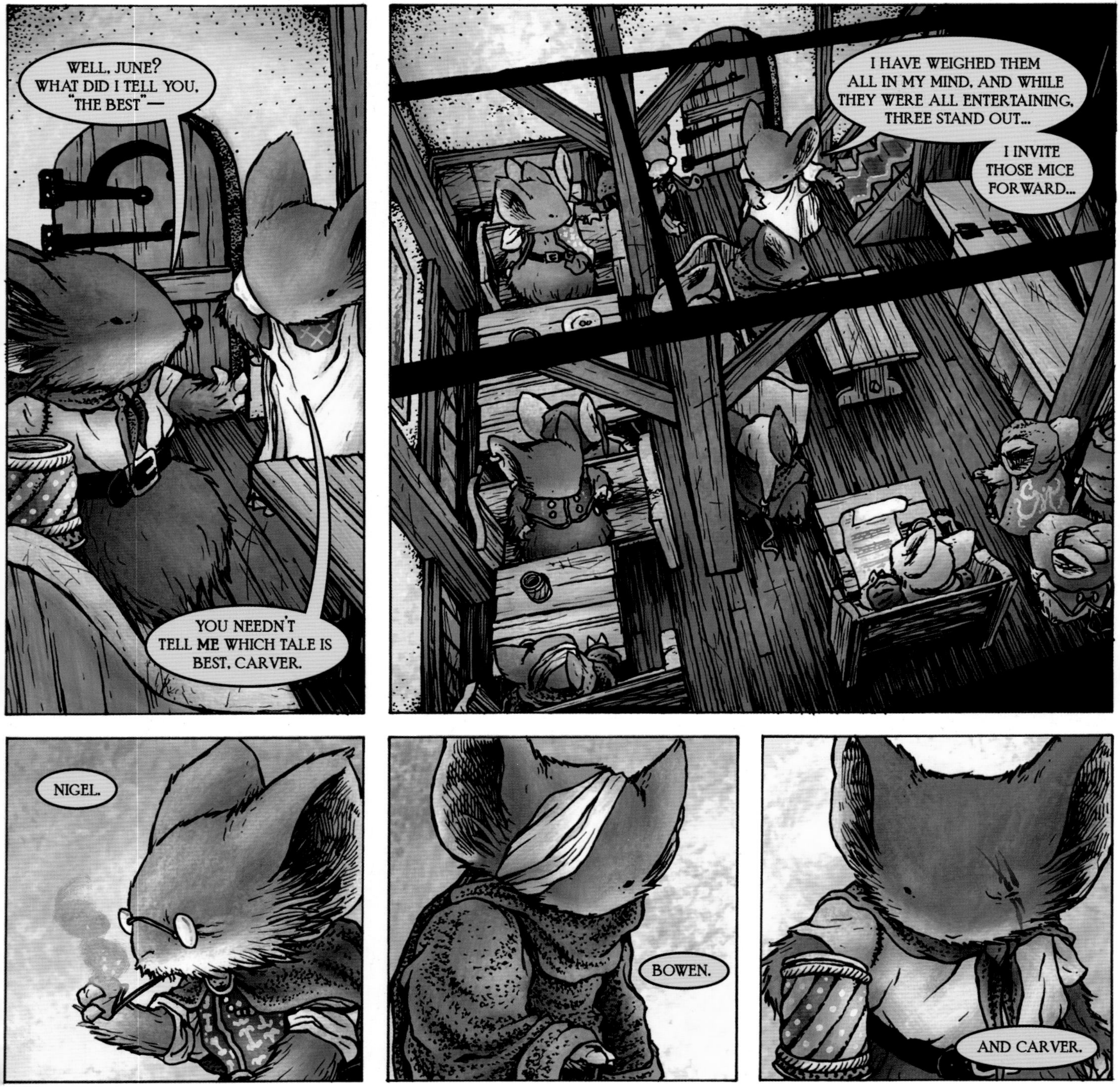
WELL, JUNE? WHAT DID I TELL YOU, "THE BEST"—
YOU NEEDN'T TELL ME WHICH TALE IS BEST, CARVER.
I HAVE WEIGHED THEM ALL IN MY MIND, AND WHILE THEY WERE ALL ENTERTAINING, THREE STAND OUT...
I INVITE THOSE MICE FORWARD...
NIGEL.
BOWEN.
AND CARVER.

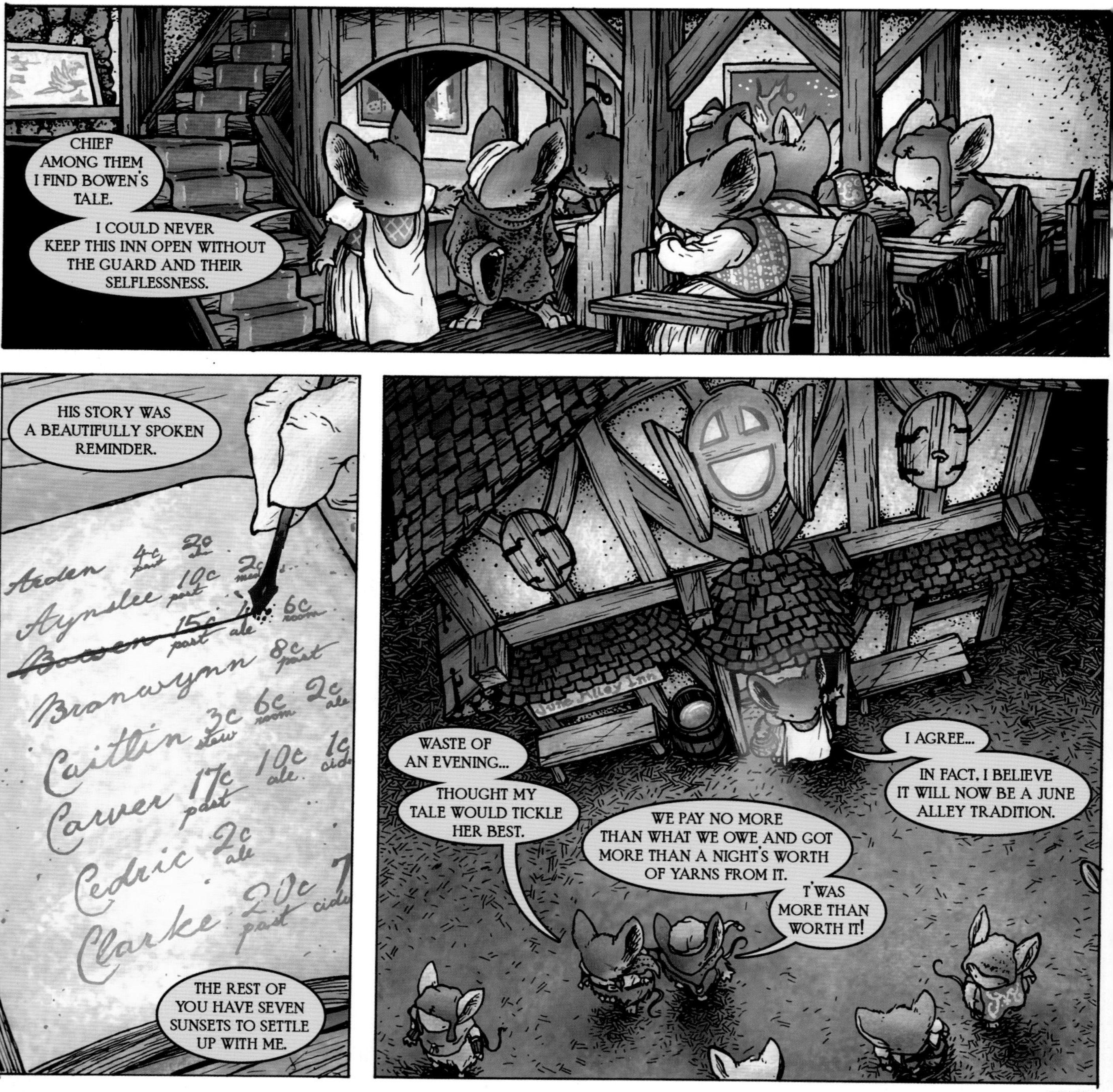
CHIEF AMONG THEM I FIND BOWEN'S TALE.
I COULD NEVER KEEP THIS INN OPEN WITHOUT THE GUARD AND THEIR SELFLESSNESS.
HIS STORY WAS A BEAUTIFULLY SPOKEN REMINDER.
Arden 4c past 2c
Aynslee 10c past
Bowen 15c past ale 6c room
Branwynn 8c past
Caitlin 3c stew 6c room 2c ale
Carver 17c past 10c ale
Cedric 2c ale
Clarke 20c past
THE REST OF YOU HAVE SEVEN SUNSETS TO SETTLE UP WITH ME.
June Alley Inn
WASTE OF AN EVENING...
THOUGHT MY TALE WOULD TICKLE HER BEST.
WE PAY NO MORE THAN WHAT WE OWE AND GOT MORE THAN A NIGHT'S WORTH OF YARNS FROM IT.
T'WAS MORE THAN WORTH IT!
I AGREE...
IN FACT, I BELIEVE IT WILL NOW BE A JUNE ALLEY TRADITION.

END

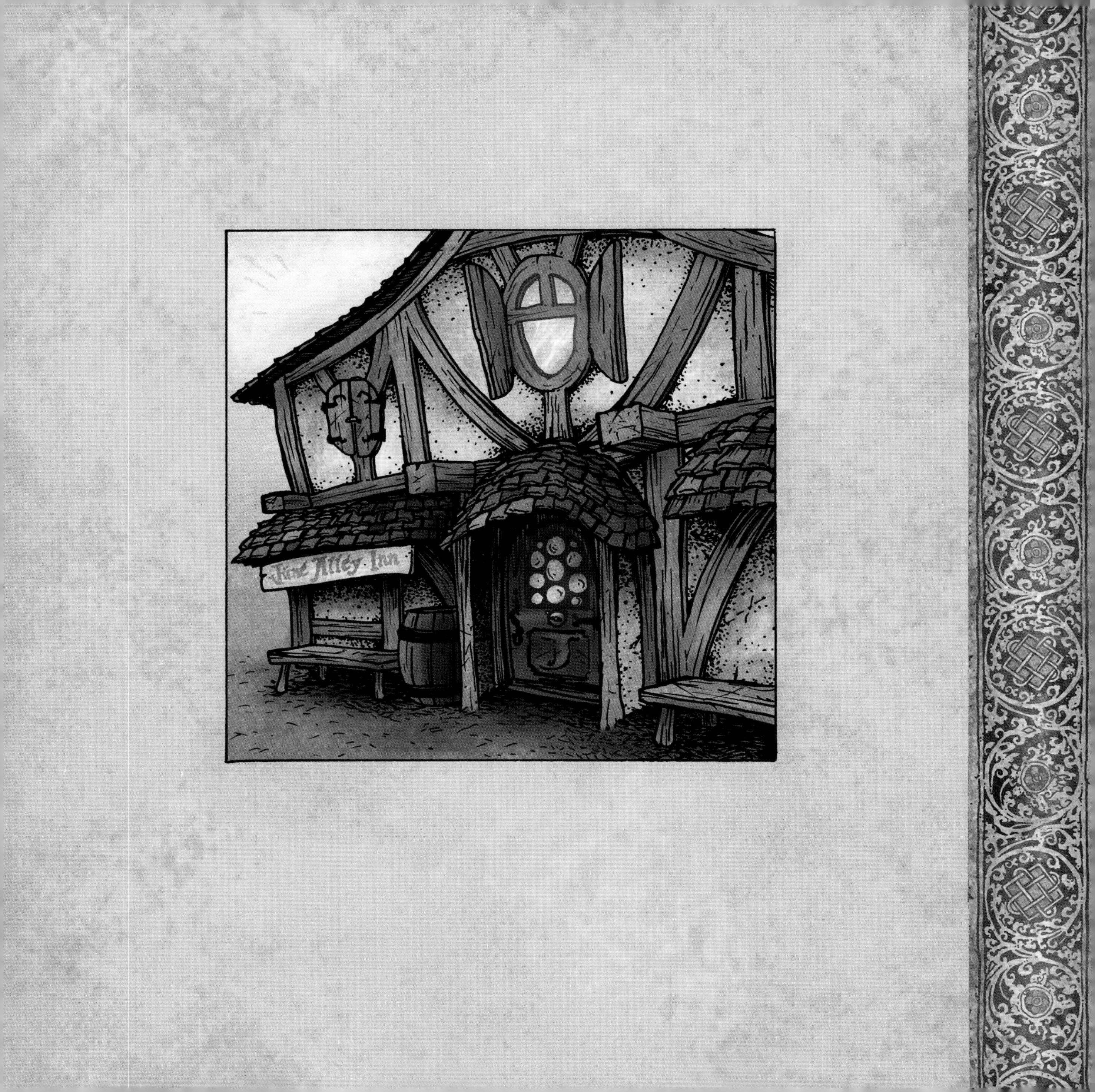
Vine Alley Inn

EPILOGUE

ART & STORY: João Lemos

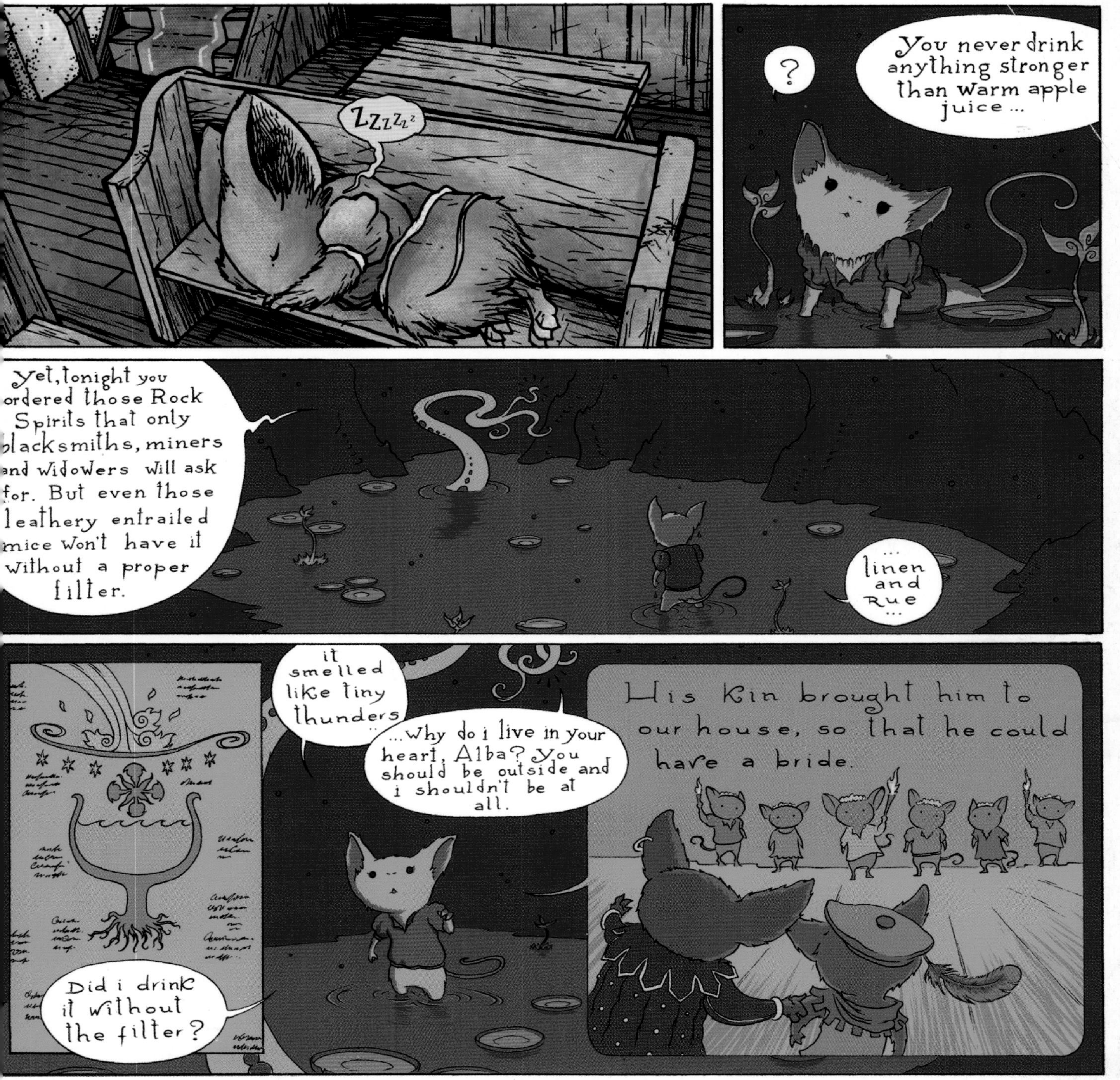
Zzzzz
?
You never drink anything stronger than warm apple juice ...
Yet, tonight you ordered those Rock Spirits that only blacksmiths, miners and widowers will ask for. But even those leathery entrailed mice won't have it without a proper filter.
... linen and Rue ...
Did i drink it without the filter?
it smelled like tiny thunders ..
...Why do i live in your heart, Alba? You should be outside and i shouldn't be at all.
His Kin brought him to our house, so that he could have a bride.

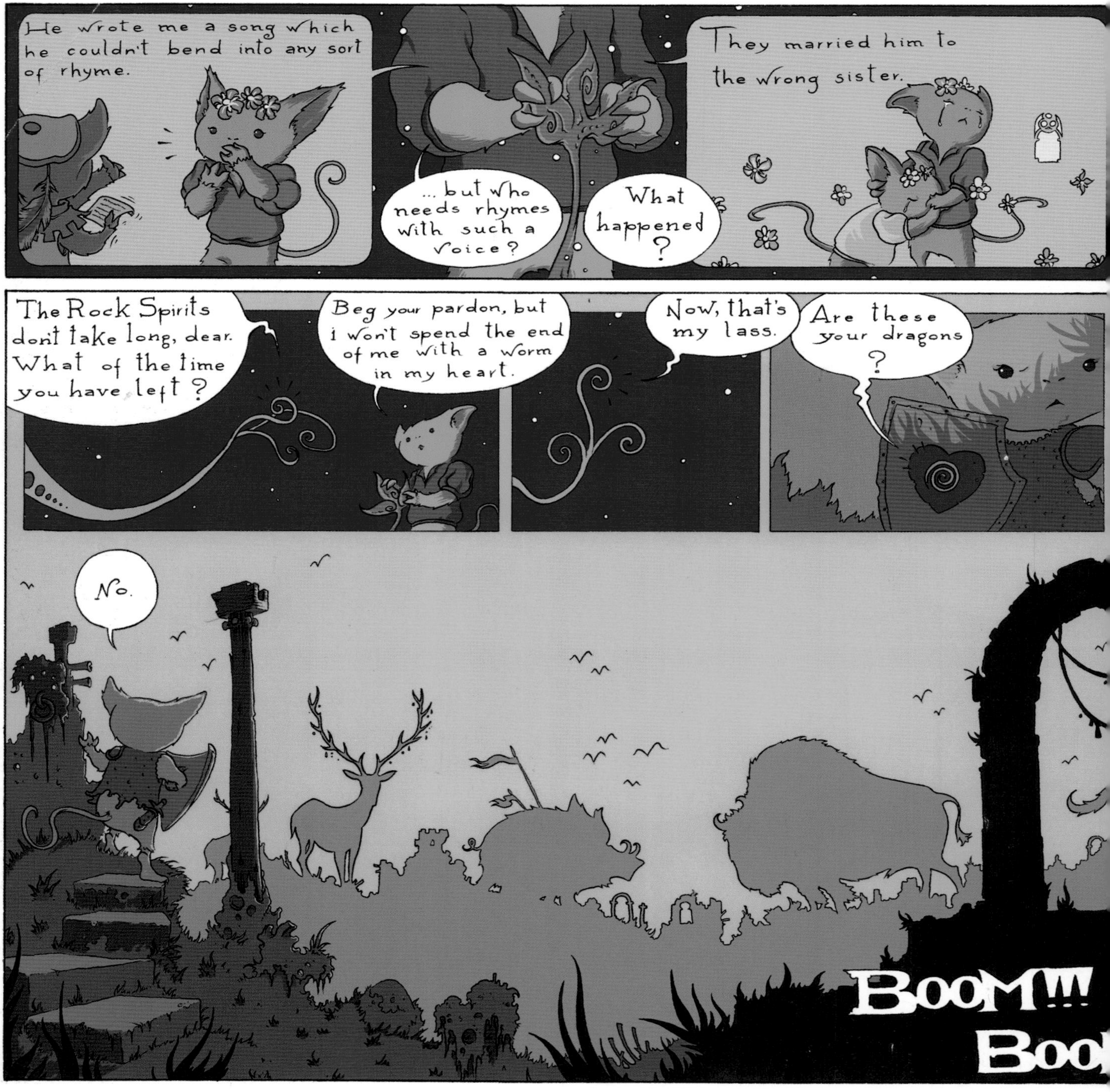
He wrote me a song which he couldn't bend into any sort of rhyme.
... but who needs rhymes with such a voice?
What happened?
They married him to the wrong sister.
The Rock Spirits don't take long, dear. What of the time you have left?
Beg your pardon, but i won't spend the end of me with a worm in my heart.
Now, that's my lass.
Are these your dragons?
No.
BOOM!!!

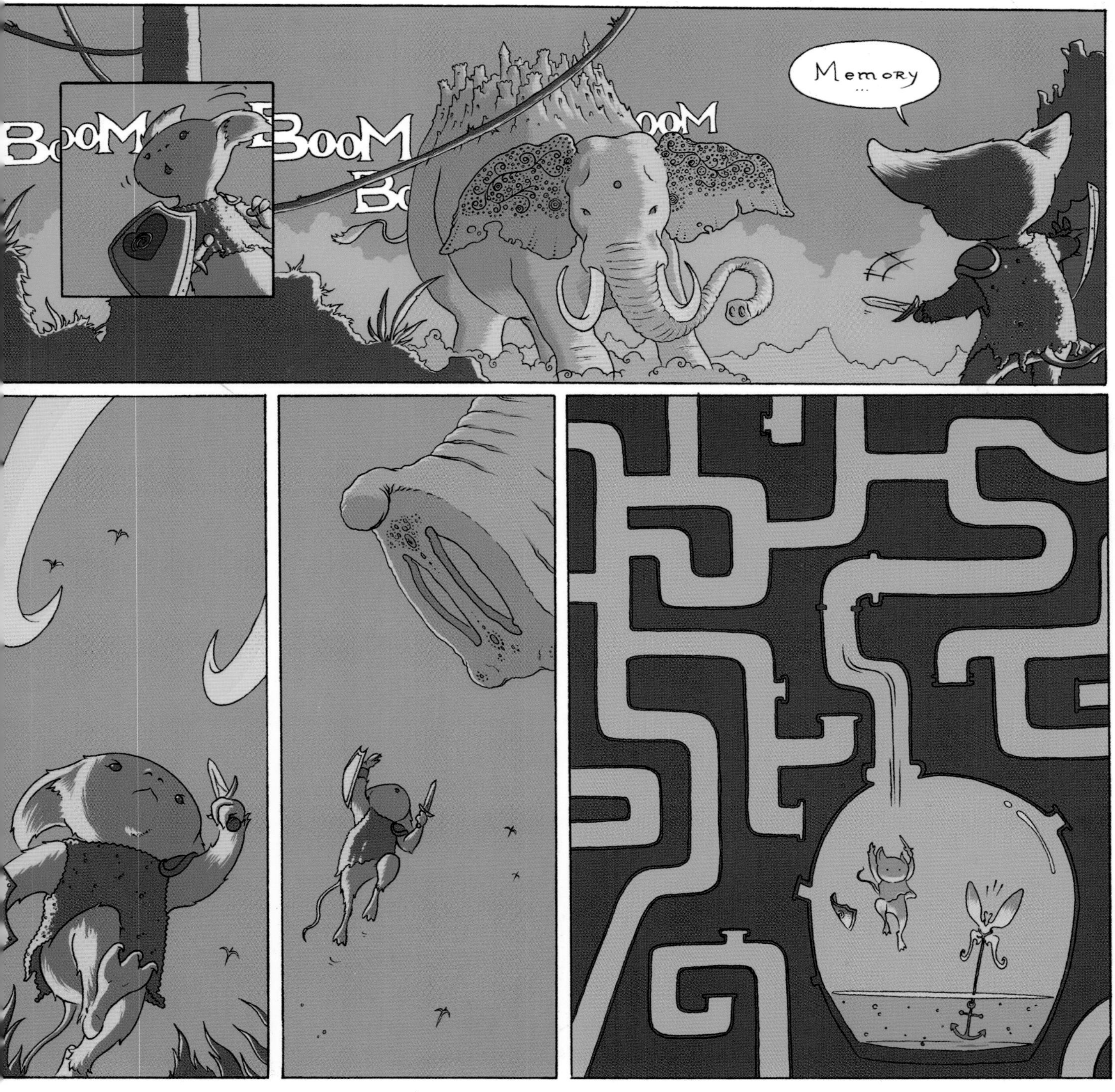
BOOM BOOM
BOOM
BOOM
Memory ...

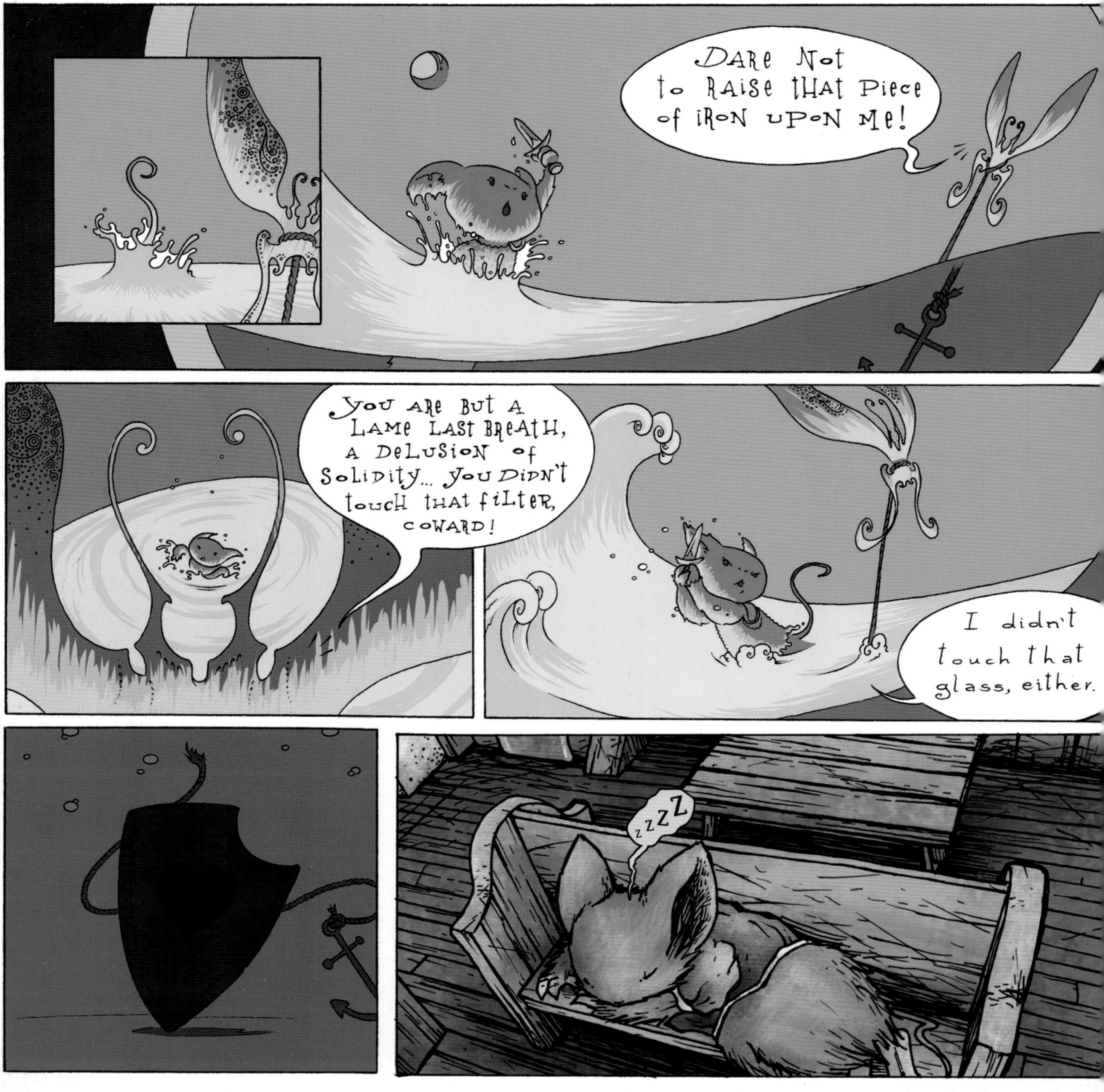
DARE Not to RAISE THAT Piece of iRON UPON ME!
YOU ARE BUT A LAME LAST BREATH, A DELUSION OF SOLIDITY... YOU DIDN'T TOUCH THAT FILTER, COWARD!
I didn't touch that glass, either.
zzzZ

Legend Cover Gallery

Legend of the War of Silver & Golden Crowns:

In 942 Rosestone and Cedarloch were ruled by King Souree of the silver crown and King Lutch of the golden crown, respectively. The kingdoms' disputes with one another boiled over due to each imprisoning the other's Queen. As Kings were more self reliant in those years, Souree fought Lutch on the bridge to the Cedarloch prison. King battled against King until they both struck a mortal blow. Both Queens were said to have never been released.

Legend of Calla's Ghost:

On the longest winter night of the year 1106 in Lillygrove, the faithful keeper of books, Gregor, was witness to the appearance of a disembodied spirit. The ghost-mouse claimed to be the first matriarch of the Mouse Guard named "Calla". When Gregor stammered out, "We have only traced back to Laria who was fourth, but have no written record of who came before her", she stabbed him with her spectral blade and vanished. At the site of the invisible wound, Gregor's fur turned a patch of bright white and ached severely before any first snowfall.

Legend of the Wythrashers:

The Order of Wythrasher was a group of eight mice who rode identical birds. The riders knew their mounts and spoke to them, without words, but subtle movements and nods of the head. No mouse knew where they came from or how they had made such kinships. Some believed they all lived in a nest atop an ash in Seyan, but such claims were never proved. Their chief Pedair and her bird Pyra were struck dead by a hawk and fell into the sea. Observers say the other seven followed, without being struck, into the watery grave never to soar in the sunbleached skies again.

Legend of the Heron Constelation:

Attempting to discover and chart a water passage leading from the north sea around the Wild Country and back to the southern waters near Lillygrove, explorers Jakob of Burl & Rupert of Darkwater set off with a crew of ten. However, due to storms they were shipwrecked on uncharted land. Using only scavenged materials, the explorers and their three surviving crew members, built a craft suitable of returning them to the Mouse Territories. Jakob said to have navigated by a constellation he found of a heron with the brightest star making up it's eye and it's beak pointing them home.

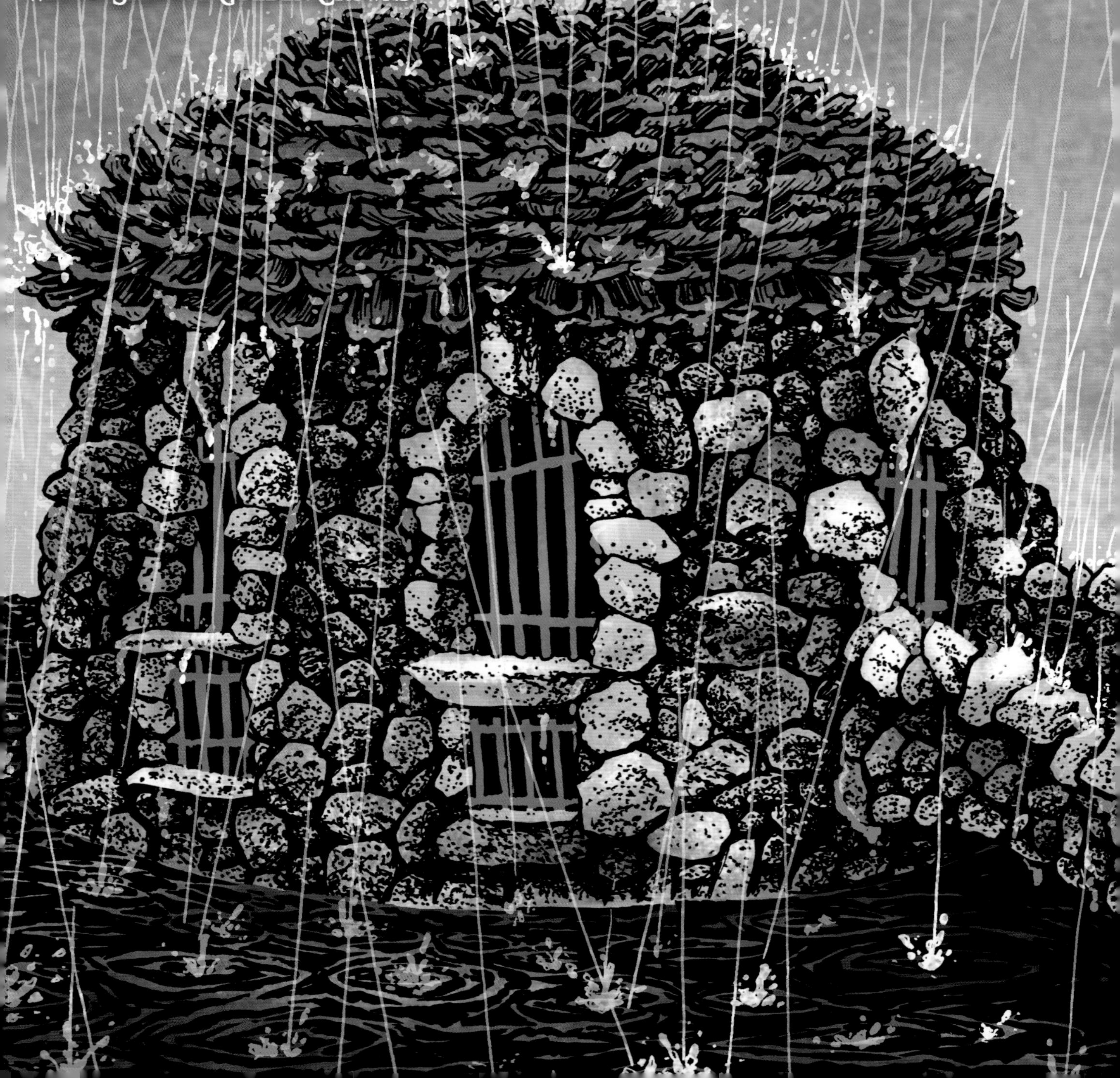

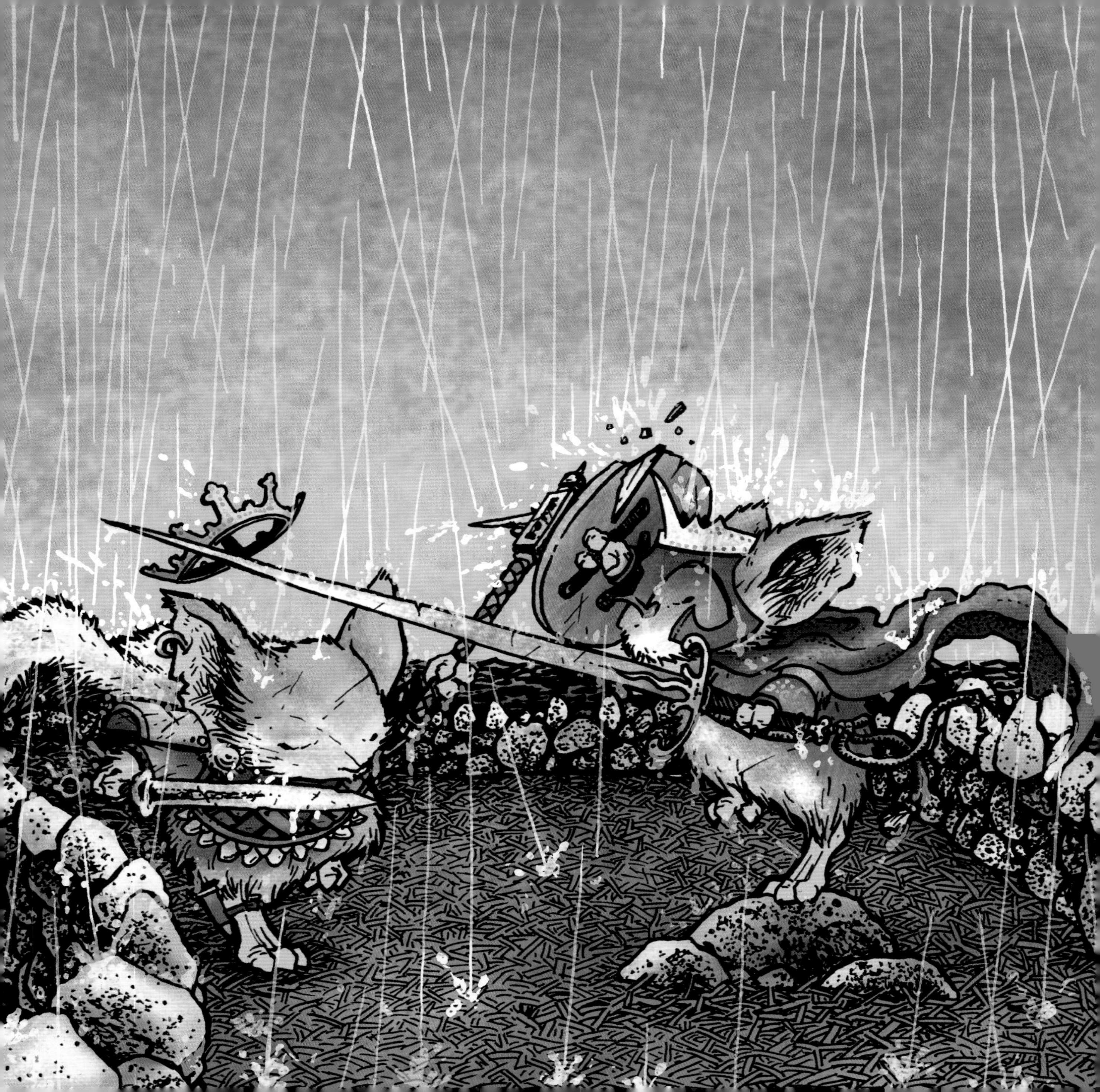

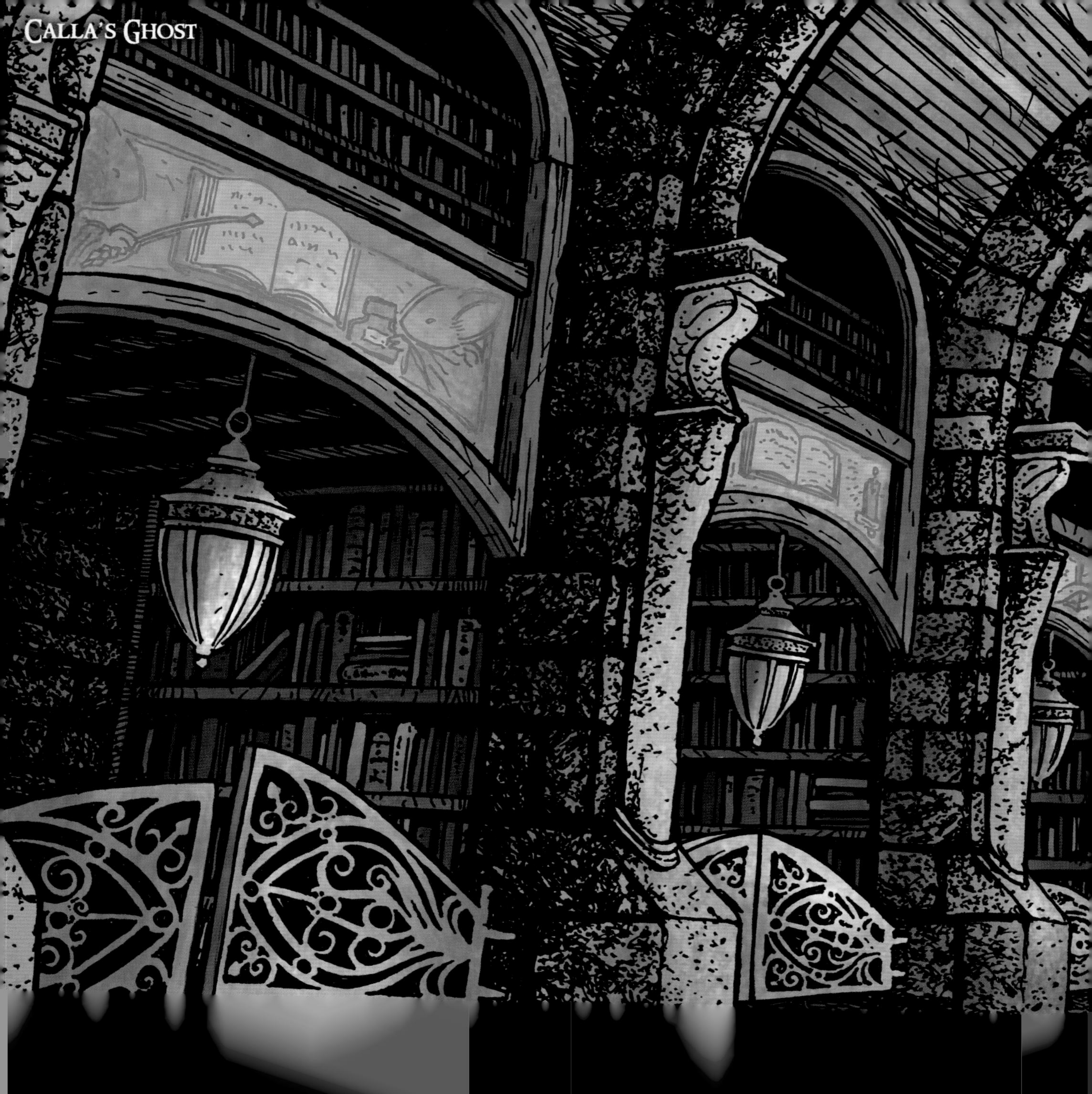

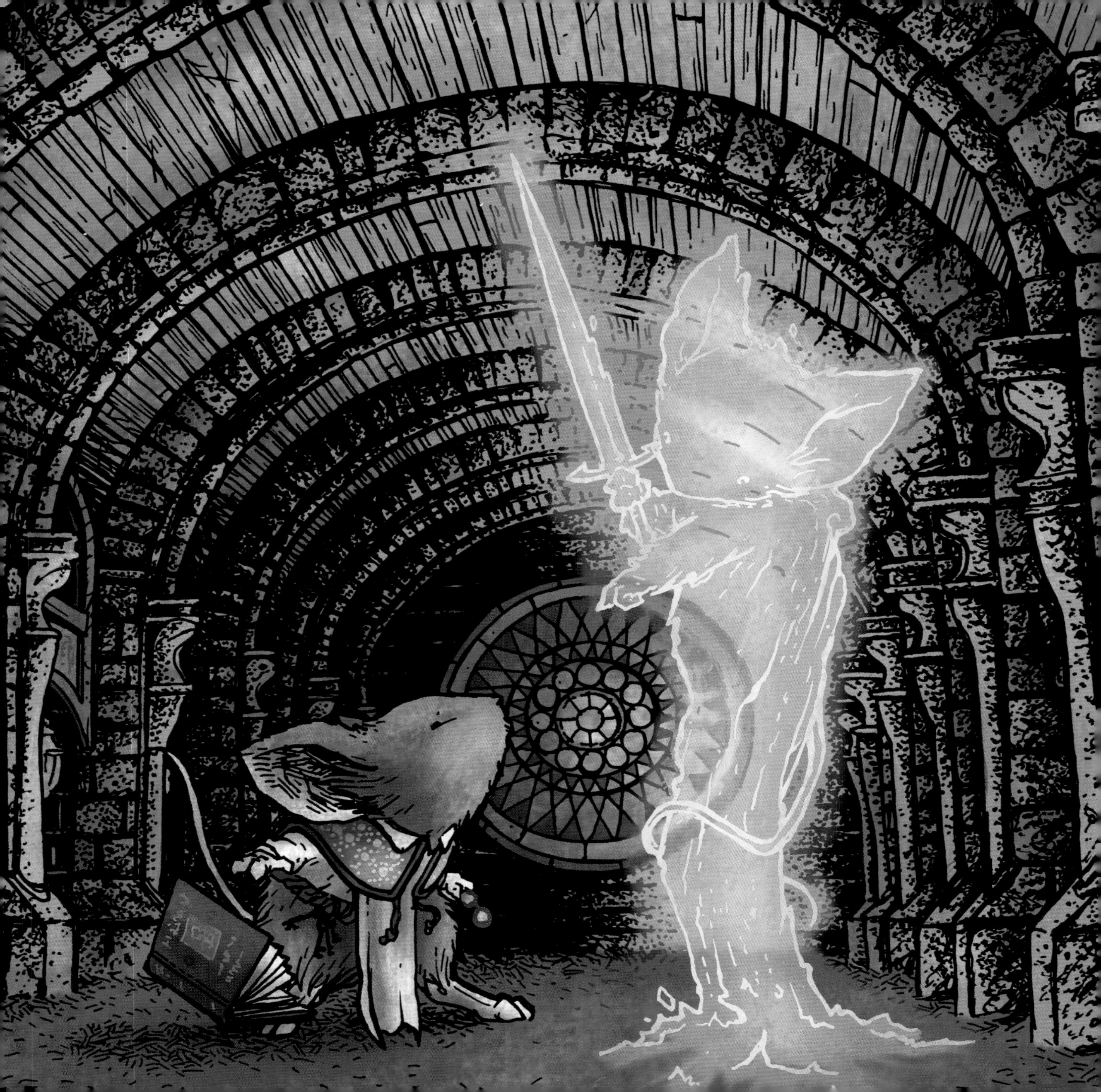

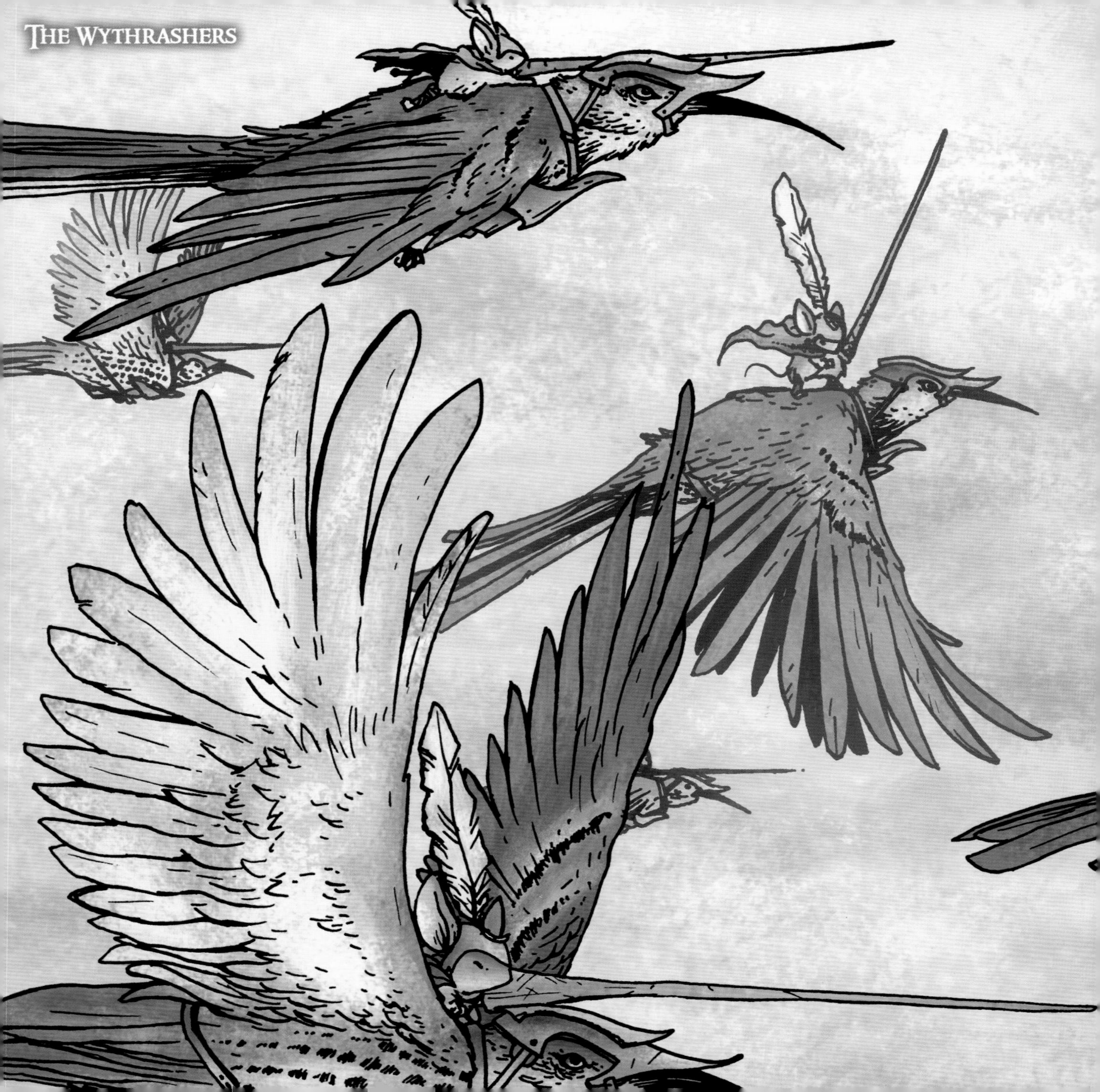

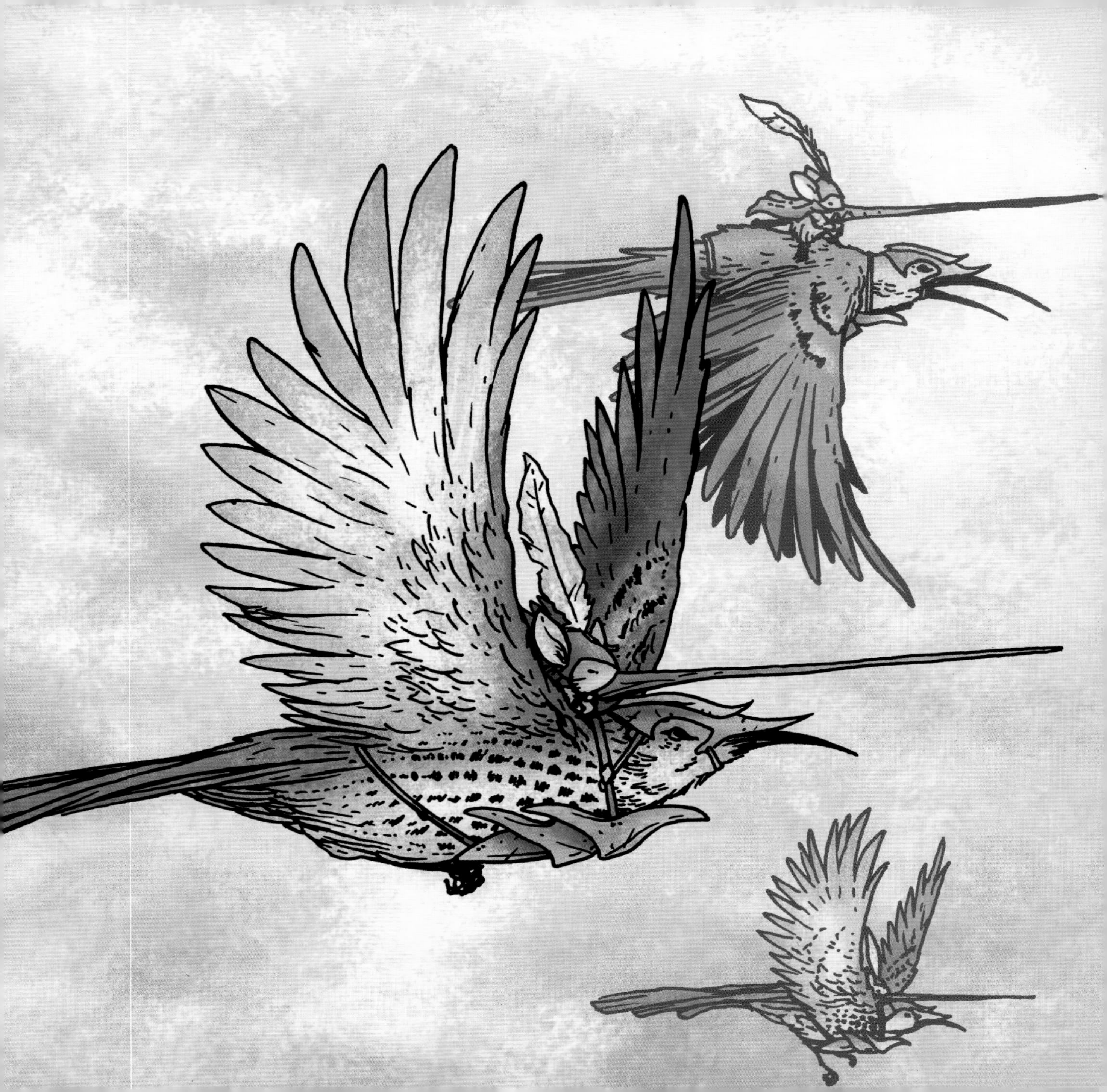

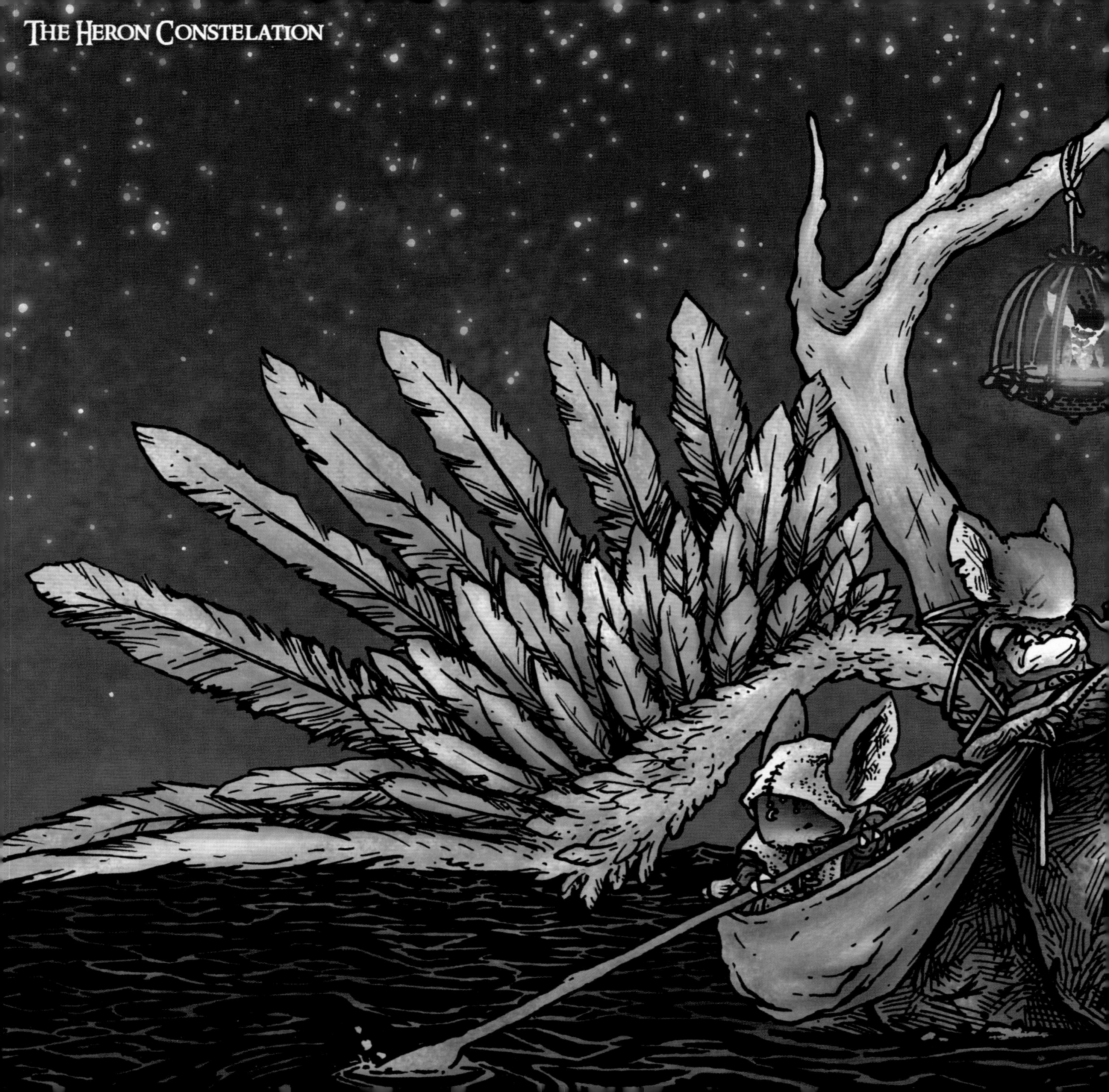

THE HERON CONSTELLATION

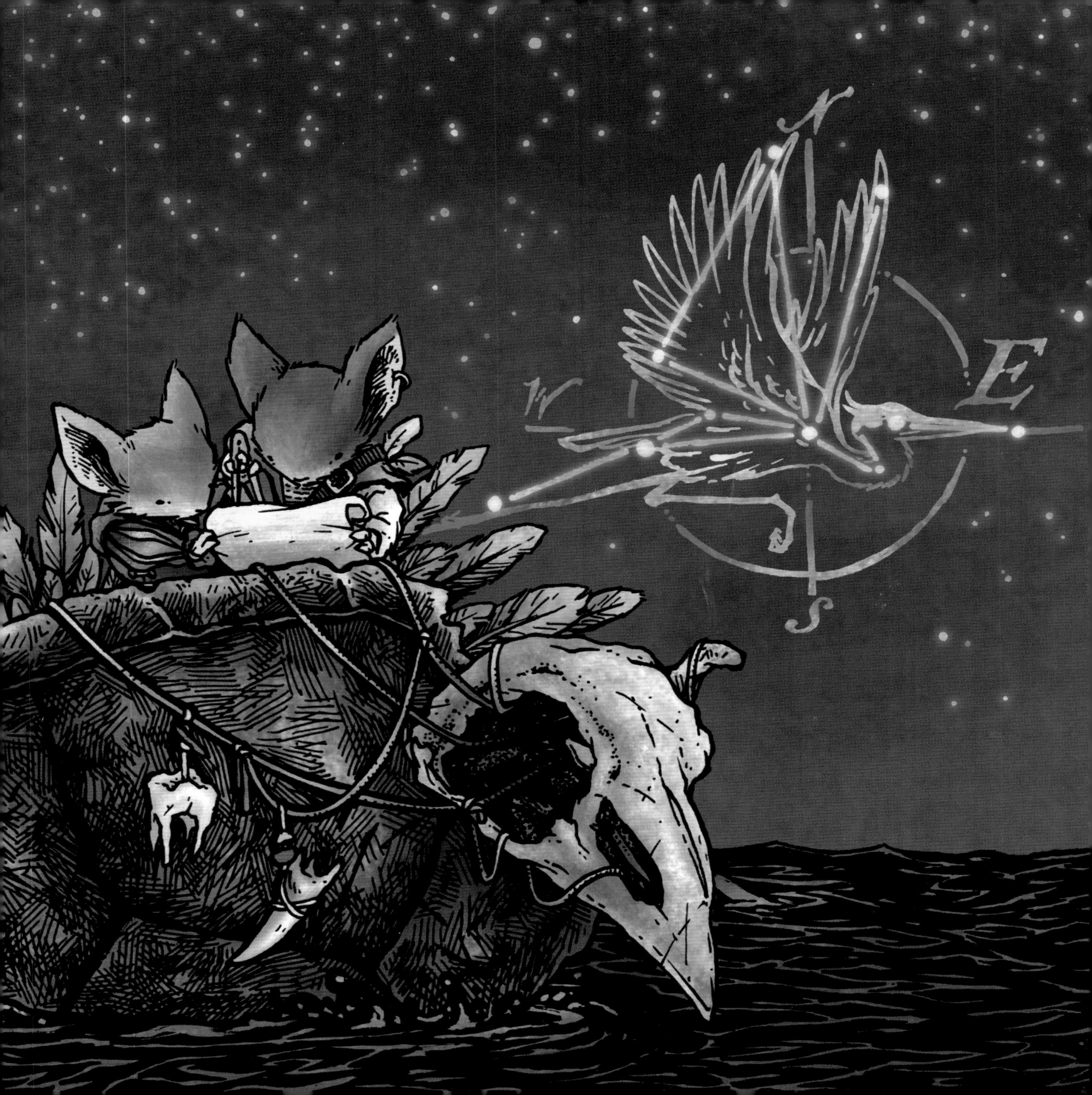
N
W
E
S

The Inn's Patrons:

June
Owner and operator of the June Alley Inn, which is known as the most hospitable inn on the west end of the Mouse Territories.

Nigel
Scholar, poet, artist, and historian from Appleloft who has moved to Barkstone for inspiration.

Kole
A peasant mouse who earns his keep processing the harvests in Barkstone & Elmoss.

Wyatt
Banker and weigher of goods for Barkstone. Known for being a shrewed but fair business-mouse.

Fenton
Plants, cultivates, and harvests grain outside of Elmoss, but is originally from Barkhamstead.

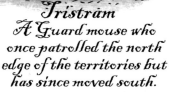

Tristram
A Guard mouse who once patrolled the north edge of the territories but has since moved south.

Aynslee
A textile crafter and merchant from Pebblebrook.

Bowen
A potter who relocated to Barkstone after the fall of Ferndale.

Vaughn
Defended his home of Woodruf's Grove in the War of 1149 before it fell.

Caitlin
Owns the Red Leaf Tavern in Maple-harbor.

Carver
A master-crafts mouse in Barkstone who shapes wood both for purpose and decoration.

Fyffe
A lighthearted street performer who is also known for slight of hand and card tricks.

Haggen
Eldest son of the former mayor of Barkstone who lost the rest of his family in a fire.

Ewyn
Bard and minstrel who has performed for food and lodging from Grasslake to Barkstone.

THE JUNE ALLEY INN

a: Entrance

b: June's Ledger

c: Barrel Storage

d: Cellar Stairs

e: Stairs to Rooms

f: Firewood Storage

g: Doors to Kitchen

h: The Legend of The War of the Silver & Golden Crowns

i: The Legend of the Wythrashers

j: The Legend of Calla's Ghost

k: The Legend of the Heron Constelation

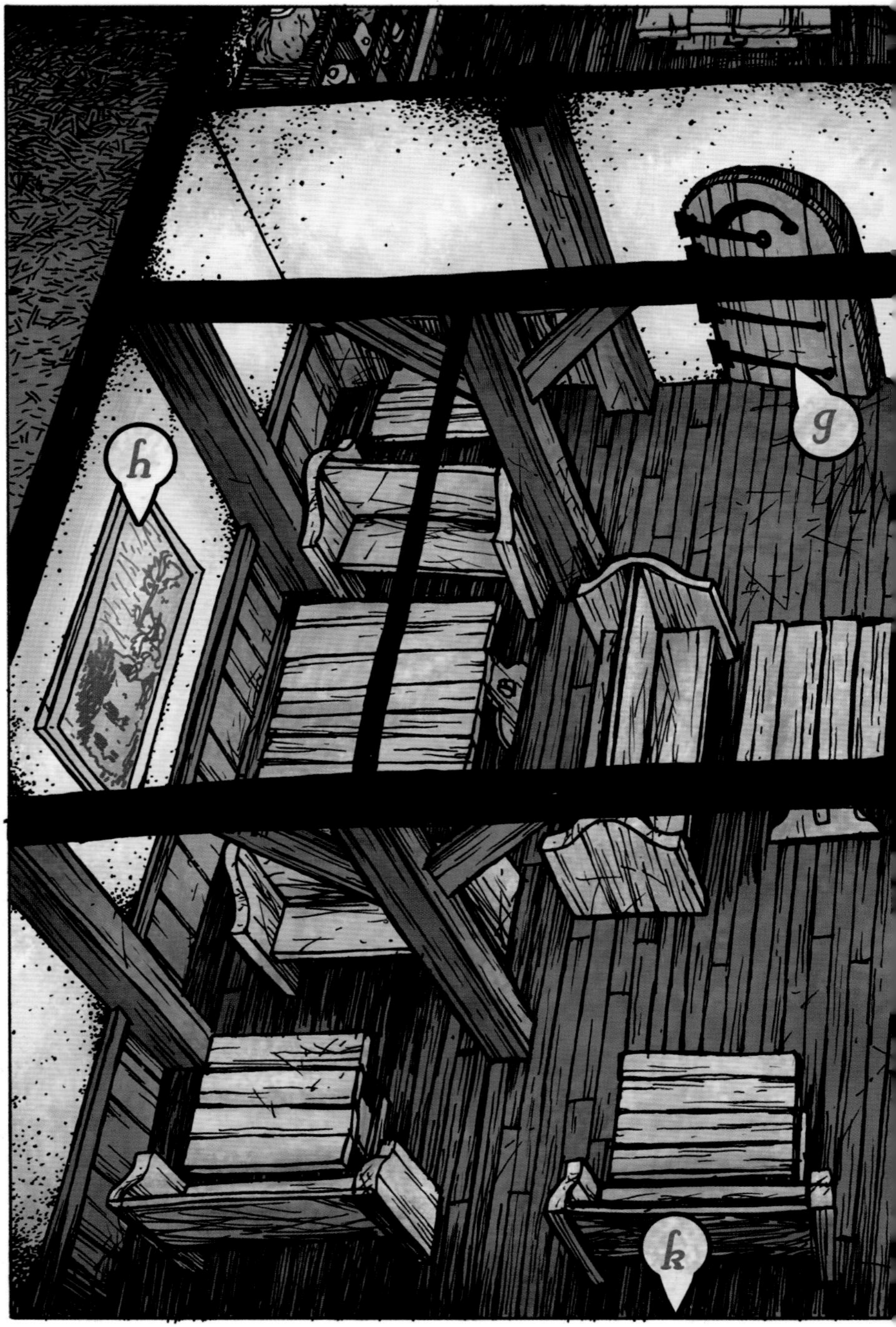
h
g
k

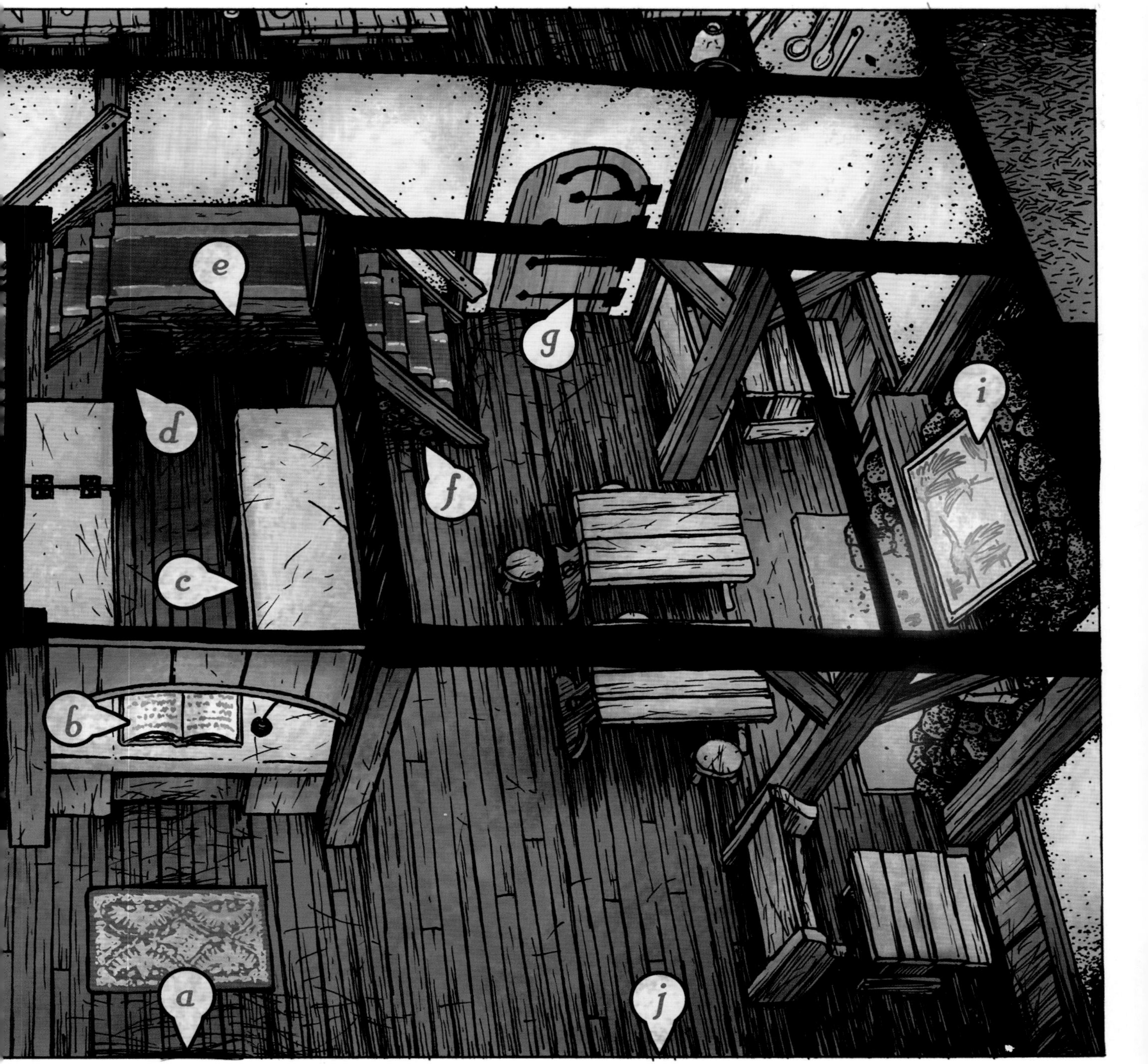

e
g
i
d
f
c
b
a
j

Mouse Territories 1150

A map of cities, towns, villages, and safepaths after the winter war
As measured by the Guard of 1149, Recorded by Clarke's Cartography
Fallen settlements listed & struck

Darkheather Entrance

Dawnrock

Calogero

Whitepine

Chistledown

Wildseed

Elmwood

Lockhaven

Ironwood

Pebblebrook

Shaleburrow

Ivydale

Blackrock

Barkstone

~~Woodruff's Grove~~

Elmoss

Copperwood

Ro

Ferndale

Spructuck

Darkheather Tunnels

~~Walnutpeck~~

Dorigift

Appleloft

Gilpledge

Frostic

Rustleaf

Port Sumac

Sent Perle

Wild
Country

Wolfepointe

arkwater

Lonefire

Grasslake

Burl

Sandmason

deharbor

one

Lillygrove

Oakgrove

Flintwist

Birchflow

ABOUT THE AUTHORS

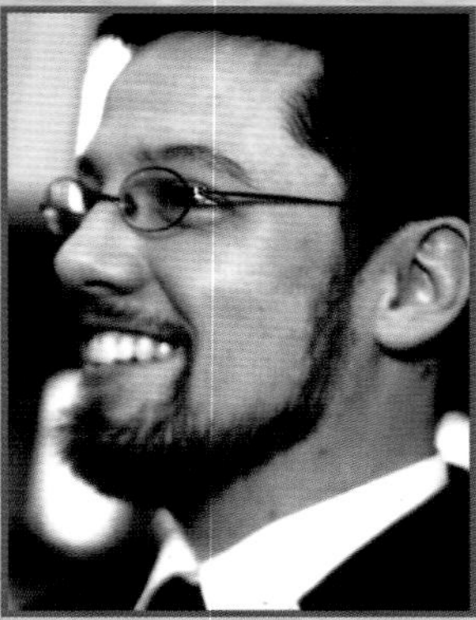

DAVID PETERSEN: WAS BORN IN 1977. HIS ARTISTIC CAREER SOON FOLLOWED. A STEADY DIET OF CARTOONS, COMICS, AND TREE CLIMBING FED HIS IMAGINATION AND IS WHAT STILL INSPIRES HIS WORK TODAY. DAVID WAS THE 2007 RUSS MANNING AWARD RECIPIENT FOR MOST PROMISING NEWCOMER, AND IN 2008, WON THE EISNER AWARDS FOR BEST PUBLICATION FOR KIDS (*MOUSE GUARD FALL 1152* & *WINTER 1152*) AND BEST GRAPHIC ALBUM–REPRINT (*MOUSE GUARD FALL 1152* HARDCOVER). HE RECEIVED HIS BFA IN PRINTMAKING FROM EASTERN MICHIGAN UNIVERSITY WHERE HE MET HIS WIFE JULIA. THEY CONTINUE TO RESIDE IN MICHIGAN WITH THEIR DOG AUTUMN.

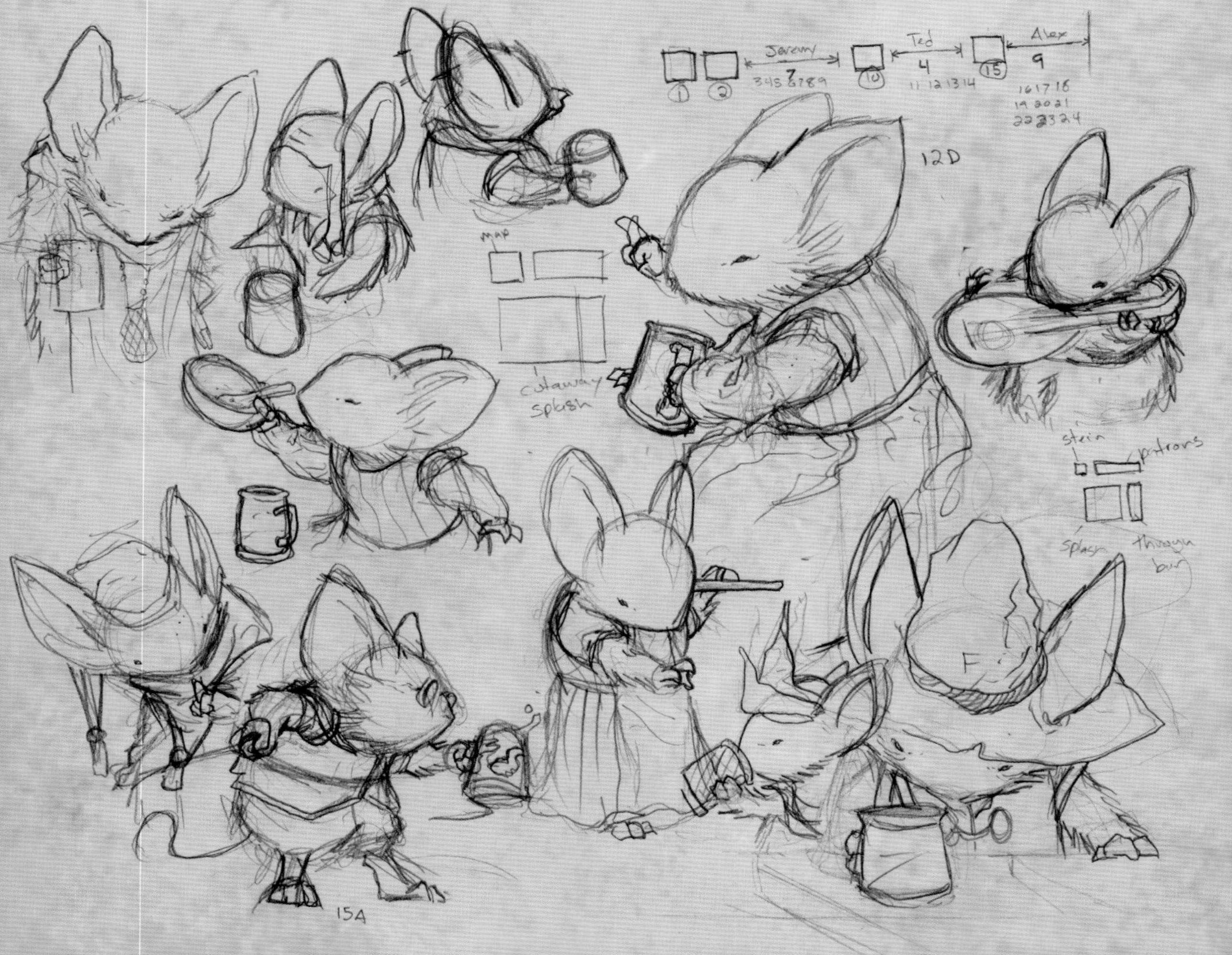
Jeremy
Ted
Alex
12D
map
cutaway splash
stein
patrons
splash
through bar
154

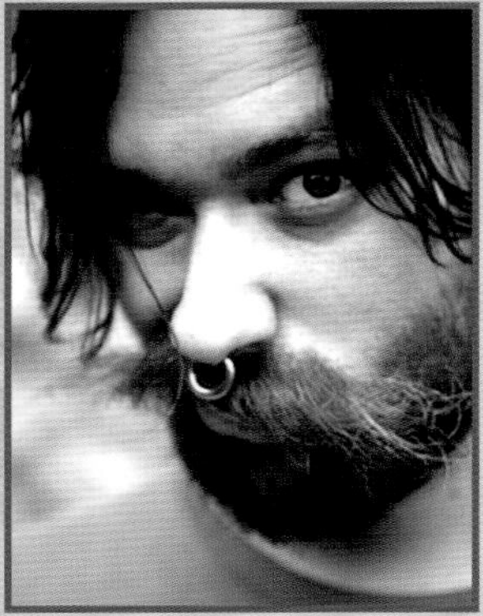

Jeremy Bastian: was born and raised in Ypsilanti, MI in 1978. He is currently living in Plymouth, MI with his wife Emily, their two dogs Connor and Basil, their two cats, Cleo and Harrison, and their four ducks, Remus, Bill, Fleur, Tonks and Luna. He spends most of the day trying to out do the extremely bizarre creature or character he just created or watching *Law and Order.* Right now he is currently working on his creator owned project *Cursed Pirate Girl* for Olympian Publishing. He is half way done though and that is good, hopefully the other half will come out before he can no longer see the infinitesimal detail he puts into every page.

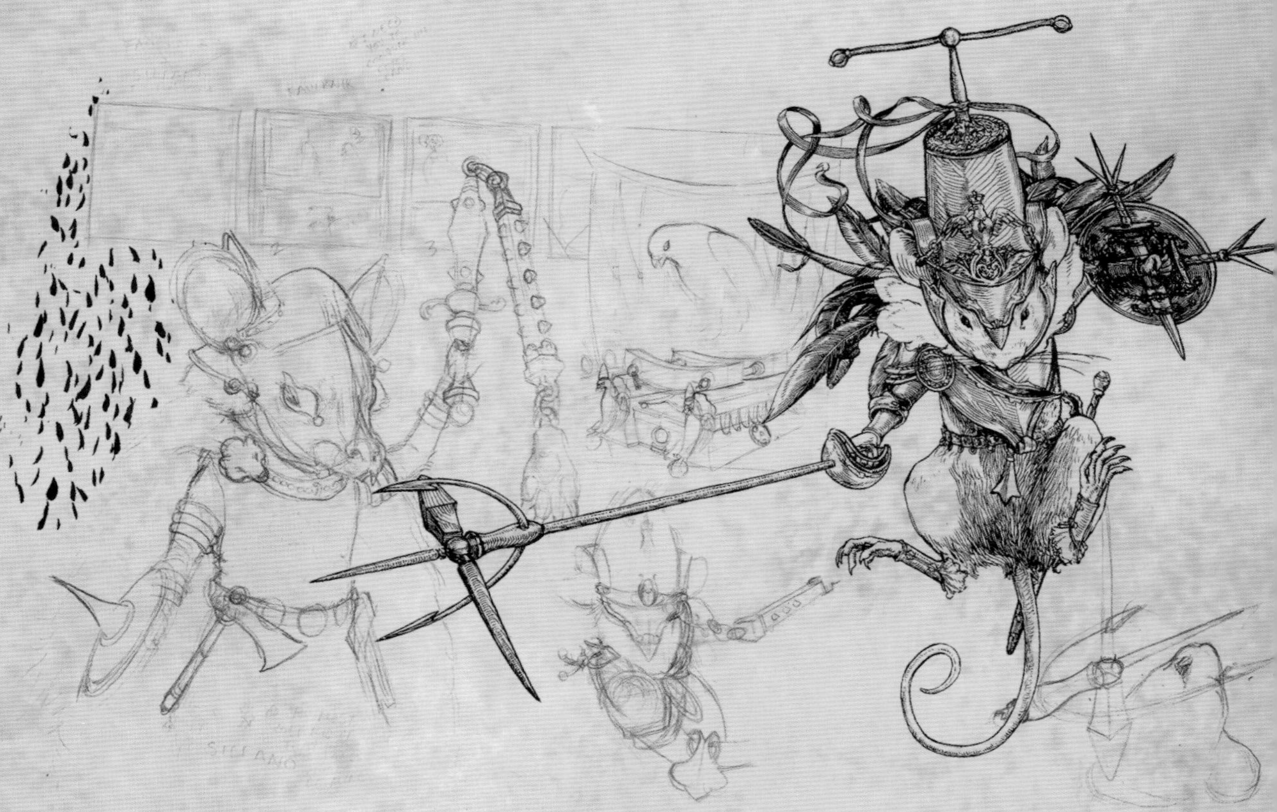

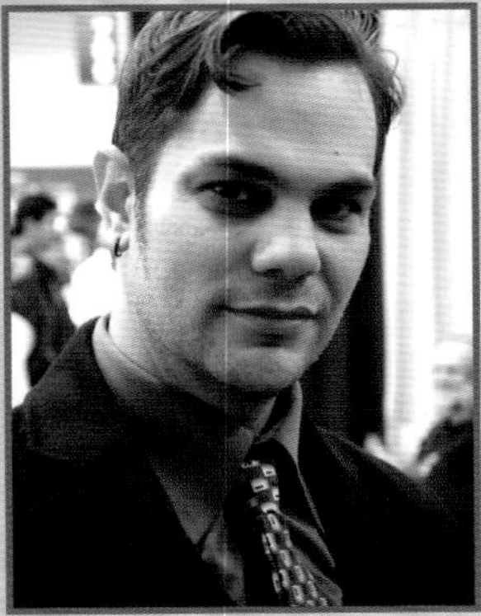

TED NAIFEH: is responsible for many dark, delicious worlds. These include the gothic romance *Gloomcookie* (with Serena Valentino), *Courtney Crumrin* (optioned for a movie by DreamWorks in 2007), and the all-ages *Polly and the Pirates*. He has just finished illustrating a graphic novel trilogy by bestselling author Holly Black.

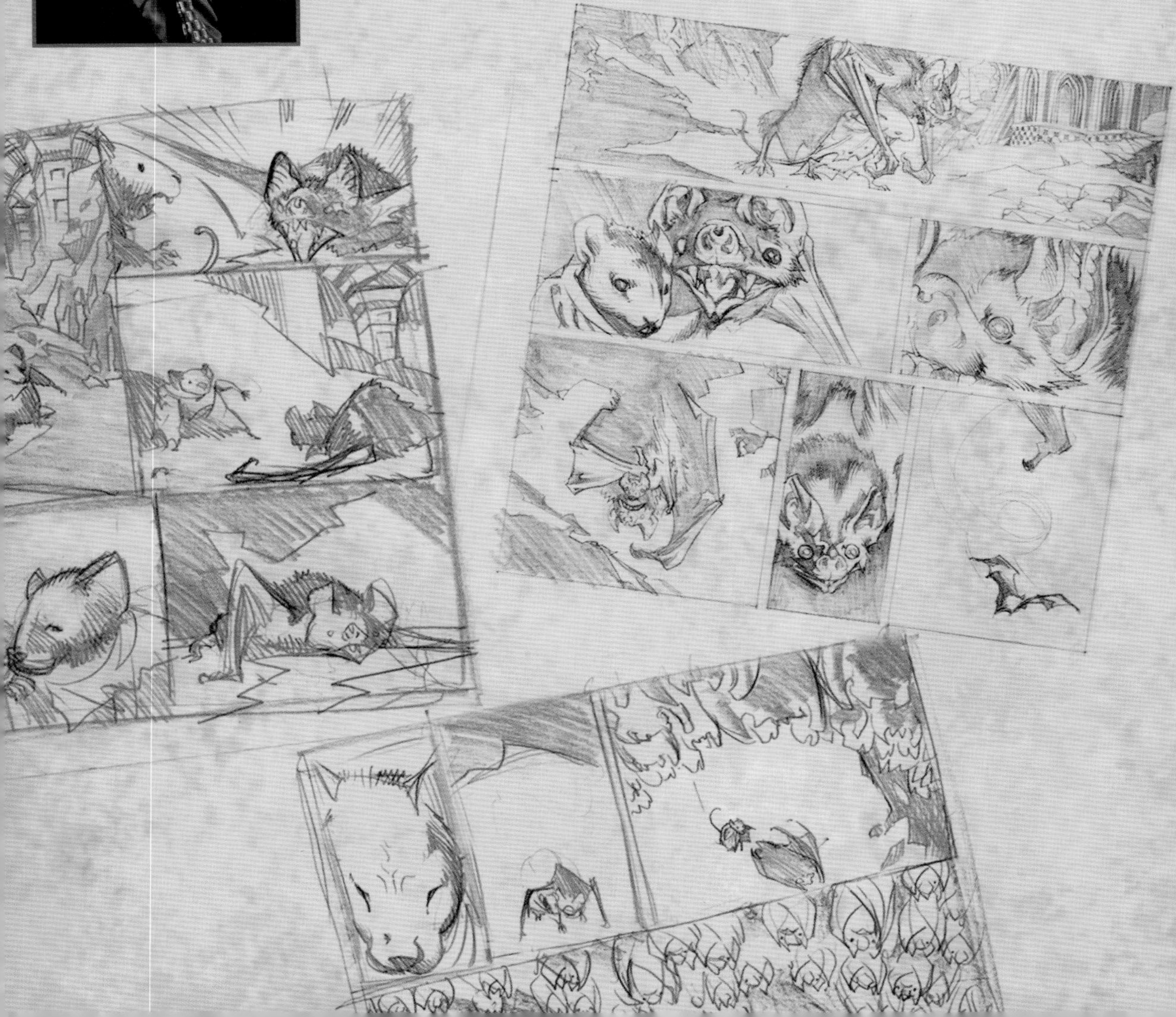

ALEX KAIN: IS A WRITER AND VIDEO GAME DESIGNER AT VENAN ENTERTAINMENT, INC. HE HAS WORKED ON OVER A DOZEN TITLES RANGING FROM THE AWARD-WINNING iPHONE ACTION-RPG *SPACE MINER: SPACE ORE BUST* TO THE BAFTA-NOMINATED COMEDIC STRATEGY GAME, *NINJATOWN*. A NEW ENGLAND NATIVE, ALEX CURRENTLY RESIDES IN THE HARTFORD AREA.

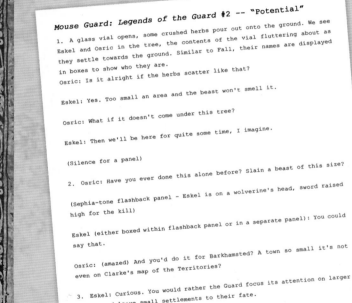

Mouse Guard: Legends of the Guard #2 -- "Potential"

1. A glass vial opens, some crushed herbs pour out onto the ground. We see Eskel and Osric in the tree, the contents of the vial fluttering about as they settle towards the ground. Similar to Fall, their names are displayed in boxes to show who they are.

Osric: Is it alright if the herbs scatter like that?

Eskel: Yes. Too small an area and the beast won't smell it.

Osric: What if it doesn't come under this tree?

Eskel: Then we'll be here for quite some time, I imagine.

(Silence for a panel)

2. Osric: Have you ever done this alone before? Slain a beast of this size?

(Sephia-tone flashback panel - Eskel is on a wolverine's head, sword raised high for the kill)

Eskel (either boxed within flashback panel or in a separate panel): You could say that.

Osric: (amazed) And you'd do it for Barkhamsted? A town so small it's not even on Clarke's map of the Territories?

3. Eskel: Curious. You would rather the Guard focus its attention on larger cities and leave small settlements to their fate.

Osric: It just seems odd. Why would a Guard risk their life for no reason?

Eskel: There is you.

Eskel (pointing to the nearby settlement): And your kin. That is enough for the Guard. We- (is looking off-panel, down at the forest floor)

4. Eskel (standing up): Excuse me a moment, Osric.

(Eskel leaps off the branch - epic shot - lands on top of the bear)

5. Eskel (battling the bear, boxed): We connect all mousekind. With [the] Guard making safe the wilds between settlements, each one would [be] isolated. A prison.

Eskel (battling the bear, boxed): One by one they would fall to our en[emies] until we all perished.

6. Eskel (battling the bear, boxed): And so we protect even the sma[llest] settlement. To the Guard, every mouse is worth fighting for.

Eskel (boxed, as he deals the killing blow): Worth dying for.

7. No text - the bear crashes into the gatehouse library. The stunned [bear?] leader stares at Eskel from within the wreckage)

8. (The wrecked library. Eskel and Osric sit at a table with the carna[ge] surrounding them. The Librarians are cleaning up the mess)

Eskel: There is potential here. For life and prosperity. For happiness. [I] would die to protect even the faintest memory of these feelings.

Osric: Eskel, tell me... could I become a Guard?

9. Eskel: Could you?

Eskel: (same scene, boxed. Eskel seems deep in thought): Perhaps this is why we train Tenderpaws... They say the path of the Guard cannot be walked alone[.]

10. (Eskel and Osric leaving Barkhamsted together. Osric is carrying Eskel's [sword) ... For the path of the Guard never ends. -Eskel, Patrol Leader, Fall 1147

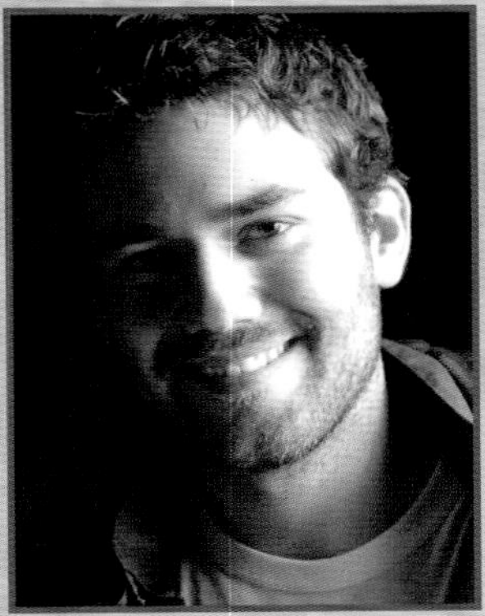

SEAN RUBIN: HAS BEEN ILLUSTRATING SINCE 1999. HE IS PRIMARILY KNOWN FOR HIS WORK ON THE *NEW YORK TIMES* BEST-SELLING *REDWALL* SERIES, INCLUDING *THE SABLE QUEAN* AND THE UPCOMING *ROUGE CREW*. BORN IN BROOKLYN, SEAN STUDIED ART AND ARCHEOLOGY AT PRINCETON UNIVERSITY AND IS A FORMER HIGH SCHOOL TEACHER. HE STILL LIVES IN NEW YORK, WHERE HE DRAWS, WRITES, AND WORKS IN A MUSEUM FOR MEDIEVAL ART. *LEGENDS OF THE GUARD* IS SEAN'S COMICS DEBUT.

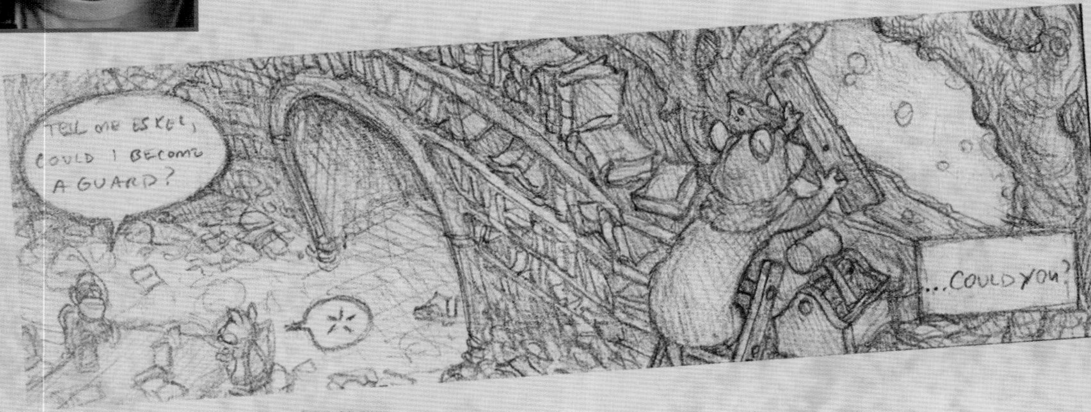
TELL ME ESKEL, COULD I BECOME A GUARD?
...COULD YOU?

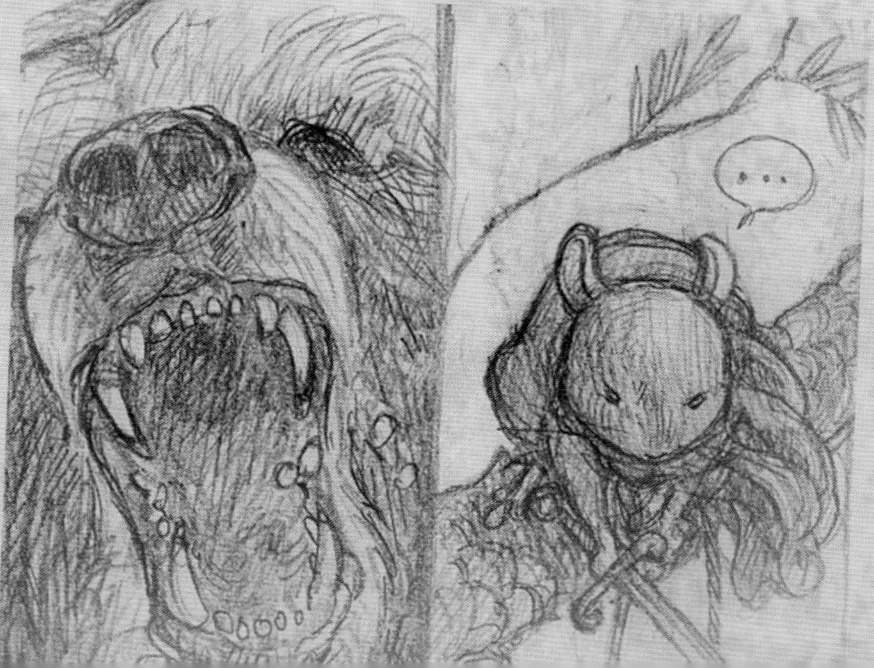
...

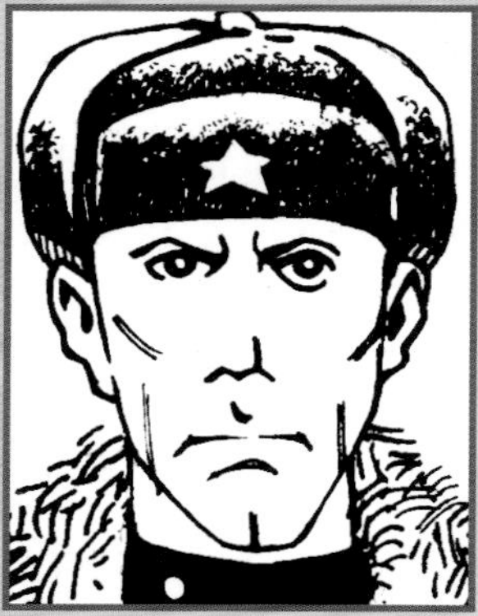

Alex Sheikman: Was born in the USSR and immigrated to the US at the age of 12 and shortly thereafter discovered comic books. Since then, he has contributed illustrations to a variety of role playing games published by White Wolf, Holistic Design, Steve Jackson Games, and Goodman Games. He is also the writer/artist of *Robotika*, *Robotika: For A Few Rubles More*, *Moonstruck* and the illustrator of a number of short stories. He lives with his wife and son in Northern California.

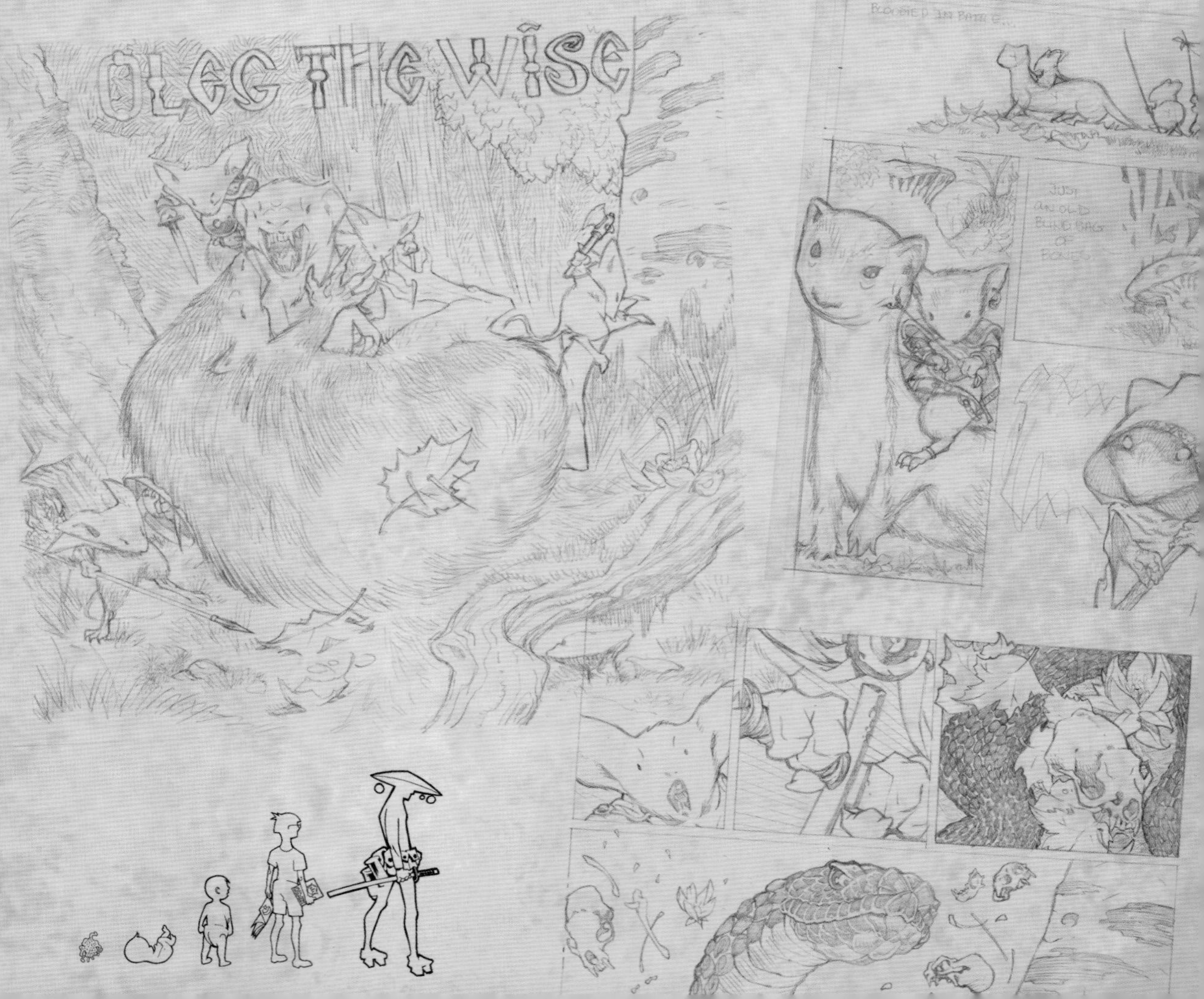
OLEG THE WISE

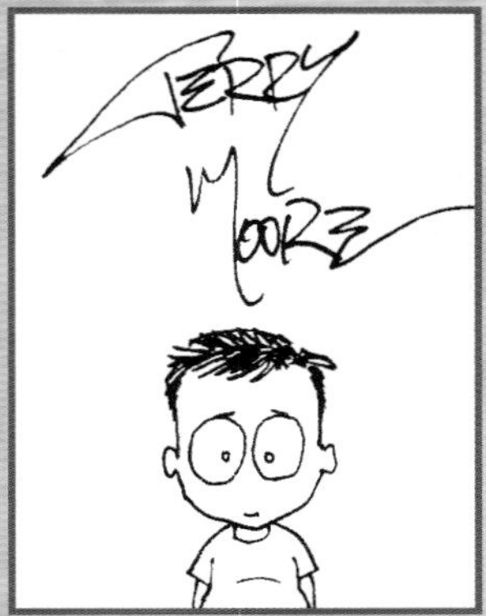
TERRY MOORE

TERRY MOORE: IS AN EISNER AWARD WINNING CARTOONIST, BEST KNOWN FOR HIS SELF-PUBLISHED SERIES, *STRANGERS IN PARADISE* AND *ECHO*. IN ADDITION TO HIS OWN BOOKS, MOORE HAS WORKED WITH EVERY MAJOR COMIC BOOK PUBLISHER SINCE HIS CAREER BEGAN IN 1993, WRITING AND/OR DRAWING FOR TITLES SUCH AS *STAR WARS*, *BUFFY THE VAMPIRE SLAYER*, *GEN 13*, *RUNAWAYS*, AND *SPIDER-MAN LOVES MARY JANE*.

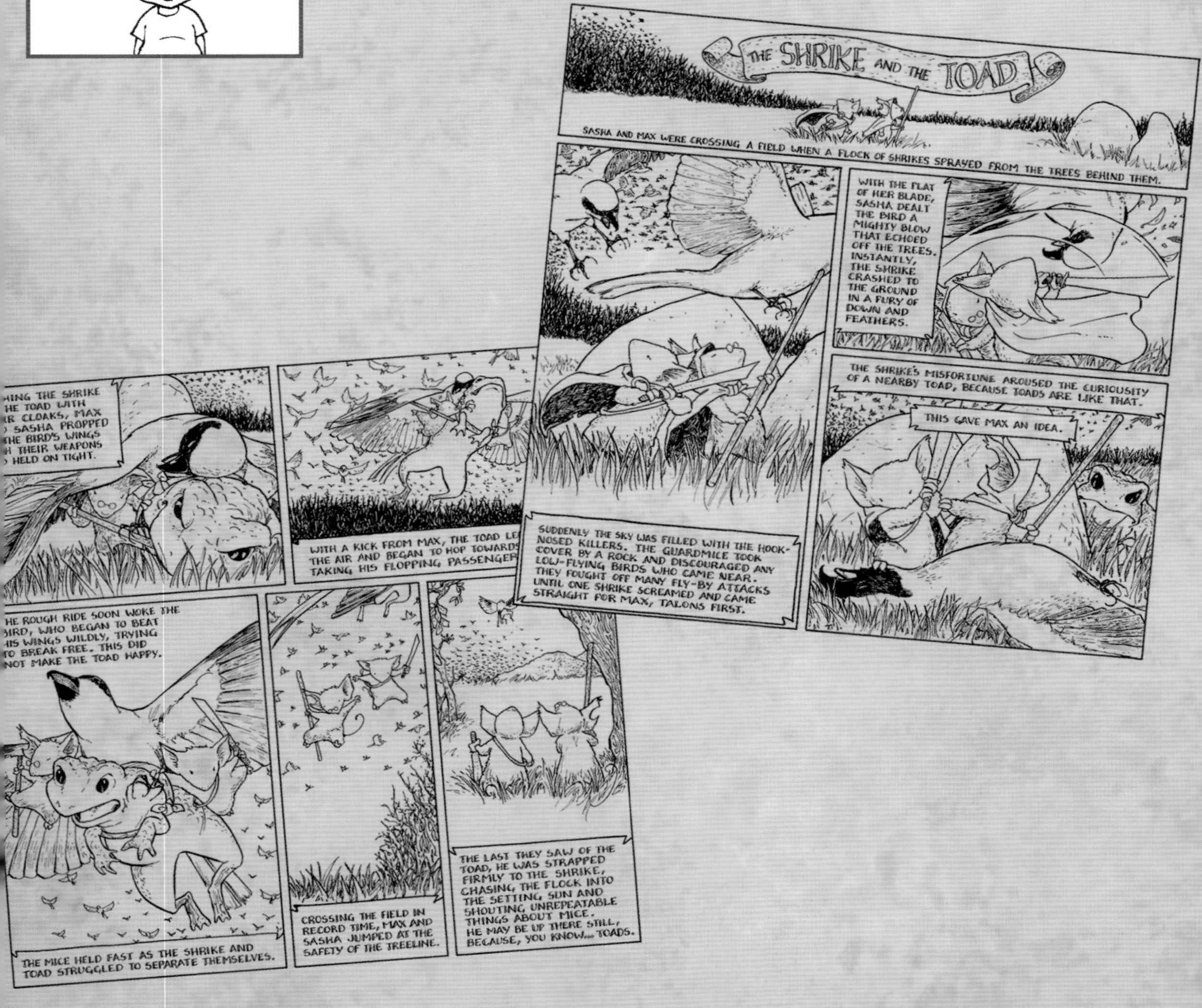
THE SHRIKE AND THE TOAD
SASHA AND MAX WERE CROSSING A FIELD WHEN A FLOCK OF SHRIKES SPRAYED FROM THE TREES BEHIND THEM.
WITH THE FLAT OF HER BLADE, SASHA DEALT THE BIRD A MIGHTY BLOW THAT ECHOED OFF THE TREES. INSTANTLY, THE SHRIKE CRASHED TO THE GROUND IN A FURY OF DOWN AND FEATHERS.
SUDDENLY THE SKY WAS FILLED WITH THE HOOK-NOSED KILLERS. THE GUARDMICE TOOK COVER BY A ROCK AND DISCOURAGED ANY LOW-FLYING BIRDS WHO CAME NEAR. THEY FOUGHT OFF MANY FLY-BY ATTACKS UNTIL ONE SHRIKE SCREAMED AND CAME STRAIGHT FOR MAX, TALONS FIRST.
THE SHRIKE'S MISFORTUNE AROUSED THE CURIOUSITY OF A NEARBY TOAD, BECAUSE TOADS ARE LIKE THAT.
THIS GAVE MAX AN IDEA.
THE TOAD WITH
R CLOAKS, MAX
SASHA PROPPED
THE BIRD'S WINGS
H THEIR WEAPONS
HELD ON TIGHT.
WITH A KICK FROM MAX, THE TOAD LE
THE AIR AND BEGAN TO HOP TOWARDS
TAKING HIS FLOPPING PASSENGER
HE ROUGH RIDE SOON WOKE THE BIRD, WHO BEGAN TO BEAT HIS WINGS WILDLY, TRYING TO BREAK FREE. THIS DID NOT MAKE THE TOAD HAPPY.
THE MICE HELD FAST AS THE SHRIKE AND TOAD STRUGGLED TO SEPARATE THEMSELVES.
CROSSING THE FIELD IN RECORD TIME, MAX AND SASHA JUMPED AT THE SAFETY OF THE TREELINE.
THE LAST THEY SAW OF THE TOAD, HE WAS STRAPPED FIRMLY TO THE SHRIKE, CHASING THE FLOCK INTO THE SETTING SUN AND SHOUTING UNREPEATABLE THINGS ABOUT MICE. HE MAY BE UP THERE STILL, BECAUSE, YOU KNOW... TOADS.

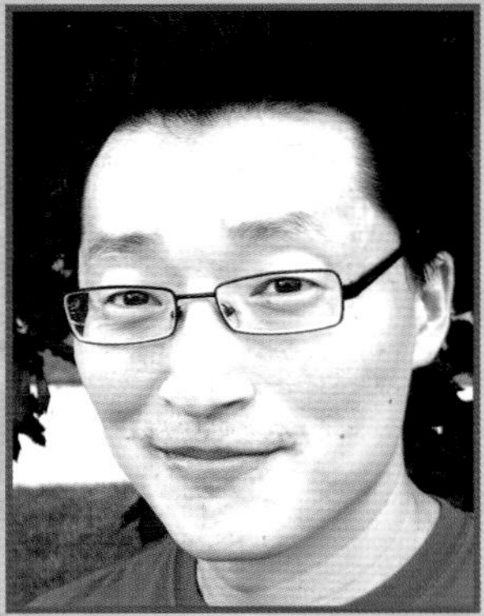

GENE HA: IS THE MULTIPLE EISNER AWARD WINNING ARTIST OF ALAN MOORE'S *TOP 10*, *THE FORTY-NINERS*, AND BRAD MELTZER'S *JLA #11*. HE BEGAN WORKING IN COMICS IN THE EARLY 90'S ON BOOKS SUCH AS *GREEN LANTERN*, *CYCLOPS AND PHOENIX*, *STARMAN*, AND *OKTANE*. HE'S DONE PAINTED COVERS FOR *THE ADVENTURES OF SUPERMAN*, *CAPTAIN AMERICA*, *JSA VS. KOBRA*, AND *GREEN LANTERN*. NORMALLY HE WORKS IN A DETAILED AND REALISTIC STYLE, BUT LEAPT AT THE CHANCE TO DO SOMETHING DIFFERENT WHEN OFFERED A *MOUSE GUARD* STORY. HE LIVES OUTSIDE CHICAGO WITH HIS LOVELY WIFE LISA AND THEIR DOG NIBBLES.

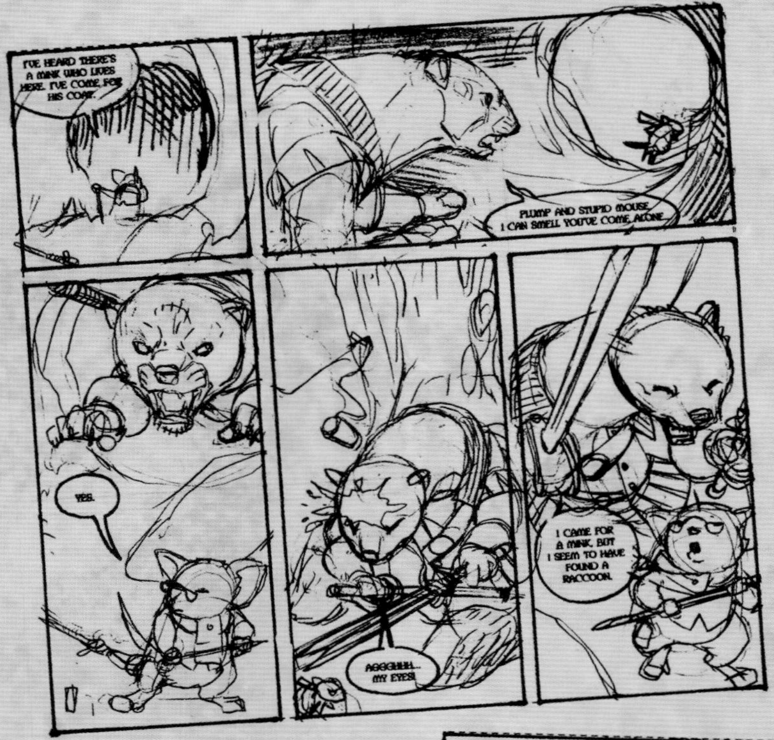
I'VE HEARD THERE'S A MINK WHO LIVES HERE. I'VE COME FOR HIS COAT.
PLUMP AND STUPID MOUSE. I CAN SMELL YOU'VE COME ALONE.
YES.
AGGGHHH... MY EYES!
I CAME FOR A MINK, BUT I SEEM TO HAVE FOUND A RACCOON.

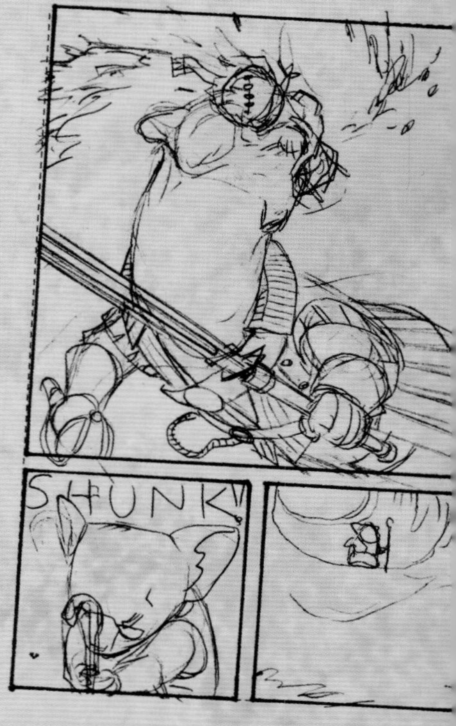
SHUNK!

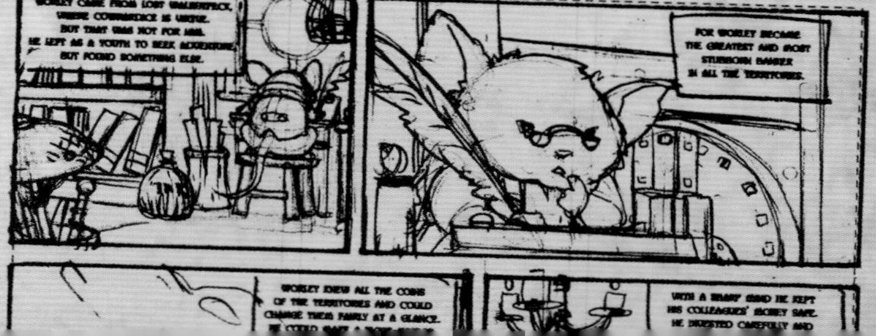
WORLEY CAME FROM LOST WALLENPECK, WHERE COWARDICE IS VIRTUE. BUT THAT WAS NOT FOR HIM. HE LEFT AS A YOUTH TO SEEK ADVENTURE BUT FOUND SOMETHING ELSE.
FOR WORLEY BECAME THE GREATEST AND MOST STUBBORN BANKER IN ALL THE TERRITORIES.

LOWELL FRANCIS: WRITES AND EDITS FREELANCE. HE LOVES STORIES--IN GRAPHIC NOVEL, PROSE OR GAMING FORM. HE'S AN AVID ROLE-PLAYER AND AMATEUR GAME DESIGNER HIS CLAIM TO FAME LIES IN HAVING GIVEN GENE HA HIS FIRST ALAN MOORE COMIC BOOK.

PAGE TWO

PANEL ONE

On a Mouse, not particularly threatening looking, in fact, more than a little harmless appearing. He's laden with a backpack, marching through the grass. Plump mice are rare, but he should notably for his bookish appearance. Glasses are an option-- Dain from the rpg book has a pair of simple pince-nez which is probably more appropriate than something more scientific (like that of the cartographer). Should have a ledger book either underarm or visibly fastened to his pack.

CAPTION (MINSTREL)

FOR WORLEY BECAME THE GREATEST AND MOST STUBBORN BANKER IN ALL THE TERRITORIES.

PANEL TWO

On Worley marching through the bad places.

CAPTION (MINSTREL)

WITH A SHARP MIND HE KEPT HIS COLLEAGUES' MONEY SAFE. HE INVESTED CAREFULLY AND MADE SURE ALL GOT THEIR SHARE WHEN AN EXPEDITION CAME HOME SAFE.

CAPTION (MINSTREL)

AND HE NEVER, EVER LET ANYONE CHEAT HIM...

PANEL THREE

Worley over-the-shoulder (OTS) as he looks at the frontier town of Wolfpoint. We're at the edge reaches of the lands, and we have a more rough and tumble looking affair here. If the cities represent a level of development akin to the Medieval or Early Modern, we're talking Dark Ages and Viking style construction here. Will need to consult on that.

CAPTION (MINSTREL)

WHICH IS HOW LATE ONE SPRING HE CAME TO WOLFPOINTE, AT THE FAR EDGES OF THE LANDS

PANEL FOUR

Worley comes into town without hesitation, while the local and bigger mice stare at him with hostility.

CAPTION (MINSTREL)

HE'D LENT MONEY TO A TRADEMOUSE WHO'D RUN OFF WITH HIS GOODS, INK, LEATHER, CLOTH AND SUNDRIES, FLEEING TO RELATIVES IN THIS DISTANT TOWN.

CAPTION (MINSTREL)

BUT HE HADN'T COUNTED ON THE STUBBORNNESS OF WORLEY.

---

use Guard: Legends of the Guard #2 -- "Worley and the Mink"

GE ONE

NEL ONE

a tavern room, with a minstrel in off-center, but with other mice
ound about-- no one particularly solid looking, these are trademice and
erchants. Note: there are some great models for minstrels and instruments
n the cover of the rpg.

MINSTREL

PERHAPS A STORY ABOUT THE MOUSE GUARD...

FIRST PATRON

NO! GIVE US A TALE OF WORLEY!

THREE PATRONS (Overlapping balloons)

WORLEY AND THE SIX STUBBORN MICE!

HOW WORLEY BOXED THE CROW!

WORLEY AND THE LONGTAIL REEVE!

PANEL TWO

On a young mouse, an apprentice sitting beside his master, he speaks hesitantly.

APPRENTICE BANKER

WHO...WHO IS WORLEY?

PANEL THREE

On the Minstrel.

MINSTREL

AH YOU'VE ONLY BEEN IN AN APPRENTICE FOR A SHORT TIME, YOU DO NOT KNOW TH
TALES...

PANEL FOUR

On the apprentice as he listens

MINSTREL (OFF-PANEL)

WORLEY'S A LEGEND AMONG YOUR NEW PROFESSION. AND THERE ARE MANY STORIE
HIM.

PANEL FIVE

Perhaps on the crowd, or the minstrel again as he continues on.

MINSTREL

WORLEY CAME FROM LOST WALNUTPECK, WHERE COWARDICE WAS VIRTUE. BUT THAT WAS
NOT FOR HIM. HE LEFT AS A YOUTH TO SEEK ADVENTURE, BUT FOUND SOMETHING
ELSE...

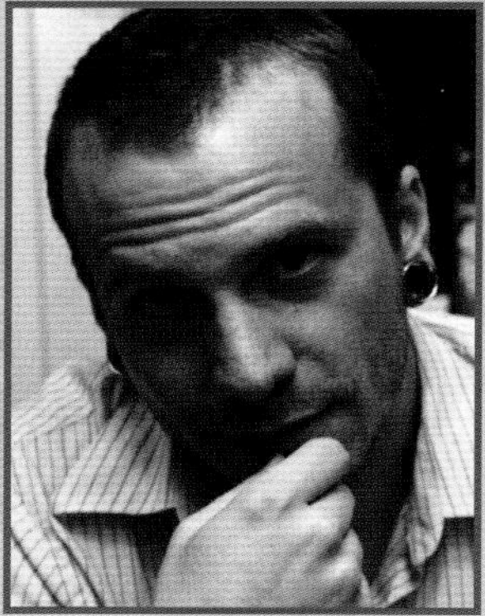

JASON SHAWN ALEXANDER: BEGAN HIS CAREER SELF PUBLISHING AND LATER, FOR HIS WORK FOR ONI PRESS ON THE SERIES, *QUEEN AND COUNTRY*, RECEIVED TWO EISNER AWARD NOMINATIONS. HE'S SINCE GONE ON TO WORK WITH DC COMICS, MARVEL COMICS, AND DARK HORSE BEFORE CHANGING GEARS TO BEGIN WRITING AND PAINTING HIS OWN BOOKS. THOUGH MOST OF HIS ENERGY NOWADAYS IS FOCUSED ON PAINTING, JASON THOROUGHLY ENJOYS TAKING ON COMICS PROJECTS WHERE HE'S ALLOWED ULTIMATE CREATIVE FREEDOM AND CAN GO NUTS. LIKE THIS ONE.

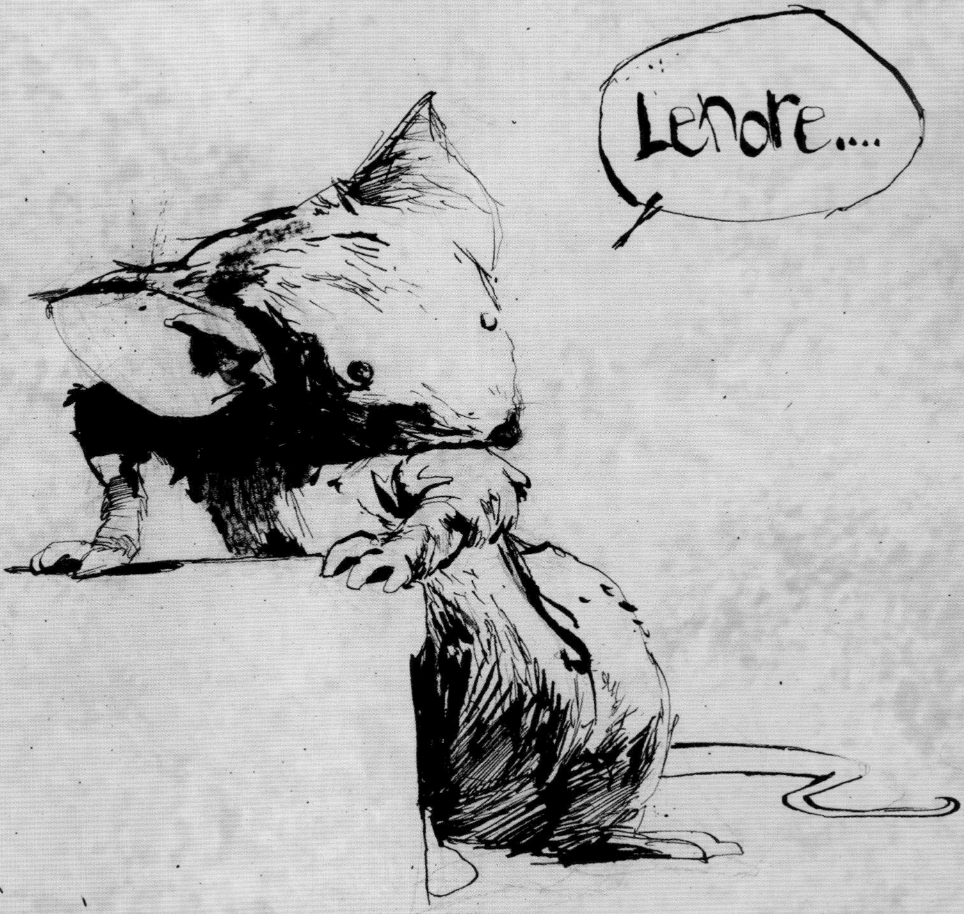
Lenore....

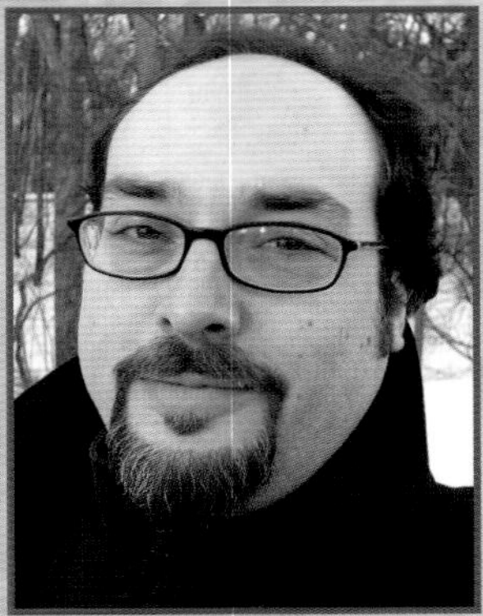

Nate Pride: was born in Ann Arbor, Michigan in 1970. His artwork has appeared in *Mage: The Awakening* and *Scarred Lands*, RPG books from White Wolf Publishing. Nate's recent illustration projects include exclusive hardcover editions for Barnes & Noble: *Library of Wonder: Jules Verne Extraordinary Voyages* and Charles Dickens *Five Novels*. He works in a home studio in the Great Lakes State that continues to inspire him.

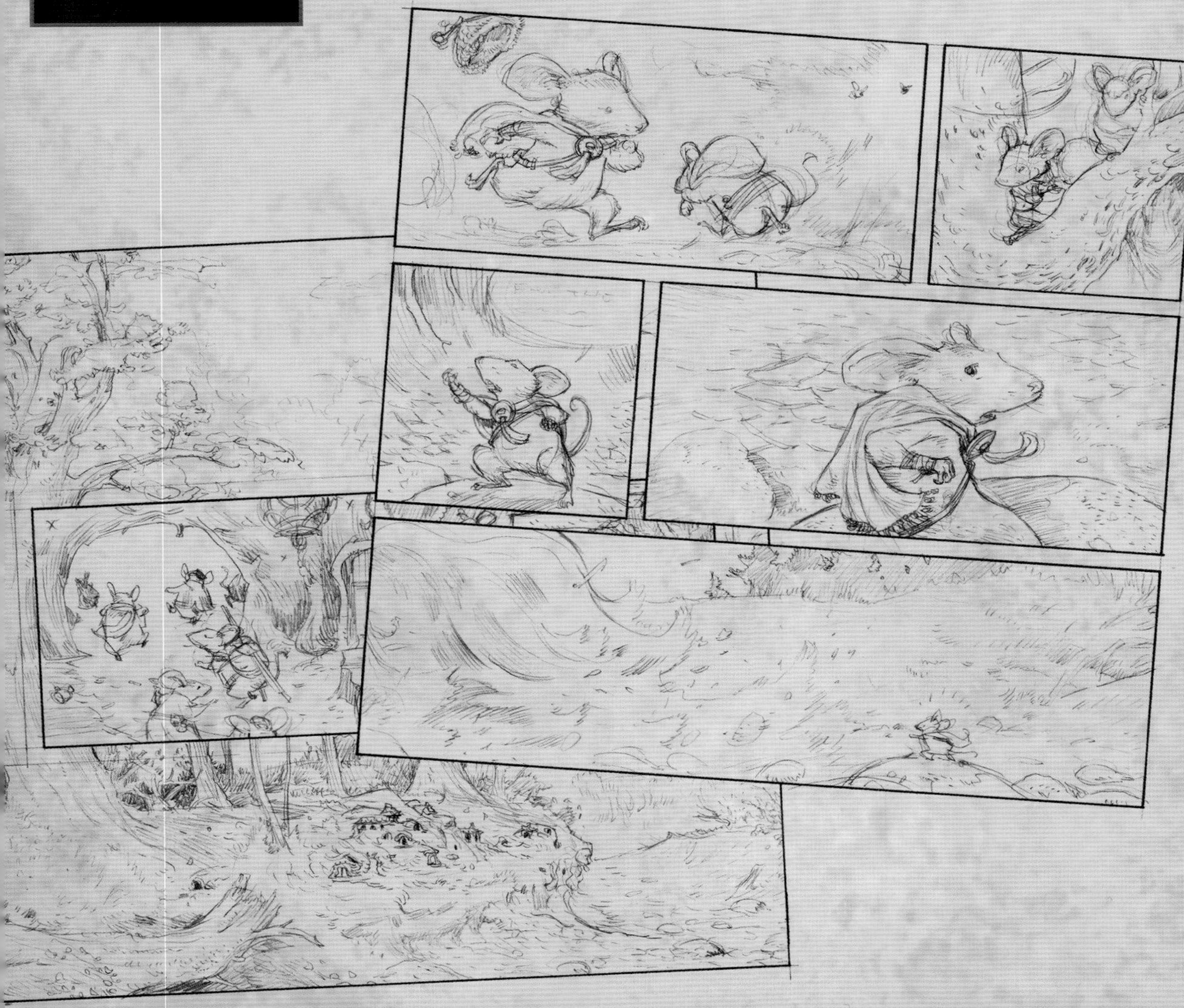

KATIE COOK: IS A COMIC BOOK ARTIST AND ILLUSTRATOR LIVING IN THE ANN ARBOR, MI AREA. KATIE IS MOSTLY KNOWN FOR HER WORK IN THE *STAR WARS* UNIVERSE... BUT SOME OF HER CREDITS BESIDES *STAR WARS* INCLUDE LICENSED WORK FOR DC COMICS, MARVEL COMICS, *THE LORD OF THE RINGS*, ARCHAIA'S OWN *FRAGGLE ROCK* COMIC, AND MORE! SHE IS THRILLED TO HAVE BEEN GIVEN THE CHANCE TO PLAY AROUND IN THE WORLD OF *MOUSE GUARD*, BECAUSE SHE LOVES THE PROPERTY SO MUCH. YOU CAN SEE MORE ABOUT KATIE, HER ART, AND HER CATS AT WWW.KATIECANDRAW.COM.

a mouse named fox

real.. fox?

SCREECH!
JUMP!

HELP!
smoke

LEAP

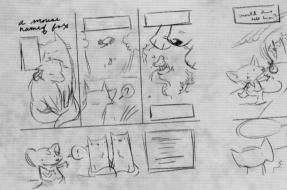

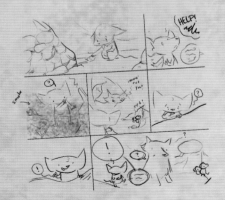

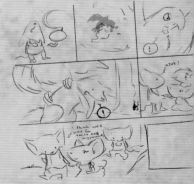

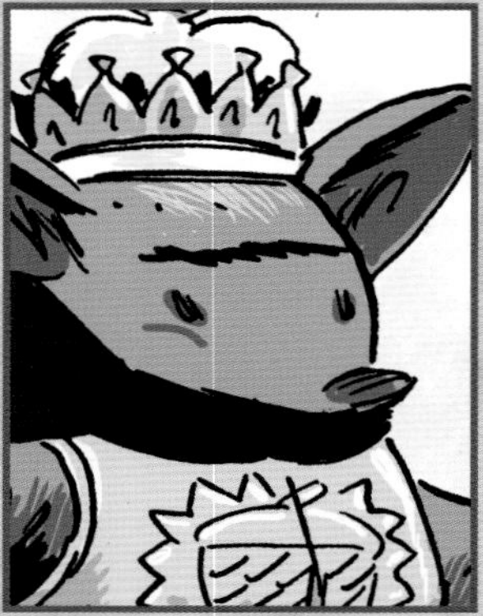

GUY DAVIS: (B. 1966~ AND STILL AT IT) IS A SELF-TAUGHT MICHIGAN BASED ARTIST WHO STARTED HIS COMIC CAREER IN 1985, WORKING ON SMALL PRESS COMICS. SINCE THEN HE HAS WORKED FOR A VARIETY OF MAJOR AND INDEPENDENT COMIC COMPANIES ALONG WITH PROVIDING ARTWORK AND CONCEPTUAL DESIGN FOR VARIOUS ROLE-PLAYING GAMES AND MULTI-MEDIA PROJECTS. CURRENTLY HE IS THE SERIES ARTIST ON THE HELLBOY SPIN-OFF B.P.R.D. ALONG WITH HIS CREATOR OWNED SERIES, THE MARQUIS, FOR DARK HORSE COMICS.

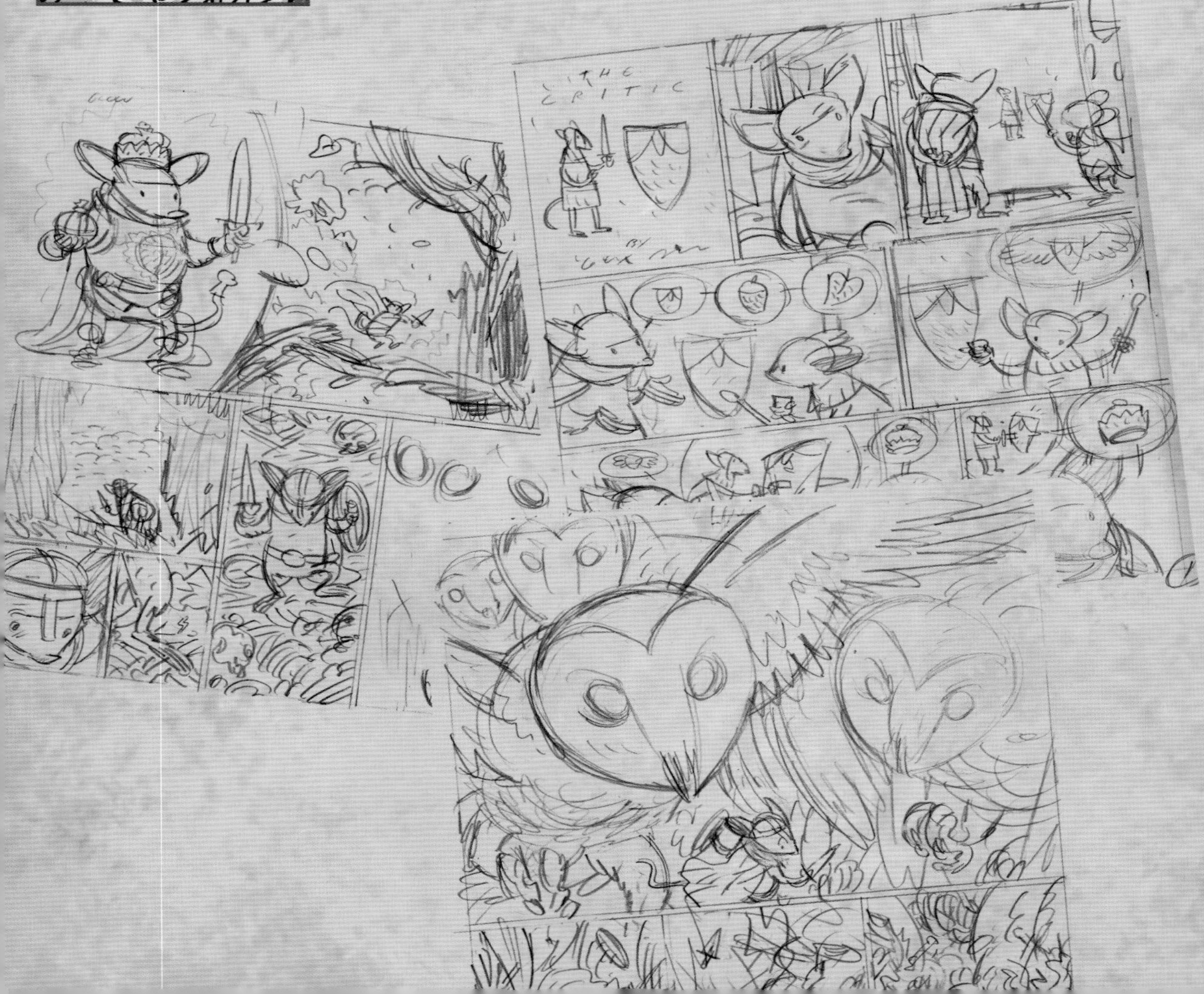
THE CRITIC

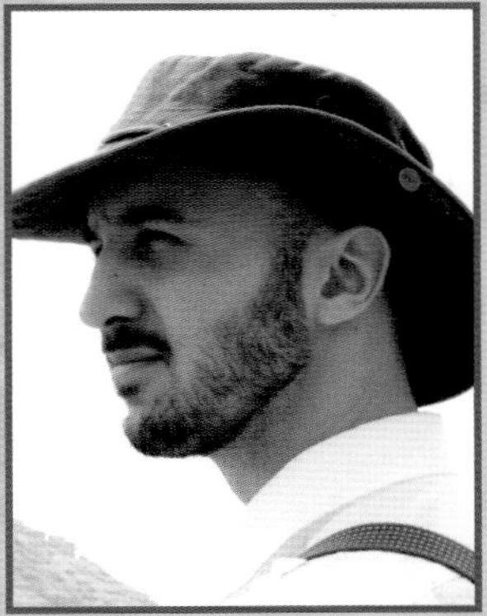

KARL KERSCHL: HAS BEEN DRAWING COMICS PROFESSIONALLY FOR 15 YEARS. HE HAS WORKED ON *SUPERMAN*, *THE FLASH*, *ROBIN* AND *TEEN TITANS*, AMONG OTHER HEROIC THINGS, AND RECENTLY ENTERED THE WORLD OF SELF-PUBLISHING WITH A COLLECTION OF HIS EISNER-NOMINATED WEBCOMIC *THE ABOMINABLE CHARLES CHRISTOPHER*. HE LIVES, VERY HAPPILY IN MONTRÉAL, CANADA. MORE OF KARL'S WORK CAN BE SEEN AT *KARLKERSCHL.COM*.

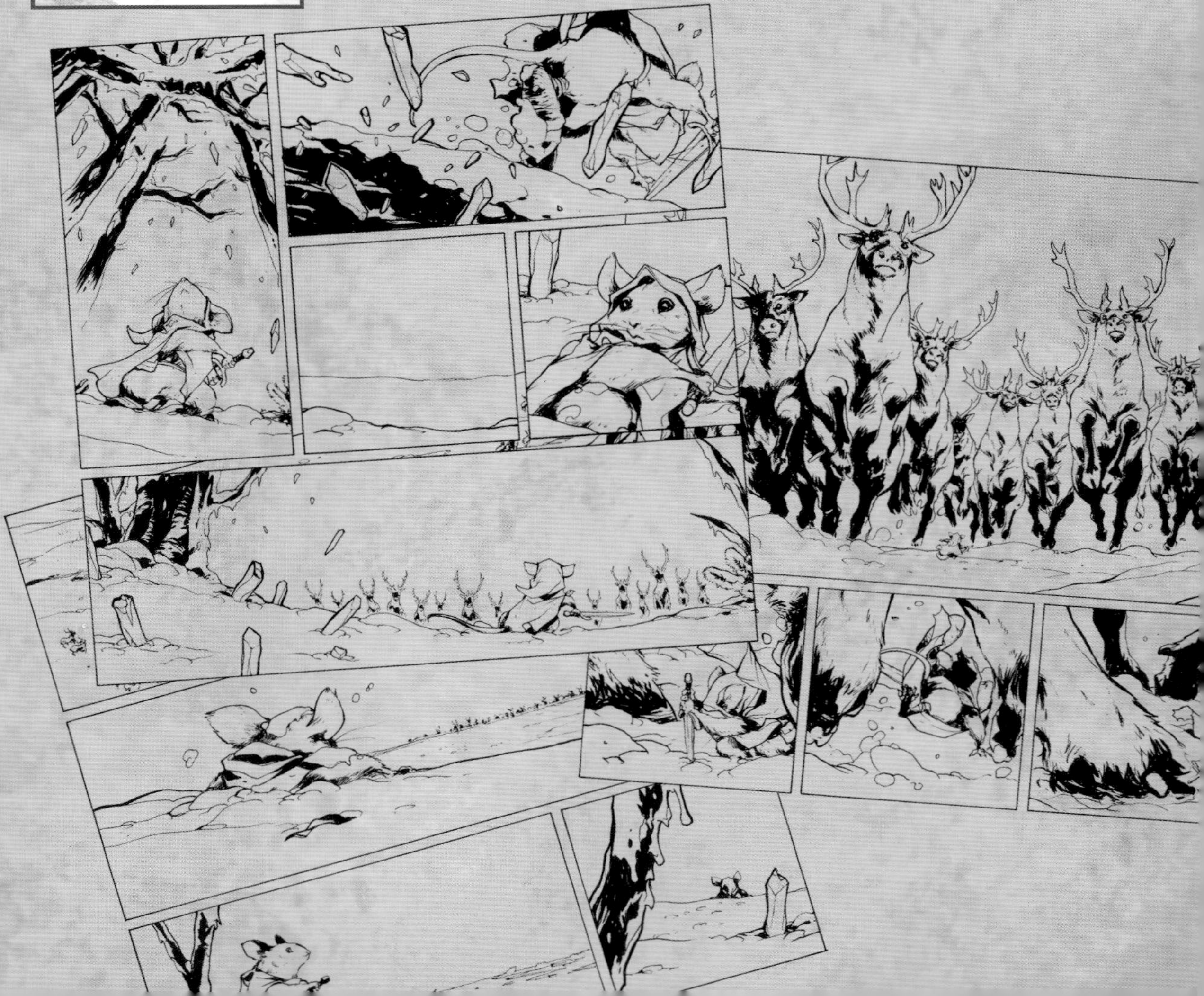

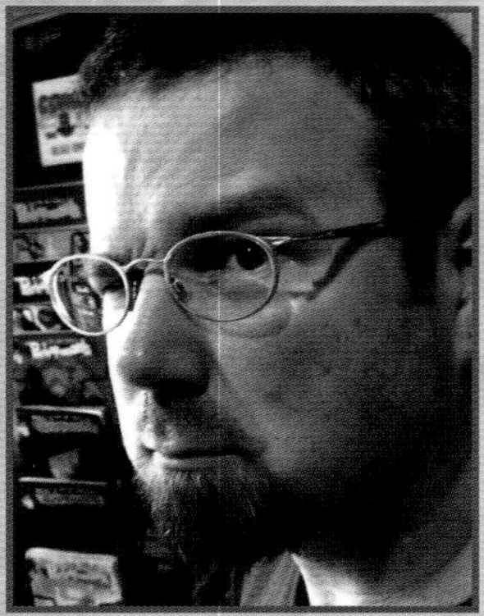

Craig Rousseau: draws comics. (And was very glad to draw one for David.)

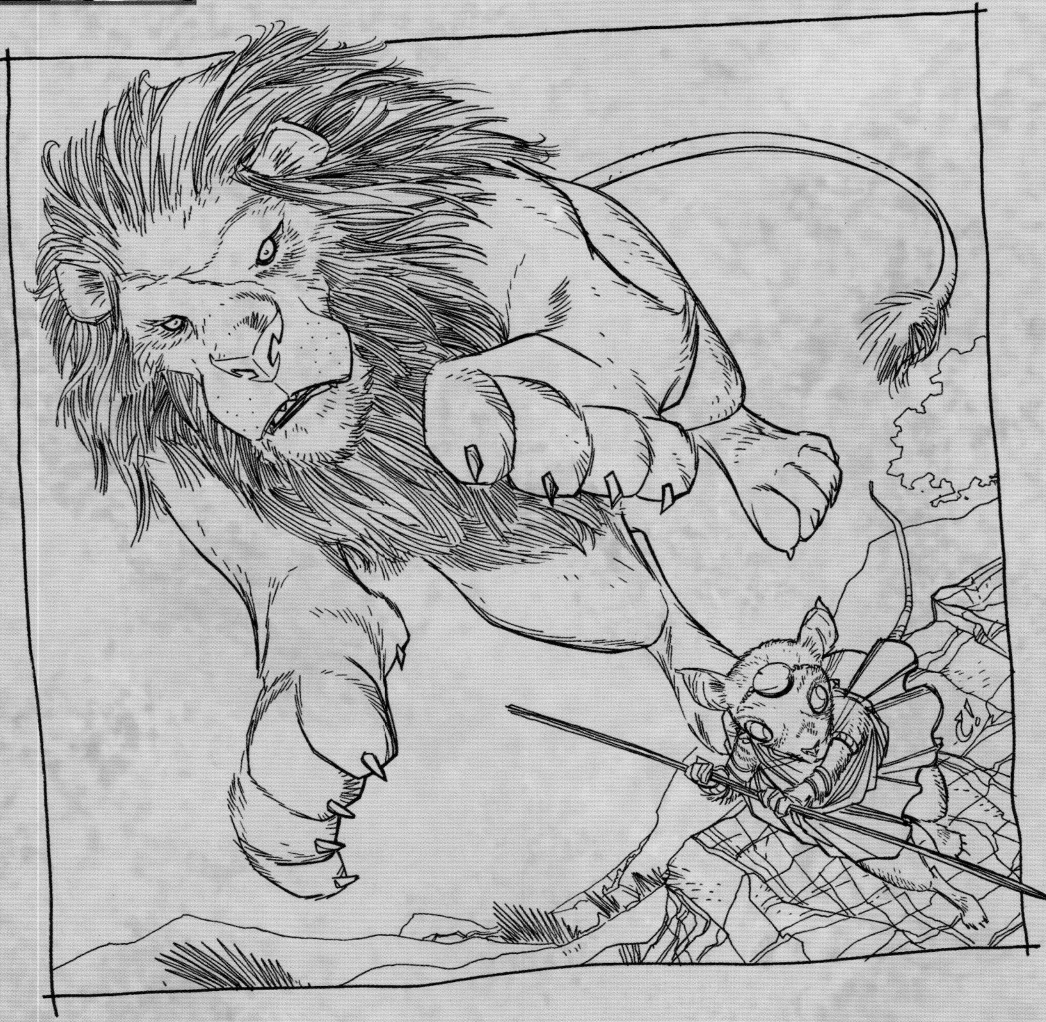

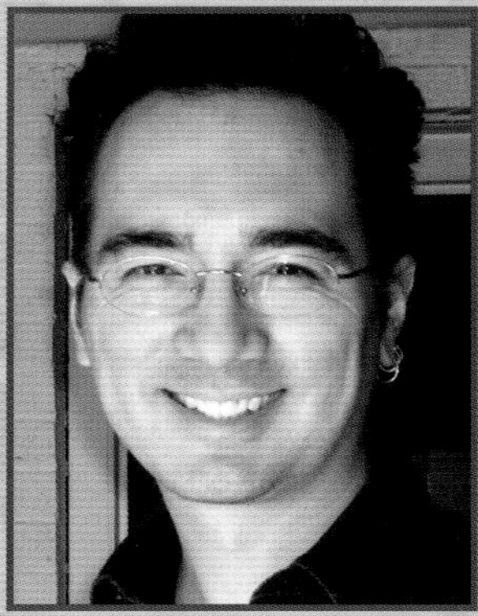

Mark Smylie: founded Archaia as a self-publishing venture for his epic military fantasy comic book *Artesia* (first published through Sirius Entertainment), and later expanded it to include a select line of comics and graphic novels from other authors as well as translations of some of Europe's finest graphic novel offerings. Mark was nominated for the Russ Manning Award in 1999, and for an Eisner Award in 2001. His illustration work has appeared in works from Wizards of the Coast, White Wolf, Brigand Publishing, and collectible card games from AEG. He designed and illustrated a role-playing game based on *Artesia* that won the Origins Award for Role-Playing Game of 2006, three Indie RPG Awards, and was nominated for six ENnies. He lives and works in New Jersey, a state he actually likes a great deal.

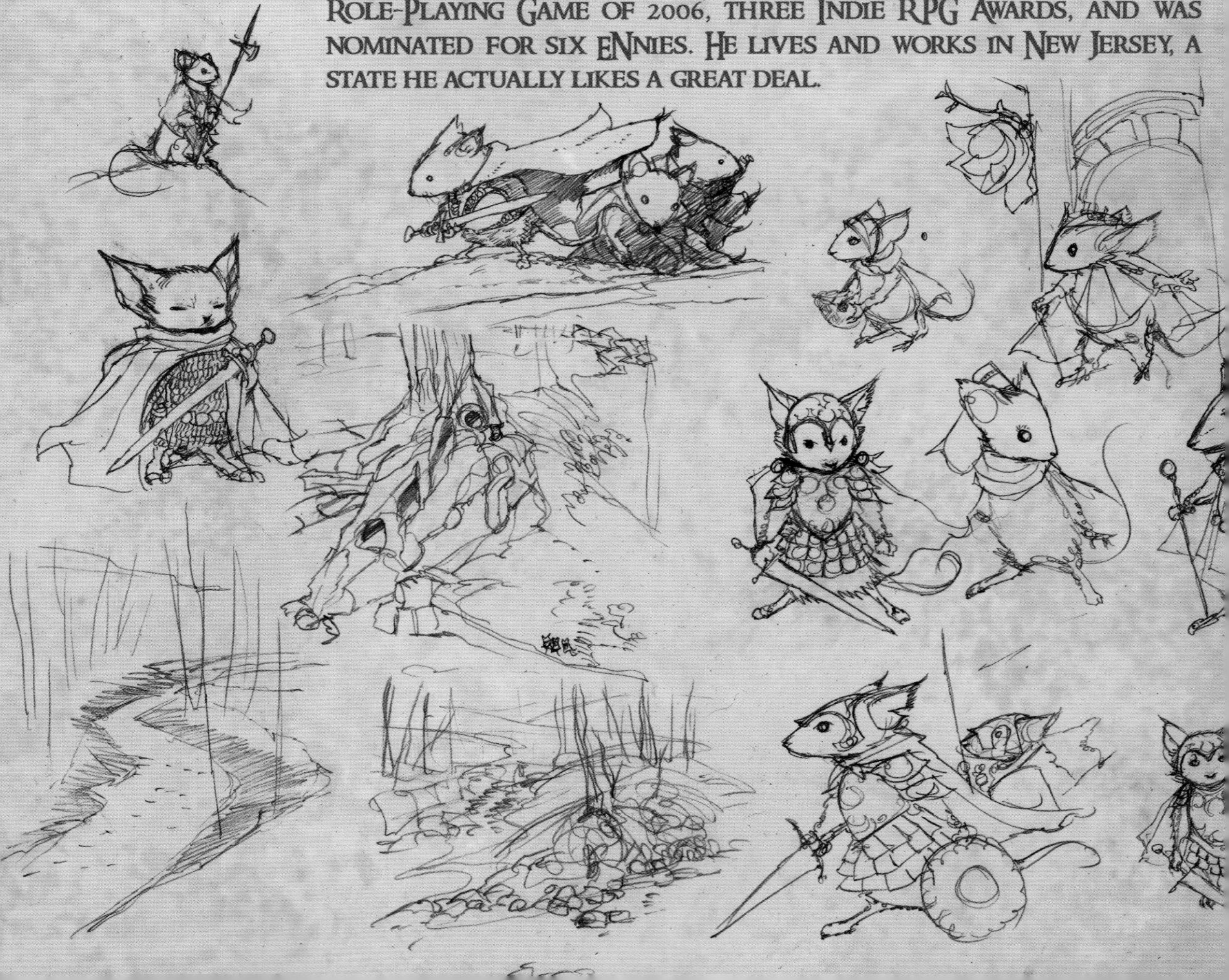

João M. P. Lemos: is still mad at David Petersen's preposterous suggestion that his original pitch for the dream epilogue was stealing anything whatsoever from *Inception*. He maintains that a rather excessive exposure to that whole Eisners affair has spoiled the man's mind and that the elegantly dressed mice tumbling and spinning out of their wits in the oneiric hotel corridor would have looked just lovely. He also penciled and inked C.B. Cebulski's take on J.M. Barrie's *Peter Pan* in *Avengers Fairy Tales #1*, drew a Wolverine story scripted by novelist Sarah Cross and keeps bragging about having scripted newcomer artist Francesca Ciregia's first Marvel story. He is now developing a group of independent projects, including an all-ages fantasy epic with fellow artist Nuno Plati. His third person contention is that they might happen to be worth it. Do confirm, if you please, at *sete-estrelo.blogspot.com*.

YET TONIGHT YOU ORDERED THOSE ROCK SPIRITS THAT ONLY BLACKSMITHS, WIDOWERS AND MINERS WILL ASK FOR
IT SMELLED LIKE TINY THUNDERS
WHY DO I LIVE IN YOUR HEART, ALBA? YOU SHOULD BE OUTSIDE AND I SHOULDN'T BE AT ALL.
DID I DRINK IT WITHOUT THE FILTER ?

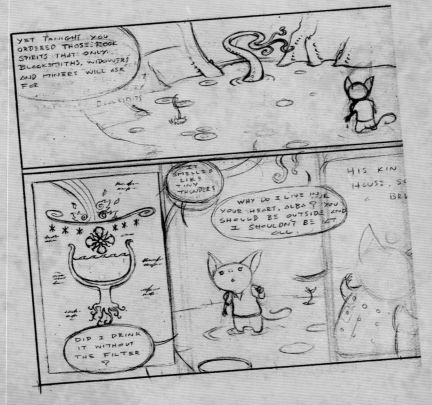

COMING
2011

MOUSE GUARD:
LEGENDS
OF THE GUARD
VOLUME TWO

Mouse Territories 1150

A map of cities, towns, villages, and safe paths after the winter war
As measured by the Guard of 1149, Recorded by Clarke's Cartography
Fallen settlements listed & struck

Dawnrock

Calog

Darkheather
Entrance

Whitepine

Thistledown

Wildseed

Elmwood

Lockhaven

Ironwood

Pebblebrook

Shaleburrow

Barkstone

Ivydale

Blackrock

Woodruff's Grove

Elmoss

R

Copperwood

Ferndale

Scout Border

Darkheather
Tunnels

Sprucetuck

Dorigift

Appleloft

Walnutpeck

Gilpledge